WIDOWS ON THE WINE PATH

JULIA JARMAN

Boldwood

First published in Great Britain in 2024 by Boldwood Books Ltd.

Copyright © Julia Jarman, 2024

Cover Design by Alice Moore Design

Cover Illustration: Shutterstock

Every effort has been made to obtain the necessary permissions with reference to copyright material, both illustrative and quoted. We apologise for any omissions in this respect and will be pleased to make the appropriate acknowledgements in any future edition.

A CIP catalogue record for this book is available from the British Library.

Paperback ISBN 978-1-78513-039-7

Large Print ISBN 978-1-78513-040-3

Hardback ISBN 978-1-78513-038-0

Ebook ISBN 978-1-78513-041-0

Kindle ISBN 978-1-78513-042-7

Audio CD ISBN 978-1-78513-033-5

MP3 CD ISBN 978-1-78513-034-2

Digital audio download ISBN 978-1-78513-036-6

Boldwood Books Ltd
23 Bowerdean Street
London SW6 3TN
www.boldwoodbooks.com

1

30 MARCH 2013

Libby

That's – er... The name escaped her as it often did these days.

Libby had been standing at the crowded theatre bar for the last five minutes, waiting for someone to notice she was there, when he – what *is* his name? – had walked in and caught the barman's eye in seconds. It must help being male and six feet tall, even if your shoulders were now slightly bowed and your once black hair turned silver. Age hadn't withered him as much as it had her, and the wine-coloured velvet dinner jacket made him look distinguished.

Don't do yourself down, Libby.

She caught sight of her reflection in the sparkling mirrors behind the long curved bar of the Cottesloe. Not bad, not bad at all. The moiré silk jacket covered a multitude of sins and Zelda's girls had done wonders with the ash-blonde balayage, emphasising what Zelda called her Grace Kelly good looks, if Grace Kelly had freckles.

'Can I get yours?'

Oh. Was he talking to her? She turned to look at him. Yes, he was.

'Er... thanks, er... Prosecco, please. Here.' She held out her credit card.

'If you insist.' He took it with a quirky lopsided smile.

'I certainly do.' *I'm not accepting a drink from a strange man at a theatre bar, even if he isn't completely strange.* Where had she seen him before?

'Same again for the interval?' His voice resonated too, deep, a bit gravelly, and posh.

'Yes – er...' A memory surfaced and she took a chance. 'Yes, Charles? Charles Montgomery?'

He raised an eyebrow. It wasn't a double take exactly, but he was surprised. 'Hmm. No one's called me that for a while. How far do we go back, my dear?' He handed her the Prosecco and her credit card, and she took a gulp. The first bell was already ringing.

'You can take it into the auditorium. Plastic.' He nodded at her drink.

But she needed that drink now to steady her nerves, for suddenly she was eighteen again. Flustered. Flushed. A girl with a crush. Pulses racing. A student like him, but not like him. At drama school.

'Had to change my name when I went into the theatre.' He brushed beer froth from his upper lip. 'Equity insisted. Seems there was another Charles Montgomery, also a theatre director, so I had to think of something else.'

They'd all wanted to go into the theatre.

'Monty, I'm Monty Charles now.' The voice was the same, still upper class, but maybe not quite so far-back as it used to be. To match his more demotic name perhaps. Not that you got a lot of Montys on the council estate where she grew up. Monty sounded a bit P. G. Wodehouse. Did he have a butler? she wondered. Memories were flooding in now. Of an improvisation class in the upper studio, where they'd had to find as many uses as they could for a chair. While she was still dithering – she'd never done improvisation before – King Charles was lowering himself onto his throne. Next thing, he was on his feet, the chair a crown on his head. Then it was something on the floor – a cringing servant? – and he was looking down on it. It wasn't surprising that he'd made a career in the theatre, but as a director? The name Monty Charles didn't ring any bells. Annoying, because for years now she'd been an avid reader of credits, cast lists and programme notes, keeping a lookout for names from her student days, keen to see who'd 'made it' as an actor or stage manager, lighting technician or wardrobe mistress, make-up artist or any of the myriad jobs listed in the credits. She'd spotted a few she recognised over the years, mostly on TV or in films, but sometimes at the theatre where she and Jim would come for treats. But she couldn't recall seeing the name Monty Charles, or maybe she could...

'*She Stoops to Conquer*! It was quite a hit!'

He sighed. 'Yes, that's the one everyone knows. Did you see it?'

'No, sorry, but I read all about it in my mum's *Daily Express*.' She thought he'd cast one of the young royals – Edward? – as the unroyal Tony Lumpkin. It may even have been on the news. Her mum, a keen royal watcher, had been very excited. 'Sorry again—' she took another gulp of Prosecco '—but I didn't get to the theatre much in those days.'

It must have been in the seventies, when she was a stay-at-home mum, looking after three under-fives, and supporting Jim setting up his own business. Mercifully, before he could ask any more questions, the second bell rang, reminding them that *Antony and*

Cleopatra was about to begin. With luck, they would be on the banks of the Nile before she was exposed as Country Mouse on a rare visit to Town. She downed her drink. 'Better find my seat.'

He took her empty glass. 'See you in the interval, then. Our order will be at the far end of the bar.' He pointed to it, and then to the credit card still in her hand. 'Don't forget to put that away.'

She nodded and put the card away but didn't note where he said the drinks would be. He was welcome to hers. Resolved to stay in her seat at the interval, she watched him heading for the door on the far side of the circle. *Phew!* Thank goodness he wasn't going to be on the same side of the auditorium because she didn't want him anywhere near her. What a nightmare if he'd been sitting beside her in the empty seat she'd offered for resale at the box office. Or, possibly worse, in a seat behind her, breathing down her neck. She'd have died. The seat beside her was still empty, she noted, sitting down, so Zelda would lose her fifty quid. *Bad luck, Zelda, but your loss my gain, and I'll make it up to you somehow.* She put her bag on the spare seat. *Libby Allgood, calm down!* Her pulse was racing, her face burning. The lights were going down. Good. But she didn't need the throbbing passions of the fiery pair on the burnished barge right now.

* * *

'Well, what do you think of it so far?' He'd ambushed her outside the loos.

Foiled by her bladder! She'd had to leave her seat to go in search of the Ladies at the first interval, and when she came out there he was, a glass in each hand. 'Thought I'd find you here.' Great, he'd been thinking about her bladder too. He moved away from the doors towards the bar.

'Brill. Absolutely brill.' She took a gulp of her second Prosecco.

'Antony and Cleopatra both brill.' She wished she could think of something more intelligent to say, but it was back to flushing incoherence. The ambush had thrown her.

'It is superbly directed.' He took a sip of beer.

'Wh-what do you mean by that?' *Well done, Libby!* It was a good question and something she really wanted to know. People were always saying '*It's superbly directed*' or sometimes '*It's very badly directed*' at the film club she belonged to, but she'd never got a good answer when she'd asked what they actually meant. They just looked at her as if she should know, and maybe she should. Fortunately Monty seemed all too pleased to enlighten her.

'Good directing is *not* directing,' he began. 'That's the essence of it.' Was he working in academia now, she wondered, in a drama department at a university? They'd sprung up since they were young. It sounded like the beginning of a lecture. 'Directing isn't telling people what to do,' he went on, almost swaying on his heels, 'it's about... loving them.'

Two women next to them were listening now.

'Simon got those brilliant performances from Ralph and Sophie —' he made them sound like his best friends '—by loving them. If you love people, they love you and give you what you want.'

Do they? Not always in her experience. Had he had children? she wondered. She loved hers and they did exactly what *they* wanted. And how did people know what he wanted? she asked.

Because he told them, he said, by describing his vision.

'Before a production begins, I spend weeks alone, studying the play and deciding what it's about. Then I choose the cast – that's an act of love in itself – also set designers, costume designers, make-up artists and so forth. Then – this is important – on our first day together, even before the first read-through, I address them sharing my vision.'

'Then...'

'It's up to them to make my vision a reality.'

'But...' It couldn't be that simple. 'What do you actually *do*?'

'Love them, encourage them, show them I love them. My dear, the days are long gone when actor-managers blocked out moves and told actors what to do. That's so nineteenth century and went out with gaslights. Believe me, Ralph and Sophie are perfect as the self-deluded lovers because Simon loves them, so they're giving him their all. Actors just want to be loved.'

'Doesn't everyone?'

'Ye-es.' He looked at her, his head slightly to one side. 'I suppose they do.'

The noisy bar had gone quiet, and he held her gaze with the startlingly blue eyes she now remembered vividly. Then the bell went. Thank goodness. Time to go back to her seat. She'd revealed too much. She finished her drink, and he took the glass out of her hand. 'You haven't told me your name yet.'

'Libby, Liberty Allgood.' What the hell? If he was going to recognise her it would be now. That was what she was called then, and now professionally.

'Great name.' He showed no sign of having heard it before. 'Next interval you can tell me where you knew me as Charles M.'

The bell went again and she headed for her seat, where she would stay for the second interval, if she had to sit with her legs plaited.

2

————

LIBBY

'I did it, all by myself!' Libby knew she sounded childish.

But Zelda, on the other end of the phone, sounded pleased, relieved and impressed. 'Well done, Libby! It's hard doing things on your own for the first time. I felt so bad letting you down at the last minute. Did you really enjoy yourself?'

'I did,' Libby, still in bed and not yet coffee-ed, reassured her new friend and neighbour, while wondering if *enjoy* was the right word to describe her night at the theatre. It definitely wasn't the whole of it. There had been moments not unconnected with meeting Charles Montgomery aka Monty Charles when she'd wished she hadn't gone. Now she still had a squirgly feeling in her stomach. Was it a hangover from yesterday, or was she getting the tummy upset that had made Zelda opt out of the trip?

'How are *you*, Zelda?'

'Okay, definitely on the mend, but really, Libby, I couldn't have done that, not seven months after Harry died. I was still in pieces.'

'Zelda, you've just flown to the States on your own!'

'But that was five years on.' Zelda had gone to America in search of her long-lost Afro-American dad and found him.

'Okay, Zelda, compliment accepted. I *am* a bit proud of myself for doing it. But I did want to see the play and I didn't want to waste two tickets. Sorry, by the way, they didn't resell yours. Too late.'

She imagined Zelda shrugging in a resigned, win-some-lose-some sort of way, possibly still sitting in bed like her, but with her two adoring Westie dogs by her side. Living three doors up, in a semi just like hers, Zelda had been Libby's lifeline since she'd moved in only three months ago. How lucky was that, meeting someone who understood? About *everything,* even getting used to hearing-aids. But most importantly Zelda seemed to know exactly how lost and lonely she'd felt since Jim had died, and she'd introduced her to two of her friends, also widows, Viv and Janet. The Three Muscateers, they called themselves. They were close friends, but had welcomed her, a fourth, to their group. They were a fund of knowledge and experience and they'd empathised with every feeling she'd described. But would Zelda, *could* Zelda, done-with-sex-Zelda, done-with-men-Zelda, resolutely single, empathise with how she was feeling now? How could she, when there was only one word to describe it?

Lust.

She'd arrived at the theatre a rational woman, proud of herself for getting there, proud of dealing with all the changes to the transport system since she'd last been to London, proud of going it alone. She'd left emotions in turmoil, convinced she needed a man to make her complete, that she needed an Antony for her Cleopatra, and that his name was Monty. *Oh no!* For the first time since she'd met Zelda, Libby felt she couldn't talk freely. She couldn't tell her what was on her mind. She wanted to tell her. Talking would help. It always did. It would defuse these ridiculous feelings. But, well, what would Zelda *think*? Libby saw the pen and notepad beside her bed and had another idea. Could she defuse the feelings by writing about them in the column she wrote for a local paper? She was always looking for a subject.

'Libby, how was Ralph Fiennes?' Zelda brought her back to the present.

'Delicious. I *was* Cleopatra.' Yes! Phew! Articulating her thoughts was helping already. She had identified with Cleopatra, acted brilliantly by Sophie Okonedo. It was Ralph Fiennes aka Antony causing this maelstrom of emotions.

'Well, you couldn't have drooled over gorgeous Ralph with Jim by your side, could you?' Zelda, a big count-your-blessings exponent, wasn't always tactful. She never missed a chance to point out the advantages of living on your own, which included, she was now saying, not having to slave over a stove and cook Sunday lunch today. 'You can have a sandwich and drool all day long over Ralph Fiennes if you like, unless you'd like to come and walk the Westies with me?'

But I'd love to be cooking lunch for...

When Zelda eventually rang off, after again extolling the virtues of dogs over men, Libby had agreed to meet her for a walk in Russell Park in the afternoon. Downstairs making coffee she decided she would tell Zelda about meeting Monty Charles, laughing at herself as she needed to do. It would help to get him out of her system. Now she was feeling too alive, more alive than she had done since Jim died. For months she'd been numb, going through the motions of living, cleaning teeth, eating and drinking, putting one foot in front of the other, mechanically like an automaton. The encounter had jolted her out of that catatonic state and she wasn't used to having feelings. Yesterday had been too much of an adventure. She was in a tizz. Whether the dazzling Ralph Fiennes was responsible for that or the less dazzling but rather distinguished Monty Charles, she couldn't be sure. But between them both they'd managed to stir up the giddy feelings of

a younger, sillier self, and it had to stop. She put back the cafetière
and reached for the camomile tea – caffeine she did not need – and
started to plan a sensible, matter-of-fact, calming day. One, put a
load of washing in, two do some overdue admin, beginning with
her bank account.

Half an hour later she was laughing, tears streaming down her
face, though exactly why she wasn't sure. Hurray for online banking, but why discovering she'd been *done* by Mr Distinguished
Theatre Director should make her happy, she didn't know. Done!
Cheated! Bamboozled! At first she hadn't believed it when she saw
how much money had gone out of her account for drinks at the
Cottesloe bar. Could two Proseccos cost that much? Thinking she
could be wrong as drinks at theatre bars were notoriously expensive, she'd googled prices and a horrible suspicion was confirmed.
She'd paid for two Proseccos and two beers. She'd paid for his and
her drinks at both intervals. What a con man! But money well spent
– that was why she was laughing – she had her independence back.
She was her own woman again. All her crazy yearnings had gone.
Her pulse was still beating faster than normal but fuelled by fury.
Who needed men? Zelda was right. They were overrated with very
few exceptions. By lunchtime she'd written a first draft of next
week's column, working title – 'Beware geeks bearing gifts!' Because
Monty Charles was a geek, a theatre geek, with his nineteenth-
century this and twentieth-century that and his fancy theories of
direction. He must have spotted her as a soft touch from the
moment he walked in. The editor, she was sure, would love this
one. He loved a cautionary tale.

* * *

'I forgot to mention I met someone from my past, last night.' Telling
Zelda was easy now. Libby had no trouble telling a tale against

herself. She liked to make people laugh.

But Zelda didn't laugh. 'That isn't funny, Libby. My flabber is gasted.' She let the Westies off their leads as they reached the gate of Russell Park and they shot into the shrubbery at the side of the gravel path, white rumps flashing among the gloomy rhododendron leaves. 'What a poo-bag!' Zelda disposed of the one in her hand in a bin. 'Tell me, where did you first come across this creep?'

They settled into the walk, keeping a lookout for little bikes and scooters and stray balls. Families were out in force on this sunny Sunday afternoon, with mums or dads pushing baby buggies or guiding ride-on toys along the wide path, still strewn with autumn leaves though spring was clearly on its way. In the borders daffodils waved their cheerful heads.

'Well?' Zelda prompted.

'We were students together at drama school.'

'You went to drama school!' Zelda's flabber was gasted again.

'Briefly.'

'You trained to be an *actress*?'

'Not quite. I dropped out, but that was the dream once, yes. Why so surprised?'

'Because... well, first because you've never said, but also...' Libby felt herself being studied '...you're... I was going to say not the type, but perhaps there isn't a type, you're shy in some ways but you cover it up with...' She didn't say. 'You can be a bit of a show-off, in an entertaining way. Anyway, what happened? If that isn't a crass question.'

'Old story, I'm afraid. Got pregnant. Still feel bad about it actually. Letting so many people down, especially my parents. That was the worst bit...'

Zelda touched her hand. 'Snap. No need to explain.'

'You mean...?'

Zelda nodded. 'Yup. Me too, up the duff, as we used to say,

followed by a shotgun wedding in my case, but I didn't get a lovely son or daughter at the end like you, and the marriage didn't work out.' She became brisk. 'So, where does Con Man fit into this sad tale?'

'He doesn't. He's got nothing to do with it. I had a bit of a crush on him, that was all. I was a naïve eighteen-year-old, straight from school. He was good-looking, in a tall, dark and handsome sort of way, and a few years older. I'd noticed him on the first day, in the registration queue, a head above the others but it was his voice more than anything, so deep and dark and, well, sexy, that got to me. You could say it reached parts that other features didn't reach.'

'And you had an affair?'

'No! *No!* Wrong end of the stick again!' She could see the way Zelda's thoughts were going. 'I said he doesn't fit into this. Jim is – was – Eleanor's father, and of my two boys. I went home and married the boy next door, well, round the corner to be exact. He was a friend of my brother's and we'd been friends for about a year, when one night it went a bit further than we intended it to. I hardly knew Monty, Charles as he was then, Charles Montgomery to give him his full name, just fancied him from afar. We were in some of the same classes, but not in the same class, which mattered more than you might think. Money or lack of was a great divider. We didn't mix much outside because our social lives were totally different. He mixed with the rich set, aristocrats some of them – they'd all been to posh schools – who dined out in posh restaurants. We, the few of us who weren't wealthy – I was a rarity with a local authority grant – well, we ate in our digs, or in the college canteen, or we had takeaways, though there weren't many of them in those days even in London. It was fish and chips or kebabs if you were feeling adventurous.'

'So why is wealthy, former posh-boy Charles now lurking around theatre bars, getting single women out on their own for the night to buy him his drinks? No, Mack, no, Morag!' Zelda pulled the dogs away from an ice-cream cone that a child had just dropped on the path.

'Pass. Total mystery.'

'I trust you've cancelled your card?' Zelda grabbed Libby's arm.

'I didn't give him my pin number!'

'But he had your card in his hands, Libby. He could have memorised the account number, or even photographed it on his phone. We're going home now to cancel it! The man's a fraud! You should report him! Mack! Morag!' She called the dogs and put them on their leads.

'Okay. Okay. I'll do it as soon as I get in!'

* * *

But the phone in the hall was ringing as she opened the front door.

'Hello!' She picked it up, hoping it was Eleanor asking her to babysit or just come round. She hadn't seen Ellie-Jo since Tuesday.

'Libby.' His deep voice was unmistakable.

Put down the phone.

'Is this really you? Please say it is.'

Put down the phone.

'Have I got the right number? Am I speaking to Libby, Libby Allgood?'

How had he got her number?

'I've been trawling through social media all day to try and find you. You're quite a celeb in your own little way, aren't you? Please don't hang up on me. I know what you're thinking and I want to explain.'

'E-explain, then.'

'You must think I'm a complete bastard...'

3

LIBBY

To go or not to go?

That was the question uppermost in Libby's mind as she joined her friends for lunch on Friday. Monty wanted to see her again. She wanted to see Monty again. On Sunday she'd had to clamp her lips shut to stop an instant yes bursting out when he'd pleaded with her to come to London. Somehow she'd managed to say she'd let him know.

But she hadn't yet and wasn't quite sure why.

'He apologised. Profusely. And he explained exactly how it happened.' Libby wanted Viv, Janet and Zelda to understand how desperately sorry Monty had been. Abject. She'd *felt* his misery. 'He's desperate to put things right, he really is.'

Zelda raised well-shaped eyebrows over the tortoiseshell glasses she'd just put on to read the menu. Libby wished she hadn't told her about the credit-card mix-up before she'd heard Monty's explanation. Viv and Janet seemed more open-minded, though they'd both already heard the Zelda version.

'Suspend your disbelief, Zelda.' Janet brushed a crumb off the red-check tablecloth. 'This might be an honest man. Let's hear what Libby has to say.'

Viv nodded. The four of them were in The Olive Branch, the Greek restaurant Libby had introduced the others to when they'd started inviting her to their monthly lunches. She'd been pleased to contribute something to the group who had done so much for her. It struck her again how different the women were. Their friendship still amazed her but she knew they'd seen each other through thick and thin since meeting five years before. Viv in denims, her red hair streaked with white, looked as if she'd just come in from the garden, which she probably had as she was a professional gardener. Janet was bandbox neat, her silver hair kept short and stylish by the girls at Sophisticutts, Zelda's salon. Zelda was as glamorous as ever with her braided hair and flowing caftan, though she'd now embraced the life of a student as well as her Afro-American heritage. She'd been busy amassing degrees at the OU since handing over the running of the salon to a manager.

'We're on the edge of our seats, Libby—' Viv touched her hand '—so tell us how you've been for the past month, including your night at the theatre. You know the format now, highs and lows, gains and losses in whatever order they come. We want to hear it all.'

It was a bit like Weight Watchers for feelings.

'And,' said Janet, giving Zelda a glare, 'we shall all, *all*, keep an open mind about this new male on the scene.'

Libby took a deep breath, but there was no need for nerves. These women were on her side even when, like Zelda now, they seemed not to be. They looked out for each other. That was why they'd formed the Muscateers. They understood what she was going through, so she didn't need to tell them how shaky she still sometimes felt, or what a big deal it had been going to the theatre for the first time by herself. Sparing them that, she quickly got to the bumping into Monty and the question on her mind.

'Monty thought he'd used my card for the pre-show drinks, his and mine, and his card for the interval drinks, his and mine, which meant we'd each paid for our own drinks, which is what I'd asked to do. He thought he'd paid in two transactions. It was only when he checked his bank statement and couldn't find any payment there that he guessed the barman had put all the drinks on my card, and he was mortified.'

They were all frowning with concentration. Then Janet said, 'Let me get this right, for avoidance of doubt, this Monty came up to you and asked if he could get your drink. You said, "Yes a Prosecco," and handed over your card?' She made *handed over your card* sound like the action of someone who should be certified.

'Yes, because I didn't want him, someone I'd just met, though as I've said I had met him before, but over forty years ago, to pay for my drink. He didn't *ask* for my card. I volunteered it. And I didn't give him my pin number so what was the harm? It was touch screen.'

Zelda rolled her eyes. 'You could have taken your card to the bar yourself.'

'But Libby didn't...' Viv intervened, 'Look, I'm trying to visualise this scene. While your card was still in his hand, he said, "Shall I get the same for the interval?" or words to that effect?'

'Yes, and I said yes again, and it was then I remembered his name and used it, which surprised him. Actually, that could have distracted him from what the barman was doing.'

'You're making excuses for him.' Zelda again.

'Did he ever show the barman *his* card?' said Viv. 'Did you see it?'

'I don't *know*. All I was interested in was my card. I was keeping an eye on it, I really was, but...'

'Ladies, excuse me.' It was Nikos, the restaurant owner, with hummus and pitta bread and large black olives. With his bald pate and strong features, he made Libby think of Kojak. Phew! She welcomed his smile and the break from what had started to feel like an interrogation. She always got Nikos's personal attention – he kept a window table for them all – because he remembered her from the days when she used to come in regularly with Jim. The two men had become friends over the years, in the way that men did, getting together over shared interests. They would chat about cricket or chess, which they sometimes played together, while she talked to his wife about grandchildren. The two men had occasionally gone to a match at the Oval.

'Are you okay, Liberty? These Muscateers aren't giving you a hard time?'

Libby shook her head and he topped up her glass with the wine, a delicious fruity Malagousia, made from grapes grown on Mount Olympus, he said, before moving to fill the others' glasses. 'Sure?' He looked round the table and Zelda opened her mouth as if she might be going to tell him what they'd been discussing. So Libby shook her head vigorously in a *Don't you dare tell him* sort of way. How much had Nikos heard? She wondered, hoping not a lot. He saw himself as her protector, she sometimes thought, a stand-in for Jim, which was nice. But she didn't want him thinking she wasn't capable of going it alone. When he'd gone back to the kitchen she carried on trying to convince the others that the card mix-up was a genuine mistake on Monty's part.

'I mean, if anyone was at fault it was me. I know I shouldn't have let my card leave my hand. Blame new-widow brain if you like. But I repeat, he didn't ask me for my card, and—' she suddenly thought of a clinching argument '—why would he have got in touch to tell me about the mistake if he wanted to get one over me?'

Even Zelda hadn't got an answer for that, so, point made, she at last asked what she wanted to ask. '*Should* I see him again?'

'Libby,' said Viv, 'we don't tell each other what to do, and try to avoid *shoulds*. We'll give you our opinions but you make up your own mind. What's he proposing?'

'Lunch at a restaurant in London called Simpson's.'

'Simpson's! Simpson's in the Strand?' Janet nearly jumped out of her seat. 'That's famous for traditional English food, roast beef and Yorkshire pudding, a nice glass of claret, that sort of thing. It's very expensive. When is this?'

'Tomorrow. I've got to tell him yes or no today.'

'Tomorrow?' Janet frowned. 'But you have to book weeks in advance.'

'He must have pulled strings,' said Viv.

'Or he booked to take someone else who dropped out?' Libby started to go off the idea – she wasn't a fan of roast beef – but Janet was growing more enthusiastic by the minute. It was an opportunity not to be missed, she said, such an iconic restaurant, and Libby would be safe in such a public place. She must check he was paying though – to apologise for the drinks debacle – and she must keep them informed about her whereabouts before and after, so they could be on standby.

'That's our only rule,' said Viv. 'You must tell one of us where you are when you go on a date. So we can rush to the rescue if needed.'

'Which has happened,' said Zelda, and Libby hoped she'd elaborate, but she didn't.

'Libby—' Viv speared a black olive '—do you fancy this Monty?'

'Y-yes.' It just came out.

'Thought so.' Viv nodded and looked sympathetic. 'Well, just be aware grief fucks up your hormones like it fucks up everything else. The pheromones will be buzzing like a swarm of bees and you won't know a dish from a donkey. Or non-existent,' she added. 'I didn't fancy anyone for years...'

It was a relief when Nikos arrived to take away the empty dishes and bring their main course. He'd cooked fasolakia lathera, he said, to go with the lamb kebabs, because the dish of green beans, onions and tomatoes cooked in silky olive oil was one of Libby's favourites. He hoped it would bring a bit of colour to her cheeks.

'Oh dear, do I look washed-out, Nikos? I think we all do compared to you.' His bald pate was bronze. 'How was Greece?' He went there to top up his suntan and his culinary skills every winter. The restaurant, only five years old, was a new venture for Nikos, and he was still learning, he frequently told them. 'Where is Evelina today?' she asked, keen to shift the focus to his family.

'Visiting the grandkids, but she made your favourite dessert before she left.'

He sat down with them at the end of the meal, when he'd brought the slices of honey-sweet nutty baklava to the table, along with coffee and glasses of fragrant Greek brandy. 'To revive everyone's spirits,' he said, raising his glass. *'Yamas!'*

Libby and Zelda left first, leaving Viv and Janet still drinking coffee, because it was three o'clock and Eleanor had said she might come round with Ellie-Jo after school. As they left, Libby assured them all that *if* she went to London next day, *if*, she would keep in close touch.

4

VIV

'She'll go. It's spring. The sap's rising.' Viv watched Libby and Zelda leaving, with the ever-attentive Nikos holding open the door. She noted that he stood for at least a minute, watching the two of them cross the square, and had no doubts where his gaze lingered. 'Nikos has got a soft spot for Libby, hasn't he?' she thought aloud.

'Soft isn't the word I'd use.' Janet lifted her head from her phone.

'Janet Loveday, you're getting as filthy-minded as I am. Nikos is a happily married man.'

'And when did that stop a man having – what shall I call them... feelings?'

'Well...' Viv chose her words carefully '...I know that you know that only too well, and that some of the bastards act on those feelings, regardless of their marital status. But Evelina and Nikos seem very happy together and I think he's a very honourable man. Did you know that he was a lawyer in his former life?'

'No, I didn't. Interesting, but I didn't say Nikos wasn't honourable. I just agreed with you that he's very fond of Libby. He admires her and finds her attractive and looks out for her in an old-fashioned chivalric, possibly Greek way. Wasn't he friends with her husband?'

'Think so,' said Viv. 'Well, I just hope that Libby goes to London and gets this Monty to buy her a slap-up lunch as recompense for the money he owes her. Or, better still, that she gets him to pay back the money he owes her and then she pays for her own lunch.'

'Why?' Janet was googling. 'Why's that better?'

'No sense of obligation if she pays her own way?'

'But why the sense of obligation, anyway? Why should a man expect something in return if he buys a woman a meal?' Janet was still googling. 'Listen to this. Monty Charles hasn't directed anything for a long time as far as I can see. Nothing at all this century. And his last success was a play about the French Revolution. Woman murders man in the bath, a bit of a bloodbath it seems, literally. "Nothing left to the imagination," one reviewer said. His production, a revival in the nineteen seventies, was quite a hit. The main character was de Sade, by the way, he who gave us sadism, but let's not do guilt by association. This Monty may be a teddy bear.'

'I bet he takes his to bed with him.' Viv was letting her prejudices show. 'Right upper-class twit, he sounds to me. Where are our second coffees, by the way? Can't help noticing that Nikos isn't so attentive now that Libby isn't here.'

They'd lingered for another cup because they both had to drive home and because Niko's coffee was delicious. Janet thought it was the cardamon seeds he added when he roasted the beans that made it special, but hadn't got him to reveal his secret. Perhaps she should get Libby to ask?

'Janet, do you think Libby was rushing off to ring the not-so-famous man from her past?'

'More like she was going to see her granddaughter, but...' Janet stopped as Nikos arrived with the coffees.

'Ladies, I'm sorry to have kept you waiting.' His English was perfect with hardly a trace of a Greek accent, just a slightly rolled r, which was rather attractive. *He* was attractive.

'I meant,' said Janet when he'd gone, 'that I'm perfectly okay with Libby finding someone else. It would be lovely. It worked, is working, for both of us.'

'But? I sensed a but.'

'It's early days, less than a year, much less in fact, and we know how careful you must be.' Janet didn't really need to say it and they relaxed into companionable silence, savouring the excellent coffee, each with their own thoughts.

'Must be great to be Zelda and Libby living in walking distance of The Olive Branch,' Janet mused. 'But I'd be the size of a house, Alan too, if we lived nearer. I'd give up cooking completely.'

Janet and Viv usually came in together sharing a car, because they lived in the same village. Today, though, Viv had come straight from work, from a job on the other side of town, so Janet had had to drive herself.

'Sorry,' said Viv, 'but it'll be our turn to walk home next time.' Their monthly meetings had got into a bit of a pattern, The Wagon and Horses in Elmsley one month, The Olive Branch in town the next.

'Ladies.' Nikos had his booking diary open, when they settled the bill at the counter. He looked disappointed when they said it would be June before they were in again. 'Two whole months!'

'Yes, Nikos. Sorry. But I'm sure Libby and Zelda will be in before that, and we will as well, with or without our partners. Your food and drink are the best in town.' Janet's words brought a smile to his face.

'I will look forward to that.' He came to the door with them but didn't linger.

'And by June,' Janet said as they crossed the square to head for the car park, 'or even earlier we'll have learned if Libby's encounter with the man from the past is the beginning of a great romance or...'

'The start of a bloody disaster?' said Viv.

5

LIBBY

'I'm here, yes, at Simpson's in the Strand, in the loo, well, on the loo, actually.'

'Too much information, Libby!' But Zelda was laughing, obviously pleased to get her call.

'It's a throne, Zelda, but so comfortable – no more plastic seats for me from now on – the mahogany is as smooth and shiny as conkers. Must have been burnished...'

'Stop there, Libby! I don't want to think about a century of upper-class bums polishing the wood to a fine patina...'

'I was thinking more of lower-class maids with beeswax and yellow dusters. Honestly, Zelda, you should see the wall panelling, mahogany too, I think, in this *room*. It's not a stingy cubicle you can hardly turn round in.'

'Room for a crinoline, I expect, when Victorian women retired discreetly to powder their noses. Keep tight hold of your mobile, by the way, Libby. If you drop that one down that loo you'll never see it again.'

'Thanks for reminding me about that, Zelda,' Libby recalled a recent disaster. 'I got here early. That's why I'm hiding in here.'

'Libby—' Zelda was stern '—you're not on trial, this Monty, Charles or whatever he's called, he is. He should be nervous, not you, pulling out all the stops to please you to make up for his appalling mistake. Remember that. You're there to enjoy yourself and find out more about him, including how he managed to get a table at such short notice. Did you clarify who's paying, by the way?' Zelda obviously still had him down as a con man.

'No, I didn't, but I'm not I can assure you. My credit card is buried in my bag. This restaurant is way out of my league, sumptuous, Zelda. Stepping out of the revolving doors into the entrance hall was like stepping back in time, that's if you were one of the wealthy elite who could afford to eat here. Don't suppose the servants came in this way and the beggars in the street outside could only have peered in marvelling at the opulence. The entrance hall is like a jewellery box, glitteringly gorgeous. There's wood panelling polished to a high sheen, and shiny leather seats and sparkling mirrors, reflecting the intricately patterned black and white tiled floor. Honestly, Zelda, the lamp on the counter glowed in the semi-darkness like a magic orange. But sorry, I'm getting carried away, may even be writing an article for Libby's World. I'd better get on. Need to check my make-up...'

'Okay, but try and enjoy yourself, right?' Zelda sounded like a mother encouraging a shy teenager.

'Will do.'

And keep your knickers on. Zelda didn't say that, but Libby heard her anyway and ended the call before Zelda came up with any more advice.

She was grateful for all the tips from the *How to Be a Widow* handbook she was sure her three friends could write, but thought she could manage this situation. Things had changed a lot since she'd last dated nearly half a century ago, they had warned her. Firstly, she must be prepared to pay for herself, which was fine by

them, they said – or fine-ish. Viv had pointed out that men and
women's pay and pensions still weren't equal so men usually had
more cash, so they should perhaps pay for more, but independence
was worth paying for. Zelda had spelt it out: 'Be wary when a man
does treat you to dinner, or lunch – or a coffee.' Lots of them, most
in her experience, expected something in return. 'Especially if it's
pricey,' she'd said. The prices at Simpson's were eye-watering. That
was why Zelda had wanted her to clarify paying arrangements
beforehand.

But Libby hadn't because there hadn't been time. She'd had a
short conversation with Monty on Friday night when he'd rung her
to ask what she'd decided. She hadn't rung him, because she didn't
want to seem too keen, and because she'd started having pangs of
guilt. Suddenly Jim's voice was in her ear. *You've replaced me already,
have you?* She'd felt his hurt and decided she wouldn't go when the
phone rang, and the sound of Monty's voice changed her mind.
'Yes,' had come out of her mouth and she'd agreed to meet him in
the entrance hall at half past twelve. Crikey. It was gone that
already. Better flush the loo, wash hands and apply lip gloss.

* * *

'How can I help you, madam?' The earringed young man behind
the counter was friendly.

'I'm here to meet Mr Monty Charles, at half past twelve.'

'Mr Charles is waiting for you, madam. I'll take you to the
dining room. Follow me.'

Monty stood up to greet her with a light kiss on one cheek, and
appraise her, she felt, not noticing, she hoped, that she was
wearing the same moiré silk jacket she'd worn at the theatre a
week ago though now with black velvet pants. As the young man
pulled out a red leather chair for her to sit down, she thought it

wasn't too bad a choice. At least it didn't clash with the furniture. The young man retreated after seating her at the table, before an array of sparkling cutlery and glasses on a thick white linen tablecloth.

'Perfect,' said Monty. 'Perfect for the setting.'

'And you look every inch the director,' she said, because it was true. The navy and orange paisley cravat and a dark shirt with pale suit gave him a theatrical air.

He laughed and fingered the cravat. 'From Victoria Richards. She's wonderful. Beautiful pearls, by the way.'

'From Jim Roberts, my husband.' It was a single string with matching drop earrings. She'd put her hair up to show them off.

'Your reward for thirty years of servitude?'

'Not at all. I was happily married.'

'Was?' He raised an eyebrow.

'Jim died seven months ago.' She waited for the customary words of condolence.

'You're available, then?'

Fortunately, the waiter arrived with the wine list and the menu, called the Bill of Fare here. 'Sorry,' Monty said when he'd ordered a bottle of something. 'No offence meant. Just checking there wasn't a jealous husband waiting in the wings, brandishing pistols.'

'None taken. I'll blame the Victorian setting.' She went along with his recommendation of roast rib of beef with all the trimmings. The wine, she noted when it came, was English too, Gusbourne rosé – why not pink? she wondered – from a vineyard in Kent.

'And what did your husband do?' he asked when they both had a glass in their hands.

'Computers. He had his own business.'

'Lucrative?' He wasn't subtle.

'Quite. Jim worked very hard.' She didn't say how hard, how

keen he was to be a success, to make it up to her for the glittering career he was sure he'd deprived her of.

'Less precarious than a life in the theatre?'

'Yes, but there was a lot of competition.'

He's trying to find out how much you're worth. Zelda was in her head. *Don't worry, Zelda.* She didn't say that she'd sold the business for a very good price, because none of the children wanted to take it on, or that she'd given them most of the proceeds to help them buy houses.

'Do you mind if I take notes?' She reached for her notebook as the starter arrived. 'I write this weekly column, see...'

'I know. You have quite a following. I researched you, remember, to track you down? Good job you didn't take your husband's name. It would have been harder.'

'But I did, then became Libby Allgood again when I started writing.'

The devilled eggs, piped with a spicy mayonnaise on a bed of crunchy chicken skin, looked like a work of art, and tasted delicious. Chicken skin, who'd have thought of serving it like that? She'd never throw it away again, or give it to the cat. And the Melba toast, wafer thin and even crisper than the chicken skin, melted in the mouth.

'Chess is a theme here.' He saw her studying the crockery, which had a chequered motif. 'That's why you see so much of that. Simpson's used to be even more famous for chess than it was for food. When it was a coffee house, back in the eighteenth century, they played matches against other coffee houses. Top-hatted runners used to carry the news of each move from one coffee house to another. There's an ancient chess set on display in one of the rooms.'

How Jim would have loved this.

'Well?' He was looking at her, fork poised, having obviously asked her something.

'Oh, sorry. Senior moment.'

'I just asked where we'd met before, where you knew me as Charles Montgomery.'

'The Central School of Speech and Drama.'

'Really?' He looked very surprised.

'Yes, I was there briefly. Two terms.' No need to go into more detail.

'Good heavens!' He studied her face as if trying to find a younger self there. 'Why don't I remember you?'

Because, she didn't say, we hardly came into contact, and the one time we did, at your invitation, well, I'm glad you don't remember that encounter.

He picked up a piece of Melba toast. 'I thought you were going to say we grew up in the same village.'

'Where was that?'

'Somerset.' He named a village she'd never heard of. 'Lived there till I was sent off to school.' He mentioned a school she'd never heard of either. Minor public, he explained, then the waiter came to clear their dishes, and he said they must prepare themselves for the main course, served from the fabled antique carving trolley. 'Sit back and get ready to applaud.'

It was a piece of theatre. The waiter, if that was a grand enough word for the man who rolled the trolley in and raised the silver dome to reveal the succulent joint beneath, was a maestro. He artistically carved off the rose-pink hunks of beef and arranged them into a perfect fan covering half the warmed plate. Another waiter added a golden-brown pillar of fondant potato, a creamy mound of cauliflower cheese, another of lustrous spinach and, to complete the picture, a golden Yorkshire pudding that looked as if it might fly away.

It tasted as good as it looked, but she didn't let it distract from her main task.

Find out all about him, Libby.

By the time they'd finished the main course, she had learned that he'd had a pony called Freddie, and coming home from school to find his parents had sold it was the worst thing that had ever happened to him. That his father was a barrister, working in London a lot, and that his mother was a stay-at-home wife, who hadn't stayed at home much. Drama was what saved him from a miserable childhood. Plays, he just loved plays from the very first one he saw. He thought it was *The Mousetrap* but it might have been *Peter Pan*. Then a charismatic English teacher at school gave him the main part in *Henry V*, and he was hooked. 'I had my escape route, knew I must go into the theatre. Forward into the breach! I was doomed. And what about you?'

She waited for the plates to be cleared away.

'Drama saved me too, but from boredom more than from unhappiness, though teenage was angst-ridden as teenage is. The town I grew up in didn't have a theatre, so it was school plays and amateur dramatics and reading novels that took me out of myself. They let me forget the everyday and humdrum for a bit. I always loved to escape into another world. My dad was a bus driver, my mother worked at the local Woolworths so there wasn't a lot of cash, and I had two younger brothers. Mum and Dad were great, really good parents who hadn't had an education themselves, so they were very keen for us all to stay at school and go to university.'

'But you went to drama school instead. How did they feel about that?'

'Thrilled. Absolutely thrilled. Other people warned them – it was all "Don't let your daughter go on the stage, Mrs Worthington" – but they were 100 per cent behind me. They were sure I'd end up as Dame Liberty Allgood, star of stage and screen, and make them all proud.'

'So what went wrong?'

'Oh, that's for another time.'

'I'm glad you said that.'

'Oh, I didn't mean...' She *didn't* mean.

'I hope you did mean. Pudding?' The waiter was back.

She shook her head. 'No, thanks.'

'Is that how you stay looking so svelte?'

Svelte? Hardly! She'd had to surreptitiously undo the button on her black velvet pants to accommodate the roast potatoes. And after treacle sponge with vanilla custard – he'd ignored her no – she'd had to retire to the palatial Ladies and undo another.

'Well,' he said over coffee and cognac, which he'd ordered while she was away from the table, 'all I can say is that I wish I'd met you earlier, Libby Allgood.'

But you did, she didn't say. Good, though, that he'd forgotten that particular encounter.

'But now—' he reached for her hand '—we're going to make up for lost time.'

6

ZELDA

'He wants to see me again.'

There was no need to ask who. Libby's face was creased, as if this Monty wanting to see her again were a problem she had to solve. For a few seconds Zelda thought Libby might have invited her round to discuss the pros and cons, but it soon became clear she hadn't. Libby had made up her mind. Libby was going to see lover-boy again. Libby was smitten. Zelda sitting opposite her saw all the signs – the number of times she said his name and the breathless way she said it. There were two of them in Libby's kitchen on Sunday morning, but only one of them was there in body *and* mind.

'It was perfect, Zelda, the food, the drink, the ambience, everything.' Libby was still in the posh restaurant with Monty Charles.

Zelda didn't believe in perfect, and said so, trying to sound like a realistic friend, not a negative grumpy one.

'Honestly, Zelda, he didn't put a foot wrong.'

'Not one?' She couldn't help smiling at Libby's dreamy expression.

'Not one.'

'And he paid?'

'Well, I didn't.' Libby laughed. 'And I don't think we'd have got out of the door if he hadn't.' The staff seemed to know him very well, she said.

'Perhaps he moonlights as a waiter? Sorry.'

Libby frowned. The re-meet was a mere four days away.

'Thursday,' Libby said when Zelda asked for details. 'Monty has tickets for *Relative Values* at the Harold Pinter Theatre. That's a play, a comedy, by Noël Coward, if you didn't know. Monty says Rory Bremner is playing the lead in his theatrical debut. Should be fun and interesting, and it's a matinee, you'll be pleased to hear, as you don't like me staying out late.'

'Libby, stop that. Don't cast me as your mother, I'm—'

'Only looking out for me. I know and I appreciate it, but you make me feel like a teenager sometimes. And I'm sure you've got nothing to worry about. Monty is perfectly lovely.'

Evidence? Zelda wanted to ask. *Can you supply proof of Monty Charles's perfect loveliness?* But Libby's ginger and white cat – Cornflake, was that its name? – had appeared on the windowsill outside and Libby was standing up, saying she ought to get on. She wanted to write a column about her visit to Simpson's while it was fresh in her mind.

'But I'm not sure what angle to take yet.'

'Just make it personal,' said Zelda, who was a big fan of Libby's World. 'That's why your readers like it, your honesty and the way you learn from experience.'

'But do I tell them about Monty?'

'Yes, not naming him, of course. Privacy and all that. Just say "my companion" like they do in foodie columns. Hey, Simpson's might pay you if you praise the food enough, or give you a free meal.'

'Don't think they need to, Zelda.'

'Was it packed? Anyone famous there?'

'Oh.' Libby grimaced, then laughed at herself. 'Sorry. No idea.'

'Because you weren't looking. You only had eyes for the person sitting opposite you. Oh dear, Libby, you've got it bad, haven't you?'

She nodded tragically.

'Well, I'd get on with your column if I were you. Your readers will love learning all about your trip to Simpson's.' *And* – she didn't say this – *it might make you think a bit harder, a bit more objectively about Monty Charles, and that 'not a foot wrong'. She might even recall a mis-step or two.*

But she didn't hold out much hope.

* * *

'We've got to have one of our suppers.' Zelda got on the phone to Viv as soon as she got home. 'Libby's smitten. We've got to get that Monty here so she can see him with us, and gain a bit of insight while we can scrutinise.' She gave as full an account as she could of what Libby had said to her, plus a few of her own perceptions. 'Nothing she said dislodged that first impression of him seeing her as a soft touch.'

'Mmm.' Viv didn't sound convinced. 'But this time he did pay?'

'Yes.'

'For a super-expensive meal?'

'Yes.'

'And he's taking her to the theatre?'

'Think so, but knowing Libby she'll offer to pay.'

'Which might be wise if she doesn't want to be beholden. Zelda, I share your concern, I really do, but I don't think subjecting him to our scrutiny at this stage would be useful. Yes, we would see his flaws, but Libby wouldn't, not if they had flashing lights attached.

Sounds as if she's in too deep. I think we've got to wait a bit, till she comes up for air.'

'If she hasn't drowned before she floats to the surface.'

'Hell, Zelda! Why so pessimistic? The man might be right for her. They seem to have a lot in common. You used to say that was important.'

'Don't know, Viv, but point taken. Let's wait, but can we try and do it before I go to the States?'

'When's that?'

'End of June, so I'm there for my dad's birthday and Independence Day.'

'Well, that's nearly three months away, and it may have fizzled out by then, or exploded, but I'll talk to Janet about it.' Viv rang off, leaving Zelda deflated, out of sync with two of her dearest friends and maybe three. What was wrong with her? Why did she feel so anti-Monty?

7

LIBBY

Libby was feeling very pro-Monty.

To say she was looking forward to going to the theatre with him on Thursday was an understatement. By Wednesday night she was ready to go, and, mindful of the Muscateers' rule, only needed to ring Zelda to give her all the details. 'As I said, it's at the Harold Pinter Theatre in the West End, which is in Panton Street. It begins at two thirty so I'm catching the twelve thirty into St Pancras and I'll catch the first cheap, non-rush-hour train back. That's the 19.03 ETA Bedford 19.43. Expect we'll have a cup of tea somewhere after the show to fill in the time.'

Zelda told her to enjoy herself and said she'd be at the station to meet her with Mack and Morag – if Libby was happy to walk? Libby said she would be happy to walk if it wasn't raining, and, aware of Zelda's reservations about Monty and dating in general, she waited for her to issue dire warnings. When Zelda didn't Libby rang off and went to try on her Joseph Ribkoff jacket again. Was red and silver too glitzy for daytime? Yes, she decided, and switched back to her all-purpose blue linen dress with a knitted crochet shrug in the same colour.

The show was great and discussing it with Monty – who didn't comment on her clothes – was even better. When she said she thought Rory Bremner as the class-conscious butler was brilliant, he said he thought the director should have helped him to find more depth, which made her think. She felt her brain waking up, her critical faculties sharpening, a few synapses springing into action, but it didn't stop her finding Caroline Quentin as the maid/companion to Patricia Hodge's countess absolutely hilarious. She regaled Zelda with it all when she met her at the station with the Westies on her return.

Though regaled with it *all* wasn't strictly true.

Ditto, a week later when she went to see *The Play That Goes Wrong* at the Duchess Theatre. Walking companionably home from the station, she told Zelda all about this 'farce to beat all farces', quoting the blurb, and how it was about an am-dram group who put on a murder-mystery play, in which everything goes wrong. She told her how she hadn't thought she liked slapstick but had laughed till her sides ached. She told her how efficiently the trains had run and what an excellent train the 19.03 was and what a boon the senior travel pass was.

But she didn't tell her where she went to have that cup of tea.

* * *

Zelda wondered, of course, though the arrangement worked quite well for her. The Westies got a good long walk to the station and back, and so of course did she. Steps! She loved steps, loved to see them mounting on the Fitbit her stepkids – ha-ha! – had bought her. She did have to make sure she was always free on Thursday evenings, with her phone at the ready, so that she got the text Libby sent when she was at the train at 19.03. But that was fine. There was nothing else pressing on a Thursday evening. As soon as she got the text she would set off with Mack and Morag to meet the train, which arrived at the station at around eight.

She enjoyed their chats on the walk home too, though Libby was less forthcoming, less open than she used to be. Her face was just as mobile and expressive but she talked mostly about the plays she'd seen and hardly ever mentioned Monty. And she didn't say what she did between five o'clock when the play ended and 19.03 when she caught the train. Two hours, Zelda couldn't help thinking, was quite a lot of time to fill, but she never mentioned going for a meal, only a cup of tea. What did they talk about to make a cup of tea last that long? Who paid for it? When did Libby eat, as she was on the train from twelve thirty to one thirty and had to be at the theatre by two?

Zelda's head was full of questions. Did Monty pay for the tickets? How about the interval drinks? Did Libby keep hold of her credit card? Libby was obviously enjoying reacquainting herself with the London theatre scene and Zelda quite enjoyed hearing about the plays she'd seen, but when she stopped talking about the shows she quickly moved to blander topics like, 'How lovely that the nights are lengthening!' or 'Can't believe it will soon be May,' or – Zelda yawned just thinking about it – how well the bloody trains ran.

But then Libby missed one, which did make things a bit more interesting.

* * *

It was a quarter past seven, ten minutes later than usual, when Libby eventually rang – rang, not texted, unusually. Zelda was getting a bit anxious and had just said so to Viv, who happened to be with her, filling time on the way to a meeting in town. Perched side by side at the breakfast bar in Zelda's mini-kitchen, Zelda had been telling Viv how cagey Libby had been lately, and Viv had opined that Libby must be sleeping with Monty, when the call came – to the phone on the wall in front of them.

Libby, Zelda mouthed to Viv, putting the speaker on loud. 'Hi, Libby.'

'Hi, Zelda, just to say sorry but I missed the train, so I'll get the next one in an hour's time. But please d-don't come to meet me, it'll be too late. I'll get a taxi from the station.'

'Libby, nine o'clock isn't too late, and I'll meet you in the car if you're tired, but... Okay, I won't if you insist. Thanks for letting me know, Libby. How was the play?'

Zelda listened to Libby's reply, alert for other voices in the background, while trying not to laugh at Viv whose rolling eyes and frantic nodding were saying, 'Told you so! Told you so!' very loudly.

'Bit upsetting actually, considering it was a comedy, but I'm hoping for better next week. You'll never guess what we're going to see. *The Full Monty*! Yes, the *play* of! Didn't even know it was a play. The film was hilarious. Just hope the seats aren't too near the front. Won't know where to put myself.' She giggled.

Zelda wondered where she was as she couldn't hear any other voices in the background.

'That,' said Viv, when Zelda had put the phone back, 'was not a woman ringing from St Pancras Station, drinking tea in a draughty waiting room or waiting on a chilly platform. That was a woman, I'd put money on it, who had just got out of bed.'

8

LIBBY

Viv was right. Ish.

Libby had just leaped out of bed to make that phone call, suddenly realising what time it was. She had been in Monty's bed. She was in Monty's house, where she had been twice before. But Monty hadn't been in bed with her. Ever. At first when he'd suggested going back to his place, after *Relative Values* at the Harold Pinter Theatre, she'd been apprehensive, or maybe excited. It was hard to interpret the fluttering in her stomach. 'Better than a crowded café,' he'd said. 'It's not far and I make a good cup of tea.'

Had he got more in mind? she'd wondered, then recalled that he hadn't commented on her worried-about appearance, hadn't as much as touched her hand in the theatre, or shown any signs of finding her physically attractive, and decided that he hadn't. Keen to see where he lived, she'd been surprised to discover how close to the West End it was. It was only a short ride on the Tube from Leicester Square, ten minutes at most, then a five-minute walk from Chalk Farm station to Rokeby Villa, his house in Elton Street. House? Rokeby Villa was a *mansion*, gobsmackingly gorgeous. She felt she'd been transported, not just in space, but also in time. It was a beautiful eighteenth-century, red-brick, symmetrical mansion, three storeys high, looking over a front garden with apple trees and grass and daffodils and a wicket gate.

'You live here alone?' she'd asked as he'd opened the gate and led her, literally, up the garden path, surprised she was so surprised as she'd known all along he was rich.

'At the moment,' he'd replied. It wasn't that big, he said, and had most likely been built as a single man's house, not a family home.

Even so, when he'd opened the blue front door, framed by a white latticed porch, and she'd stepped into an oak-floored sitting room, finding the whole Bennet family in residence, with Mr Darcy about to call in, would have seemed quite possible. But it was smaller than it looked from the outside, she realised as he turned right, straight into the kitchen on the other side, and was maybe only one room deep. The kitchen was spacious though, with a dresser filling the back wall and a shiny black Aga on the side over-looking the lovely garden, and a square oak table in the centre. She'd asked for the loo and been directed to a staircase leading from the back of the sitting room. When she'd come down, after only the quickest of peeps into two bedrooms, he had already laid tea on the kitchen table and not just a pot of tea. There were scones and clotted cream and strawberry jam, on fluted white china so delicate she was almost afraid to pick it up.

'So, where do you stand on the great scone debate, Ms Allgood?' he'd said. 'I'm a Somerset man so I go as the fancy takes me. Maid's day off, by the way.' Was he joking?

She had played along, feeling like the housekeeper, Mrs what's-her-name, in *Downton Abbey*, being honoured by the family, because she was retiring perhaps. 'I'm strictly cream first, Mr Charles, and I say scones to rhyme with dons, not scones to rhyme with drones.'

It had all been light-hearted, not relaxed in her case, but not nerve-wracking either. And when, after a second cup of tea, she'd looked at her watch, he'd immediately got to his feet and said that he would walk her back to Chalk Farm Tube station. Within minutes she'd been back at St Pancras and had caught the 19.03 with time to spare. It worked well the second week too. She went to the theatre. She went back to Monty's for tea. She caught the train home.

Now, today, was the problem.

It was because, perplexingly, the play, *Blithe Spirit* by Noël Coward, had upset her. It was a famous comedy, for heaven's sake! But she'd started not enjoying it during the second half when she'd realised everyone around her was laughing, and she wasn't. It was about a man called Charles, a widower, who had remarried, very happily. One night, for fun, Charles invited a famous medium, Madame Arcati, to hold a séance for his new wife, Ruth, and some guests, to try and contact 'the other side'. Charles, convinced Madame Arcati is a fraud, was shocked rigid when she didn't just contact Elvira, his late wife, but brought her back to haunt them. Hilarity ensued when Elvira's ghost took residence in her husband's house and started to persecute his madly jealous new wife. The ghost had been funny. Eighty-three-year-old Angela Lansbury cavorting around the stage as the medium had been *very* funny and so had the rest of the cast. The cast's comic timing had been perfect and the audience had been in stitches, some of them crying with laughter.

But Libby had just been crying.

The trouble was that at some point she'd started to identify with Charles, the grieving widower, who yearned for his first wife, though happily married to Ruth. Was that Noël Coward's genius, to show passionate feeling beneath the witty, superficial repartee? Whatever, Libby had started to feel desperately sorry for Charles, then dangerously, desperately sorry for herself. She missed Jim.

She longed for Jim, yearned for him, ached for him. Waves of misery had started welling up inside her. It happened from time to time. Not so often lately, and Zelda and the others said this was how it was, and it was best to give into it, let it out, but not for too long. Janet, ever practical, thought Elgar's 'Cello Concerto' was long enough.

Thankful for the dark, Libby had managed to find tissues and mop up the tears. Monty hadn't noticed, she was sure. Again, he hadn't as much as brushed her hand. Again he hadn't commented on her appearance, and she'd wondered if he might be gay.

Time to go home and lick her wounds, perhaps?

But when the play was over and she'd said, 'Sorry, Monty, I'm feeling a bit under the weather, I'm going to go straight home now,' he had reminded her that she would need to buy a new ticket to travel in peak time, and how expensive it would be. He'd said, 'Why not come back to mine and lie down for an hour?' She'd agreed, confident that he'd leave her in peace. When they'd got in she'd accepted his offer of a cup of tea, and gone upstairs to the loo, leaving him filling the kettle. She'd given her nose a good blow, taken some deep breaths, and splashed her face with cold water. Fine, she'd be fine, she'd thought, if she could take her tea back upstairs and have a short nap. But when she'd got back to the kitchen, something had changed. He'd changed. The kind, but not-too-concerned Monty had looked angry. She'd hovered in the door-way, watching, wondering what to do.

He'd been reading a letter that she'd seen him pick up from the doormat when they came in, and clearly it had affected him for the worse. What was in it? His mouth had been a snarl and he'd shaken his head as if he couldn't believe what he was reading. Then he'd looked up and seen her and his expression had changed. He'd seemed to study her, then, stuffing the letter in his jacket pocket, he'd opened his arms wide. 'Darling... darling Libby. I do love you, you know.'

'What's the matter...?' she'd started to say but stopped when she'd realised what he'd said and her tears had overflowed. Which had come first she would never know – her tears or the tender look in his eyes.

'Darling.' He'd enfolded her. 'It's nothing, nothing we can't deal with together.' She would never forget how safe she'd felt wrapped in his arms and the comforting smell of him as she'd buried her snotty nose in the velvety needlecord of his jacket.

9

ZELDA

Zelda got Libby's call saying she'd missed the train at a quarter past seven. Two hours later, she was worrying because she hadn't had another call from Libby saying she was on the later train. Why hadn't Libby rung or texted? If she'd caught a train an hour later and then got a taxi she should be home by now. She wasn't. Zelda had been keeping a lookout and she hadn't seen a taxi delivering Libby to her door. Zelda was on her own now, sitting on the end of the sofa so she could see out of her front-room window. Viv had gone off to her meeting, none too concerned about Libby, though convinced that she was having a torrid affair. Good luck to her! seemed to be Viv's position. Now Zelda was on the phone to Janet, to update her and share her concern and hopefully get some empathy.

'Libby hasn't rung to say she's on the train yet. The last I heard was when she said she'd missed the train, the one around seven that she usually gets, and she was getting the next one. But the next one was only half an hour later, not an hour. And even if it was an hour, she should be home by now.'

'What time is it?' Janet was brisk and breezy.

'Nine fifteen.' Zelda got up to check the clock on the mantel-piece. 'If she got the just-after-eight she should have been home by now. When she gets the seven o'clock she's home at around half past eight.'

'So she missed the next train too. She's enjoying herself. Stop worrying. She'll be home any time now.'

Zelda wished she hadn't told Janet what Viv had said about what she thought Libby was up to. Now Janet was doing Woman of the World, which was funny when you remembered what a prude she was before she began her one-woman mission to put the sex into sexagenarian.

'But *why* and why hasn't she *said*?'

'Do you wait up for her, Zelda?' Janet was sarky.

Zelda bridled. She was the same age as Janet give or take a year and resented the implication that she was old enough to be Libby's mother. 'I'm not sitting by the window anxiously twitching the curtains, if that's what you're thinking.' Zelda sat down again but not near the window. 'I'm on the sofa with Mack and Morag, and I've just had a nice glass of Sav. I'm worried because I thought our guiding premise was "all for one", in other words looking out for each other, and that requires knowing where to look. Where is she? That's what I want to know.'

Where had Libby made that phone call from? They didn't know. They didn't know where Libby was. Libby had broken their golden rule – telling each other where they were when they were on a date. Being worried was reasonable. You heard such things. They didn't know the man Libby was seeing. Libby hardly knew him. She'd known him briefly, and distantly it seemed, forty or fifty years ago. She'd seen him – how many times since she'd met up with him? Zelda said all this to Janet, while reaching for her diary, half hidden beneath Morag.

'She's known him four weeks,' said Janet, ever precise, but

sounding a bit more concerned. 'It's May next week, by the way, so Muscateers is coming up.'

They met on the first Friday of the month.

'And by my reckoning...' Zelda leafed through her diary '... Libby's seen him five times, mostly in the theatre, which isn't exactly the best place for getting to know someone.'

'But didn't you say she had a couple of hours to kill after the show, before catching the cheap train home? What does she do then?'

'That's the crux, Janet! That's what I want to know!'

Janet wasn't usually this slow. She must have had a few.

'I'd better get off my phone.' Zelda stood up again. 'Libby might be trying to ring or text me right now. And I ought to take Mack and Morag round the block. I'll check her house when we walk past. We might even bump into her if she got a later train.'

But Zelda didn't.

Libby's semi, three doors up, was in darkness. There was a porch light on but that was all. Cornflake, her overweight cat, white fur glowing, was miaowing at the door and didn't move away even when she saw the dogs.

'You've got a cat-flap at the back door, silly.'

Clearly Libby wasn't in.

'She isn't back.' Zelda rang Viv from the landline in the kitchen when she got home. 'Oh, hold on. A text coming in.' She read it out. '"Don't worry! I'm fine. Had a bit of a wobble earlier so went to lie down for a bit. On the 9.00 from St Pancras ETA 10.05. Will get taxi from station. Lx".'

'Well, then.' Viv didn't need to say, 'Told you so'.

'You think your hunch was right?'

'*Lie down* is a bit of a reveal.'

'But open to interpretation. Perhaps she wasn't well. Do you think I should meet her from the station?'

'It's gone ten. I think she'll be in the taxi by now. Let's hope she'll enlighten us next Friday. I'll book The Wagon and Horses.' Viv rang off.

Zelda, hoping for enlightenment before next Friday – a whole week away – was in her front garden, dead-heading daffodils by moonlight, when she got a one-word text from Libby.

Home x

Straightening up, she saw Libby getting out of a taxi, then hurrying to her front door.

10

LIBBY

Libby had coffee with Zelda next morning and told her all about the wobble, and why she was so late home. She guessed what Zelda – and Viv and Janet – were thinking and it was good fun watching Zelda's face as she explained that she'd simply overslept. That after the lovely man-hug, Monty had insisted she went upstairs for a lie-down, and promised he'd wake her in time to catch the 19.03, but he hadn't. He'd said he couldn't bear to because she looked so peaceful, and he'd let her sleep on for two whole hours. Then he'd brought her a cup of tea. He hadn't got into bed with her.

She didn't tell Zelda how disappointed she was.

On the following Thursday she went to London to see *The Full Monty* with Monty and it was back to the old routine, except that Monty now held her hand in the theatre and on the walks to and from the Tube. Progress? She hoped so, but he showed no signs of wanting to delay her departure after tea and scones, and she caught the 19.03, wondering all the way home again if he was gay. *Well, that's all right, he'll make a lovely friend.* Walking home from the station, she told Zelda that she would pick her up at twelve the next day to drive to the Muscateers lunch at The Wagon and Horses in

Elmsley. But at twelve the next day she was on the 11.17 to St Pancras, rushing to Monty's bedside.

* * *

When she had rung earlier this morning to thank him for taking her to see *The Full Monty*, he'd sounded dreadful. Croaky. Wheezy. Breathless. At death's door. She could hardly make sense of what he was saying. He was still in bed, he'd said, trying to sleep it off, but it was just a bad cold, no, no, not the flu, he'd had the jab. 'Oh, look after yourself,' she'd said, then immediately realised he wouldn't because he was a man and wouldn't know how. 'Have you got soup?' she'd asked, knowing he hadn't or only something from a tin. 'Have you got paracetamol? Have you got tissues? Don't worry. I'm on my way!'

It had taken her only half an hour to gather what she needed, and tell Zelda she wouldn't make Muscateers, but only briefly why. She hadn't got all the ingredients for the classic cock-a-leekie soup, which she felt sure would boost Monty's immune system, but she had most of them. She thought he'd like the traditional Mary Berry recipe with prunes, rather than Jamie Oliver's more modern take without – Monty was a traditional sort of man – but she had brought prunes and potatoes so she could cook whichever version he liked. Her bag was heavy as she lugged it to the door of the train as it drew into St Pancras. She still needed to buy a chicken or some chicken pieces, but reckoned she could get them from M&S at the station, before getting the Tube to Chalk Farm. Was the way to Monty's heart through his stomach? Libby fervently hoped so!

Libby had told Zelda the truth about her wobble last week. Truthfulness was in her DNA and in her name. Liberty Allgood. She had always found it hard to tell even the whitest of lies, and only managed it then if she had a very good reason, like not hurting someone's feelings. She'd told Zelda in some detail about the lovely man-hug, how she'd wept on Monty's shoulder – or more accurately his needlecord-clad chest as she was quite a bit shorter than he was – and how it had lasted about a minute, but not how she'd wanted to stay with his comforting arms around her for ever.

And then some more, please.

Up to that point she and Monty had hardly touched. And after she'd wiped her eyes and blown her nose on the white linen handkerchief that he'd pulled from his pocket, he'd said, 'You're exhausted, darling. Grief is exhausting,' as if he knew about it. 'Go upstairs and have a sleep.' Then he'd led the way up the wooden staircase to a bedroom she'd peeped in earlier. It had a pair of old-fashioned wooden wardrobes and a smallish double bed, small compared with nowadays, an antique with a carved wooden bedhead. He'd pulled back the covers, sheets and blankets – not a duvet – and some sort of eiderdown and she'd climbed in – it was quite high – after removing her shoes and coat. That was all. He'd taken her coat and she'd heard him going down the wooden staircase but had soon fallen asleep, or almost asleep, because she remembered a chambermaid putting a hot-water bottle, the china kind, at her feet. But she must have been asleep and dreaming because there wasn't a chambermaid, only Monty. The hot-water bottle had still been slightly warm when she'd woken up.

He's lovely. She wanted to tell Zelda, she wanted to tell all her friends how lovely he was. She wanted to tell everyone.

The dive into M&S was successful. She picked up, not only chicken pieces, but also some soda bread and fruit. Then, realising she couldn't get into Monty's house unless he opened the door, she texted him from Chalk Farm station to say she was on her way. He texted back to say he'd leave the door on the latch, and to lift up the latch and walk in. The wicked wolf came into her head – Ellie-Jo loved the story – and she was smiling as she turned into a blossomy

Elton Street, picturing him sitting in bed waiting for her, wearing a granny's nightcap and nightdress.

Monty was sitting in bed, but wearing old-fashioned winceyette pyjamas, the striped sort, rather faded and threadbare from the bits she could see. But the paisley dressing gown, silk or polyester, hanging on the door, looked newer. It was the same bed he'd helped her into over a week ago. He was lying in the same spot. It was a sort of togetherness.

But he backed away as she went to kiss his pallid brow. 'This cold's a stinker.'

He perked up when she told him about the cock-a-leekie – he liked with-prunes – but then worried that she might not know how to use the Aga. When she reassured him that she did, she used to have one, he relaxed against the pillows and picked up the book he'd been reading.

She'd had an Aga before she'd downsized and moved to the semi. When Jim was alive they'd lived in a five-bedroomed detached in a village a bit like Elmsley where Viv and Janet both lived now. She'd loved those years, though might, she realised, be looking at them through rose-tinted glasses. Looking after three children and a husband and various pets hadn't been easy all the time, and very definitely not when the kids were teenagers. Eleanor and the boys had been far from angelic. It had taken her children longer than most to get the necessary bits of paper together and go to university, or get an apprenticeship in Ben's case. He'd been the last to leave home, but when he did whoopee!

She and Jim had both seen being child-free as liberation and had loved spending more time together – and in her case spending more time by herself. Empty nest syndrome? It had been in the news, but hadn't registered, and she'd refused to feel guilty about it. She'd done her bit. Now she could pick up her life at the point where it had taken a different direction all those years ago. She didn't regret her decisions, least of all marrying Jim and having the children, but the ambitious young woman had re-emerged. Not as an actress obviously, too late for that, but discovering she could write when she'd gone to a creative writing class a few years previously had been great. And her writing had grown more important since Jim had died, absorbing her for hours.

As she opened drawers and cupboards looking for pots and pans and implements in Monty's well-equipped kitchen, she wondered about his past. What had he been doing for the last forty years or so, on the domestic front, that was? She knew quite a lot now about his professional life, the various plays he'd directed, some television, mostly soap operas, the different theatres he'd worked in, the famous people he'd met. Google helped. But he'd never ever mentioned a wife or partner. Was he divorced, separated or widowed? Had he remained single? A bachelor pad this was not, unless said bachelor did a lot of entertaining. This was a family home. Had he inherited it? He gave that impression but hadn't actually said. There was enough crockery and cutlery for a large family, sets of six or eight, mostly blue and white Spode, and lots of large platters and heavy iron casseroles, the traditional bright orange Le Creuset, one of which she used for the cock-a-leekie. When it was bubbling away at a gentle simmer on the top, she went for what she had to admit was a snoop.

There was a utility room behind the kitchen with a washing machine and tumble drier and a back door that led into a small courtyard garden with an array of terracotta pots not yet planted up for summer, and a shed in the corner. She peered through the shed window. Very tidy. Garden tools hung on the walls, an unopened bag of compost stood ready to fill those pots perhaps and – aha! – some children's toys including a ride-on dinosaur, exactly like Ellie-Jo's. Who rode on that? she wondered. But it was the letter she found back in the utility room pinned to a noticeboard that riveted her attention. Oh dear, it must be the one that had brought that worried expression to his face last week.

Dear Mr Charles,

...you must vacate Rokeby Villa by 30 June...

'Do you make a habit of reading other people's correspondence?' He was standing in the kitchen doorway wearing his paisley dressing gown.

'Sorry, b-but it didn't seem private, not being on there...' She felt caught in the act as he reached past her and took the letter off the board.

'Electricians, they have to rewire the place. I have to get out for a bit. That's all, Paula Pry.'

Was he cross or amused?

'Guilty as charged.' She held up both hands. 'Sorry, but I'm a compulsive reader. Sauce bottles. Cornflake packets. Last wills and testaments. Won't pry, but if you don't want me to see hide it away. You have grandchildren? I saw the dinosaur.' She followed him back into the kitchen.

'Dinosaur?' He looked puzzled. 'Oh. One granddaughter. She lives in the States. Smells good.' He lifted the casserole lid. 'My daughter's daughter.'

'What's her name?'

'Imogen.'

'Daughter or granddaughter?'

'Granddaughter. My daughter is Cordelia.'

'*How* very Shakespearean!'

And what's Cordelia's mother called? she wanted to ask. Is she American? How long were you together? Did you marry? When did you split up?

'What else can you cook, Ms Allgood?' Head tilted on one side, he was almost flirtatious.

'What would you like me to cook, Mr Charles?'

'Afternoon tea. It's time, I think. We can have the soup for supper.'

Supper? Was she staying for supper?

She made a batch of dropped scones, which they ate at the kitchen table with strawberry jam and cream left over from yesterday and a cup of tea. He put the kettle on, saying he was feeling much better.

'Do you make the scones we eat on Thursdays?' she asked.

'God no. There's this stall...'

It was companionable, and when they moved into the sitting room to sit side by side on the comfortable flowery sofa with their feet up, even more so. They closed their eyes, after each confessing – she went first – that they liked, even needed, an afternoon nap these days, and the thought drifted into her head that she was like a stranded whale, on the beach but getting vibes that the tide was turning. Soon water would be lapping over her parched body. She was staying for supper after all. He would open up; he would tell her what he was going to do when he had to vacate Rokeby Villa.

11

ZELDA

'No Libby?' Janet asked, patting Mack and Morag, who went to greet her.

'No. And sorry I'm late.' Zelda eased herself into the seat opposite Janet and Viv. It was a corner booth. 'She sends her apologies, but she had to rush off to London. It was all very last minute.'

Janet raised a knowing eyebrow.

Viv filled Zelda's glass with fizz. 'Thought Thursday was Libby's go-to-the-theatre day?'

'It is. Was.' Zelda took a sip. 'They did *The Full Monty* yesterday.'

'I bet.' Viv laughed.

'They went *to The Full Monty*, the play. She said it was very funny and moving.'

'So what's the latest? Why isn't she here?' Viv lowered her voice. 'I assume she's off to see lover boy. Can you give us an update?'

The pub was busy. The booth next to theirs was full and Zelda had to adjust the hearing aids she was still getting used to, to cut down background noise. 'All I've managed to glean is that she has been going back to his after the show for a cup of tea – and scones and strawberry jam and cream – for several weeks now. She divulged that much without thumbscrews, and that he has this amazing old house in Chalk Farm, a mansion, eighteenth century she thought. Called Rokeby Villa. Must be worth millions, so she thinks he's seriously rich. She thinks the house has been in his family for aeons. Some of the furniture and the crockery and cutlery are really old. Solid silver. Seems it's become a bit of ritual, a habit they've got into, going back there after the theatre. "So much nicer than paying London prices to sit in a crowded café where you can hardly hear yourself speak," to quote Libby. It all sounds very sweet and friendly. They sit in the kitchen drinking tea, discussing the finer points of theatre, just like when they were students.'

'And then lie down?' said Viv. 'Like she said last week? "I went to lie down for a bit." Didn't she say that? Sorry, that sounds a bit...'

'...prurient,' Janet finished Viv's sentence for her. 'But carry on. I'm googling Rokeby Villa, by the way.'

'Libby said she lay down because she'd thrown a wobbly. Something in the play they were watching had made her miss Jim badly – you know how it happens – and when they got back to his place it suddenly overwhelmed her. She cried on his shoulder, well, a bit lower down. Seems he's tall. Then he suggested she go and have a nap. He took her upstairs to this ancient bed, and left her to sleep, but for a couple of hours instead of waking her up after an hour as she'd asked him to. That's why she missed the train, several trains.'

They looked at each other, thoughtful.

'It rang true.' Zelda patted her dogs' heads. They were now by her side. 'She said he closed the door and left her to sleep, except for coming back with a hot-water bottle. She sounded disappointed. I think she was telling the truth.'

Zelda really did.

'But,' said Viv, 'was it the whole truth and nothing but the truth?'

'And why's she rushing back to him today?' said Janet.

'I'll try and find out.' Zelda declined the top-up of fizz. She had to drive home.

'I've got an address for Rokeby Villa,' said Janet as a waitress brought the specials menu. 'It's on Rightmove.'

* * *

Zelda met Libby from the train, almost certain now that Viv and Janet were right and she was wrong. She hadn't heard from Libby all day and was assuming she was staying the night with her lover, when she got a text saying her ETA at Bedford station was 8.37. It was already half past eight, but fortunately she'd just left the house with Mack and Morag. Had Libby been in a dream for the half-hour she'd already been on the train? Why hadn't she let her know earlier? All answers led to the same conclusion. Zelda texted back.

Walking M & M so will head for station via Brickhill Drive and Kimbolton Road. Walk back with you unless getting taxi?

There was no reply, but ten or twenty minutes later, as she was turning into Kimbolton Road, she saw Libby in a bright red coat, coming towards her, quite a spring in her step.

'How was your day? We missed you,' Zelda said when they met up only seconds later.

'Fine!' Libby beamed. 'I love him, Zelda, I love him.' She linked arms as they turned to walk back up Brickhill Drive. 'It's the real thing. Not just a crush. Not like when we were students. I've got to know him. I know that he's kind and decent and honest and, well, just *gorgeous*.' As they reached the upper school, she slowed down a bit, holding Zelda back so the Westies strained on their leads, to savour whatever memory she was having. 'It's fate, Zelda.' She clearly had no doubts. 'Fate that we met all those years ago, fate that we both went to the same bar on the same night in March...'

Something significant had happened, obviously. Zelda didn't need to ask what.

Watering the World's Pots 59

Clearly had no doubt, Zara, that we had all those years ago, late that we both went to the same bar or the same café in Madrid. Something significant had happened, obviously. Zara didn't need to say what.

12

LIBBY

Libby couldn't put into words what a life-changing day she'd had, well, not words for public consumption. She couldn't, wouldn't, write about it for Libby's World. She couldn't 'share' – modern parlance – how Monty had turned to her when they'd woken up from their snooze on the sofa. How he'd looked at her with those deep blue eyes and reached for her hand and told her how hopelessly, how helplessly, he was in love with her. 'I can hide it no longer. I must see more of you. These Thursday matinees aren't enough.'

She'd agreed – oh, how she'd agreed! – and they'd gone upstairs to the ancient bed and at last lay down *together*. She had come home that night, she had *floated* home in a dream, her body singing, and then the pattern of her life changed. When she went down to London on the next Thursday morning, she took an overnight case with her. She didn't come back on Thursday night. She didn't come back on Friday night either. She did the same the next week, and the next, and the next, and it was totally wonderful!

Till she asked him what he was going to do when he moved out of Rokeby Villa.

13

ZELDA

Zelda missed Libby.

They had never lived in each other's pockets despite their houses being so close. They had always respected each other's privacy, but they had always been there for each other. They'd always found time for a natter on the phone or over a cuppa or glass-of, at least once a week. But things had changed. Now Zelda felt that she was there for Libby – and her cat, Cornflake – but Libby wasn't there for her. It was difficult to fit everything in, she knew that. They both had busy lives with lots of commitments. Zelda had her studies, the salon to keep an eye on, the dogs, and her grandson, Albert, to look after one day a week. Libby had her writing, her mother to visit in the care home, her granddaughter, Ellie-Jo, to look after one day a week – and now Monty.

Zelda wasn't jealous – at least she didn't think she was, and she did interrogate herself – but she did resent Monty for occupying such a big chunk of Libby's time. Especially when that chunk included the first Friday in June. Zelda thought Libby might break into her new routine and come home for the Muscateers lunch –

she had missed the last one after all, and this one was at The Olive Branch – but she didn't.

Libby wasn't coming up for air, Zelda was telling Viv and Janet, when Nikos appeared at their table by the window, menus in hand, his tanned brow furrowed. 'Liberty, where is she?' She was his favourite, they all knew that.

'I was just explaining,' Zelda adjusted what she'd been about to say, 'that er... she's in London, er... staying over with a friend.'

'Libby's having a summer of love, Nikos.' Viv took the menus from his hand.

Zelda kicked her hard under the table. *What* had she said that for? Had she no respect for Libby's privacy? She hoped against hope that Nikos hadn't understood, but one look at his face showed he had.

'You mean...?' The furrows in his brow deepened.

Viv didn't reply but it was too late.

Janet said, 'Libby's got a new friend, that's all, Nikos, and he's taking up quite a lot of her time.'

'He? A boyfriend?' He looked alarmed.

Janet nodded and he turned to Zelda, as she'd hoped he wouldn't. 'Is this true?'

There was no point in saying she didn't know. Nikos knew that she and Libby lived near each other and were close. They knew each other's comings and goings. He knew she fed Libby's cat when she was away, and looked after her plants, but not how often that was these days. How much should she tell him? How much *could* she tell him?

Viv tried to smooth troubled waters. 'Libby's very busy, Nikos—'

'I know how busy Liberty is,' he snapped, unusual for him. 'Sid tells me.' Sid was the owner-editor of the local paper Libby wrote for, and a business friend of Nikos. 'I know she's writing theatre reviews now as well as her own column, and that Sid is very pleased. Some London theatres have started advertising in the paper so it is bringing in extra revenue. It's good for everyone. Liberty is a talented writer.'

And I think you're in love with her. Zelda put down the wine list. 'And she has a lot of family commitments, Nikos. There's Ellie-Jo on Tuesdays—'

'I know all that.' Nikos brushed something off the red-check tablecloth. 'She is good mother, grandmother, daughter, but these lunches with you, she never missed. They are important to her.'

But not as important as they were.

'We're miffed too, Nikos.' Janet voiced Zelda's thoughts. 'She's missed two now.'

'That is concerning.' Niko's usual perfect English faltered. 'This new friend, she have for how long?'

'Two months,' said Janet, 'since she met him, well, re-met him actually. He's someone she knew when she was a student.'

No need to tell him Libby's life story, Janet.

Fortunately, Nikos walked away before Janet supplied more unnecessary detail. Unfortunately, he picked up the menus and took them away with him. Evelina brought them back a few minutes later, with a carafe of the house white. She apologised for Nikos, who usually brought their wine, and again when she came to take their orders. 'He very fond of Libby, so a bit upset.' Zelda didn't catch everything she said because one of her hearing aids chose that moment to fall out, but she got the gist, that they were both worried about Libby. 'Because early days,' she heard when she'd pushed the device back in. 'Only one year. Poor Jim.' She wiped away a tear with the corner of her apron. 'They like brothers.'

* * *

Evelina returned later with their food.

The three of them had just done their 'weigh-in', reporting on the gains and losses of the past month, getting the negatives out of the way before moving on to the positives. They were the wine club, they reminded themselves, not the whine club, but didn't rule out a therapeutic whinge. It was like old times, before Libby joined their group, Zelda thought, but it felt a bit odd being in The Olive Branch without her, and a bit flat. Libby had added an indefinable something to their gatherings. Zelda gauged her own reactions as her friends reported. Was she really happy hearing about her friends' new relationships? Was she as happy as she thought she was single? Didn't she envy them a little? Viv's partnership with her architect lover, Patrick, seemed idyllic. They spent quite a lot of time in Greece restoring an old monastery together. Janet's marriage to Alan seemed to be working well one year on. They divided their time between Elmsley and Brighton, sometimes spending time together, sometimes not.

Janet was tapping Zelda's hand; her attention must have wandered.

'I was saying that if any of you want the flat in July or August...' Janet was generous with Alan's seaside flat. 'So, Zelda, if you'd like to go there with Tracey and Albert...'

'Thanks, Janet, that's really kind, but I'm off to the States to see my dad.' That was something else she was having to fit into her life, her new-found family.

'Ladies, sorry for delay.' Evelina had returned with another carafe of wine. 'This white new one Nikos introduce to the list, an Assyrtiko. What you think?' She pushed back a lock of heavy iron-grey hair.

'Bouquet good, Evelina.' Janet, the connoisseur of the group, held the glass to her nose. 'Do I detect jasmine and maybe melon?'

Viv took a mouthful. 'Very gluggable, but I'd better go steady. Driving.'

Zelda held out her glass. 'More, please, Evelina. I'll have Viv's share as I walked here.'

Evelina cast an eye round the restaurant, a bit less busy now, and sat down on the spare chair. 'A moment okay, I think. We *verr-y* worried about dear Libby. She not been in to see us lately, not even for takeaway. New friend, what he like?'

Zelda wondered who was the more worried, Evelina or Nikos. Did Evelina think Nikos was taking a little too much interest in Libby? Was she jealous? She looked stressed. Was that what was stressing her?

Zelda tried to be tactful. 'Sorry, Evelina, but we don't know what he's like. None of us has met him yet. We feel a bit shut out too, but, as Viv says, we've just got to wait till she comes up for air.'

'Come up for air?' Evelina's English wasn't as good as Nikos's.

Zelda wished she had put it better.

'Till reality sets in.' Viv was having a go. 'You know how it is when you first fall for someone. It takes time before you know if it's infatuation or the real thing. We all hope that this man Libby is seeing is as wonderful as she thinks he is...'

'You do?' Evelina looked from one to the other. 'You *want* Libby serious about this new friend?'

Not really, I've got doubts... Zelda didn't get the words out.

'Ye-es,' said Janet. 'We want Libby to be happy.'

'Well, then...' Evelina stood up.

To say she left the room like an avenging fury would have been an exaggeration, but she moved faster than they'd ever seen her move before, and the swing doors crashed against the walls as she pushed through them into the kitchen.

Janet said, 'Did I say something wrong?'

14

LIBBY

Meanwhile, Libby was in heaven, or more accurately the garden of Rokeby Villa. She was having lunch with Monty sitting at a bistro-style table under the apple tree and she felt as if she were in an Edwardian play, or a Monet painting, though her clothes were completely wrong. She should have been wearing a long flowing dress with a pinched-in waist and low décolletage, not her old standby, the plain blue linen button-through, from the Rohan sale of umpteen years ago. The colours toned in though. The round table and slatted chairs were also blue and she'd found a yellow tablecloth in one of the drawers. Circular, it reached almost to the ground and could have been bought for the purpose. By whom? she'd wondered, but when she'd asked, complimenting Monty on the décor inside and outside the house, he would take no credit for it, except to say he had a talent for finding the right people. A small green apple dropped into the grass from the gnarled old branch above them. There were more at their feet. The tree was laden. Monty had just said he hoped she had lots of apple recipes ready for autumn when they'd be bigger and juicier. He adored her cooking.

They'd spent the first half of the morning shopping in Camden Market, buying dewy fresh produce, and then come home to cook. Well, she had come home to cook, while he'd looked on, but she'd loved every moment. Having someone to cook for again was wonderful, and only slightly nerve-wracking because she was so out of practice. The sea bass cooked with saffron, sherry and pine nuts had gone down very well. She'd followed Nigella's recipe to the letter, except for substituting pan-fried potatoes for basmati rice and 'muddy lentils'. Monty wasn't a rice or lentil fan. Now they were about to start on one of Nigella's puddings, and Libby was a bit apprehensive because the recipe said it needed three hours in the fridge, and it had had that but only just.

'What's this one called?' He adored puddings.

'Slut-red raspberries in Chardonnay jelly.'

'Perfect.' He filled his dish with a smile on his face.

After coffee they would go to bed.

That was the new pattern. They met at the theatre on Thursdays, came back to his afterwards and she stayed for two blissful days and nights. On Saturday afternoon she went home again. It was like the arrangement that Janet and Alan had, and Viv and Patrick, but on a shorter timescale, and they were right: it was perfect. You really did get the best of both worlds. Absence made the heart grow fonder and familiarity didn't have time to breed contempt. Familiarity was in fact breeding contentment.

She had gleaned a few more biographical details now. He had been married to Cordelia's mother, Martha, for seven years. They'd tried but it hadn't worked out. Martha worked in the film industry as an editor, mostly in America. He had tried getting work in America but they didn't like his style. Too British. He saw his daughter and granddaughter intermittently, when they came over, and, yes, he did go over there from time to time to see them but they lived in California, which he didn't much like. Too hot. She didn't exactly prise this information from him but he never volunteered facts and figures about his American family and he was a bit vague about details like his granddaughter, Imogen's age. Libby worked out that she must be four like Ellie-Jo. He was rather more forthcoming about his own family, especially his older sister, the one married to a baronet.

What was a baronet, she had asked, a little baron, a teeny-weeny one? She'd held up finger and thumb to make him laugh, but he hadn't. And he hadn't answered her question, so she'd had to google. 'A member of the lowest hereditary titled British order, with the status of a commoner but able to use the prefix "Sir"' she'd read. It was below a baron but above a knight. So his brother-in-law was Sir Somebody, his sister Lady Something Else. They were in banking, Monty said. Had been in banking for centuries, ever since his brother-in-law's ancestor had *walked* from the lowlands of Scotland, where they had a bank, to establish a branch in London.

It was interesting and intriguing, but a tad annoying if she was honest, because he wouldn't tell her their family name, only that his sister was called Marianna. Why not? she'd asked. Because she might reveal it to her friends, he'd said, or, worse, the press. She might write one of her columns about them. He had to respect their privacy. He said he'd got ticked off for talking about them when he was young because it had brought them unwelcome publicity.

Some of this rang a bell. At drama school he'd given the impression that *he* belonged to the aristocracy. He'd been a bit of a name-dropper but she couldn't remember any of the names he'd dropped. He'd mixed, socially, only with upper-class types – there had been a lot of those – and people with money. He hadn't taken any interest in her. Except once when she'd auditioned for a play he was directing, a kitchen-sink drama by Arnold Wesker, *Chicken Soup with Barley*, that was it. She thought she'd auditioned quite well, and had been hopeful when she'd seen him coming towards her in the canteen afterwards, carrying a coffee, but he'd said that though he *thought* she'd be perfect for the part of Ada, he wasn't quite sure yet. Would she like to come back to his place and talk about it? No, she'd replied, suspecting his motives. She'd said she would do another audition if he wanted her to, in the studio, or she could talk about it there and then, but she didn't want to go back to his place. She remembered blushing and stuttering a bit, because she had fancied him, and he'd laughed and said, 'I just wanted to have a friendly chat, Miss Too Good. I thought you might enlighten me about the trials and tribulations of working-class life but suit yourself.' After that, she'd got Miss Too Good from a few of his posh chums, male and female, and she'd wondered if she had jumped to the wrong conclusion but decided she hadn't. She hadn't wanted to get the part like that.

It was good that he didn't remember.

And things were different now. Times had changed and so had Monty. *She* had changed, was no longer a rather puritanical eighteen-year-old. And – this was the big thing – now she was sure Monty loved her.

'That was delicious, darling. Shall I make coffee?' He was getting to his feet.

She loved having someone to care for and having someone care for her. Eating was a social activity, living was a social activity and food and drink tasted so much better shared. She gathered the empty dishes and joined him in the kitchen. They stacked the dishwasher companionably. 'I've been meaning to ask you something, darling,' he said later, as he carried their coffees out to the garden. 'You know I've got to get out of here at the end of the month.'

He'd explained that the whole house had to be rewired.

'Yes, but do you really have to leave?' She'd mentioned it to Viv, who'd said most people just lived with the mess.

"Fraid so, darling. Seems they turn off the electricity and make a frightful mess chipping away at the walls to uncover the wires.'

'Poor walls! Poor beautiful walls!' The thought of those smooth greys and earthy reds being hacked into by workmen was painful.

'Yes, and the dust would trigger my asthma. And when the electricians have finished I'll have to have the house completely redecorated, which will mean staying away even longer.'

'So where are you going while all this is happening?'

She assumed he'd say he had another property somewhere and hoped it wasn't too far away. It was hard enough fitting in these two nights away with all her other commitments. If he was moving down to deepest Somerset that would make it even more difficult. So would staying with his titled sister in her ancient pile, wherever that was, as Lady Marianna might not welcome her brother's friend coming to stay over, though she'd heard the aristocracy were anything-goes. Her worst fear was that he would move so far away their tryst would end, but what he said next left her stuttering.

'Darling—' he'd reached over the table for her hand '—I was rather hoping... that you would ask me to come and stay with you.'

15

LIBBY

I d-don't want you to!

Her certainty surprised her even two days later.

I don't want you to come and stay with me!

She didn't want him to move in. It wasn't that she didn't love him – when she wasn't with him she longed to be close – *but not at my house. It wouldn't work out. There isn't room.*

Libby looked round her tiny kitchen, all of which she could see while swivelling on the stool at her breakfast bar. She could see her back door and her front and the little hall leading up to it. Monty wouldn't fit. He was too tall, too bulky, too loud, too *Monty*. A three-bed semi-detached was the wrong setting for him.

But she hadn't said so, though honesty was her first impulse. Or maybe the second. Unwilling to hurt his feelings, she'd stuttered, 'I-I-I'll have to think about this, Monty,' suppressing the 'No, you can't!' that was her surprising-to-her gut reaction. But even that had brought such a hurt hangdog look to his face that she'd followed it quickly with, 'Don't worry, I'll think positively about it, I really will.' Which was why she'd got on the phone to Zelda on Saturday afternoon, soon after she'd got back.

'He wants to move in, Zelda, and I don't want him to! What shall I do?'

'Well, tell him so, obviously. It's good that you know your own mind.' Zelda had been sympathetic. She'd said she knew how difficult telling someone what they didn't want to hear could be. 'We women are far too eager to please.' But then she'd come up with the perfect solution. 'He can have Janet's flat, well, Alan's flat, in Brighton. He can rent it. She offered it to us all yesterday, for July and August. Ring Janet and say you need it for your friend.'

Fingers crossed, Libby had rung Janet as soon as she'd said goodbye to Zelda. It would be the perfect solution. They could carry on with the same arrangement, but in a different location, a glamorous location. The flat was very stylish. She'd been there. Of course she'd explained to Janet that it was for Monty, not herself – though she would be there some of the time – and that she didn't expect it for free. Monty would pay a proper rent, she assured her. He wasn't short of money and would insist on it. Janet had said she thought that would be all right – she was really glad things were going well with her and Monty – but she'd have to talk to Alan about it first. It was his flat, after all. She'd said she'd get back to her asap but hadn't by the time Libby went to bed.

* * *

Hurry up, Janet.

On Sunday morning Libby still hadn't heard from Janet. And now there was something else on her mind that needed sorting. Quickly. She hadn't told Eleanor about Monty yet, and it was beginning to feel as if she had a dreadful secret. It was another reason why Monty couldn't come to stay. That would be much too much for Eleanor, who was coming to lunch today with Ellie-Jo and Derek.

Libby was willing Janet to ring as she got on with prep for the meal. She was doing picnic-fried chicken from her current favourite recipe book, and planned to eat in the garden as it was such a beautiful summer's day. It was warm and getting warmer. She'd already filled the paddling pool for Ellie-Jo, who loved water. The little girl loved her food too – wasn't faddy like so many children – and adored chicken done this way as she was allowed to sit on the grass and eat it with her fingers. The prep wasn't difficult, mostly opening packets, as she'd bought salads and crusty bread from M&S at St Pancras yesterday.

An email from Janet pinged its arrival. Excellent, Alan had agreed to let Monty have the flat, but see attached, he was putting terms in writing as he didn't know Monty yet and thought they should keep things businesslike. He had given Monty mates' rates though, trusting they would be mates in the future, but he needed to cover himself in case Monty turned out to be a con man. Ha ha ha! Libby had just had time to glance at the terms, which seemed generous, when Cornflake exited, heading upstairs, as Ellie-Jo burst in through the back door, little pigtails flying. 'What's for dinner, Granny?'

Steadying herself against the breakfast bar – as Ellie-Jo hugged her knees, nearly felling her – Libby, made a mental note to ring Monty later.

* * *

'You've told me, Mum!'

Libby had taken the first chance she got to tell Eleanor about Monty, but Eleanor had cut her off almost before she'd begun. They were in the kitchen after lunch, and Derek was keeping an eye on Ellie-Jo in the paddling pool.

'When? When did I tell you?' Libby was getting milk from the fridge.

'Weeks ago. You said that you'd run into this old friend at the theatre and got on like a house on fire.' Eleanor poured coffee for herself. 'Isn't this the one you've been staying over with?'

'Oh, yes, did I really say?' *When did I say? What did I say?*

'Yes, Mum!' Eleanor raised critical eyebrows. 'You're not losing it, are you? You said you'd met this friend you were at drama school with. I've been meaning to ask if she made a career in the theatre or dropped out like you.'

Fortunately, Ellie-Jo chose that moment to give an ear-piercing scream and run into the house, closely pursued by her Derek-Daddy-shark, who needed a coffee.

'I'll get a towel for Ellie-Jo.' Libby headed upstairs, pursued by worrying thoughts.

She? Had she lied to Eleanor? If she had she hadn't intended to. Or had she? Now she remembered mentioning that she'd met 'an old friend' at the theatre some weeks back. And yes, she had told Eleanor when she was staying over with that 'old friend' because she always told Eleanor when she was away from home, in case she needed to get hold of her. But had she made her comments deliberately gender-neutral? Yes, she probably had. Libby tried to be honest with herself. She had, to avoid explanations, and Eleanor had made assumptions. It hadn't entered her head that her mum might have a male friend, or that she might 'stay over' with him, and that had been convenient. But now she must come clean.

Eleanor was looking at family photographs on the back of the kitchen door when Libby came downstairs with the towel, not needed now because Ellie-Jo was back in the pool. 'I do miss Dad, Mum.' She was dabbing her eyes.

'Me too, darling.'

'Simon and Ben miss him too. Si said so the other night when he rang. He wanted to know when we were going up to see him, by the way, and I said when the Highlands are midge-free. End of summer most likely, but before schools go back, obviously.'

Eleanor was a head teacher, who had taught maths and occasionally still did. She looked a lot like Libby, with the same fair colouring, but she had a brain like her dad's. All three children were more like Jim than they were like her, Libby often thought, and they were very fond of him.

'There's no one like Dad.' Eleanor blew her nose, and Libby knew exactly why she hadn't told her about Monty.

Eleanor would be shocked. The boys would be shocked. It was too soon for them. She would tell them of course, eventually, and hope they would be happy for her, but it had to be done sensitively. If she needed another reason to tell Monty he couldn't come to stay, this was it. What if her sons came home while he was there? Simon and Ben both lived away, Simon in Scotland, Ben abroad, but they both visited from time to time and needed to stay over, sometimes with their partners, sometimes not. She needed to keep a room, or even two, free. And there was Ellie-Jo. One spare room was hers already, for when she stayed over just because she liked staying with her granny. Monty couldn't have a room.

But I don't need a room of my own. I'll sleep with you. She heard his voice in her head.

But he couldn't. He really couldn't. Thank goodness she had Plan B.

* * *

When the family had gone, she rang Monty and told him about the flat in Brighton, that he could have it for a month at least, and that their current arrangement could continue. 'I'll come to Brighton every Thursday, not London, that's the only difference. It'll cost me a bit more on the train but that's okay. Janet says they have a good theatre scene in Brighton, with lots of shows coming there first that go on to become London hits, so we can even carry on with our matinees.' She told him about the mates' rates terms Alan was offering him as a hoped-for mate.

Silence. She thought the phone had gone dead.

'Monty, are you still there?'

'Yes.'

She burbled on a bit more about how lovely the flat was. 'It's very stylish... What's the matter, Monty?' His lack of response became too obvious to ignore. 'Are you okay?'

'You're putting me in an embarrassing situation, darling...' He cleared his throat.

'How?' She was mortified. What had she done?

'I feel my manhood shrinking trying to explain, but... well, as you know there's been no work coming my way for some time, my face doesn't fit any more, so I have this cash-flow problem. I'm afraid paying rent, however reasonable, is out of the question.' There was a break in his voice. 'I *need* to come and stay with you, darling.'

16

LIBBY

How do I tell Eleanor?

On Monday morning Libby was in her little office under the stairs, a good use of space she'd copied from Zelda. She was trying to write her column, about shoplifting, but she couldn't concentrate.

Why did I say, 'Well, yes, I suppose you must, then'?

She couldn't believe the words coming out of her mouth. She didn't want Monty to come and stay but he was coming. Now she must find a way of telling Eleanor that a man was moving in, because she couldn't keep it from her, well, not for much longer, three weeks max.

Her mobile pinged – it was Eleanor. There was her face. Libby had mixed feelings about FaceTime. She didn't mind it by arrangement but didn't like it sprung upon her. She could be anywhere looking a fright. She could be on the loo. Eleanor was at school in her office. Libby could see a computer behind her. She'd rung to remind Libby to bring Ellie-Jo's swimming costume, she said, left behind yesterday, when she came to look after her tomorrow.

'Yes, I will, I've got it ready. No, don't go yet, Eleanor, there's something I have to tell you.'

'Okay. But be quick, the bell's about to ring for break.'

'It's about the old friend I mentioned meeting at the theatre, the one I stay over with. Well—' *say it* '—he's a him not a her, male not female.' *Said it!*

'Oh, *Mu-um!*' Eleanor smirked, there was no other word for it. It was an all-knowing patronising smirk. Eleanor was patting her dear old mother on the head. 'It's all right, Mum, people are doing it all the time. Hold your phone up a bit higher, Mum, or I can't see you.'

Libby's hand had dropped to her side.

'That's better.' Eleanor reappeared.

'What are people doing all the time now, Eleanor?' Libby strongly suspected her daughter was jumping to a very wrong conclusion.

'Changing gender, Mum. It's no big deal. Honestly. We've got kids in school doing it. Look, I've got to go, the bell's ringing. Talk tomorrow.'

Monty hasn't changed gender! And he's coming to stay!

But the screen went blank before she could put her daughter right.

* * *

She tried again next day, when she went to Eleanor's to look after Ellie-Jo. Not in the morning, when Eleanor was rushing out of the house. That would have been crazy. She waited till she came in from work when Ellie-Jo was having her tea of pancakes, which they'd just made together. Eleanor was sitting down at the table with a cup of tea in her hand.

'Eleanor...' Libby helped Ellie-Jo squeeze lemon juice onto her pancake '...the friend I mentioned yesterday, I need to tell you he's coming to stay, as my lodger.'

The lodger bit had been Monty's idea after she'd phoned to explain the delicate situation with her children. Not that he'd seen it as delicate, not at first. It was her house, wasn't it? Her life, therefore her decision. You don't *ask* your children how to live your life, you tell them. Cordelia hadn't turned a hair when he'd told her Libby stayed over with him. She was pleased for him, pleased he had a new friend. Why wouldn't Libby's grown-up children, he emphasised *grown-up*, be pleased for her?

'Because their dad has died, only recently. And because they're *around*, they're *here*, well, Eleanor is, and your daughter is in America...' She'd spelled it out. 'Eleanor would know we were sleeping together. It would make her feel awkward.'

'Sweetie, she has sex, doesn't she, with her husband? Are you sure it's not you feeling awkward, that this isn't little Libby Too Good speaking?'

So he does remember.

But he had come up with his brainwave, that he had his own room and she told the children he was her lodger, paying her to help out. He wouldn't, sadly, because he couldn't, but they might feel better if they thought it was a business transaction.

'Do you need the money, Mum?' Eleanor looked anxious.

'It's not just the money. I'm helping him out.'

Eleanor nodded. 'Oh yes, I suppose it is a difficult time for him.' Libby realised she hadn't corrected that misunderstanding either. 'Because, if you are short of cash, Mum, Derek and I could rejig our finances, remortgage or something, and give you back some of the money we've had from you.'

'Eleanor, there's no need for that. I was pleased to help and still am. I'm not rolling in it, but I've got enough, thank you.'

'You're so generous, Mum—' Eleanor poured more tea, clearly

relieved '—and super-kind but I'd have another think about this Monty situation if I were you. It could be more complicated than you think. There's hormone treatment for a start. I do know a bit about these things—'

'Eleanor—'

'You're right, Mum, now's not the time and place.' Eleanor stood up and turned to her daughter. 'You've demolished that pancake, Ellie-Jo! Do you want another?'

* * *

'Monty, I'm having second thoughts.'

Libby had rung Monty as soon as she got back from Eleanor's – well, as soon as she'd fed Cornflake and poured herself a fortifying glass of Pinot, to aid fluency. Now she was in her sitting room, on the sofa with her feet up, but she wasn't as relaxed as she looked. Cornflake was on her lap, and she'd had half a glass of Pinot already, but she was rigid. She was tired. It had been a very full-on day as it always was with Ellie-Jo, but the walk home had given her time to take in what Eleanor had said, and she was determined to tell Monty that coming to stay wouldn't work.

'Darling...' His voice sent shivers through her.

'No, let me have my say, Monty. There isn't a room for you here. My house is too small. My family too close. I live in a three-bedroomed semi. One of my spare rooms is full of boxes that I haven't unpacked since I moved. The other spare room is Ellie's. Or Simon's when he comes home. Or Ben's. I like to keep a room free for my children when they want to visit, and for my grandgirl. I'm sure you would be happier staying with your sister. Didn't you say she said you could, and she lives in an old Georgian vicarage?'

Silence. *Had he put the phone down?*

'Monty? Are you there?'

'Yes, yes, I am. I'm just waiting to see if you've finished burbling.'

'Ye-es, I think I have.'

'Well, you're right, I could stay with my sister... but, I've told you before, Marianna and Lawrence, they're so – how do I put it? – exacting, formal, not relaxing at all. They still live in the nineteen twenties. They dress for dinner. I'd have to dig out my white tie and tails.'

'Wouldn't you like that? Do they have a butler?'

'No, they don't – they have a housekeeper-cum-cook – and no, I wouldn't, I wouldn't like it at all. What I would like is to come and stay with you in your dear little house because that would mean I was never far away from you. And, darling, you don't think I really want my own room, my own bed, do you? You can keep your spare rooms for your family. I want to share your bed and go to sleep holding you in my arms.'

17

LIBBY

If only he hadn't got so much *stuff*!

Libby was parked in Elton Street, outside Rokeby Villa, in her little blue Hyundai i10. She'd thought Monty would come on the train with a suitcase, maybe two. But he'd asked her to bring the car, even though she'd been taking bags full of his things home with her for weeks, lugging them on the train. The spare room was half full already. He'd just put another suitcase and some bags in the boot but was now coming down the garden path carrying more clothes, some on hangers, some in overflowing plastic bags. Was he bringing his entire wardrobe? It was summer, for heaven's sake. Did he need thick sweaters, quilted jackets, and woolly hats, and when did he think he was going to wear that dinner jacket?

When he'd suggested she drive into London to pick up a few bits and pieces on the Sunday before he had to be out, she'd asked why. She hadn't fancied driving into London, but he'd said it was okay on Sundays, no trouble parking outside the house. There wasn't much traffic and the area wasn't in the congestion zone so she didn't have to worry about charges. So here she was helping him – well, she'd been helping till she'd thought they'd finished, but here he was, ducking under the gate-arch now, dodging an over-grown rambling rose, with yet another load.

'Monty, are you a man or a centipede?' She kept the tone light as she got out of the car and joined him by the boot. 'Do you really need all those shoes?' No, he said – he referenced *King Lear*! – it wasn't about need, it was also about protecting things from all the dust the electricians would create when they started next day. Things included board games and quite a lot of books, which he put on the floor behind the passenger seat.

'Is that it?' She was ready to close the boot.

'Not quite.' He headed inside again before she could say, '*You don't have to bring everything. We can come and get anything you've forgotten when we come to London for Thursday matinees.*'

Waiting for him to reappear, she texted Eleanor to say she hoped they were having a lovely lunch at The Olive Branch. She'd treated the three of them to a meal there as an apology for not having them to hers. Eleanor had been a bit miffed when she'd cancelled. They'd discussed whether to change the timing and make it an evening meal and include Monty but decided against it. She, Libby, had decided against it, because things were still a bit awkward. She had tried putting Eleanor right about their misun-derstanding, but the words '*Monty is male. He's a man. He has always been a man. There has never been any question of a gender-change. Sorry, Eleanor, but you jumped to a wrong conclusion*' had never managed to leave her mouth.

And here he was again. But *what* was that caught up in a whippy branch of the rambling rose? A golf club? He'd never mentioned playing golf, but now a set of golf clubs and a tennis racket were going into the boot of the car, alongside a fold-up bike and a safety helmet.

'Think that's everything.' He closed the boot and got into the front seat beside her.

'Sure you haven't forgotten the kitchen sink?'

'Not like you to be waspish, darling.'

'A joke, Monty, a joke.'

He leaned over and kissed her ear. 'Sorry, darling, but what I love about you is that you're not like other women. You don't try to trip a chap up. My ex had this book, the *SCUM Manifesto*?'

'SCUM! The Society for Cutting Up Men? How horrible! What made her so bitter?'

He did up his safety belt and she started the car.

What I love about you! He'd said it again. *You're not like other women.* She was unique. He made her feel so special. She must make this work. She *would* make this work. It was only for a few weeks, after all.

18

VIV

'Chattanooga Choo Choo' was pulsing out of the sound system when Viv and Janet arrived at The Wagon and Horses, adorned with stars and stripes. It was the fourth of July, Independence Day in the USA. A super-size photograph of Glenn Miller, a regular at the pub during the war till he vanished so mysteriously, was on the wall behind the bar. All the tables sported little star-spangled banners on sticks stuck into potatoes.

'For us to wave?' Viv eased herself into their corner booth, wondering if Libby would join them, or if this would be the third time in a row that she hadn't. Zelda had predicted that she wouldn't before leaving for North Carolina to visit her new-found family. She had texted Viv to say that Libby was no longer her own woman.

'Well, is Zelda going to be proved right?' Viv was keeping an eye on the door.

'I think Libby would have said by now if she wasn't coming.' Janet was checking the time on her phone. 'She said she was and is only eight minutes late so far. Why did Zelda think she wouldn't? Tell me again.'

'She thinks she's under The Director's baleful influence. Oh, here's our bottle of Sav and the menus.'

'Evidence?' Janet filled their glasses.

'Not a lot, she admitted that. Seems they've hardly put their noses out of the door since he moved in.'

'Which was?'

'Five days ago. Zelda was at pains to say she wasn't a puritan. She wasn't against Libby having a lover, it was the *timing* she queried. She thinks it's too soon for him to be moving in.'

'But he isn't, is he? Not permanently.' Janet took a sip. 'I thought it was just while he had some work done on his house.'

'Then why,' said Viv, 'to quote Zelda again, is there a fur-collared winter coat hanging on the newel post, a pair of UGG boots on the stairs with a lot of other stuff, and woolly hats on the hallstand? Zelda saw them when she dropped by to leave her key, so that Libby could look after her plants, and also noted more boxes *and skis* in the garage. She saw the skis being delivered by Hermes. Oh. Here's Libby now. Perhaps we'll get some answers.'

Viv stood up and waved till Libby saw her.

'Sorreeee!' Libby was a bit red-faced and dishevelled, though as blonde and beautiful as always, as she slid into the seat opposite them both. She was wearing jeans and a pink linen top, with sparkly Fitflops showing off toenails painted pink to match the top. 'Sorry I'm late. Had to hang on a bit to get a casserole out of the oven for Monty's lunch. Oh, thanks.' Janet had handed her a glass.

'Can't lover-boy get his own lunch out of the oven?'

Careful! Janet voiced what Viv only dared think.

'Oh, Janet, *don't* be like that. I'm enjoying having him. Let me, please, while this stage lasts. I *love* looking after Monty. I *love* cooking for him and caring for him and being cared for. I hadn't realised how much I'd missed all that and I thought you two would understand.' She looked a bit hurt. 'I've been longing to share with you.'

But she couldn't share with Zelda, that was what she didn't say.

'And we've been longing for you to share!' Viv raised her glass in solidarity. 'To you and Monty! We want to hear all about him. We want to meet him as soon as possible.' She clinked glasses with Libby and then Janet. 'Gosh, I remember wanting to *merge* with Patrick.'

'Time and place, Viv.' Janet looked round but smiled. 'But yes, Libby, we do understand. We have been there and done that and come out the other side. I'm glad you see what I call the doting stage as just that, a stage. There's a time when you believe the man is perfect, and another when you discover he is not. If you come through both stages and find you have someone you still love and respect, then you are truly blessed. Viv and I have both been very lucky and we hope you will be too.'

Well said, Janet.

Libby sighed. 'Oh, it's great talking like this. I did want to tell Zelda, but she's so resolutely single, and seems, well, almost anti-Monty...'

'Zelda's on your side, Libby—' Janet was firm '—but she's made mistakes in the past, as indeed have I, and knows how easy it is. Now, let's order, though I fear it's burgers and fries or fries and burgers with or without ketchup.'

There were hopeful signs there, Viv thought, during a lull in the conversation, when they were all working their way through the burgers. Libby was smitten but also aware she could be at the love-is-blind stage of the relationship. And it was good that she said she loved being cared *for*. If this Monty was caring, if he cared for her as much as she cared for him, that was a very good sign. 'I'm glad you said you loved being cared *for*...' she said, hoping she didn't sound as if she was prying.

'Oh, yes.' Libby beamed. 'Tea every morning in bed, just like Jim did. Bliss.'

Well, that was a start.

'You'll love him, you really will,' Libby went on, looking dreamy, 'both of you will.'

'Well, then.' Janet paused and reached for her handbag. 'Let's get a date in the diary. Heh, I could do supper tomorrow night, at mine, I mean. Mack and Morag would love to see you, Libby. You know they're staying with me? And Alan could do a barbecue.'

'I'm free.' Viv didn't need to look at her diary. 'Patrick's here but we haven't got anything planned for this Saturday. Libby?'

But Libby was shaking her head. That was a bit soon, she said, she didn't think Monty was ready, especially as he was meeting Eleanor on Sunday and that was, well, problematical. She needed to sort that first.

'Can we help?' Viv and Janet spoke as one.

Libby felt better for sharing with Viv and Janet at the Muscateers lunch but was no nearer a solution to the Monty and Eleanor problem by the time she got home. It didn't help that Viv and Janet saw things rather differently from each other. Viv had been most understanding. She'd said some of her family had found it hard to accept her relationship with Patrick, so she knew exactly how Libby felt. She'd advised ignoring the gender issue, as it wasn't an issue except in Eleanor's head, and not telling Eleanor anything at all about sleeping arrangements. 'We don't have to explain our love lives to our children, do we?' she'd said. 'Do we ask them about theirs? Would we dare?' There was a fine line between privacy, good, and secrecy, bad, she'd said, and this was privacy. Janet disagreed. Not telling would look as if she was keeping their relationship a secret and when it was discovered – as it surely would be – there would be trouble.

Libby was recalling their conversation as she cleared Monty's lunch dishes from the table. He'd left a note saying he'd gone for a walk.

'Just tell the truth, Libby. Tell Eleanor that Monty is male and always has been, and you're sleeping with him.' That had been Janet.

'But I've told her that he's my lodger and has his own room.'

'Well, tell her he isn't and hasn't.'

'But I'm sure that would upset her.'

Janet had shrugged, which was all very well for someone whose only child lived in New Zealand. If Eleanor lived on the other side of the world and not a few streets away, Libby wouldn't be worried. She wouldn't have told her anything about her private life. And that was what Viv advised for the time being – not telling Eleanor anything. 'Leave it to Eleanor to see what she wants to see, and believe what she's comfortable believing, but maybe keep bedroom doors closed?'

* * *

By midday on Sunday Libby had followed Viv's advice. All the bedroom doors were closed – except the door to the room she thought of as Ellie-Jo's. There were toys there and Ellie-Jo went in and out freely, sometimes taking herself off for a nap. Libby had in fact gone a bit further – in a just-in-case frame of mind – and done some stage-managing behind the closed doors. Remembering her own snoop round Monty's house, she feared that Eleanor might be a snooper too so she'd made sure the lodger's room looked lived in. Yesterday, she'd made up the bed after putting all the sports equipment Monty had dumped on top of it under it. And, last-minute thought, she'd put his pyjamas, unworn since he'd been here, under the pillow. Even more importantly, she'd removed anything from her own bedroom that might suggest Monty had ever been inside it. She'd changed her bedding so a super-snooper wouldn't find any white hairs on the pillow next to hers. Monty didn't share her en suite, so there were no worries there. His toiletries were in the bathroom. She was prepared for anything, she thought, but nevertheless her stress levels were high as she came downstairs to get on with the Sunday lunch. She'd just checked – again! – that the doors were closed. Fortunately the door handles were way too high for Ellie-Jo, who loved to 'explore'.

'Darling, calm down.' Monty got up from the chair where he'd been reading the Sunday papers, to follow her into the kitchen and kiss the nape of her neck. It was his last chance, he said, before the Morality Squad arrived.

'It's not like that. I've asked you to be sensitive to other people's feelings, that's all. Now, remember you're my lodger and we're just good friends, and let me get into the oven.'

'Oh, dear. Not that bad, is it?'

'Ha ha. I need to baste the chicken.'

She was doing a roast though it was hardly the weather for it, temperatures already soaring. But Monty – slight sore point – had declined to do a barbecue, when she'd asked him, thinking it would earn him brownie points. He'd said, 'Sorry, darling, not part of my skill set.'

She glanced at the kitchen clock. The family could be here any moment.

'Monty, do you think you could make a dressing for the salads? The recipe's there.' She pointed to *Delia's Summer Collection*, open at the right page.

'Salads?' He looked alarmed. 'Roasties too, I hope?'

'No. Sorry.' She hated to disappoint. 'But bread, nice bread. Oh, here are our guests, well, the youngest. Hello, darling. Do come in.'

Ellie-Jo, who usually burst in, was standing in the doorway, head on one side, giving Monty a searching look. 'Are you Granny's new friend?'

'I'm Granny's new *old* friend,' Monty replied. 'I have known her for a very long time.'

Ellie-Jo considered that. 'Do you like my bunches?'

Monty considered them. 'Yes, they're very wavy.'

'That's because I usually have plaits.' She took a step inside.

'I think I like bunches better than plaits. They are less constrained. My name is Monty, by the way.' He stuck out his hand and they shook hands solemnly.

Libby awarded him brownie points. He was being delightful, his comments perfectly pitched. Perhaps there was time to do roasties or pan-fried if she started them off in the microwave.

'Mummy has told me all about you.'

Uh-oh! Libby's stress levels soared. Why did modern parents think children had to know *everything*? But surely Eleanor hadn't... Oh, here she was now with Derek in tow as bag-carrier.

'Good morning, everyone!' Eleanor filled the doorway in a voluminous purple caftan.

This isn't a school assembly, Eleanor.

'Eleanor, meet Monty. Monty, meet Eleanor.' Libby did the introductions. 'Monty, meet Derek.' She took a bottle of red from Derek, then, leaving them all to weigh each other up, she escaped to the oven to see if there was room for a small pan of roasties.

'How *are* you, Monty?'

Libby hoped she was imagining the over-concern in her daughter's voice. 'Beers and white wine in the garage fridge, chaps,' she called from the floor as she rearranged the oven shelves. Had they heard her? She heard Ellie-Jo asking Monty if he could put more water in her paddling pool, as they headed outside. Was Monty joining her staff?

'He's very masculine, isn't he?' Eleanor was pouring red when Libby straightened up. 'Such a rich *deep* voice.'

'Yes, Eleanor, because—'

'I did ask Ellie-Jo not to stare.'

'Eleanor, Monty *is* a man!'

'Of course, Mum. Shush. He's coming in.'

'I have orders to get a funnel, the jug with the up-and-down lid, the colander and... oh, darling!' Monty saw the potatoes Libby had just put in the sink and looked as if he was going to kiss her.

'Here.' She grabbed the colander from the draining board and thrust it into his hands, then the jug and funnel and squirty bottle that she guessed Ellie-Jo had also asked for. 'On your way, Monty, or your new mistress will be displeased.'

Whoops. Bad choice of words perhaps? But Eleanor's thoughts were going in a different direction. 'How much is he giving you, Mum?'

Awkward, but there was worse to come.

* * *

It was Cornflake's fault. No, Libby took full responsibility, *she* should have noticed the cat was missing and done a room search before she went round closing doors. But she had assumed he was outside because he often disappeared on these hot summer days, returning hungry in the evenings.

Unfortunately not today.

It was mid-afternoon when Ellie-Jo came into the garden where the grown-ups were gathered in various stages of post-prandial somnolence, to announce that she'd just 'rescued' Cornflake. Libby didn't immediately register a problem. The little girl had gone upstairs soon after lunch had ended, but no one had worried because that was what she did, and Derek had been up to check a couple of times and reported that all was well. He'd found her napping first time and playing with the doll's house next. She was, he said, 'as good as gold'.

Now here she was standing by the sunlounger where Libby was lounging, awake, but only just.

'I rescued Cornflake, Granny,' she said again.

'Thank you, darling.'

'He was trapped in your room.'

It took a few minutes for what her granddaughter had said to sink in and signal alarm. 'Wh-what, darling? What did you say?' Libby struggled into a sitting position.

'I opened the door all by myself standing on my chair.'

'Clever Ellie-Jo.' Her doting father applauded.

'Because Cornflake was miaowing and scratching at the door,' said Ellie-Jo. 'Miaow! Miaow! Scratch! Scratch!' Her impression of a distressed Cornflake got her another round of applause from Derek, who said she definitely had Granny Libby's theatrical genes.

Libby told herself there was nothing to worry about, except perhaps a hole in the carpet, or, worse, an 'accident' she'd have to deal with.

'Cornflake's very hungry, Granny.'

'No worries, stay where you are.' Derek was on his feet. 'I know where the cat food is and I'll put the kettle on while I'm at it. Tea, anyone?'

'And I found this under your bed, Granny.' Ellie-Jo held out her hand and Libby froze.

She hoped Eleanor was as fast asleep as she looked.

'What is it, Granny?'

'I don't know, Ellie-Jo.' Stupid dishonest answer. She knew exactly what it was and reached out to take it from Ellie-Jo's hand, but the little girl was running off.

'I'll ask Mummy, then. Mummy! Mummy, wake up!'

20

Monty seemed to think it had all gone rather well.

He was stretched out on the sofa, where he'd headed as soon as Eleanor, Derek and Ellie-Jo had left half an hour ago. 'I think they liked me, and I rather liked them. Derek's everything a modern man should be, isn't he?'

Take lessons? Waspish wasn't the word for how Libby was feeling. Hornetish, was that a word? She had just joined Monty on the sofa, after clearing tables, putting leftovers in the fridge, wiping down surfaces and loading up the dishwasher yet again. Monty hadn't helped.

'Ellie-Jo found one of your cufflinks under my bed.' Libby would never forget the look of disgust on Eleanor's face as she'd handed it to her. 'My four-year-old daughter found *that* in your bedroom.' How had Monty managed to miss that little episode?

'Oh, I wondered where that had gone.' He obviously saw no cause for concern. 'I'm not sure that it works for Eleanor though.'

'*What*? What doesn't work for Eleanor?'

'Derek doing everything. Being modern man. What's left for Eleanor?'

Being a wife, mother and head teacher, and that was just for starters, but Libby didn't bother to answer. Monty wasn't showing enough concern about the cufflink, cufflinks, which he must have left on her bedside table. Of course he wasn't to know that the cat would find them, which was what must have happened. He couldn't be blamed because the cat had batted them onto the floor, and then batted them around a bit, so that one ended up under the bed, the other under the wardrobe where Libby had found it. But he could show some *interest*.

'Why was she so concerned about me?' Monty was still on about Eleanor. 'She went on and on. "How's it going, Monty? How's it going?"' He did her voice. '"You can tell *me*, you know." As if she were some sort of counsellor.'

'Because she thinks you're undergoing gender reassignment.'

'What?'

'A sex-change, Monty.'

That did shut him up long enough for her to tell him how upset Eleanor had been about the cufflinks, solid gold with the monogram CM, the two letters intertwined. Her brown eyes, just like Jim's, had filled with tears, as she'd said, 'M for Monty, I presume? I think I'm most hurt that you didn't feel you could share with me.'

'Eleanor, I've been *trying* to share this with you for weeks!' She hadn't shouted, she hadn't.

'You were dishonest, Mum! I'm not sure I can forgive this!'

But Monty didn't get it even after she'd explained.

'You need music.' Monty lifted her legs so he could get off the sofa. He had brought his extensive CD collection with him, believing that life, like film, needed background music. What would *Brief Encounter* be without Rachmaninov's surging rhythms? he frequently said.

But right now Libby craved silence so she could think.

What exactly was troubling Eleanor? Was she upset because her mother was sleeping with a man who wasn't her father, or because she thought her mother was sleeping with a man undergoing gender reassignment who wasn't her father? Or because she hadn't 'shared' that she was sleeping with a man who wasn't her father, who might or might not have been undergoing gender reassignment?

'Darling, stop worrying and listen.'

But the music wasn't helping: 'Cavalleria Rusticana' – didn't it once advertise Kleenex? – even before a shocking text pinged in.

Not comfortable with Ellie-Jo coming to yours now. Think best if you come to ours on Tuesday. E

'E-Eleanor says she thinks it's better if I go round their house to look after Ellie-Jo on Tuesday.'

'But I thought that's what you always did.'

'No, I went there one week, Ellie-Jo came here the next. She should be coming here this Tuesday, but Eleanor thinks...'

What *did* Eleanor think?

Libby reached for her phone and keyed in Eleanor's number but didn't even get the answerphone.

'She's punishing me.'

'What on earth for?' Monty was back on the sofa, eyes closed, entranced.

'For having you to stay.'

Was it only a week ago that she was driving Monty here with all his stuff, vowing to make it work? Was it only two days ago that she was telling Viv and Janet how she was loving having someone to love and look after? That it was all working out much better than expected? Was it only yesterday that she'd thought how lovely it

would be if this lasted forever? Why hadn't she followed her first
instinct? *I don't want you to come and stay with me!* She had known it
wouldn't work.

'Monty, turn that bloody music off!'

21

LIBBY

Monty crept towards the sitting room, as if he were playing Grandma's Footsteps, then closed the door behind him, leaving Libby in her mini-office under the stairs. She had seen his reflection on her computer screen and had in fact heard him. He wasn't as quiet as he thought he was, but he was being super-considerate. The row yesterday had cleared the air. They had sorted a few things out, like her need for silence, especially when she was writing, like now.

It was Monday morning, her designated time for writing her column. She'd made it clear that she hated background noise of any kind, and that she mustn't be disturbed, even for tea or coffee. If she wanted a drink she would ask for one, or get it herself. Her office wasn't as private as she would have liked. It had worked when she was living on her own but wasn't so good now there was another person passing through the hall to go upstairs to the loo or into the kitchen to make himself a drink. Now she hankered for a room with a door to close, not a nook in a main throughfare. But she tried to be positive; he was trying very hard to respect her wishes.

She had a subject for her column, thank goodness, an unjust parking fine. A sickening example of Rip Off Britain, it was something she needed to warn others about, because it could happen to anyone. It had given her CPTMP – Car Park Ticket Machine Phobia and PBPP – Pay by Phone Phobia. Sid would love it. So would lots of her readers, well, the ones who preferred human beings to machines and devices with tiny screens and tinier keyboards, and automated robot-voices.

Nine weeks ago – it was a Friday – I parked at our local station and paid for parking by PAY BY PHONE. I paid by PAY BY PHONE because the ticket machine at the station kept rejecting my credit card and my debit card. Feeling like an idiot – what was I doing wrong? – and afraid that I would miss my train, after three attempts, I gave up. I made a note of the telephone number for PAY BY PHONE, displayed on a board nearby, and started trying to pay as soon as I got on the train. I got through on the fourth attempt, but not to a human being. I had to speak to an automated Daleky voice, which I found disconcerting, and even more disconcerting when it asked for my pin number. Had it really said that? Surely you weren't supposed to give your pin number to anyone? I hesitated, not least because I was still getting used to hearing aids, recently acquired. The train was rattling along noisily. The carriage was full of talking people. The Daleky voice repeated the question, which I now heard as 'What is the car park number?' But I didn't know the number of the car park – how could I know? – so I gave the name of the car park. Dalek moved on to another question and eventually I completed the transaction. The Daleky voice said I had completed the transaction but I couldn't help worrying throughout the day in London, where I had gone to meet an old friend. Had I paid?

Would my car be there when I returned? Would I find it clamped? Phew! I was very relieved to find my car in the car park when I got back that evening, and not clamped. I was even more relieved when I checked my online bank statement next day and there in black and white was the transaction. TO PAY BY PHONE £8.50 02/05/14. Phew again! But then, a fortnight later, I got a letter, a real letter, not an email, through the post, Royal Mail no less, saying I hadn't paid and had incurred a fine of £100 or a mere £60 if I paid immediately. Of course I didn't cough up. This was clearly a mistake so I wrote straight back enclosing the evidence that I had paid. I photocopied the bank statement showing very clearly that I had paid £8.50 to PAY BY PHONE on Friday 2 May. It was the day...

Libby hesitated. It was the day she'd rushed to Monty's bedside when he wasn't feeling well. Should she include that in her article? Yes, because her readers liked the personal detail, but without naming him, obviously. Decision made, she carried on, telling them how she'd thought sending the evidence would be the end of it, but it hadn't been. The horror had mounted. She'd got another letter rejecting her evidence, demanding £100 now, but also telling her she could appeal to an arbitrator, POPLA, an acronym for Parking on Private Land Appeals, as long as she agreed to abide by their decision.

What was that?

Music. From the sitting room. Surely not. Yes, it was. How could Monty have forgotten so soon? The door was pulsing to the rhythms of film music, *The Magnificent Seven*. There were cowboys in the sitting room, hooves pounding across the prairie. Rage rose within her.

Think positive, Libby. Harness the rage.

Could she use its surging rhythms to speed up her word count?
Yes, she could, typing faster...

Convinced of my innocence I appealed to POPLA – Parking on
Private Land Appeals – as they could come to only one conclusion. I HAD PAID! Filling in the online appeal would take a mere
fifteen minutes, it said. Not true! One hour and a quarter later,
when I had just finished scanning in my bank statement, my PAY
BY PHONE history, a photograph of the offending ticket
machine, a photograph of my rail ticket proving that I was where
I said I was, a photograph they had sent me as their evidence
that I had parked illegally, proving I was where I said I was.
Because, incredibly, 'they' were now saying that I had paid to
park in another car park in another town!

Then, as if some malevolent force was at work, as she looked on,
the whole lot, every word of what she'd written that morning,
vanished.

Vanished. She was staring at a blank screen.

'*What* have I done?' She howled, burying her head in her hands,
and as she did the door behind her opened and her cries were
drowned by thundering hooves.

Go away, Monty!

But his hands were gripping her shoulders. 'Can one of the
good guys help?'

'Doubt it.' She felt his stubbly cheek brush against hers.

'How about clicking on the bendy arrow thing?' He pointed to
the left-hand corner of the screen, and without much hope she
reached for the mouse and clicked and... watched entranced as her
words returned, filling the screen.

Nine weeks ago – it was a Friday...

Monty was the comeback kid. All he needed was a Stetson. Every time she wrote him off, he bounced back, like her script today – and her love for him. She got to her feet *filled* with love and gratitude. 'Have a shave, Monty. I'm taking you out to lunch!'

22

LIBBY

Energised, while Monty was upstairs, Libby got on the phone to The Olive Branch and booked a table for two. Monty was an asset. He was a darling. He deserved a big treat. She finished the article in record time, recounting the dismal result that would appal her readers, as it had appalled her. Her appeal had failed. She'd had to pay the £100 fine, for an £8.50 parking fee that she *had* paid. The injustice still rankled, but at least she had got a good article out of it, *and* she'd discovered that Monty had hidden talents.

'I didn't know you had computer skills.' She tucked her arm into his as they set off for town on foot, resisting his pleas to take the car. Monty wasn't keen on walking but it was good for his health so she jollied him along. And she pretended not to hear when he said he wasn't keen on foreign food. They reached the river and she paused to enjoy the view of the picturesque white Japanese bridge and the swans and ducks floating under it.

'Couldn't we go there?' He was pointing to the building on the other side of the road, a smart Tudoresque gastro pub, very popular with businessmen.

'No, because I've booked The Olive Branch and I want you to meet Nikos and Evelina.'

'How about that one?' He pointed to The Swan, another black and white half-timbered building, when they reached the town centre.

'Another time, Monty. You'll like The Olive Branch. Honestly.' They were waiting for the lights to change so they could cross the high street. 'Greek food's great. There's a lot of roast meat if you want it. The lamb kebabs are delicious.' She pulled on his arm as the lights changed. 'Not far now. Come on.'

Two birds with one stone was what she'd thought when she'd got this urge to treat Monty to reward him for rescuing her article. One, she was introducing her friends to each other, two, she was supporting Nikos and Evelina, who needed all the business they could get. There was a lot of competition, not just from The Swan Hotel and gastro pub, but also restaurant chains that had moved into the relatively new square, which they'd now reached. It had once been a derelict car park, but the council had made it into an attractive plaza with a continental feel. It was paved attractively and planted imaginatively with tropical-looking trees in pots and raised beds full of colourful flowers.

Nikos had been delighted when she'd rung to book but had reminded her she didn't have to. 'There will always be a table for you, dear Libby, even if you eat in the kitchen with Evelina and me.' He was pleased she was coming today, a Monday, as they were trying to attract customers earlier in the week, with a BOGOF. He'd cooked her favourite, he'd said, fasolakia lathera, a delicious slow-cooked bean dish, as one of the specials. 'Your table by the window, right?'

'Right.'

'I will be waiting for you.'

And he was of course. Nikos was a man of his word. She saw him before he saw her. The Olive Branch, though small, stood out with its vivid Santorini blue tables and chairs, some of them outside today. And Nikos stood out too, standing in front of the door, flanked by his trademark spherical olive trees. Every inch the proud proprietor in his black apron, his handsome bronze head shining like a Belisha beacon. He raised his hand and beamed when at last he saw her, bringing a smile to Libby's lips.

Then he didn't.

Nikos had the most expressive face she'd ever seen. It registered every nuance of feeling, she'd often thought, but there was nothing nuanced about the look he was giving Monty right now. Mouth down and eyebrows close together, he was an emoticon of dislike.

'Hi!' Libby raised her hand in a wave, but Nikos had gone inside.

Evelina showed them to their table by the window.

'Monty, meet Evelina, joint proprietor of the best Greek restaurant outside Greece and creator of the most amazing baklava in the world. Evelina, meet Monty, computer whiz extraordinaire and old friend going back to our drama-student days.'

Monty stuck out his hand, bowing a little, and Evelina took it and shook it formally. Formally was the word. Stiff was another. Stilted another. Strained another.

'Any friend of Libby's is a friend of ours,' said Evelina, but the words lacked her usual warmth and she didn't stay to chat. She gave Monty a menu when he sat down and turned to the next table.

'Er, excuse me.' Monty raised his hand and for an awful moment Libby thought he was going to click his fingers. 'Doesn't the lady get a menu?'

Evelina spoke over her shoulder. 'We know what Libby likes, sir. I'll be with you in a minute.'

Sir? What was the matter? Had they thought she was coming

with Zelda? Was that the problem? She'd said she was bringing a friend.

Monty perused. He would like a steak. With chips. Did they do steak? Were they any good? Libby said she was sure everything was good but could only vouch for what she'd tasted, and she hadn't had steak here. 'If you want grilled meat I recommend the lamb kebabs, which you could have with chips, maybe with some faso-lakia lathera, which is one of the specials today.' She didn't like to point out the BOGOF as she was treating him, and it seemed a bit cheapskate, but she did want him to honour their cooking. 'Faso-lakia lathera is a mix of fresh vegetables, onions, garlic, tomatoes, potatoes and green beans, lots of green beans, cooked slowly in olive oil and spices. It's delicious and goes well with kebabs, lamb or pork.'

Monty said he really fancied a rump steak and Libby urged him to have anything he liked. When Evelina came to take their orders, she pointed out that steak wasn't part of their two for one. Monty raised an eyebrow in Libby's direction and she said that was fine, absolutely fine.

She just wanted everyone to be happy.

'Is Nikos okay?' she asked Evelina, when she brought meze to their table, and Monty had nipped to the loo.

'He is cooking. We are very busy. As you see.' The restaurant was quite full.

'But is he okay?' Libby caught Evelina's eye and held it.

'He is a man, Libby. He is a man.'

What was that supposed to mean? Oh, who was she kidding? *Nikos was jealous.*

'But that's so unfair, Evelina!' *Unfair to you too,* she meant, but Evelina sprang to his defence.

'Nikos is fairest of men! He spend whole life fighting for justice! What you think Olive Branch about?'

'Wow!' Monty, returning from the Gents, stood back as Evelina stormed off and the doors to the kitchen crashed against the walls. 'We don't have to go to the theatre for drama, do we?'

The meal was delicious, every mouthful. Even Monty said so. *Even Monty said so?* His steak and the chips were perfectly cooked, he said. Phew! Why *phew*? Libby questioned herself. Because she'd thought Nikos might flavour it with arsenic?

Get a grip, Libby. Get a grip.

* * *

When they'd finished she longed for Monty to get up and go and pay the bill, or at least say they'd go halves, which was silly and unfair because she'd told him she was paying. And she knew he had a cash-flow problem. But when Evelina put the bill in front of him she wanted Monty to pick it up, stride to the bar, wield his credit card and pay. She even thought of asking him to pay, saying she would reimburse him later. She spent a few seconds examining her own thought processes. *Why don't I want Nikos and Evelina to see me paying for Monty? Because they're old-fashioned and will think he should pay for me. They'll think he's using me.* She hoped Monty would intuit how she was feeling and spare her the embarrassment, yes, the embarrassment. She felt sick with embarrassment, which was silly in this day and age. But Monty didn't intuit anything. He handed her the bill. Then she took it to Evelina at the counter, where Nikos suddenly appeared, took it from Evelina's hand and redid it. 'You came for the two for one.' He handed it back, halved.

'But—'

'That's okay, Liberty. It was good to see you.' Nikos always called her Liberty. 'Please come again. Bring Ellie-Jo perhaps? We loved meeting her.'

'Oh, thanks, I'll tell her. I'm seeing her tomorrow, actually.

And... er thanks for the... er bill. I was treating Monty because he'd helped me with a computer problem...' She was burbling but it was good to be talking to Nikos at last.

He nodded, so did Evelina, but sympathetically, she thought, as if they were sorry for her.

23

LIBBY

Ellie-Jo was sitting on the stairs in her pyjamas when Libby arrived at Eleanor's house at half past seven on Tuesday.

'No, she hasn't had her breakfast, I've got to fly!' Eleanor and her briefcase rushed by Libby, who was still at the door.

The new arrangement worked rather well for Eleanor, Libby couldn't help thinking as her super-charged daughter reversed down the drive, but perhaps best not to think about her motivation. Ellie-Jo made no comment on the change of routine, and maybe hadn't noticed.

'Would you like to go into town and feed the ducks on the river, Ellie-Jo?' Libby asked as she closed the front door. 'I've downloaded an interesting leaflet for you. Here.' She handed it to Ellie-Jo, for modern granny had also printed out the info and made it into an attractive booklet. 'All About Ducks' was full of activities and up-to-date information and dire warnings from the Canal & River Trust. Libby tried not to feel guilt-ridden about all the ducks whose health she'd ruined in years gone by with hunks of white bread as she headed for the kitchen. Today's ducks would get healthy snacks.

'I'll ask Hippo, Granny.' Ellie-Jo shared the leaflet with her most beloved soft toy, sitting beside her on the stairs. Confusingly to the uninitiated, Hippo was a lamb, knitted by Libby some years ago, but any resemblance to a lamb or a hippo or any other animal was long worn away by love and affection and time in the washing machine when he could be wrested from Ellie-Jo's hands. Nowadays he mostly just slept with Ellie-Jo, but today he might be getting a day out.

'What does Hippo say?' Libby wondered what to give her grand-girl for breakfast.

'He's still thinking about it.'

Excellent. A slow day. Libby adjusted her pace. How lovely! What a privilege to be able to give herself up to this experience! If she resisted the urge to vacuum or tidy or throw a load of washing in the washing machine, which was not hard, she had absolutely nothing else to do except have fun with Ellie-Jo.

'I'm going to have a cup of coffee while Hippo is thinking, Ellie Jo.'

'All right, Granny.'

Two hours later, when she'd got Ellie-Jo dressed and break-fasted, and Ellie-Jo had got Hippo dressed and given him his break-fast, and she'd washed Ellie-Jo's face and got her to clean her teeth, and Ellie-Jo had washed Hippo's face and got him to clean his teeth, and Ellie-Jo had done a jigsaw and they'd both done a lot of colouring in, Hippo was strapped in his buggy and they were outside the front door ready to go.

'Are you sure you don't want to ride in your buggy, Ellie-Jo?'

'Mummies don't ride in buggies, Granny.'

Ellie was being Mummy today, pushing Hippo in his buggy, and, to give the grandgirl her due, she pushed the little buggy for at least half the walk into town. Then Hippo enjoyed riding in Granny's bag and the buggy hooked over Libby's arm was awkward but not as heavy as she'd feared. Ellie-Jo, unlike Monty – Libby couldn't help comparing – didn't complain about the walk into town. She did wonder about the change to the ducks' diet though, when they reached the embankment.

'Peas, Granny?'

'That's what the leaflet says. Tinned, fresh or frozen, though if frozen they must be thawed. And they are thawed now.'

'Sweetcorn?'

'It's very good for them, Ellie-Jo.'

'Lettuce?'

'They love it.'

'Birdseed?'

'Mad for it.'

'Flapjacks? You're joking, Granny!'

'No, they're good for them because of the oats.' It was a surprise to Libby too but, assured that even made with sugar and syrup they were fine for ducks in small quantities, she'd set to and made a batch while Ellie-Jo and Hippo were doing a jigsaw.

'Here.' She'd brought a slice each for the humans too and it was while they were eating them, sitting on a bench by the river, that she got a call from Sid, the editor of the paper. Could she come in for a chat about a business matter?

'Yes, of course I can.' How intriguing! 'When were you thinking of?'

'Asap.' Sid was even terser than usual.

'Now?' Libby was terse back.

'Fine.'

And before she could ask if bringing Ellie-Jo was okay and tell him they were only round the corner and would be there in ten minutes, he'd put the phone down.

* * *

'Why have you got your foot on a bucket?' Ellie-Jo wasn't fazed by meeting the editor of a provincial newspaper, even after climbing three flights of stairs to reach his untidy office at the top of the building in Mill Street.

'Because I have an ingrowing toenail. And it's a waste-paper bin, not a bucket.' Sid was clearly in pain. His big toe, un-socked, looked swollen and sore.

'Ellie-Jo...' Libby got her breath at last '...here.' She got Hippo out of her bag. 'I don't think Hippo has ever been to a newspaper office before, and I'm sure he'd like to look round, quietly. Sid—' she turned to him '—you're clearly suffering. Let's get to the point. What's this about?'

'Syndication. I've had an offer to syndicate your column.' He had to explain that other papers, local papers, free sheets like his, wanted to buy the right to print her column in their papers.

'Other papers want to buy my column?'

'Several.'

'And they want to pay?'

'Both of us, 50–50. If you agree. It's great news. Makes the paper viable and you're quids in.'

'Quids in?' She felt like a parrot.

Sid winced. 'Operation tomorrow. Contract later. Will send. Talk to Nikos if you have any questions.'

'Nikos? Why?'

'Because he's my legal adviser.' He closed his eyes.

Curiouser and curiouser, but Sid wasn't going to answer any more questions. Libby gathered her things and got to her feet. 'We're going out to lunch, Ellie-Jo.'

* * *

'Nikos, guess who's here!' Evelina, serving customers near the door, saw Libby walk into The Olive Branch with Ellie-Jo.

The reception couldn't have been more different from yesterday.

Nikos stepped out from behind the counter, held out his arms and Ellie-Jo rushed into them. Then Evelina joined them and got a hug from Ellie-Jo too. Libby's grandgirl had obviously made fans when she'd come for Sunday lunch with her mum and dad a couple of weeks ago. It was early lunchtime, about half past twelve, and the restaurant was busy, but Nikos quickly found Libby and Ellie-Jo a table outside. Then he brought them drinks, juice for Ellie-Jo, Malagousia for Libby and a platter of meze, including his wonderful home-made hummus and pitta bread. Later there was ice cream.

'She'll be fine,' said Nikos when he'd cleared the table, seeing Libby watch Ellie-Jo go into the restaurant holding Evelina's hand. 'They've gone to seek out Oedipuss, the restaurant cat,' he added, seeing her questioning look. 'You haven't had the pleasure? Oh, cue for a story? But first, well, when I've brought coffees, I'll try to explain this syndication business.'

Sid, he'd managed to say earlier, had been on the phone.

Now he sat down with her. 'Firstly, yes, since you ask, I am Sid's legal adviser. Secondly, though you haven't asked, I am qualified. This—' he nodded towards the restaurant '—is what I do for love. Law is the day job, or was till I retired, but Sid wouldn't let me retire from advising him, so I still do that.'

There was a lot to take in.

'But back to business. Sid is right and wrong. I do understand this stuff, and you can ask me anything once you've read the contracts – there will be several – but strictly speaking I'm acting for Sid so you shouldn't take my advice.'

'But you think it's a good deal? For Sid and me?'

'It's excellent. You'll get twenty, maybe thirty times more money than you're getting at the moment, depending on how many papers buy in.' He topped up her cup with coffee. 'Just one more thing – I'd keep this under your hat for a bit, as it isn't signed and sealed yet. Don't tell anyone.'

Don't tell Monty, that's what he means.

Monty was the elephant in the room, though they weren't in a room and Monty wasn't an elephant.

'There's no need to rush, Liberty. In fact, it might be a good idea to get your own solicitor to look at the contract, or a trusted family member, one of your children perhaps? Eleanor, she has a good brain.'

'But you think it's good for me and I should sign the contract?'

He nodded, clearly pleased for her.

And she nodded because she'd trust him with her life.

24

LIBBY

'How was your day, darling?' Monty was standing by the open front door.

'Perfect.' She longed to tell him about it, *all* about it. 'What's with the tea towel?'

It was tied round his waist waiter-style. 'Oh.' He seemed surprised to see it there. 'Darling, come here.' He held her close and kissed her. 'I've missed you.'

'Oh...' She hadn't, she realised, missed him. No time.

'I was worried, darling, when you didn't reply to my messages.'

'Messages?'

'Texts, darling. I've been texting you all day, wanting to know how you were. Where you were. Doesn't matter, not now. Look at them later. Come and sit down.' He led the way to the sofa in the sitting-cum-dining room, past the table already laid for supper with wine in a carafe and a candle not yet lit.

What was this?

'Red okay?' He poured her a glass of wine. 'We're having coq au vin. Now put your feet up while I check on things.'

Shoes off, glass in hand, a lovely velvety Malbec, she scrolled through the 'Love you's and 'Miss you's sent at hourly intervals throughout the day, and the 'What's your ETA?' sent only an hour ago.

'All right?' He looked round the door.

'No, I'm feeling dreadfully guilty.'

'Not your fault, darling. I'm sure that little girl was running you off your feet.'

'Oh.' She saw the vacuum cleaner behind the sofa. He'd been cleaning too!

'Sorry.' He saw her noticing. 'Didn't have time to put it away.'

'I wasn't criticising! I...' She watched him pick up the cleaner and carry it out, the hose coiling after him, looking at her, a serpent accusing her of gross neglect. Sssss! But another memory was surfacing, another feeling about another too-tidy house. She'd come home from a short shopping trip and Ben, aged ten or eleven, had greeted her at the door.

'Monty, what is this?'

'What do you mean?' He looked hurt.

'All this... er helpfulness?'

Ben had taken her bags. Simon had insisted that she sat down while he made her a nice cup of tea. They'd both put the shopping away for her and then had come the confession. They had broken one of her favourite things, a Royal Doulton plate, one of a set depicting Shakespearean characters. Hamlet was in bits, the victim of a ping-pong ball hit so hard it had knocked him off the dresser.

Monty hadn't broken anything, he said over dinner, but he had got a confession. He had been a lazy bastard, he said. He hadn't done anything, that was the trouble. He hadn't done anything at all to help her. He hadn't been pulling his weight. He'd been letting her wait on him hand and foot, like a nineteen fifties housewife. That was why she got waspish sometimes, he'd realised in a Damascene moment. It was because she was exhausted and couldn't do what someone like her should be doing. He was like all the others who drained her energy...

'Oh, Monty...' She was overwhelmed.

'No need to say anything—' he held up his hand '—because things are changing. I'm changing because I love you.'

Because I love you. Did he really say that?

Yes, he said it again, his deep blue eyes looking into hers. He was going to help so she could get on with her life's work. She might have to teach him a few skills, like how to stack the dishwasher and programme the washing machine, and fix all the different bits of the vacuum cleaner together – sorry, he hadn't done the stairs – because he was a traditional sort of chap, badly brought up no doubt – servants, sorry – but he truly madly deeply wanted to learn how to support her in any way he could.

'Except, of course, financially, darling.' He looked abject as he explained that he still had the same old cash-flow problem.

'Monty, eat your dinner.' He'd hardly touched his. 'It's all right. It doesn't matter, I...'

Keep this under your hat for a bit.

Fortunately Monty cheered up without her telling him her good news, and over strawberries and ice cream for afters, he told her he had a plan.

'You need to start thinking big and focus, darling. First, stop writing that column.'

'But—'

He held up his hand. 'Sorry, but it's a complete waste of your talent, brings in peanuts and is cat litter next morning.'

'Actually...' but no, she couldn't.

'Second, those little stories you write for kiddies...'

Libby sat back in her chair. She'd heard that disparaging tone before, usually at parties, usually from a man, when she'd been unwise enough to say she wrote for children. 'Oh, have you thought of writing for adults?' As if writing for children weren't as important as writing for adults, as if children weren't as important as adults.

'Thirdly, if you were more professional, if you stopped being at the beck and call of every Tom, Dick and Harriet, you would be able to write something worth reading.'

'You don't think I've written anything worth reading?'

'Not yet, darling.'

It hurt, but he ploughed on unaware.

'Thing is, darling, you're an artist and artists are different, but only if they devote themselves to their art.'

'Live in an ivory tower, you mean?'

'Sort of. Like Vita Sackville-West. She lived, well, worked in a tower. You don't read about her looking after the grandchildren, do you?'

'She had servants.'

'Precisely. Artists don't do the cleaning. They serve their art so it doesn't shrivel and die.'

'While lesser beings wait on them hand and foot?'

Libby disagreed with every fibre of her being. Creativity, art, whatever you called it, was or should be part of everyone's life. It was what made human beings human. Artists weren't a race apart. All human beings needed time and space to express themselves and create. To dance or make music, to paint or draw or write, to make beautiful things. They couldn't if they were bowed down with everyday work and worries, but they could if they had some time and space. She wished Viv were here. Viv had made a study of the subject and would put Monty in his place with a few well-aimed expletives.

'Monty,' Libby started to say, 'I'm sorry you don't think anything I've written is worth reading, but I'm proud of what I do, *all* that I do, including being there for my family—'

But Monty was still in full flow. He would do his bit to help, he said, but she must stop looking after her granddaughter for a whole day every week, unappreciated by her ungrateful daughter. She must cut down on her visits to her mother, who by all accounts didn't recognise her anyway...

'Monty—' There were a lot of *musts*, she couldn't help thinking.

'Hear me out, darling.' He held up a hand. 'If you stopped doing all these other things you could write something important, a novel.'

He had a brilliant idea for a novel, he said, and he'd already worked out the plot. He felt in his jacket pocket and brought out a folded piece of paper. 'Read that,' he said, 'then get writing it. It will earn us a fortune.'

25

LIBBY

It won't work. Libby didn't want to say that.

Well, not before she'd heard Monty outline his plan. She was sitting at the table in her dining room, now designated as the office. She was in a meeting, a formal meeting, convened by Monty. It was beginning at ten and ending no later than twelve – she'd said – because she was going to see her mother. It was Wednesday. Monty had refused to divulge his plan last night, because it needed her serious attention, he'd said, not the slightly sozzled attention of a woman who'd had several glasses of Merlot with her coq au vin. *Her* coq au vin in more ways than one, she'd realised when she was putting the ice cream back in the freezer, not too sozzled to remember to do that, though Monty had been. Monty hadn't cooked the meal from scratch, he'd thawed and reheated a family-sized coq au vin that she had made earlier. Not that she was holding that against him; he had thawed and reheated it successfully. Not everyone could do that. Now, though, he was sitting at the end of the table, opposite her, waiting to inspire her with his vision. That was how he worked, she'd remembered, how he began any project, by inspiring the company with his vision.

'That's you and me, Cornflake.' The cat was on her knee. 'We're the company.'

'Does it have to be here?'

'Sorry.' She put the cat on the floor.

'Are you sure your mobile is off?'

She nodded.

'And the landline is switched to voicemail?'

She checked.

'Right, let's begin.' He was pen poised, with a notebook in front of him, a few notes already written. 'You and me, we met in the wrong place at the wrong time. Yes? When we were young. Then met again years later in a bar. Yes?'

'Ye-es.' It wasn't the opening she'd expected.

'So, what classic film does that remind you of?'

Blank. Having questions fired at her made her go blank. She was no good at quizzes.

'Clue.' He began to hum. 'Mm mm m mer, mm mm m mer...'

'Got it!' Words were coming into her head. 'A kiss is just a kiss...' she joined in '...m mm mmm' and yes, a title was coming up... 'Give me a mo, yes, got it! *As Time Goes By*! Love that sitcom, Judi Dench...'.

But Monty was shaking his head.

'Film, darling, film, not sitcom. Further back, nineteen forties... but come to think of it, the sitcom must have been inspired by the film.' He hummed again and it dawned.

'*Casablanca!*' Phew! Of course. It was possibly her favourite film of all time but she still wasn't sure where this was going.

'One work of art inspires another, right? There's no such thing as originality, right?' He waited till she nodded, tentatively. 'So, *Casablanca* inspired the sitcom *As Time Goes By*, and, in your case, the sitcom and the film inspire the brilliant new novel – and then the film – *A Second Summer*.'

'Sorry?' She wasn't following.

'*You* are going to write a brilliant novel, about us, inspired by us, but also by *As Time Goes By* and *Casablanca*.'

She still didn't get it.

'You *must* see the parallels. You and me, Rick and Ilsa, Jean and Lionel. They all meet in the wrong place at the wrong time, when they're too young, then meet again later *and it works*. Think about it, wartime Paris, Ilsa meets Rick and feels a strong attraction, and he for her. She thinks her husband is dead. Passionately in love, they plan to flee from Paris before the Germans arrive, but when he arrives at the station she isn't there. He waits but she doesn't turn up. Distraught, he assumes he's been jilted and taken for a fool. Bitter, bereft, angry, he makes his way alone to Morocco where he sets up a bar, Rick's bar in Casablanca—'

'I know the plot, Monty—'

He held up a hand.

'Rick becomes cynical about women, about life, he wants to forget Ilsa but can't get her out of his mind, there's no other woman for him... then one night, years later, she turns up in his bar, *just like you turned up in the bar at the Cottesloe*.'

'But—'

He held up his hand again.

'It's us, isn't it, a classic love story? Two people meet and fall in love. They're prevented from being together, but eventually they overcome all the obstacles and find each other. Rick and Ilsa meet in the nineteen forties in Paris. Libby and Monty – we'll change the names obviously – meet in the nineteen sixties in London. Rick and Ilsa fall in love not knowing her husband is alive. I fell in love with you not knowing you were bound to another... I made plans for us to be together...'

'What plans?' She got a word in.

'The play I wanted you to be in.'

'Roots?'

'Yes, that one, but you never turned up to the meeting we'd arranged...'

So he did remember.

'I wondered where you'd gone... and tried to forget you, but, like Rick, I couldn't get you out of my mind. That's why I've never made it work with anyone else.'

Was there any truth in this?

'So when forty or so years later – the time scheme is different, obviously – you turn up in a theatre bar, one spring evening... I turn to see you standing there, a beautiful woman, a beautiful older woman, but even more beautiful than I remembered because, because... the years have given you a... a *patina*, that's the word, they really have. You're like... like a beautiful piece of old furniture, improved by age, but when I recognised you, I could hardly believe my eyes. Can this really be Libby Allgood?'

'Or Libby Too Good?'

He smiled and took a drink of water. 'This is going to be such a hit. Aren't you longing to get started?'

* * *

She got away by twelve o'clock despite Monty's protests. 'The old dear won't know you're there, darling.'

'Monty—' she moved his restraining hand and opened the door '—I've got to go.' She didn't need his negative thoughts. She had enough of her own, which she would try to remove from her mind as she made the hour-long drive to see her mum in the Hell House, in *Holly* House, the so-called care home.

They do care, the carers do care, probably more than you. They wipe her bottom.

In the car she stopped to check yet again she'd put everything she might need in her bag, ticking them off the list. Nail varnish and remover and cotton-wool pads because Mum still took pleasure in having her nails done. Yes. Little bottle of wine and a wine glass because Mum still took pleasure from drinking her favourite Liebfraumilch. Yes. A table mat, one of the set of table mats her mum had made her to match her dining room curtains. Yes. That was when she was an accomplished patcher and quilter, the doyenne of the local group, included because it might remind her of happy times and spark a few dying synapses. The Duchess, the other members used to call her. Mum was their oldest member and the cleverest, an inspiration to them all. Till she wasn't.

How quickly it seemed to have happened, the fall from high to low like a tragic heroine. But it must have happened gradually, the ability to piece together complicated patterns with agile fingers getting less and less, day by day and week by week, till one day, she'd looked at a pretty piece of fabric and wiped her nose on it. Would she recognise her own work today? Would she remember how she'd taken home the off-cuts from Libby's curtains, and made the mats secretly? Would she know that *she* had pieced together the intricate shapes, and delivered them to her daughter as a surprise on her birthday? Probably not.

'But I've got to go and see!' With a glance in the rear-view mirror, she started the engine, ignoring Monty's glum face as he waved her goodbye.

'I can't write a novel, Monty.' She'd said that. 'I don't want to.' *You're living in cloud cuckoo land!*

She hadn't said that.

* * *

Mum was in cloud cuckoo land or, more precisely, Australia.

'Stralia! Stralia! We're on our way!'

Libby could hear her mum even before she reached her room at the far end of the corridor. Relieved she was going to find her mum in a happy place, heading for one of her favourite destinations, she quickened her pace. What did the other residents make of her mother's still surprisingly strong voice? she wondered as she passed their rooms, identical to her mother's as they lay curled up on their cot-beds, looking like overgrown babies.

Mum was, at least, sitting up, on the plane at a guess.

'Stralia! We're on our way! Yes, we are!'

Mum had mostly gone on her own, maybe four times, but Libby had gone with her the last time. Was that what she was remembering now? Three of Mum's brothers, all younger but long gone, had emigrated to Australia and Mum had loved to visit them. And they, it seemed, had loved her visits, feting Big Sister Queenie as she progressed from state to state, Ted in Victoria, Tom in New South Wales and Lennie in Queensland, each outdoing the other in their warm antipodean hospitality.

'Stralia! Stralia!'

'A glass of duty-free, Mum?'

Suspicious eyes stared at her. Who was this? that stare said.

'Glass of wine, Mum?' She held up the glass, hoping the officious carer who disapproved wouldn't come in. 'Liebfraumilch, your favourite.' She held up the bottle.

'Leeb. Frou. Milk.' Mum peered at the label.

'Like a glass?'

A slow smile was her answer.

Mum held the long-stemmed glass with all the aplomb acquired from a lifetime's happy drinking.

'Cheers, Libby Lou!'

Did Mum really say that?

'Cheers, Mum!' Tears in her eyes, Libby raised one of the horrible plastic feeding cups that she found on the side, for want of anything better. *Must remember to bring two glasses next time.* The lidded cup was full of a cold gloopy liquid, maybe tea, maybe soup, that her mum had declined to drink. Why did they use these things? In case she choked, Libby had been told when she'd asked. It was because they hadn't got enough staff for one of them to sit with her mum while she drank tea from a proper cup. Staff were leaving in droves because they could get better wages serving in supermarkets. But the CEO of this chain of care homes was taking home two million pounds a year and had just given himself a rise to reward himself for raising their profits.

A really loving daughter would be looking after her mum herself. The only reason bastards like that can profit is that you won't.

'More! More, more, Libby-Lou!' Mum held out the glass for a refill.

* * *

'She recognised me!' Libby near burst through the front door.

Monty poured her a drink and raised his own glass. 'Here's looking at you, kid.'

He'd set up her computer in the spare room, he said, the one she didn't need for Ellie-Jo now. She needed to be able to work uninterrupted and could get started while he cooked dinner.

26

VIV

'Have you heard from Libby?' Viv put the cafetière on the table in front of Janet, who had just popped in for coffee.

'No, not since... when was it?' Janet, head back, eyes closed, was topping up her suntan. 'Friday at The Wagon and Horses.'

They were on the terrace outside Viv's kitchen door and Viv stretched luxuriously, unknotting her back. How good it was to sit down after an hour weeding the vegetable patch, and simply enjoy the garden at its midsummer best. The pergola was a frenzy of humming bees, going mad for the nectar in the Kiftsgate's creamy white blossoms.

'Six days, if it's Thursday today?' Janet had opened her eyes and was counting on her fingers. 'Your garden's stunning, Viv, a feast to all the senses.' She took a deep breath. 'What is that heavenly scent wafting over from the steps?'

'Lilies, lilium regale. I'm growing them in pots this year to keep them out of the way of Claudia and neighbouring cats as the pollen can be fatal. Zelda asked, by the way, that's why I'm on Libby alert. She rang last night from North Carolina.'

'Zelda? Oh.' Janet sat up straight. 'We promised to keep an eye, didn't we?'

'Yes, Zelda wanted an update. *Is the director still directing*, to quote?'

'She doesn't like him, does she?' Janet poured Viv a coffee, then one for herself.

'Let's say she's waiting to be convinced.'

'Of what exactly?' Janet took a tentative sip.

'That's he's good for her? That's all Zelda wants, to be fair.'

'That's all we want,' said Janet. 'So what *are* we doing to further our investigations? Good coffee, by the way.'

'Zilch?' Viv felt guilty.

'Not good enough!' They spoke together but the words were Zelda's. They could feel waves of disapproval surging across the Atlantic.

But ten minutes later, diaries open, they had a plan that would, they hoped, put them back in Zelda's good books, and find the info she wanted.

'Are you texting Libby or am I?' Viv eyed the mobile in Janet's hand.

'I can, but think the invitation would come better from you—' Janet put her phone down '—as you'll be hostess. I'll let Zelda know what we're proposing. Let's just hope the weather holds and we can eat outside – and that the invitees accept, of course. It is rather short notice. Libby declined last time we asked, didn't she? Your garden will be the perfect setting, especially if you can persuade those two to stay to set the tone.'

'Who? Oh, them.' Viv followed Janet's gaze to the top of a birch tree halfway down her garden. 'The love birds, they're always here!' A pair of collared doves were throbbing softly, billing and cooing tenderly as they preened each other, first he her, then she him. Well, that was what she assumed, but there was no way of telling.

'Janet, do you think it would be easier if we humans couldn't tell the difference, except for hidden parts?'

'Pardon?' Janet was refilling her cup. 'You've lost me.'

'I was thinking about Libby and her fall-out with her daughter, because of the mix-up about this Monty's gender. There wouldn't be this confusion if they were doves...'

'But they're not doves,' said Janet sharply, 'and in my opinion there would be even more confusion if we didn't know. But I would like to say that if the man is half as loving to Libby as that dove is to its mate, he would get my seal of approval.'

'And mine,' said Viv, 'but perhaps not in front of us? Not that I'm against a show of affection, but I'll need more than that to convince me he's worthy of her. Right, I'm sending the invite now.'

27

LIBBY

'Darling, no more Mum.' Monty reached over the train table and put his finger on Libby's lips. 'Mum day was yesterday. Today's our day for fun.'

Libby lifted his hand away, wishing his marvellous theatrical voice weren't quite so carrying. She was keen to hear Monty's thoughts about the show they'd just seen, but the other passengers in the crowded carriage didn't need to hear them. They were on their way back from London, after going to see an amazing production of *Miss Saigon* at the Prince Edward Theatre, riveting but not what she would call fun. She still felt harrowed by the tragic story, but it was magnificent and – bonus – Monty hadn't mentioned The Novel once. She hoped she'd made clear last night that she wasn't going to write one. She thought she had because this afternoon had seemed like old times. After the show she'd suggested going to Rokeby Villa to make it seem even more like old times, and see how work was progressing, but Monty hadn't wanted to. He'd had a better idea, high tea at Searcy's on St Pancras station, with a celebratory glass of champagne.

'What are we celebrating?' she'd asked.

'Life,' he'd replied.

Now they were on the crowded 19.03, the first non-peak train out of London, just a little bit high from champagne.

Libby kept her voice low. 'I was only saying that my mum would have loved *Miss Saigon*. I think she saw one of the first performances back in the nineties. She loved a musical.' It was hard to believe that that was maybe twenty-five years ago, when her mum would have been in her mid-sixties.

Like I am now.

'Okay.' Monty leant back. 'That's allowed, if it was a happy thought.'

She didn't say that happy wasn't quite the right word. Remembering her mum years ago, gallivanting all over the place enjoying herself, reminded her how much things had changed.

'I said happy, darling.' Monty was reading her face. 'Happy thoughts only. Carpe diem.'

It was his motto and she was trying to make it hers. Live for the day.

'It has been a lovely day. Thank you, Monty, for thinking of it.' It had been his idea to get back into their old routine of Thursday matinees.

'Thank you, sweetie, for funding it. I will pay you back, honest. You know that *Miss Saigon* is a retelling of *Madame Butterfly*, don't you?'

'Yes.' She nodded, closing her eyes.

'That Boublil and Schönberg used exactly the same plot as Puccini?'

She nodded again, keeping her eyes closed, hoping this wasn't going where she suspected.

'Same plot *and* same theme, men being bastards, sadly, just time and place changed. Same characters even. Puccini's 1890s' American naval lieutenant and a geisha girl become 1970s' US marine and a South Vietnamese bargirl.'

'It's in the programme, darling, and...' She opened her eyes, and gave a sideways nod to the other people in the carriage, who had gone very quiet. To give him credit, he did lower his voice.

'Bet you don't know this though,' he almost whispered. 'Puccini got his plot from a short story called *Madame Butterfly* by a chap called John Luther Long, and John Luther Long based his story on an 1887 French novel called *Madame Chrysanthème* by Pierre Loti. See what I'm getting at?'

'I do, Monty, I do, and—'

'But wait for it, darling, because it gets better.' It was clear now he was googling on his phone. 'John Luther Long's version was dramatised into a one-act play, also called *Madame Butterfly*, by a playwright called David Belasco. It premiered in New York in 1900 – and then came to London where Puccini saw it and nabbed the plot!'

Someone in the carriage clapped a single sarcastic clap.

Monty shrugged. 'So, have I made my point, darling, that all writers steal from one another?'

'You have, Monty, but...' They were nearing their station, so she let it go, and a text pinged in to her phone.

Can you and Monty come to supper on Saturday night? There will be just the six of us, Patrick and me, Janet and Alan, you and your beau. Do say yes, Viv x

She held the phone up for Monty to see as the train drew into the station.

'Good idea.' He got to his feet. 'It will save me cooking, and we can ask your friends what they think.'

'I just wish she believed in herself as much as I believe in her.' Monty touched Libby's cheek with a finger.

Viv, watching from the other end of the table, thought, *Tender or possessive or both?* And decided to give him the benefit of the doubt. She was trying very hard to keep an open mind. The man seemed fond of Libby. Near the back door for easy access to the kitchen, she had a good view of the whole table, but her focus was on Monty, and of course on Libby sitting next to him, on his right. How was Libby feeling? What had she thought when Monty had sat himself down at the head of the table?

Be fair.

Viv reminded herself this was an informal supper party and she'd asked everyone to sit where they wanted. There was no seating plan, and that end of the oblong table could just as well be described as the foot, not the head. It didn't matter where Monty sat, anyway. Was he good for Libby? Libby's well-being was all that mattered. Did he make her happy? Was he kind? Was Libby at ease with him? At the moment she looked – what? – a tad embarrassed?

'Oh, Monty.' She shook her head in an amused or bemused,

what-are-you-on-about? sort of way. Then she topped up his glass with the delicious Sancerre that Patrick had supplied, to distract him from saying more perhaps.

So far so good. The evening was going well, Viv thought. Murmurs of satisfaction had greeted her tomato and mozzarella salad starter, made with home-grown tomatoes of course, Marmande for flavour. Now her main course, a not bad salmon en croute, if she did say it herself, seemed to be going down well, and her medley of veg was drawing accolades. But now a distraction as Alan pointed out a pair of red kites wheeling overhead, and the eating paused as they all leaned back in their chairs to watch the birds' acrobatics. Or not all. Monty's voice was ringing out again. 'Of course, I was the first to spot Libby's talent, all those years ago.'

Is that praise for Libby's talent or his own perceptive powers? Viv wondered.

'It was when she was still at The Central, at the auditions to get in, in fact. That was the first time I saw her. She just *shone*.'

Oh, that was definitely praise for Libby, she decided as the others turned to listen to him too. Monty admired Libby. Rated her. She would text Nikos later to reassure him of that at least. He'd been so worried when she'd met him in town yesterday, convinced that 'the fellow' was a freeloader taking advantage of her sweet nature. He and Evelina both thought so, he'd said.

But Monty was stroking Libby's cheek again. 'Spotting talent is what I'm good at... That's how I made my name... *so* when I moved from theatre to TV...' *Had someone actually asked him about his brilliant career?* '...and got a commission to direct *Dombey and Son*...'

Dombey and Son. That rang a bell. With Janet too, it seemed. 'You directed that serialisation of *Dombey and Son*?' Janet sounded almost impressed.

'It was acclaimed,' Viv murmured to Patrick. 'If he did direct that he's really good.'

'Well, he certainly thinks so,' Patrick murmured back.

But fair dos, if it was the production she was thinking of, it was a brill dramatisation of Dickens's novel. She remembered showing it to her A level English class, when she was still teaching, back in the eighties before she switched careers. She might have the DVD somewhere, if it wasn't on something even more ancient, like video. She tried to catch his eye to ask but he wasn't looking her way.

'Casting is crucial...' The next-door neighbours could probably hear him. Was that what was getting up Patrick's nose? 'I chose the cast, all of them unknown at the time, but several of them big names now. And Libby could have been one of them if she hadn't been so self-effacing. I would have cast her as the divine Florence Dombey, but...'

Libby was shaking her head.

'Instead I cast the unknown...' Viv didn't catch the name because Patrick was getting up, scraping his chair '...as the lovely Florence and... she is of course a huge name now, a star of stage and screen, but completely unknown – I think it's fair to say – before I lifted her from obscurity.'

Now Libby's hand went to her face.

'See what I mean?' Monty laughed. 'My self-effacing Libby!'

Patrick started clearing the dishes. Libby got to her feet.

Viv said, 'I'll get the pudding.' And headed for the kitchen, with Libby close behind her. Once inside Viv closed the kitchen door, but it didn't shut out the arsehole's resounding voice. 'Family first, that's Libby's trouble, that's what's holding her back. Believe me, I'm a witness...'

Viv said, 'You can assemble the pavlova if you like. I need to whip up some more cream for the top, but the meringue base is on the dish already, there's some cream and the strawberries are over there.' She got the hand-mixer and whipped the cream, loudly, but could still hear him.

'...and on Wednesday it's off to see her mother, though the batty old dear doesn't know if she's there or not...'

Viv whirred louder still.

Libby said, 'Sorry, I'll finish this when I come down. Need the loo.'

Viv tipped cream onto the top layer.

'...and when she is at home, on her so-called writing days, if the phone rings or a text pings her hand springs to the phone in case it's one of her offspring, her *adult* offspring, needing her help... which is all very well if all she wants to do is write the odd article or a little story for kiddies...'

Viv arranged the strawberries in a circle on top of the cream.

'...but if she wants to write something that's any good...'

Had he really said that? Viv glanced over her shoulder to check that Libby was still upstairs.

'If she wants to write something really worthwhile...'

Viv opened the door and saw the idiot pouring himself another glass of wine, oblivious, it seemed, to the stunned silence and waves of loathing coming from around the table. Janet was the first to gather her wits. 'Monty, please tell us what family responsibilities have prevented you from producing anything, anything at all, in the last, what is it, twenty-five years?'

Alan, Janet's husband, said, 'Try reading Libby's World. Her latest on the parking-meter scam is brilliant. Those rogues should be exposed.'

'With respect—' Monty smiled '—you're missing the point, old chap. I'm not denying Libby is talented. I'm not saying she can't write. I'm just saying that, with my guidance, she could write something worth reading.'

How dare that man rubbish Libby's work? Viv felt her hackles rising. What a pompous arse! Had he finished? She didn't care if he had or hadn't. She didn't care if her guests got pudding or not. It might be better if they didn't. All that sugar was bad for them. After propping open the door, she picked up the pavlova. How that ring of strawberries glistened on its soft bed of whipped cream as she held it aloft with both hands. How the pillowy peaks quivered. As she stepped outside she caught Patrick's eye and he shook his head, reading her mind. But it was made up. She was on her way to the table, taking the long way round to get to her seat – so she had to walk past the incredibly talented Mr Monty Charles.

Oh dear! Whoops!

29

LIBBY

He's gone. He's left me!

Libby's mouth went dry when she saw her car wasn't in the drive. She'd just got back from lunch at Eleanor's. Monty must have taken the car and driven away, to get as far away from her as he could. Why not, after yesterday? She would never erase the sight of him with strawberries and cream dripping down his face, would never forgive Viv. An accident? That, she would never believe. Her hand trembled as she fumbled in her bag for her keys. What time was it? Just gone four, and he hadn't sent any of his little loving texts since she'd left him at twelve noon. And he'd been very quiet at breakfast. Not himself. Down. Understandably. She'd left Eleanor's earlier than usual because she was so worried about Monty, left on his own, though by his own choice. He hadn't wanted to come – and now she knew why. He had been planning to leave.

'Miaow!' Cornflake greeted her from the top of the stairs.

'You won't miss him, will you?' Libby closed the front door behind her, her spirits rising a little when she spotted a pair of boots in the corner, and then sandals on the stairs and a sweater on the newel post, and, moving into the kitchen, more shoes and his coat hanging on the back door. Maybe he hadn't gone, well, not for good.

She put the kettle on. It had been nice at Eleanor's today, easier, she had to admit, without Monty. Derek had barbecued, while she and Eleanor had chatted amicably, aided by a few glasses. Ellie-Jo had put on one of her shows, a dramatisation of *The Very Hungry Caterpillar*. Ellie-Jo was of course the caterpillar gobbling her way through a week's supply of food, and then of course emerging as the butterfly. Her transformation dance was quite amazing, in this doting granny's opinion. Monty hadn't been mentioned, except by her when she'd said, 'Monty sends his apologies,' which he hadn't. They were pleased he hadn't come, she thought, because they didn't understand him. Like last night – she was there again – Janet had got him completely wrong. So had Viv. They saw Monty as an egomaniac, when in fact he had been trying to boost *her* morale.

'Miaow!' Cornflake was winding round her legs.

'Janet *asked* him to tell her about *Dombey and Son*...' Crikey! She stopped herself, mid-filling the cat's dish. She was getting like Zelda talking to her dogs.

Get a grip.

What had Monty said, while she was upstairs, to incense Viv? That was the question. The last thing she'd heard him say was that she was wasting her time visiting her mum. That *had* annoyed her. She hadn't needed the loo, she just hadn't wanted to hear any more, and Viv had probably sensed that, and decided to shut him up. But why such an *extreme* action? What else had he said to incense Viv to make that attack? Yes, *attack*. Afterwards, she'd been all concern. Well, she'd said sorry, and urged him to go inside, take off his clothes and have a shower, while she put his clothes in the washer – 'Don't want to make work for Libby.' Yes, that had been her main concern. Patrick had offered to lend Monty some of his own clothes but Monty had declined. He had been *so* dignified. He'd simply said, 'We're leaving.' They'd left together.

But it must have been humiliating. You'd only got to put yourself in that situation to know how foolish he must have felt. *Don't shrink my manhood, darling.* Those words haunted her. But *that* was exactly what Viv had tried to do. It was so unlike her. Oh, good, a text. Monty was on his way home. ETA 6 p.m., so she must hurry. Viv had knocked him down so she must build him up again.

* * *

Cornflake heard him first. Well, he heard the car in the drive, put two and two together and shot into the back garden as Libby rushed to open the front door.

'Darling, darling Libby!' He hailed her from the car and didn't seem down at all. 'What sort of day have you had?' Monty had bounced back.

The hug he gave her when he'd straightened up and stretched – 'Long drive!' – was warm and long.

It was a while before he held her at arm's length, looking down at her frilly pinny. 'What's with the fifties-housewife look?'

'Wait and see.'

'Wow!' When he saw the table, laid with flowers and candles, and best cut glass and china, he hugged her again. 'Thought you didn't believe in all this meal-on-the-table-when-your-man-gets-home stuff.'

'Hope you haven't eaten?'

'Not since lunch.' He took the glass of Saint-Émilion she offered.

'Where have you been?' She was keen to know.

'Aha!' He touched the side of his nose. 'Now it's time for you to wait and see.'

'Tease!'

'Not at all.' But he made her wait till he'd eaten the steak and chips she'd cooked for him, with sauce Diane, his favourite, before divulging, and then not straight away. 'Darling.' At last he put down his knife and fork and wiped his mouth on the linen napkin. 'That was so wonderful. You spoil me. I'm speechless!'

'Hope not. I want to know what you've been up to.' She hoped she sounded jokey.

'O-ka-ay.' He refilled their glasses with the red wine. 'I, Monty, your devoted swain, have been up to London, to see – no, not the queen, and I didn't chase a little mousie under the chair. I went to see an old friend.' He took a tantalisingly long sip of the wine, savouring it in his mouth, before at last coming out with his news. 'I have booked us a holiday!'

'A holiday?'

He nodded a long, slow, very-pleased nod. 'A– ho-li-day. You need a holiday. I need a holiday. We both need to get away.'

'But...' *Where? When? How? I thought you didn't have any money!* She was full of questions.

'No buts, darling.' He put a finger over her lips. 'Just say yes.'

'I can't do that.'

'Course you can. Trust me. Now, dare I ask what superwoman is offering superman for pudding?'

30

'I'll answer all your questions when you agree to go.'

His unreasonableness made her angry. Still. It was Monday morning, her writing-her-column day, and she'd got to her desk under the stairs an hour ago, straight after breakfast. With her laptop because she found it easier working downstairs than on her PC, now set up in the 'spare' room, Ellie-Jo's room as she couldn't help thinking of it. So far, though, she'd only written – how many words? She counted – eighty-eight. On a completely new theme, not the one she'd told Sid she was going to cover, a fun piece about garlic, to celebrate the fourteenth of July and the storming of the Bastille. *Let's storm Sainsbury's!* But she hadn't written one word of it because all she could think about was The Surprise.

'I can't agree to go till I know where we're going and when!'

Why couldn't he understand that? She'd said it last night, several times, ditto this morning, but he wouldn't take her concerns seriously, which was infuriating.

'I want to give you a lovely surprise,' he'd said and kept saying. 'I want to lead you blindfold to the door of the secret destination, then – ta da! – whip it off and see the amazement on your face.'

'But, Monty...'

'Shhh, darling.' Nothing could come between him and his vision.

It was intriguing, she had to admit – it would make a good scene in a play – but was utterly impractical in real life. She couldn't agree to going away without telling Eleanor when and where she was going. Eleanor would need to arrange for someone to look after Ellie-Jo on Tuesdays. There was also Cornflake to make arrangements for, and her mother. Who would visit her? Monty would give in, she kept telling herself, he couldn't hold out for ever. She'd just got to find the right approach, that was all, the right moment, the right questions. *Will I need my passport, Monty?* That would be a good opener. *What clothes shall I pack?* But first, she must write her article.

Dear Readers,

How do you feel about surprises? Are you for or against? Do you like surprise presents or do you prefer to be asked what you want well before the big day? Do you like surprise visitors or would you rather people let you know they were coming well in advance? Or better still ask you if or when a visit is convenient? Would you like a surprise holiday? I thought I liked surprises till a...

This was where she'd broken off, unsure of how to continue. Her readers loved it when she wrote about real-life situations but she had to be careful.

...a dear friend sprang a surprise on me.

A 'dear friend' was good...

...my dear friend, Cindy...

Even better, a made-up imaginary friend! Monty wasn't likely to read her column, but she needed to hide his identity, so as not to expose him to the public eye – and in case he did read it. Her readers accepted that she changed names to protect people's privacy.

Monty was outside cleaning her car, being helpful and co-operative in every way except the one she most wanted him to be. He would leave her in peace, he'd assured her several times, but if she wanted a tea or coffee, or *anything*, she had only to put her head out of the door, and he would leap into action. Or she could text him. He'd check his phone regularly, he said. He was there to attend to her every need so that she could get on. He was trying to help her be more professional. She had the attention span of a goldfish, he'd said recently. The slightest thing could interrupt her writing – and it was true. Look at her now. She'd jumped from one topic to another and still wasn't yet sure if she was going to write about surprises in general, or this one in particular. She was tending towards this one in particular. It was the sort of dilemma her readers liked to be involved in. Should she go along with this friend to preserve their friendship, or refuse and risk bringing it to an end? What should she do? She could invite them to write in with their opinions.

Talk to Monty, you've got to sort this out with Monty, not your readers. That was what Viv would say. Why was she thinking of Viv? She was finished with Viv. And Janet. And Zelda. They'd got a down on Monty. And talking to Monty was easier said than done. It took two to talko – ha ha! Two to tango, two to talko. Would her readers get that?

My dear friend, Cindy, has booked a holiday for us both as a present but will not tell me where or when! She is enjoying keeping me in suspense, and finds my frustration amusing. Should I be pleased? Cindy thinks I should be grateful and can't understand why I'm not. 'Why don't you trust me to plan something you will really like? I know you well.' I DO appreciate her generosity and I think she knows what I really like. But. I am trying to be positive about this. It is, for one thing, a learning experience. I have discovered I DON'T LIKE SURPRISES. I like to plan ahead and choose for myself. Does that make me a control freak?

Put like that, her question looked ridiculous. Her readers would think she had lost her mind. Libby's World was about how she'd re-invented herself since Jim died, how she'd had to re-invent herself because she was *not* the same person. She was no longer someone's wife for a start. It was about the pluses and minuses of life on your own, and one of the pluses was doing what you wanted. It could feel lonely at times, having to decide things yourself, but it was freedom. It was liberty. It was Liberty Allgood. Parents might take children away on holiday without telling them where or when, but one adult couldn't make that sort of decision for another.

I don't want to control anyone else, just run my own life. I don't want to control Cindy's life. I wouldn't plan a holiday for her. Surely, if anyone is a control freak here it's Cindy. She isn't thinking about me at all, well, only a little bit. She thinks she can plan my life. The more I think about what she has done, the more high-handed and inconsiderate it seems, the more I feel ANGRY!

The phone rang. Goldfish-brain picked it up.

'Libby, are you okay?' It was Viv. 'I'm sorry about last night. It wasn't the right thing to do...'

'Oh, Viv, I under—' But the phone disappeared from her hand before she could finish.

'Libby is busy at the moment. Please call back later.' Monty – when did he come in? – put the phone back on its stand. She felt his lips on the back of her neck. 'I thought you deserved a break, darling, you've been working so hard. I've brought you a coffee. Look.' It was beside her on the desk. 'How's it going? You've written quite a lot. Let me see. Oh, Cindy, I like being Cindy... Cindy sounds fun...' He was reading from the screen, over her shoulder. 'But, oh, darling... she isn't fun... you're upset? I hadn't realised. I didn't mean to upset you.'

'I – am – not – upset.' She stood up. 'Read on. I am angry. There's a difference.'

'And you think I'm a control freak! Oh. I'm sorry if that's what it looked like.' He looked sorry, really sorry, hurt even. 'W-wait, wait a minute.'

He went upstairs, head down. Libby was about to ring Viv when she saw him coming down, holding the banister with one hand, something behind his back in the other.

'There,' he said, putting it in front of her. 'There's control freak's terrible surprise.'

31

VIV

Viv rang Libby again on her mobile.

She was in her Range Rover, outside a client's house. Libby didn't pick up the phone this time and the answerphone kicked in, the real one, not someone pretending to be one. The impersonator – no prizes for guessing who he was – must have snatched it from her. He was probably still lurking.

'Sorry. I can't come to the phone at the moment. Please leave your number and a short message and I'll get back to you as soon as I can.'

Yes, that was the answerphone, the real one, with a message recorded by Libby. But Viv didn't leave a message because she didn't see the point. Libby's calls were being monitored by The Director. The Controller. Libby wasn't in charge of her own life.

Viv made another call, but this time to Janet. 'We need to talk about Libby!'

32

LIBBY

'Is it so very terrible?' Monty put a thick glossy brochure in her lap.

It was for the Villa Adelos, a beautiful white house surrounded by lush gardens with a swimming pool at one side, against a background of mountains and clear blue sky.

'Where is this?' It looked Mediterranean or perhaps Caribbean.

'Look inside.' He reached over and turned a page.

'No, not here.' She got up. 'There's no room on my desk. Let's take it into the sitting room – and look at it over coffee.' She picked up the cup he'd made her, playing for time.

He went into the kitchen, and she took the brochure into her dining-cum-sitting room and sat down at the table to read it.

Set among vineyards, the Villa Adelos, formerly a winery, is a luxurious two-storey holiday residence with private pool and sea and mountain views. There is a beach nearby, yet it is only twenty kilometres from Athens airport and all the cultural delights of the city: theatres, museums, art galleries and ancient ruins...

Greece! But he didn't like Greece, well, not Greek food. She read on.

> Large well-equipped family kitchen, capacious lounge with comfortable sofas and large TV and sound system, five bedrooms, all en suite, two family bathrooms, can sleep twelve...

Twelve? Why twelve? But it sounded wonderful even allowing for travel agent's hype, but OMG, she saw the eye-watering price per *night*. 'Who else is coming, Monty?' He was back with a coffee for himself. 'Who's sharing the costs?'

'No one, darling. It will be just you and me.'

'But *how*? Who's paying?' Not her, she hoped. She couldn't.

'Me, darling. It's my treat for helping me out. I'll be solvent by then. My cash-flow problem will be sorted. Oh, darling, you're going to love it. *We're* going to love it, being together, just you and me in our own private idyll. See—' he turned another page '—it's got everything you might need, Internet access, a computer for residents' use and Wi-Fi. You'll be able to write your column and email it to Fred or Sid or whatever he's called, if you really have to, but I hope you'll just relax. Look, there's a hot tub by the pool and gardens with fig and olive and date trees. Can't you see us stretched out on those sunbeds?'

'Ye-es.' But there was still the question of, 'When?'

'Last two weeks of August, darling. Sunday 17th to Sunday 31st. It will be the school holidays. See, you'd marked them in on the wall calendar in the kitchen. I saw. I noted. I checked.' The calendar was on the tray with the coffee. 'You'll be off duty by then. Eleanor will be able to look after Ellie-Jo herself, and your cat too, if Zelda isn't back from her jaunt by then. But I think she will be. You've pencilled in her return date too. See, I've thought of everything.'

He really had, except maybe, 'Flights?'

'On my list, darling.' Then he looked a bit down. 'Actually, slight prob there...'

It was obvious he hated asking but eventually she got him to say he couldn't yet pay for the flights, so if she could see her way to lending him the cash for the tickets, he'd be eternally grateful.

'Of course, Monty, I'll get the air tickets. It's the least I can do.' Fares were steep in August and getting steeper by the minute. She couldn't bear that crestfallen look. His crest should be bright and shining. 'I'll put them on my credit card.'

'You really are a darling.' He kissed her cheek. 'But I don't want you to go to the bother of making the booking. A loan will be fine. Just transfer the money. This is my treat, remember.'

How she'd misjudged him! No wonder he was looking pleased with himself.

'I'm only sorry...' Oh, glum again.

'What?'

'That you didn't trust me enough to go through with my blind-folding-you vision.'

Why didn't I?

'Of course I'd have told you which part of the world we were going to nearer the time, so you packed the right clothes. Must get the costumes right! And you'd probably have guessed the location when we got to the airport, by watching the screen in the departure lounge...'

'Sorry, Monty.' She felt she'd let him down. Her lack of trust had hurt him. 'But we'll still have a wonderful time.'

How could they not? She turned the pages of the brochure to look at more photographs of the idyllic setting, the white house sparkling in the midday sun, the stone staircase up to the front door foaming with bougainvillaea, the terrace at sunset with a couple leaning over the balustrade looking at the mountains silhouetted against a blazing sky, the pool at midnight, a crescent moon reflected in the water. And then there were the breath-taking interiors, every room stunningly beautiful, especially the master bedroom, which looked like something out of *Arabian Nights*. Yes, the old feelings were coming back. She turned to him to give him a kiss.

He kissed her back. 'I'm glad you approve of the director's vision.'

'I'm inspired. When do rehearsals start?'

'No time like the present?' He took her hand.

'Yes!' She followed him to the stairs. Her article could wait. She'd changed her mind. Surprises could be okay.

But not the one that happened next.

33

_____

LIBBY

Someone was hammering on the front door.

'Libby, are you okay, pet?'

No prizes for guessing whose voice that was.

'The Valkyrie!' Monty was in the stairwell, looking out of the side window. 'Ignore them. Let's pretend we're not in.'

'Can't, sorry. I'll join you asap. You go ahead.' Libby went downstairs and opened the door.

Viv and Janet were on the doorstep.

'We came as soon as we could.' Viv, in her work clothes, looked as if she'd been pulled through the proverbial hedge backwards, and might have been, by Janet, in her determination to get her here quickly. She kept her voice low, but the words came out as if fired from a gun. 'Cut off. The bastard. Pretending to be a fucking answerphone.'

'Where is he now?' Janet peered inside and Libby, peering out, saw Janet's little white Fiat with its red and green stripe parked in the road outside, the famous get-away car, engine still running, puffing out exhaust fumes. The two of them had done this before. She'd heard about it from Zelda, who she'd once saved from a dodgy encounter, but it wasn't like that now. She had to put them right.

'Viv, calm down.' Mistake.

'He stopped you speaking to me, Libby!' Viv was furious.

'So I could get on with my work.'

'He has no right.'

Where was Monty? Was he listening to this? He'd think her friends were mad.

'What's happened to liberty, Libby?' Viv was on her soapbox. 'What's happened to Liberty Allgood?'

'Viv, I'm okay. Honestly. You've got it all wrong. I'm fine. I don't need rescuing.'

'Where is he?' Viv peered through the half-open door.

'Can we come in, Libby?' Janet rejoined Viv on the doorstep after going back to turn off the car engine. 'Are you allowed visitors?'

'I – I...' Libby was on the rack, in an agony of indecision, pulled in two different directions. 'It's not like that, honestly.'

Monty was probably packing his bags at this moment, thinking she didn't love him, but if she turned them away they'd think she was his slave.

'Darling...' Oh, here he was, coming downstairs. 'Aren't you going to invite your friends in for elevenses? I'm coming to put the kettle on.'

* * *

Now, they were outside on her little terrace, the four of them sitting round her pretty mosaic table drinking coffee, made by Monty, the perfect host.

'Ladies, are you reassured?'

They didn't look reassured, though Monty had just explained

why he'd interrupted the phone call, and apologised. He'd been not just charming, which wouldn't wash with those two, but reasonable and generous and forgiving, considering their treatment of him on Saturday night, which he'd passed off as a joke, saying he'd keep his distance from Viv in case his coffee ended up in his lap. He'd left the table but then returned with a packet of amaretti biscuits, which he'd said he'd been keeping for a special occasion.

But Viv and Janet remained stone-faced. Viv hadn't even commented on the garden, which was looking at its best, Libby thought. Bees were buzzing in the hollyhocks by the fence, the buddleia was alive with peacock and red admiral butterflies and Cornflake was rolling in the catmint.

Monty tried again. 'I was *trying* to act in Libby's best interests, and if I came across as a high-handed autocrat, I'm sorry.' He looked from Viv to Janet and back again to Viv. 'I do know a bit about the creative process, and I've been encouraging Libby to be more protective of her own time, more selfish even, to allow fewer intrusions on her privacy.'

'I am easily distracted.' Libby wanted them to see that Monty had a point.

'You multitask,' said Viv, 'like all women do, but only because we have to. That's why we're more in touch with everything that matters. Your garden looks lovely, by the way.' No signs of contrition there.

Nor from Janet. 'I can see what you thought you were *trying* to do, Monty.'

'So can I.' Viv got to her feet. 'But maybe let Libby decide who she's going to speak to in future?' She had to go back to work, she said, so if Janet had finished her coffee…

'Up the workers!' said Monty, seeing them to the door. 'And thank you for coming, ladies. I'm delighted that Libby has such supportive friends.'

'They were rather wonderful,' he said when they'd gone, 'the way they rushed round. I mean, if you had been in danger... but if I remember rightly we were on our way upstairs?'

'Yes, but you had distracted me from writing my column, which I must now go and finish.'

'Really?' He touched her arm. 'Are you hoisting me with my own petard?'

'I am.' The mood had passed.

'Okay, but a thought before you return to your keyboard. They *are* lovely, your friends, so well meaning... I like them a lot and can see that they'd go to the ends of the earth for you, that they'd lay down their lives, but...'

'What? But what? Spit it out, Monty.'

'They're so impulsive. I wouldn't say don't trust them, darling, but, I'm not sure I'd rely on their *judgement*.'

34

JANET

Janet was questioning her own judgement. 'I think Monty Charles really admires Libby.'

'He's a smarmy sod.' Viv wasn't questioning hers.

'Be fair.' Janet slowed down for a roundabout. 'He has succeeded in a world we know little about, albeit some years ago.'

'And might have insights denied to us lesser mortals, you mean?' Viv sniffed. 'So what made him rubbish everything she's written?'

'I'm just saying we shouldn't be black and white about the man, that's all. Let's try and see his good qualities and wait for Libby to get a more balanced picture.'

'But how much time have we got? What if it's like that Stockholm syndrome, where the hostage falls in love with the captor?'

'Viv, get a grip! She's not his prisoner. He's staying in her house, for a month maybe, till he can go back to his own. Meanwhile, she's free to kick him out whenever she wants. And if we're talking syndromes...' Janet stopped for traffic lights '...how about the other one, the Helsinki, where the captor falls in love with the captured? I repeat, he seemed very fond of her today.'

'I'm not sure that syndrome exists, Janet but I agree he was very lovey-dovey. Gawd! He can "darling" for England. He's a donkey, Janet, not a bloody Prince Charming!' Viv threw her head back and waggled finger-ears in a not-bad donkey impression. 'Daa-hling! Daa-hling! Daa-hling!'

Janet had to laugh and agree. The man wasn't as wonderful as Libby thought he was, but was he as bad as Viv feared? 'He can't force her to write a novel, Viv. He's not going to chop off her head if she doesn't tell him a story, like some latter-day Scheherazade.'

'Okay. Okay. Point made. I'll take him off my hit list – for the time being.'

'Libby isn't crazy, Viv, well, only temporarily, and she will eventually see this Monty for what he is, whatever he is.' Janet wanted to believe this.

'Meanwhile she knows we've got her back. If she needs us. We really are all for one.' Viv looked a bit more cheerful.

'If we haven't blown it by going in today.' Janet couldn't help voicing her doubts.

'What do you mean?'

'That we burst in today when there wasn't really any need.'

'So?'

'Won't she hesitate before telling us her troubles in future – in case we rush to the rescue when not needed?' They were back in the village and had reached Viv's house. Janet pulled into her drive, but Viv didn't get out. She looked worried, maybe contrite.

'I see what you mean. I need to apologise for jumping to the wrong conclusion, and assure her that we won't barge in uninvited. Isn't Muscateers coming up?'

Janet turned off the engine and got her diary. 'Two weeks' time, first of August. I've booked The Olive Branch. By which time Monty Charles should have gone back to his stately residence in north London, and Libby will be free to come.'

'Unless Zelda is right and he's moved in for good. She says that's what it looks like. Will Zelda be back by then?'

'I don't think so.' Janet flicked through her diary. 'No. And we need to talk to Libby before then, reassure her we're on *their* side. Because if Monty treats her well and makes her happy, then we are on their side, aren't we? What we think of his personality doesn't matter, does it?'

'Okay.' But Viv didn't look entirely convinced as she opened the car door. 'We suspend judgement but stay vigilant.'

Janet watched her walking up the drive to her front door, deep in thought, obviously still worried. But how worried should they be?

35

LIBBY

When Libby got back from visiting her mum on Wednesday, she needed a hug and a drink and a 'Well done you for going!'

It had been upsetting. Queenie had clung to her hand as she was about to leave, saying, 'Don't go, Libby Lou,' and there had been tears running down her cheeks. It had been worse than when her mum didn't recognise her, when she was in a world of her own. At least then, when she was on her way to 'Stralia', for instance, she seemed happy. Today, it was as if she was aware of her predicament and sad. She kept beginning sentences that she couldn't finish, most of them beginning, 'I don't...' or 'I don't know...'

But Libby didn't get a hug or a drink or a compliment. Monty was at the door waiting for her when she drove in, but all he said was, 'You're late,' and he closed it with almost a slam. As she followed his bowed back down the hall, she thought he looked dishevelled and old. His hair needed brushing, and a bit of his shirt wasn't tucked into his trousers.

'Yes, I am a bit later than I said. Sorry, darling. My mum didn't want me to go – she recognised me today – then the manager caught me as I was leaving. The care-home fees are going up.'

'I've got a summons.' They'd reached the kitchen, where a bottle of red stood half empty on the surface near the coffee machine.

'Oh! What have you done, or not done? I'm sure it's not your fault!' She thought immediately of her unjust parking fine.

'Not that sort of summons. The elder sister, Marianna, the one who's married to Sir Lawrence Devers.'

Libby poured herself a drink, silently registering that he'd revealed his rellies' name and title, which he'd refused to tell her before.

'She's been asking me when I was coming for some time and I hadn't answered. Capital crime. Now she's given me a date for my annual visit.' He topped up his glass.

'Annual visit?' She managed to kiss him before the glass reached his lips. 'Sounds official like...' She couldn't think of a comparison, but it didn't sound like the casual, hastily arranged pub lunch she had once or twice a year with her brothers.

'It's a total bore, darling. Once a year is all I can bear.' He groaned and took a gulp of wine. 'I think I told you how the pair of them live in a time warp, nineteen twenties at a guess. Dress for dinner, that sort of thing, *fish* knives, but at least this is lunch, sorry, luncheon – must get the lingo right or I'll be excommunicated – so we'll be spared evening dress.' He groaned again. 'O-oh, I'm just not sure I'm up for another bout of time travelling.'

We'll be spared evening dress? Must be a slip of the tongue.

'Monty.' Libby was hungry, but there was no sign of dinner though she'd left a lasagne in the fridge with instructions to put it in the oven at half past five. 'It probably won't be as bad as you fear. Best get it over with.' She turned the oven on. 'Where do they live?'

'Warburton Manor, have done for the last three centuries, in deepest darkest Surrey.'

'And when is the dreaded event?' She suppressed a smile. He *had* to be dramatising.

'Friday! This Friday! Two bloody days' time!'

'Okay, so you'll need a lift to the station?' She – secret pleasure! – would then have a lovely day on her own, once she'd seen him onto the train. He couldn't drive himself, though he had on Sunday, she'd belatedly realised with alarm, without insurance.

'But, darling—' he topped up her glass '—it's in the back of beyond. I'd rather hoped you'd drive us there.'

Drive *us*? She got the lasagne out of the fridge. 'You'd like me to chauffeur you, would you? Will I have to wait outside in the car, or stay in the kitchen with the other servants?'

'Darling, don't be silly.' He kissed the nape of her neck. 'We're going together. I want you to meet Sir Lawrence and Lady Devers, and I want them to meet you.'

Interesting. Why the change of mind? And why was he telling her all this now? So she could address them properly? Sir this and Lady that? *Sod that.* She heard Viv's voice in her ear. *Off with their heads!* Heavens, would she have to curtsey? She'd have to do a bit of googling about etiquette and think about what to wear. And there wasn't long to do it. It was the day after tomorrow, for heaven's sake! But *I want them to meet you*. As she put the lasagne in the oven and she heard his words in her head her heart gave a flip. *We're going together*. It flipped again. Could it, could it possibly be that he had had a change of heart? That he now saw her as part of his illustrious family?

36

LIBBY

Libby wished she'd had more time to prepare for the visit to Monty's sister, more time to adjust to his changed attitude. It was, as he'd said, a bit like time travelling. Marianna must have seen them arrive, because she'd appeared in the gravelled driveway, at the bottom of a flight of stone steps, while she was parking her little Hyundai i10 next to the maroon Rolls Royce at the side of the house. Then, after introductions that had gone okay – no curtseys or titles – Marianna had led the way up the steps to the open studded-oak door and into the spacious entrance hall. That was where they were now, standing beneath the gaze of several generations of Sir Lawrence Devers' ancestors, surveying them from gilded frames on the walls.

'Wa-aa wa-aa warsh?' Monty's sister sounded a bit like the Queen in very early radio broadcasts, but more quavery and not as clear. Libby had no idea what she was saying. In her sixties, maybe seventies, Marianna had a wrinkled face that made her look a good ten years older than Monty, but she was still very upright, like Maggie Smith in *Downton Abbey*.

'Would you like to wash?' Monty translated, murmuring in her ear. 'Do you need a pee, in other words? Upper classes don't do excretion.'

But I thought they were very earthy. Libby didn't say that and she hoped that Marianna was deaf as Monty's murmur could reach the back of the stalls.

'Oh, yes, Marianna, thank you.' Libby realised she needed a pee quite urgently and Marianna led the way to a downstairs loo at the far end of the hall.

No servants so far. It wasn't quite *Downton Abbey*, Libby thought as she closed the loo door. Phew! It was good to have a few minutes to herself. The large room reminded her of her visit to Simpson's in the Strand, on her first date with Monty. How long ago that seemed! The lower walls and floor had the same black and white tiles in a chequered pattern, and the loo had a similar mahogany seat. The lavatory bowl, though, wasn't white, but willow patterned, which was a bit disconcerting, like peeing into a soup tureen. As she 'warshed' her hands in the basin, also willow patterned, she checked her appearance at a gilded mirror that filled half the wall. Was she overdressed in her see-you-anywhere navy-blue linen button-through dress, this time with a long linen jacket in reds and blues, with pearl necklace and earrings? Marianna was wearing pearls too, she'd noticed, but with slacks and a Liberty print blouse.

There was no one about when she stepped back into the entrance hall, but as she was looking at a portrait of a frock-coated, bewigged gentleman, wondering if he was the one who'd walked all the way from Scotland, a middle-aged woman appeared. It was another almost-*Downton Abbey* moment, as Mrs Burton, who had a Scottish accent, introduced herself as the housekeeper. She had come to take Libby to the drawing room, she said. Plump and curly-haired, Mrs Burton looked nothing like Mrs Hughes, the house-keeper without whom *Downton Abbey* couldn't have functioned, but she had a similar dignity. Did Mrs Burton hold this place together, Libby wondered, and what was Libby Allgood's role in the drama of Warburton Manor going to be?

Libby followed Mrs Burton through several rooms, into an elegant dining room where the table was laid for lunch with a white damask tablecloth and heavy silverware. But the family were clearly in the adjoining room, beyond double doors, from where a reedy voice carried Libby to a completely different place.

'Matter'orn! Matter'orn! Up we go!'

The words were different but the intonation the same, just like her mum's 'Stralia! Stralia! We're on our way!'

'Matter'orn! Matter'orn! Up we go!'

'Sir Lawrence is in his happy place today,' said Mrs Burton, but she didn't sound happy.

'You mean...?'

Mrs Burton nodded before knocking on the door. 'It comes and goes, sometimes he's here, sometimes there, but I don't think Mr Charles will be learning much about his allowance today.'

Allowance? As Libby reminded herself that Monty was Charles Montgomery here, Mrs Burton opened the door and stood back to let her enter the drawing room.

Monty and his brother-in-law sat either side of a magnificent Adam fireplace, filled by a splendid arrangement of deep blue delphiniums and other flowers, mostly white. In the mirror above the mantelpiece Libby glimpsed herself facing the room and Mrs Burton's retreating back, and Marianna facing the hearth. She was very upright in what Libby thought was a Hepplewhite chair, close to Sir Lawrence, who was almost S-shaped, in his hearthside wing-back chair. Libby wondered if there was a safety belt stopping him from falling out.

'Darling.' Monty saw her, and got to his feet. 'Sherry? An Amontillado?' He walked to a side-table and lifted a cut-glass decanter.

'Or there's Fino, Charles.' Marianna had moved to her husband's side to right his sherry glass as it was about to tip. Marianna was every inch the aristocratic elderly lady, but, it soon became obvious, she was also her husband's nurse, anticipating his every need.

Later, at the table, sitting by Lawrence's side, Marianna cut a piece of chicken into bite-sized pieces before he began eating, and from time to time throughout the meal, when he dribbled or missed his mouth with his fork, she wiped away specks of gravy with a napkin, in a practised way, without making a fuss. She was so discreet Libby wouldn't have noticed if she hadn't been observing closely and been familiar with the situation. She noted how for longish stretches Lawrence made social conversation using stock phrases, as her mum did when she had a new visitor. 'How was your journey?' 'Was the traffic bad?' 'Would you like more wine?' If they didn't stay long, people would go away saying there was nothing wrong with her mum. But Lawrence couldn't stay off the Matterhorn for long, and when he returned there Marianna tried to weave it into the conversation. 'Lawrence climbed the Matterhorn in 1936. He was one of that famous party.'

Monty preferred to change the subject. 'Did you make this excellent coq au vin, Marianna?' She had, and the summer pudding, which was to follow, she said, with Mrs Burton's help. She didn't know what she'd do without her. Libby would have liked to ask if Mrs Burton was the only help Marianna had. She knew that poorer people were often carers with no help at all, but couldn't help admiring Marianna for doing a difficult job very well indeed.

She hadn't put Lawrence in a care home.

* * *

Monty's admiration for his sister was tempered by loathing for his brother-in-law. On the way home he vented. 'He knew what he was bloody doing!' He was in the passenger seat and his fingers drummed the dashboard. They were on the M25, stationary, stuck in traffic. Monty, keen to leave as early as possible, had declined afternoon tea, so they'd left mid-afternoon and hit the motorway at rush hour.

'What do you mean?' Libby wanted to know more.

'That when he married her the calculating bastard got himself a nurse, a cook and a full-time carer, preparing for his old age. Twenty years older than her, the first thing he did when they got married was send her on a cordon bleu cookery course, after he'd made her give up her career, of course. She was a nurse when he met her on that Matterhorn climb. He fell and broke a leg and several ribs and there she was, working in the hospital he was taken to.'

'Sounds romantic.'

He snorted.

Libby really wanted to ask him about the 'allowance' that Mrs Burton had mentioned. Was that where his cash flowed or didn't flow from? She'd hoped the subject would come up when she and Marianna had 'withdrawn' after luncheon, but had quickly realised that wasn't the conversation that Marianna wanted to have. They'd gone up to Marianna's bedroom, where she'd been invited to 'warsh' again, this time in Marianna's private bathroom, which did have a bath, large and free-standing with brass taps, and a loo.

Libby had gone in and turned the tap on, pretending to wash her hands, as she hadn't needed the loo again but had needed a few minutes on her own to gather her thoughts. When she'd come out the first thing that had caught her eye was a silver-framed photograph on the table beside the ornately carved double bed. It was of a very handsome young man. 'Charles,' Marianna had said, before

Libby had realised it was Monty, though with his black hair falling, almost foppishly, over one eye, he did look like the man she remembered from drama school.

Family was everything to her, Marianna had said, and Charles too, though he didn't always show it. They were very close. She'd recounted a few childhood incidents, like how upset she'd been when he was sent *orff* to school. Then, when they were sitting in the window-seat overlooking the grounds, had come the surprise question, 'Where is Charles living at the moment?'

Libby had hesitated before answering, thinking it a bit odd that his 'close' sister didn't know. Hadn't Monty told her he was staying with her at the moment? Did he think she would disapprove? After what she'd hoped wasn't too long an interval, she'd said, 'Rokeby Villa.'

'Oh, where's that?' Marianna had looked puzzled. Had she got memory problems too, Libby wondered, or had they got so many properties she didn't know where they all were?

Monty had resumed drumming his fingers on the dashboard. They were still stationary.

'What did you talk to Lawrence about when Marianna and I went upstairs?' Libby hoped he'd welcome conversation to relieve his obvious boredom.

'Nothing, absolutely nothing. He was back on the bloody Matterhorn, the high spot – ha ha! – of his illustrious life.'

'You didn't talk about banking, then, or family business – or finance?' *Or your allowance?* She didn't say that.

'No.' He sounded cross.

'Or Rokeby Villa? How's the work going, by the way?'

He stopped drumming. 'I've been meaning to talk to you about that.'

It wasn't going as well as he'd hoped, he said. The workmen kept disappearing. The job was taking longer than expected. He might have to stay with her a bit longer, if that was all right? Then he said she needed to concentrate on the driving if they were going to get home safely today. Well, the traffic was moving again, which was something. But Monty, she realised, wasn't moving. He was staying put – in her house. She wasn't sure how she felt about that.

37

LIBBY

It was First Friday again.

Libby was finding it hard to believe it was August already, and she was back in The Olive Branch with Viv and Janet, after missing two – or was it three? – Muscateers in a row. She had been looking forward to it, had lots to discuss, not least the pros and cons of living with a man, but the atmosphere wasn't as receptive as she'd expected. What was it with these two? They'd welcomed her warmly when she'd arrived late but – it was hard to put it into words – they were less spontaneous now, more guarded. Were they miffed because she hadn't told them she was going on holiday before they'd read about it in Libby's World? Or – she thought this was the crux – were they miffed because she had just told them that Cindy was Monty?

Why did they have such a down on Monty?

'Eleanor isn't too pleased about it either.' Libby took a gulp of the red wine Nikos had brought to the table as soon as she had sat down. 'She said she had invited me to go with them to the Lakes that week, and that I'd accepted, but I can't remember her asking.'

'We're not *not*-pleased,' said Viv carefully, before raising her glass in their customary toast. 'All for one!' They clinked together.

'No, no, we *are* pleased,' Janet corrected Viv. 'We are very pleased that you're going on a wonderful holiday, Libby, paid for by a kind friend. We're just adjusting to the fact that the kind friend is Monty. We fell for the Cindy story and were about to say we'd like to meet her. Now we think we ought to know a few facts, like the address of the location, bearing in mind our golden rule.'

Libby hadn't put much about the location in the article, which she'd changed a lot after Monty's revelation about the Villa Adelos. She hadn't said a lot about the holiday at all. It had ended up more about the pros and cons of surprises and the fictitious Cindy's gift of a holiday in Greece was just one example she'd given. She certainly hadn't named the villa and she'd changed the emotional tone. She'd been annoyed and irritated with Cindy, not angry, and very grateful for her friend's kindness. The article had generated a good response from readers, including Nikos, who'd already said how pleased he was she was going to Greece.

Oh. A jolt of reality hit her. Nikos probably believed the Cindy story too. She would have to put him right, which might be difficult. And here he was, carrying a deep blue bowl of hummus and a basket of warm pitta bread, which he put on the table before pulling out a chair and sitting down with them.

'Evelina says she can hold the fort for a few minutes. We aren't too busy and Tomos is helping out. What do you think?' He nodded at the carafe of red wine. 'It's on the house, by the way, as I'm market-testing.'

'Beware a Greek bearing gifts,' said Janet and he laughed.

They all agreed that the Mega-something-or-other – Libby didn't catch the full name of the wine – was very good and would go well with the kleftiko they'd ordered for their main. Viv said she thought she'd tasted something like it on one of her trips to the

Peloponnese, and Nikos complimented her on her palate. It was, he said, from the Nemea vineyards in that region.

'And the hummus? How is that today?' He looked to Libby for approval.

Very good, they all agreed again, delicious. Libby said she half regretted ordering the kleftiko, which she loved. But the slow-cooked lamb was a substantial dish, and she could have feasted happily on hummus and bread. Nikos made the best hummus ever. The swirl of deep green olive oil on the top was an inspired touch and he beamed when she said so.

'Now, Liberty, where exactly in Greece are you and your friend going?'

A question hung in the air. *Who's going to tell him?*

Not me, not yet. Libby bottled out, wishing she'd brought the brochure with her, so they could see how much money Monty was spending, as well as the exact location. 'It's near Athens, I know that much.' But not much more, she realised. 'We're flying to Athens and then it's a half-hour drive from the airport to the villa, which is really luxurious.' That was what she remembered Monty saying.

'What's the villa called?' Janet had her mobile ready to google.

'Adelos,' said Libby as Nikos got up, to go and get a map, he said.

'There are several Adeloses coming up,' said Janet. 'One in the Elliniko district, most are on the islands though...'

Nikos came back with a map, spread it over the table, and pointed out that a half-hour drive from the airport was about twenty miles in all directions, and that covered a wide area. Adelos was a popular name for a villa, he said, very common. He needed to know the name of the district the villa was in at least, although the precise address would be best, if he was going to recommend restaurants and places of interest to visit. He had family all over Greece, some in the Athens area, who would love to welcome Libby and her friend into their homes. It wasn't unusual, he said, for eigh-

teen of them to sit down together for a meal at his uncle Spiro's in
the Peloponnese area.

'That would be lovely, Nikos...' Libby took a deep breath '...but I
do need to make something clear first.' She started to explain as Viv
and Janet picked up knives and forks.

'Thank you,' said Nikos, but he left before she had finished.

* * *

Evelina brought their main course and said they must forgive Nikos
for being abrupt. He had been surprised, that was all. He had
believed in her old friend, Cindy. He had assumed Libby had
changed her name, but not the gender. He'd thought it might be
Viv or Janet. He'd liked the sound of Cindy from Libby's description. What a kind and generous friend to treat her to a holiday in
Greece! He had looked forward to putting them both in touch with
their family in Greece.

'But when Monty is kind and generous...' Libby gave up. It
wasn't fair. *They* weren't fair. They wouldn't see the best in Monty.

'Dear Libby—' she felt Evelina's hand on hers '—please, try to
understand. He, Nikos, he love you very much, *we* love you very
much. Nikos was good friend of Jim and he feel protector to you. He
good man, very good man. He look out for you, yes? He just a bit
suspicious of new man in life, who he do not know.'

But he won't get to know him! He won't give him a chance! Libby
wanted to scream.

Evelina was rummaging in her apron pocket. 'Look what he do
for you – and Cindy.' She pulled out a notebook headed 'Useful
Phrases' and gave it to Libby. Nikos had written them himself, the
English and the Greek translation, in Greek script and phonetically.
'So you can say out loud,' said Evelina. 'Or show to someone if you
need help.'

It was a very thoughtful present. There were pages and pages of phrases, covering what looked like every contingency. Nikos must have spent a lot of time on it. *So* kind.

'Thank you, Evelina. Thank Nikos. I know you both care for me, and I care for you both, but...' Libby couldn't say what she wanted to say, because she was too choked up, and would feel pathetic saying the words.

I want you to like Monty! I want you all to like each other. I want you to get to know him!

Viv and Janet had stopped eating. She was sure they'd been listening avidly but hadn't said a word. They were either keeping an uncharacteristic diplomatic silence or they hadn't got an opinion on the matter, which was unlikely. Though they had never met Jim and they hadn't met Nikos or Evelina till recently, or herself.

They've known me for less than a year.

'Enjoy your meal,' Evelina said before bustling off to the kitchen.

Viv watched her go. 'She can't bear for anyone to think badly of Nikos, can she?'

'That's how I feel about Monty.'

They didn't answer, which was perhaps as well. Then Libby's mobile rang. It was Eleanor.

'Mum, can you call in on your way back from your girls' lunch?' She sounded headmistressy – or even cross. 'I think we need to have a word.'

38

LIBBY

'Coffee, Mum?' Eleanor had greeted her with a hug, which was nice.

Libby wondered if she'd misjudged the tone of the phone call as she followed Eleanor into the kitchen.

'Sorry, Mum, if I sounded head-teachery on the phone.'

Gosh! Libby reminded herself that there were two Eleanors. One, the stressed-out teacher of term-time who couldn't find time to speak to her mother, and snapped when she did. Two, the at-home-on-holiday mum, trying to make up for all the times she'd bitten her mum's head off during term-time.

'You go outside and sit down, Mum. Put your feet up. Have a snooze if you like. I'll bring the coffee out. Ellie-Jo has a play date, by the way, so we can have a proper chat later.'

A *proper* chat – were they going to have a heart-to-heart? Libby suppressed concern and settled herself on one of the two comfortable-looking sunbeds on the patio. Side by side with a low table between them, they were perfect for a chat, close but looking out over the garden, so they weren't eyeballing each other. She needed a few minutes of shut-eye first though – the lunchtime wine was kicking in – but, oh dear, here was Eleanor with the coffee, already.

'It needs a few minutes to brew.' She put the tray bearing a cafetière and cups and saucers on the table. 'While we're waiting you might like to look at that.'

That was a brochure for a holiday cottage in the Lakes. Had it been there all along? It was beside the tray. Yew Tree Cottage looked very picturesque, white with a slate roof, pretty front garden, a wicket gate and a background of sheep-dotted mountains.

Libby closed her eyes. *I have been summoned for a purpose.*

'Derek and I were looking forward to it so much.'

Were, Libby noted – *were*.

'It's in the back of beyond, quite remote. We thought it would be restful.'

Libby kept her eyes shut.

'But if we did want to go out in the evening, say for a meal, we couldn't, unless we had someone to look after Ellie-Jo.'

Libby pretended she'd fallen asleep.

'Who, of course, we wouldn't dream of leaving with a stranger... Coffee's ready, Mum.'

Libby opened her eyes. 'What are you saying, Eleanor?' As if she didn't know!

'That we took this cottage assuming you were coming with us.'

Assuming. She didn't say that. *Assuming that I wouldn't have anything else to do.*

She was determined not to have a row.

'I'm sorry, Eleanor—' she was sorry '—but I-I've made other arrangements.'

Silence, except for the birds twittering round the bird-feeder.

Then – 'You mean you've had a better offer.'

'Not better, *earlier*. So flights, accommodation, everything, has been booked.'

'And you'd rather go with *him* than your own granddaughter.'

'No.' This was true – she wished Eleanor had asked first. 'I'd love to go on a holiday with Ellie-Jo, I'd *prefer* to go with Ellie-Jo, but I have committed to this fortnight in Greece, so I've got to go.'

'Even if...' Eleanor looked at her wedding ring. 'I didn't want to worry you but...'

'What? What's the matter?'

'Derek and I are going through a bit of a bad patch at the moment, and we were rather hoping that this holiday would give us some time together, on our own, so we could try and work through a few difficulties...'

Bad patch. Difficulties. The words were like knives. Would the next be divorce, heartbreaking for Ellie-Jo?

'It doesn't matter.' Eleanor pressed the plunger of the cafetière.

But it did. Very much.

'I know you've said you can't come, Mum, but, well, I thought you might like to reconsider, in the circumstances.' Eleanor poured coffee.

Libby tried to keep calm and think clearly despite the sick feeling in her stomach. It was fear, fear that Eleanor and Derek would break up, that Ellie-Jo's world would fall apart. It had happened to so many of her friends' children. She tried to keep a sense of proportion. Bad patches, all couples went through bad patches – she and Jim had had bad patches, which they'd worked through. They didn't all end in divorce. Eleanor and Derek could work through theirs, and, and – she started to feel positive – the sooner they began, the better.

'Eleanor—' Libby kept her voice steady '—there's no need to wait for your holiday, which is more than two weeks away, nearly three. I can come and look after Ellie-Jo any time you like. I will make myself available, so you and Derek can have time together. You could go away together for a few days, or stay at home undisturbed. You could talk to Derek tonight. I could take Ellie-Jo home with me...'

Eleanor snorted. 'Mum, I think I've told you. I'm not allowing my daughter to come to yours while your so-called lodger is in residence.'

'Yes, yes, you have told me—' Libby took a deep breath '—and I have respected that. So, I will carry on coming to yours to look after Ellie-Jo as we've agreed. I suggest you book a few days away with Derek—'

'Mum, you don't get it, do you?' Eleanor was on her feet looking down at her. 'Things have moved on. Your refusal to help me out when I need you, to look after Ellie-Jo when she needs you, to support our marriage, well, it changes everything. It makes me wonder how much you really care. Family first, that's what you've always said...'

Eleanor was right, it was her guiding rule. Libby rapidly revised her plans. She would have to disappoint Monty. She would have to tell him that she couldn't go with him, well, not for two weeks. She would join him for the second week perhaps. 'Eleanor...' She was about to say so when Eleanor tossed her head and strode off.

'If that's how you feel, Mum, I'm not sure if I want you to look after Ellie-Jo any more.'

39
LIBBY

'How are you feeling, Libby darling?'

'All right.' But she wasn't. She shouldn't have come. She'd known as soon as she'd boarded the plane. She'd overreacted to Eleanor's outburst, which had felt like blackmail at the time.

'Not long now, darling.' Monty patted her knee.

They had been in the back of the taxi for half an hour. The cab, pre-booked by Monty, had picked them up at Athens airport. He was trying very hard to please her, as he should be, as she'd come on this holiday to please him. Wrong! Wrong! Wrong! They were heading for the suburban town of Artemida, and the conversational cab driver was telling them that it was named after the goddess Artemis, 'probably better known to you as Diana', and was one of the twelve towns of the ancient district of Attica, united by Theseus. A man of many roles, currently cab driver and tour guide, he had introduced himself as Georgios, and asked them about themselves, in the manner of a genial chat-show host. Monty had delighted him by telling him he was a theatre and festival director, specialising in the classics, and to her alarm had told him she was a writer, 'Here to write a novel about your beautiful country.'

I will write a column about your beautiful country.

But beautiful it wasn't, well, not the bit they were driving through, which could only be described as scrub. They'd left the main road several minutes ago and were now following what seemed like a bumpy track through sandy terrain and stunted vegetation. The sky above was stunningly blue and cloudless, well, the bit she could see through the window, and she remembered reading that the ancient Greeks didn't have a word for blue – hence the famous 'wine-dark sea' – but found that hard to believe. She bet they had words for faded brown and dingy green, the predominant colours of the shrubs and cactus-like plants growing among clumps of dry grass in the mostly bare earth. She recognised olive trees so small they were more like bushes, and here and there red poppies stood out against the parched greys and browns, and there was the odd patch of yellow. but it all looked a bit run-down and depressed – or was that the lens she was looking through? She lurched against Monty despite the seat belt as they rounded a bend.

'Steady on, old girl.'

Old girl? Had they come to that?

Georgios slowed to a halt by the side of a solid double gate. 'There it is, the Villa Adelos, on your left.' He pointed upwards to a flat-roofed white building just visible behind a wall topped by a fence.

Really? It wasn't quite as depicted in the brochure. There were no other buildings in sight, for a start, not a single house that she could see. Hadn't the brochure said it was on the outskirts of town 'within easy reach of shops and restaurants and the sea'? No sea either.

Monty was leaning forward, settling the bill and asking for a receipt. Georgios was saying the receipt had his mobile number on it. If they wanted taking anywhere, shops, restaurants, the beach, museums, art galleries, temples, theatres ancient and modern, anywhere, they had only to text or call. 'I or a colleague will be at Villa Adelos in very short time.'

'How far away are all these facilities?' Libby found her voice.

'Twenty, thirty, forty minutes. No trouble,' said Georgios.

'By car?' She had to check.

'Yes, of course. Nice walk to beach through vineyards, if not too hot. Say, one hour – for young people.'

We're twenty, thirty, forty minutes away from civilisation – by car! Libby wanted to stay in the cab and tell him to drive straight back to the airport. But Monty was already getting their luggage from the boot and Georgios got out to help him.

'Come on, old girl.' Monty opened the door on her side.

'*Don't* call me old girl!'

Georgios coughed. 'Just one more thing. Best to book for return journey to airport now.' He said the firm got booked very quickly for the turnover trips at weekends, and he wouldn't like to disappoint. But Monty shook his head and said he'd be in touch later. He needed to look up the return date.

'A fortnight today, 31 August.' It was seared into Libby's memory.

But Monty was busy studying a paper he'd just got out of his holdall. They needed to find the key-safe, which was on the white gatepost, he said. Libby wondered where their welcoming host was as Georgios shrugged, got in the cab and drove off. Libby found the key-safe on the far side of the gatepost, half covered by ivy, and keyed in the number that Monty read out from the info sheet. 'Open sesame!' he said as a narrow metal gate beside the double gates slowly opened, and it did feel a bit like magic when she saw the view beyond. A transformation!

The arched gateway framed a flight of stone steps leading up to a sapphire-blue front door. Purply-pink bougainvillaea did indeed 'cascade' over the white walls as the brochure described, and other colourful plants filled pots on the steps, sky-blue plumbago scrambling up a trellis, and spiky dark blue agapanthus in another pot were a good contrast. Libby made a mental note to send photos to Viv.

'It's beautiful. They've even got a cat.' A pretty tortoiseshell was on the top step, washing herself.

But Monty was more struck by the climb ahead of them. 'Should have got that driver to help. Can you manage a couple of cases, darling?'

At least she was darling again.

They stopped at the top of the first flight of steps to gather their breath. Wow! It gave them a great view of the truly stupendous grounds. There was the swimming pool, very blue, sparkling in the sunlight, surrounded by palms and other trees, maybe olives giving shade to sunbeds, though there were sunshades too and little tables for their drinks.

'Come on. Last leg.' Monty had got his mojo back, and hers was returning.

From the top step, puffed now, she saw the villa was surrounded by vineyards and remembered that it had been a winery once. And when she turned to look behind her, she got that view of distant mountains and the sea not too far away. If she couldn't enjoy this for a fortnight there was something wrong with her. Even the cat was making her welcome, winding itself around her legs and purring. And Monty had found another key-safe by the door all by himself and was letting them in.

'Ta da!' He stepped aside to let her see the lovely entrance hall. Wow again! This was no ordinary holiday home, minimally furnished for visitors. This was a luxurious lived-in home. White Lladro figures, a mother and child, stood on the table opposite the door; a woven rug in blue stripes covered the marble floor; a framed mirror on the wall reflected her own smiling face. How could she not smile? She had done the right thing, she had, she had. The sitting room had lots of comfy sofas, and more colourful woven rugs covered shiny wooden floors. The walls were hung with interesting pictures including huge flowers by Georgia O'Keeffe, which she loved. It could have been furnished for her. The kitchen-cum-diner was a cook's paradise, with a six-ring hob, two ovens, well-stocked cupboards and a wall of plate-glass sliding doors opening onto a balcony with that gorgeous view of sea and mountains. *And* there was wine chilling in the fridge! What were the bedrooms like? she wondered, but upstairs could wait. She couldn't climb any more stairs. It was time to open a bottle and collapse.

'Sorry, I've been grumpy, darling.' She gave Monty a hug. 'This is perfect. It's exactly what we both need. This will do us the world of good.'

Four days in, Libby was getting used to waking up in the super-king-size bed, then sipping coffee brought to her by Monty as she watched the morning mist slowly clear to reveal distant mountains and what she now knew was the Aegean Sea. But however many times she woke to the view, she would never stop being amazed and delighted. It was the perfect start to the day, especially knowing Monty was downstairs getting breakfast ready. What would it be today? Fresh figs from the tree growing by the pool, sweet little grapes from the vine that grew below the balcony, cherries with real Greek yogurt, thick and creamy with honey on top, crusty white bread with delicious sour cherry jam and soft white cheese? As, coffee cup empty, she rose from piles of frilly white pillows to go and get a shower she was Aphrodite, goddess of love, rising from the foam...

'Breakfast, darling!' Monty's rich dark voice – like the coffee he made – brought her back to reality, but what a reality!

'Ten minutes, darling!' she called back. 'No, twenty, please!' There was no need to hurry. She was on holiday! Completely switched off now, she realised how fraught she'd been before she came. Monty was right. Away from home all her troubles seemed eminently soluble. When she got back she would sit down and talk to Eleanor. Calmly. Over a glass or two of wine. They'd have a friendly woman-to-woman and clear up all the misunderstandings. Eleanor would have learned that it wasn't fair to use Ellie-Jo as a bargaining chip.

* * *

Monty was at the table on the balcony when she got downstairs, surrounded by cats, including the one they'd met on Sunday night and her three leggy kittens.

'Go away.' Monty tried to shake one off his sandalled foot but it clung on. 'I've fed you.'

'Miaow!' More. More. The cat already knew him for a soft touch. He'd started feeding them on Sunday night after he'd had a phone call from Helena, the owner of the property, apologising for not being there to greet them. She had been called away suddenly to the USA on family matters, she'd said, and was very sorry, not least because she had to ask Monty to do a few things that she and her husband would normally do, like feeding the cats and watering the plants and looking after the swimming pool. Monty had reported all this to Libby because of course she couldn't hear the conversation.

'No worries,' she'd heard him say, all obliging, before he put down the phone, but now he was beginning to find it all a bit much. 'I'm knackered already,' he joshed. 'Been up since six. This lot were yowling. Need to go back to bed.' At first he'd gone downstairs to feed the cats where they were used to being fed, on the terrace of the basement flat, where Helena and her husband lived when they let their house to holiday tenants. But they'd quickly found their way upstairs, where there was a more constant supply of food.

Now he gave her a kiss and poured coffee. She could take her morning dip straight after breakfast, he said, as he'd already tested the pool water, and it was fine. Swimming-pool maintenance was causing him most stress. 'Check chlorine and pH levels daily' was scary. He wasn't a bloody scientist! The whole process seemed to take him hours because, terrified of dissolving her skin if acid levels were too high, he read and reread the instructions each time, and treble-checked the measurements. 'Vacuum the pool once a week,' also sounded easy as there was a robotic cleaner, a 'turtle', to do it, but it wasn't as easy as it sounded, as the instructions advised not leaving it in the water 24/7. How did you get the bloody thing out? Then there was the pump to check and filters to clean, jobs for a bloody engineer, not a creative artist. He was okay with 'skim off leaves and debris'. That was easy enough, quite a leisurely process with the implement provided, a net on a long handle, but it took a long time, and how the hell did you 'brush sediment from the pool walls' without drowning?

'I'll water the plants, Monty.' That was another time-consuming job as there were so many pots and planters, but she didn't mind as she enjoyed looking at the flowers close-up, and it upped her step-count in a leisurely way and gave her time to think. She wanted to write a column, 'Libby Allgood reports from Greece', but hadn't hit on a theme yet. And she wanted to help Monty because he was working so hard – she'd never seen him work so hard – which couldn't have been what he'd been expecting when he'd booked a luxurious holiday. Also, he'd confided in her that he had an idea for a business project, so he could start paying his way, but he needed time to think about it and contact local vineyard owners to get it off the ground.

'I hate sponging off you, darling.'

'You're not, you're not. You're spoiling me.' It was lovely. He was lovely. 'But by all means go and see what you can do.' It would be good for his self-esteem if he was earning.

* * *

He took off next morning in the little Fiat that Helena said he could use free of charge, as a thank you for helping out. It was in one of the outhouses at the back of the property, buildings that had been used for winemaking. He already had an appointment with a vine-yard manager, he said, and would call in at a couple of bars, as he was thinking along the lines of a buying and selling business. He'd pop into a supermarket, to top up supplies on the way back. They'd eaten all the food that they'd found in the fridge and quite a lot from the freezer and store cupboards in the three days they'd been there. She'd offered to go shopping herself but he'd said she wasn't insured to drive the car.

'Expect me back late afternoon,' he said as he drove off.

Libby had a dip – she loved swimming – then settled by the pool with her laptop. She had an idea relating to people's attitudes to foreign countries, their love-hate relationship. Why did so many people love the people they met when they went abroad but hated having the same people in their country? But she hadn't written more than a few sentences before she saw a car coming through the gates. At first she thought Monty had come back, but then noticed it was a different car. Someone must know the codes. Friend or foe? Could someone have seen Monty drive out, assumed the place was empty, and driven in? They had memorised the code earlier perhaps, after keeping an eye on the property.

The car was parked by the side of the house now, by the base-ment. She couldn't see who got out or where he or she went, or even if they had got out, because the driver's door was close to the house. She hadn't seen anyone climbing the outside stairs to the front

door. They could have gone in by the basement, but only if they had
a key. Unless they'd broken in. Should she investigate – or turn a
blind eye? Even as she had the thought, she got to her feet. Libby
Allgood did the right thing. There was a pile of sticks on the ground
near the barbecue on a terrace above the pool. With a sturdy stick
in her hand she felt braver.

She found the intruder in the kitchen. 'What...' *do you think
you're doing?* she wanted to say but the words died on her lips. It
didn't help that the woman, a shaven-headed, nose-ringed,
youngish woman in slashed denims was wielding a blood-smeared
knife.

41

VIV

'Janet, do you realise we don't know where exactly Libby is?' Viv was on the phone speaking to Janet's voicemail. 'Nikos has pointed out that the brochure doesn't give the actual address of the Villa Adelos.' She waited for Janet to pick up the phone as she sometimes did when she realised who was calling. But she didn't. Damn. Viv put down the phone.

It was Thursday morning and she'd just got back from dropping into The Olive Branch with the photocopy she'd made of the Villa Adelos brochure. Libby had brought the brochure round on the morning before she'd left, but wouldn't leave it. Monty wanted to take it with them, she'd said, but she'd been okay with Viv photocopying it to share with Janet and Nikos and Evelina. In fact she'd been very keen, and had pointed out the astronomical price Monty was paying to rent the lovely villa. 'So-o-o-o *generous!*'

Viv had said yes, it was, because it was hard not to agree when Libby wanted her to so much, but had also reminded Libby that she had been very generous to Monty, giving him a home for the last month and a half.

Nikos and Evelina, not Monty's biggest fans, hadn't been

hopeful about tracking down the Villa Adelos without more information. The brochure said it was near Artemida, a small town in the Attica district, but that covered a wide area, and the name of the villa was quite common. Nikos had urged Viv to text Libby and ask her for the postal address, which she had done, but so far hadn't had a reply. In fact, she hadn't heard from Libby since she'd texted from the airport to say that she'd landed safely four days ago.

Viv wondered what else she could do. Would Libby's daughter know her address? She didn't have Eleanor's contact details but Zelda, still in the USA, might. Then she remembered that Libby had fallen out with Eleanor. Her daughter had given her an ultimatum, she'd said – Monty called it blackmail – threatening that she wouldn't let her see her granddaughter again if she went on this holiday to Greece. But Monty had also blackmailed her, it seemed to Viv, though Libby said he had been very sweet. He'd said he would feel very hurt if she went with Eleanor, and wondered if their relationship would survive the separation. Libby had said there were tears in his eyes, and she had remembered that he'd often felt abandoned by his parents as a child, when they'd gone on holiday leaving him behind with a nanny.

Man up, Monty!

Poor Libby, caught not so much between the devil and the deep blue sea as between a devilishly manipulative daughter and a deeply devious dickhead.

42

LIBBY

Libby was shaking inside, though she now saw that the blood on the knife wasn't blood. It was red cherry jam. The young woman, a teenager maybe, was standing by the sink, where she and Monty had left their breakfast things, and didn't look threatening at all. She'd been washing up. Her hands were wet and covered with suds. She looked surprised to see Libby.

'Who...?' She didn't seem to have much English.

'No, who are you?' said Libby, then, regretting what might seem like an accusing tone, she said, 'I'm Libby, Libby Allgood.' She let the branch fall to her side. The girl looked at home here. She wasn't an intruder. She was, it looked like, a cleaner, used to coming here, drying her hands now after reaching for a towel from a hook on the inside door of a cupboard. She knew her way around, and was now walking over to a backpack on one of the chairs in the dining area. She pulled out some papers, which she studied briefly, before walking back with them to Libby.

'Meester Charles Mont-gom-er-y, no-o?' She shook her head from side to side.

'No.' Libby smiled. 'I am Libby, Mr Montgomery's friend.' Libby wished she were wearing more than a swimsuit and a wrap, hastily put on. The young woman was casually but fully dressed in cut-off denims torn at the knee, and a sleeveless black top showing her tattooed midriff. Libby felt at a disadvantage.

'I am Andrea. I help Helena.'

'I am a guest,' said Libby. 'We, Mr Charles Montgomery and I, we are guests of Helena. We are staying here.'

The girl raised thickly pencilled black eyebrows, then pulled a phone from the pocket of her jeans. She tapped for a bit then held it out to Libby, showing she'd logged on to Google Translate. Then she tapped again. 'Meester Mont-gom-er-y, he look after house. Yes?'

'Yes.' Libby nodded. 'He is looking after it at the moment, yes.' In a manner of speaking, she didn't say. She was doing quite a lot of it.

Andrea leafed through the sheaf of papers again, then she extracted a few pages and handed them to Libby. 'Leest, for Mr Montgomery, from Helena. Remind.'

It was a list of jobs, a long list, several pages of it, divided into daily, weekly and monthly tasks. Libby didn't bother to say 'we're only here for another ten days' – as the girl probably wouldn't have understood, or she might already know, as she seemed to be in touch with Helena. Instead, after making polite 'I'll leave you to get on' noises, she took the papers with her back to the poolside. After a quick peruse, she was amused to see so many instructions about toilet arrangements – Monty wouldn't be so amused – then went for a dip in the pool.

And that was where Andrea found her an hour later. 'I come show you,' she said, 'so you know and tell Mr Montgomery.'

Libby got out and was taken on a tour of the house and grounds, beginning at the barbecue area above the pool. Mr Montgomery must keep check the gas bottles, the girl said, and change them when they needed changing. He must check stocks of charcoal and vine twigs and re-stock when low. He must inspect the poolside toilets, like all the toilets, every day and be meticulous about emptying the bins. He must remind guest to obey the golden rule – *Do not put toilet paper down the loo!* The brochure for the Villa Adelos stated the rule in bold type and several languages. The same warning was on all the loo doors, she pointed out as they went round. The villa wasn't connected to the inadequate main sewage system – it had its own septic tank in the grounds – but putting paper down the loo would still cause a blockage and dire consequences. Andrea demonstrated a poonami with arms thrown wide. She exploded. Libby had to admire her dramatic skills, but it was a tad shaming. When they went upstairs Andrea wasn't impressed by the standard of hygiene.

'Poo-ooo!' Andrea stood at the door of their en suite and held her nose. Then, donning plastic gloves, she demonstrated how the plastic bag containing the soiled toilet paper should be tied up *every day*, before being transferred to the outdoor all-purpose dustbin, *every day*. Not the paper-recycling bin, not the plastics bin, not the waste-food bin, the all-purpose bin. She led Libby downstairs again to a row of assorted coloured bins behind the house, and pointed out the purple all-purpose bin. They mustn't ever, she repeated, flush toilet paper or anything else down the loo. She thanked Libby for not doing that, but Libby felt more than ticked-off, nevertheless. She'd thought she'd been dealing with that side of things quite efficiently.

Monty, of course, had had nothing to do with anything lavatorial. He'd been appalled when he'd discovered what he had to do even for himself. She suspected that he didn't always follow the rule, and had to admit that was easily done. Flushing came automatically. It was the one drawback of the idyllic setting. Greek plumbing simply wasn't up to dealing with toilet paper. Nor was the country's sewage system. Andrea again mimed the consequences of putting loo paper in the loo. She then turned her attention to the overflowing cat-litter trays on the basement terrace. Monty, she said, Mr Montgomery, hadn't been emptying them. They had to be emptied every day – into the all-purpose bin. The cats didn't poo in the ground, it was too hard. Libby began to feel a bit sorry for Monty, till she remembered that she would be doing most of this, not him.

Back in the upstairs kitchen, sparklingly clean now, Libby offered to make coffee and Andrea accepted. She went onto the balcony with her phone while Libby operated the coffee-making machine. When she took the coffees outside, Andrea held up her phone showing the word 'House-sitter' on Google Translate.

'House seeter, that right word, yes, for Meester Mont-gom-ery?'

'No, Mr Montgomery guest.'

Andrea consulted Google Translate and frowned.

Libby didn't want to argue, so she said, 'Sort of, temporarily,' though it was wrong. House-sitters moved into people's houses when they went on holiday, to look after their pets and water their plants, and make the house look lived-in to deter burglars. They might even be paid a small remuneration to cover food costs.

But Andrea had the wrong end of the stick and was hanging onto it. 'So, Meester Mont-gom-ery... he leeve here in house while no guests – then, he go downstairs to flat when guests arrive.' She pointed to the basement flat. 'That what Helena say. She have exciting life. New York! New York!' She put her phone in her pocket and picked up her coffee.

Libby got her own phone from her pocket. For the four days they'd been here she hadn't been able to text or make calls. Annoyingly, her mobile network seemed to have no coverage here. She'd tried switching to WhatsApp and Facebook Messenger but they hadn't worked either, presumably because the Wi-Fi was down. But

Andrea had just been googling on the Internet, so it must be up now. She messaged Eleanor to say she hoped she was having a restful time in the Lake District – and yes, it went. Hurray! She sent another one to Viv to share with Janet, a simple 'having a great time' to reassure them. Then one to Monty.

> What time will you be home? Don't forget the shopping or you'll starve!

A few messages were coming in now, one from Viv:

> Please send us your address! We need to know where you are!

She didn't know it, but Andrea might. She turned back to the girl, who seemed to be going.
'See you next week, Leeby.'
'Wait a mo.'
But she had gone.

43

LIBBY

Monty didn't get back till evening.

At six o'clock Libby was on the balcony looking out for him, anxiously. He hadn't replied to her messages. She'd sent him several throughout the day. She saw him driving in, skirting the gatepost, and coming abruptly to a halt, the automatic gates closing behind him. She watched him get out and walk to the house, walk not stagger, *not* stagger, but he did seem a bit unsteady on his feet. Surely he shouldn't have driven home like that.

She hurried to open the front door, and he greeted her warmly, kissing her on the mouth with lips tasting of Metaxa. She didn't recoil, which would have hurt his feelings, but she wasn't as warm as she could have been. He didn't seem to notice though, luckily, because he was in far too good a mood, and she wanted to keep him that way. Clearly, he'd had a good day meeting lots of viticulturists and barkeepers *and* theatre people and he was very optimistic about his business plan's success. The difference between the price of buying wine direct from the vineyard and selling it to bars and restaurants was colossal. He'd make a fortune. The words, 'This time next year, Rodney, we'll be millionaires' came into her head, and she told herself off for being sniffy as she led the way to the kitchen and started to make coffee, though he was in the fridge looking for another bottle.

'And if I can get an export business going—'

'Monty—' she was sorry in a way to interrupt as it sounded like good news, but she was hungry '—what are we going to eat?' Had he been to the supermarket as he'd said he would? There was no sign of shopping bags. Were they in the car?

She made the coffee, settled him on a sofa in the sitting room with a cup, then went out to see. She'd noticed he'd emptied his pockets onto the hall table, and his keys were among the assorted debris. There was no shopping in the car, and when she got back to the house, she found him asleep on the sofa. He could do that, she'd noticed, close his eyes and drop off. Hoping he wouldn't sleep too long, she made an executive decision, and a few phone calls. Soon she'd managed to book a table at the Taverna Artemis in Artemida for supper at eight and, finding Georgios's card among the contents of Monty's pockets, she'd booked a cab for seven thirty.

When Monty woke just after seven she told him what she'd arranged and sent him for a shower. He protested a bit about Miss Bossy Boots telling him what to do, but not too strenuously, and he was downstairs by seven thirty looking his gorgeous cravated self, every inch the English gentleman in slacks and white shirt. He gave an approving nod to the all-covering black and white caftan she'd chosen with jet drop earrings. When the taxi came it wasn't Georgios driving, she was a bit sorry to see, but an older man, who said he was Makis, but not much else. He drove in silence to The Taverna Artemis, which was on the beach.

They were welcomed by a waiter who recognised Monty, who she gathered had been here before. It was Libby's first night out since she'd been here, she realised, and she hoped not the last. It was a lovely setting. The waiter found them a table where their toes

were almost lapped by the waves, and the view of distant mountains against a glorious sunset was stupendous. The sea looked as if
it were on fire. Monty ordered a bottle of white Malagousia, which
she'd first had at The Olive Branch, she remembered. The waiter
recommended the bourdeto, a fish and tomato stew, as their main,
and they both agreed. The wine was delicious, like drinking orange
blossom, Libby thought, making a note to tell Nikos, and the meze
were pretty good too, though not as good as Nikos's, obviously. She
found a smile coming to her lips as she had that thought, but
Monty fortunately didn't notice or ask why she was smiling.

Monty started telling her about his day at last. The really
exciting development, apart from the wine business, was meeting
up with someone from a theatre in Athens and the prospect of an
arts festival in Artemida next year.

'Let me guess.' She took another swig of the delicious wine.
'They've asked you to be the director?'

'Bingo! *How* did you know that?' He was amazed. 'Though actually, they haven't, not yet, but I think they will, if I play my cards
right.'

'That would be wonderful, Monty.'

She began to relax. This wasn't the time to tell Monty about the
day's not-so-good developments. He didn't need to hear about the
bossy young cleaning lady who seemed to think he was a fellow
employee. This wasn't the time to talk about changing over gas bottles
and emptying toilet bins. She pictured the horror on his face if she
mentioned them now. Or even if she told him what Andrea had said
about them moving down to the basement if visitors arrived. *We're the
bloody visitors!* That was what he'd say. *Why didn't you tell her?*

'Darling—' he touched her hand '—the future looks bright.
Let's drink to it.'

They raised their glasses as the waiter arrived with the bourdeto, and they ate it as the sky darkened to a purply blue studded with stars.

* * *

On the way back to the Villa Adelos, in the back of the cab, Monty found a message on his phone from Helena asking him to ring back. He said he'd do it in the morning, first thing.

'Will that work, darling?' she asked tentatively. 'I mean, will she still be awake? What's the time difference?'

'The USA is seven hours behind Greece, well, New York is.'

Libby did calculations. It was eleven o'clock at night here in Greece, so it was four o'clock in the afternoon in New York, a good time surely? Early morning here would be night-time there.

'Darling.' She touched his arm.

'No,' he said, 'I'll ring in the morning.'

* * *

He was as good as his word though. When she woke up he wasn't in bed beside her – must be making the call, she thought – but when he appeared with her morning coffee he looked cross.

'Sorry, darling, we've got to slum it for a bit. Sorry, don't mean *got to*. We've been *asked* if we wouldn't *mind* moving into the flat to do Helena a favour.'

This was ringing bells, chiming with what Andrea had said.

'Helena has double-booked the villa for next week. She's very sorry but there's a family moving in here at the weekend. She did say she'd reduce our rent by half for the duration.'

'Why can't the new people have the basement flat?' Libby didn't want to believe Andrea's story.

'Not big enough. There are six of them, Germans, parents, three kids and a granny.'

Libby wanted to believe Monty's story. She stretched her toes in the super-king-sized bed. 'What's today, Friday?' It was hard to keep track.

'Yes, but it seems there's a cleaner who needs to clean the place before the new people move in on Saturday. We've got to get out today.'

Andrea arrived soon after breakfast, with a smirk on her face.

44

LIBBY

It didn't take them long to move out, a couple of hours at most, and the basement flat was far from spartan. The kitchen was well equipped, the sitting-room-cum-diner perfectly adequate for the two of them, with a comfortable sofa, and the one bedroom had a double bed, not king-sized but big enough. The kitchen opened onto the terrace where Monty – or more often Libby – fed the cats each morning and evening, and the cats were now a near-permanent source of entertainment. The mother cat was clearly fed up with feeding her brood and took the odd swipe at them when they encroached. The kittens, aggrieved, looked to Libby for support.

'She loves you really, but wants her body back, that's all.' Libby identified with the mother of three. Been there done that. She remembered it well.

All in all, it wasn't bad. The view from the basement was of the garden and the perimeter wall, not the sea and mountains, but they still had the use of the lovely pool and poolside. Monty went out to do some food shopping and Libby rustled up meals. They went back to the Taverna Artemis on Saturday night, a bit annoyed that the promised family hadn't turned up. Had they moved out for nothing? Libby couldn't help suspecting Andrea of a bit of behind-the-scenes-plotting, even lying so she had less to clean? But the Kaufmanns, all six of them, arrived on Sunday morning.

The pool became a little less exclusive, the gardens a bit less peaceful, though they were a charming family with well-behaved children, ranging from a teenager to a toddler and one in between. Libby estimated that Granny Kaufmann was about the same age as she was, but, unlike her, was waited on hand and foot by the rest of the family. Libby found herself sighing, and hoping Eleanor was sorting out her problems with Derek.

Andrea returned the following Thursday to clean the house but not the flat. She made that clear by going straight upstairs. Soon afterwards, the Kaufmanns left. Libby saw them piling stuff into the car – to go to the beach, she thought, to get out of the way of the cleaner. Libby saw Andrea on the balcony above when she was on the basement terrace saying goodbye to Monty, who was going out on business again. The girl called out something that Libby didn't understand, and pointed to Monty's retreating back, miming holding a gun to her head.

What was that about? Libby hated the way people mocked Monty, but didn't dwell on it. Life was too short. They had only two days left of their wonderful holiday, three if they counted today, which of course they must. They must count every day. How quickly the time had passed! She must remind Monty to check in online when he got back. He'd gone to visit another vineyard and revisit a couple more to seal some deals. He'd been working very hard all week, working on his business plan, and trying to firm up the arts festival directorship. They had only got to the beach a couple of times, but she didn't mind. He'd been cheerful at breakfast today.

'Hopefully, I'll have something to celebrate when I get back.'

'Better buy some fizz, then,' she'd said. 'I'll start to think about packing.'

'Not yet, darling! We can do it together in five minutes flat when we have to. Go and enjoy yourself in the pool while you can. I've checked the levels.'

He was right, of course. Live for the moment, though she was starting to look forward to going home. There wasn't really a lot to pack anyway, as she'd put a lot of her clothes into a case to bring them to the downstairs flat and hadn't unpacked them. A morning on her own by the pool would be lovely. She could relax and read and start to think about what she had to do when she got home, and about presents for the family, an inflatable dinosaur for Ellie-Jo, she'd decided, a lovely caftan for Eleanor from that seller on the beach, not as expensive as she'd thought they'd be... if they got to the beach again.

The kittens had left the mother cat in peace for a bit and she was stretched out in the sun, revelling in the heat and solitude. 'I'm off to do the same,' said Libby. She went inside to put on her swimming costume and get a towel. But when she came out onto the terrace again, Andrea appeared.

'Okay in flat, yes, Leebee?'

'Yes, it's quite comfortable.'

'Best I think you stay now.'

'Yes,' said Libby, 'as we're going on Sunday.'

'You go Sunday?' Andrea frowned. 'You leave Meester Mont-gom-er-y?'

'No, we both go on Sunday.'

Andrea frowned again, her thick eyebrows almost meeting in the middle.

'Come.' Libby beckoned her into the kitchen where there was a calendar on the wall. She pointed to Sunday 31 August. 'We fly home.'

'You go.' Andrea nodded. 'Mr Mont-gom-er-y, he stay.'

'No.' Libby stuck out her arms, feeling like a toddler playing aeroplanes. 'We fly home.' She could mime too.

'Ah.' Andrea nodded.

'Yes.' Good. She got it Libby thought.

But then Andrea pointed to the list of jobs on the noticeboard. 'Poor Mr Mont-gom-er-y he do all by self!'

'No! We fly. We *both* fly!' Libby tried not to raise her voice, arrogant-English style, but how did she get through to this young woman? Idea! She got two dining chairs and put them side by side. Then she sat on one of them. 'Me Libby.' She pointed to the other beside her. 'He Monty'. She mimed doing up her seat belt. She mimed doing up Monty's. 'We fly.' She got up, stuck out her arms and did her aeroplane impression again.

Andrea looked puzzled.

Was her acting that bad? What else could she do? 'We go home. We *both* go home. Sunday.' Libby spoke as clearly as she could.

Andrea frowned. 'I tell Helena. Later. She sleep now.' She shot off back upstairs.

Had she got it? Hoping so, Libby picked up her towel and headed for the pool as planned.

* * *

But when she went back to the flat to make herself some lunch, Andrea was on the terrace with a pile of equipment of some kind, pipes and tubes, hoses.

'Job. Mr Mont-gom-er-y, yes?'

She picked up a long-handled something and pointed it at the window, clearly miming washing the outside windows. Then she went inside and mimed cleaning the kitchen window, with a blue and white J Cloth and a bottle of pink Windolene. Her instruction was clear: Monty was to clean the outside windows, she, Andrea would do the insides. She pointed to the instruction on the list under 'Monthly'.

Libby didn't bother to explain yet again that they were leaving or say that she was sure Monty wouldn't clean the windows before he left. There didn't seem to be any point.

* * *

Monty tripped over the equipment when he got home, quite late.

'What the fuck?' He nearly fell into the kitchen.

Libby put out a steadying hand, which he brushed off. She had already eaten and had been tidying up. 'Sorry, I should have moved it out of the way. Andrea, the cleaning girl, thinks you should clean the windows.'

He was sinking onto the sofa now. 'She can sod off. I won't be doing this bloody houshe-shitting for much longer.'

'What did you just say?' She'd have laughed if she didn't want to cry.

'Doeshn't matter.' He was the worse for drink.

'But it does.'

But this wasn't the time to talk. She moved the equipment to one side so he wouldn't fall over it again, put his dinner on the table, and said she was going to bed.

45

LIBBY

'Sorry about last night, darling.' Monty was standing by the bed holding a drooping bunch of flowers, what sort she couldn't say.

Libby struggled into a sitting position. Monty was dressed in the same shirt and slacks he'd worn yesterday. The blue shirt looked crumpled, as if he'd spent the night in it, and yes – she checked the other side of the bed – he must have fallen asleep on the sofa. She started to remember what had happened last night.

Houshe-shitter.

'I was a bit the worse for wear, but I can explain.' He noticed her noticing the flowers. 'Meant to give them to you last night but left them in the car. Sorry, and for being squiffy.'

He looked sad-clownish with hair flopping over his eyes, but she didn't find it endearing.

'There's your coffee, darling.' He nodded at her side of the bed. 'Brought it in earlier but you were asleep.'

'Explain, then.' She picked up the cup.

'Can I sit down, miss? Or should I go and stand in the corner?' He sat on the bed.

Yesterday had been very busy, he said, intensive. He'd had so many business appointments, at vineyards and bars, and of course had to be sociable. It was how things were done here, so he'd ended up drinking more than he should. But he had found some wonderful wines and come to some great deals, not signed and sealed yet, well, not all of them, but very close. They needed a bit more time, that was all, and he needed time to sort out storage for the wine and distribution. And it wasn't just the wine business he'd been attending to. The festival directorship was a real possibility, a probability now. How lucky was that? So he'd gone to talk to some people from the local council, who he'd needed to talk to anyway, as he had to have all sorts of permissions to start the wine business, it seemed. It was all very bureaucratic and time-consuming.

She guessed where this was leading.

'So, darling—' he reached for her free hand, but she put it round her cup '—this is the bonus: we'll be having a bit longer in the sun.'

'*You* will, Monty. I'm going home on Sunday.' She wasn't making this easy for him.

'But, darling, Helena says we can stay on.'

You've got to stay on. You're the house-sitter.

'I'm going home on Sunday.' It was straight talking from now on.

'But you can't, darling.' He stood up. 'Will explain later. I've got to get on. Need a shower and a bite of breakfast, then I'm out again for another day negotiating and before I go I need to take some measurements in the outbuildings.'

'I'm going home on Sunday, Monty.'

It was as if she'd never spoken. It was finding the outbuildings that had inspired him, he said, remembering that the Villa Adelos had once been a winery. So why shouldn't it be again? The machinery was still there, a bottling plant and a labelling device. He was getting someone in to give them an overhaul. Then he would buy wine in bulk direct from the growers and bottle it himself under his own label.

'What do you think of Lord Monty's Cellar?'

She didn't answer, which didn't matter because he wasn't listening. He walked out of the door with his dreams. Monty was a complete dreamer, she'd realised with a thudding sense of reality. He would never get this enterprise off the ground, because he hadn't got the skills. Monty knew quite a lot about drinking wine, but he hadn't got a clue about making it. He didn't understand machinery or the more scientific side of viticulture. Hygiene was important. She knew that much from when she and Jim used to make home-made wine in the seventies, when they were hard-up. They'd made it from tins of concentrated wine juice and yeast, which they'd bought from Boots. They'd brewed it in glass demijohns, which they'd kept in a row on the worktop in the kitchen, or sometimes in the airing cupboard in the bathroom to speed things up a bit. The right temperature was important for fermentation. They'd had a special thermometer. It had been a right faff sterilising all the bottles, with sodium metabisulphite if she remembered rightly. Monty would find that side of wine-making irksome, like testing the swimming-pool water.

She got out of bed when she heard Monty getting out of the shower, feeling like the most practical, mundane, down-to-earth person on earth. And that was okay, because that was what she had to be to get herself home. She must get her return ticket from Monty before he went out, do the checking-in online, pack her case and go. She'd have to book a taxi if Monty was going to be too busy to take her to the airport. Energised by resolution, she showered and dressed quickly, but by the time she reached the kitchen it was clear Monty had gone. He'd left a note on the table.

Back late tonight. Will eat out. Don't wait up. Monty x

The cats and kittens were wailing. Monty obviously hadn't fed them. Before having her breakfast she filled their dishes and changed the litter trays, which had become one of her regular tasks. Yes, certain aspects of her luxurious holiday had become a lot less luxurious. It had been going downhill for a while, if she was honest. Monty came home tipsy more often than not, after she had gone to bed.

She made more coffee then reached for her mobile, to remind her friends that she was coming home on Sunday. She messaged Viv because she wasn't 100 per cent sure when Zelda was getting back from the USA, Saturday or Sunday.

Home Sunday. Alone. Will let you know ETA asap but will get train from Luton then taxi home. Looking forward to seeing you all! L x

But it didn't go. Bloody Wi-Fi or lack of it. That was something else she was looking forward to, decent Internet – and plumbing that would flush away loo paper! She tried several times during the day, but the Wi-Fi hadn't come on by the time she went to bed. And Monty wasn't home.

* * *

He didn't come home that night.

'Know you don't like me driving when I've had a couple over the limit, darling.' He didn't say where he'd stayed, when he appeared after breakfast.

Libby was on the basement terrace having coffee and quickly got down to business. She said she needed him to take her into Artemida, to find an Internet café, so she could send messages and check in online – unless he could fix the Wi-Fi so she could do it all from the villa.

'Sorry, why?' He poured himself coffee.

Had he got amnesia?

'So I can fly home tomorrow!'

'But you can't.' He sipped. 'At least I don't think you can. Can you get a flight at this short notice – in the holiday season?'

What was he saying? She didn't need to *get* a flight. She'd *got* a flight. He'd booked it. She'd given him the money to book a return flight. She managed to articulate this – though near speechless with disbelief – and he shook his head. Where did she get that idea from? There was no return flight booked, well, not an actual date.

No return flight booked! This was worse than she'd feared.

'Darling Libby, I'm so sorry about the misunderstanding. I never said our return flight was booked. I don't know where you got that idea from. It was always open-ended.'

'You said we were coming for a fortnight's holiday, Monty!'

'I didn't, I know I didn't. You must have imagined that, darling.'

Some people would call that gaslighting. Libby called it lying. But not to his face, not at the moment. That would escalate the conflict, and she needed him on her side if she was to get home quickly. She hadn't completely given up hope of going tomorrow, if she could contact EasyJet and request a cancellation...

'Monty, I know you're employed as a house-sitter—'

'Wouldn't call it *employed,* darling—'

'Let's not quibble, Monty. I've accepted that you're staying here for however long you're contracted for, but *I am going home*, tomorrow if possible. So please will you drive me into Artemida, or Athens, somewhere, anywhere, with a travel agent's, so I can try and book a ticket home?'

'No can do, darling, sorry.' He looked abject, as if he really cared. 'I've got to stay in today. I've got a chap coming – not quite sure when – to look at the machinery and talk about the pros and cons of corks or screw-tops for the bottles. What do you think? I think corks are classier...'

'Monty—' she spoke through gritted teeth '—I wish you well with your business, I really do, but my priority is getting home. If you won't drive me into a town, I'll drive myself, insured or not.'

He smiled. 'Don't think you'll do that, Miss Too Good, but I'll keep a close eye on these in case you act out of character.' He jingled his keys and stood up. 'Look, I've got to get on, but a word of advice. Chill, darling. Enjoy your time here. Relax by the pool. Is it really so bad spending a bit longer in a luxury villa?'

'We're in the basement, Monty.'

'But it's not rat-infested, is it? And the Kaufmanns are leaving today or tomorrow, so we'll be able to move upstairs again.'

Chill? She was seething inside like a pressure cooker, and when Monty came in at lunchtime and said he'd made some useful phone calls, she very nearly exploded.

'How come you have Wi-Fi and I don't?' She'd been trying on and off all morning to send messages to Viv, Janet and Zelda.

He shrugged. 'It comes and goes, doesn't it? You have to keep trying.'

'I have been trying!'

'Serendipity, darling – if you were flying home on Sunday you wouldn't be able to come with me to this.' He held up his phone so she could read the screen. 'Isn't that exciting?'

46

ZELDA

Zelda had been home a few hours.

She was feeling a bit groggy and jet-lagged but was determined to keep awake, and go to bed at her normal time. Her Sunday morning rituals helped, *The Archers* omnibus and now *Desert Island Discs*, and so did the coffee she was drinking. Kirsty Young was interviewing someone Zelda hadn't heard of, a drama teacher called Anna Scher, who had launched the careers of a lot of famous actors. Zelda bet Libby had heard of her and wondered if she was listening too. Probably not, unless, like her, Libby had been on a very early flight from Athens to Luton. Libby was definitely due home today – it was in Zelda's diary – and she was surprised she hadn't had a message with her ETA. When this programme was finished she would give her a ring, and if she didn't answer she'd get in touch with Viv and Janet to see if either of them had heard. She needed to talk to Janet anyway to arrange a time to collect Mack and Morag, who'd been staying with her. If the timing worked out she'd be able to collect the darling dogs then walk them to the station to meet Libby.

The programme was too good to miss. The lady's taste in music was very different from Zelda's, none of the classics she loved so far, but her life-story was inspiring. She was a peace campaigner whose heroes were the same as Zelda's: Martin Luther King, Desmond Tutu and Ann Frank. Zelda stopped drinking coffee to listen to disc number four with a pang. It was Martin Luther King giving his 'I have a dream' speech. What an unusual choice, but wonderful. It made her want to be with her American family. Was this how it was going to be from now on, with a part of her always wanting to be in North Carolina, with her dad and newly found brother and sister?

A message from Janet pinged.

Welcome home, Zelda! Mack and Morag are fine so collect them any time you like. Do you know Libby's ETA btw?

She replied:

Sorry no about Libby's ETA. Hoped you did. Will be along for M & M in half an hour.

Later, as Buddy Holly was singing 'Raining in My Heart' she remembered that Libby had gone on holiday with Monty Charles, so would be arriving at the station with him. Rapid change of plan. She wouldn't go and meet her with or without the dogs. Monty wouldn't want to walk. They could get a taxi from the station. She didn't want to meet them in the car. Was that petty? Should she try harder to like him? As she argued with herself the landline phone rang and, seeing from the display that it was Viv, she picked up.

'Zelda, welcome home!' It was great to hear Viv's voice.

They did a bit of catch-up and confirmed that Muscateers was on Friday 5 September at The Olive Branch again, because they wanted to see Nikos. Then, at the same time, they both said, 'Have you heard from Libby?'

Neither of them had. No one had. Viv was apologetic because she and Janet had promised to look out for Libby, but once she'd gone to Greece that had proved impossible. 'I hardly dare say this, Zelda, but we haven't even got an address for her.'

'You let her go away with that man without telling you where she was going?' Zelda couldn't believe it. 'You let her break our golden rule?'

Viv said she and Janet had sent lots of texts and emails asking for the postal address of the Villa Adelos, once they'd realised they hadn't got it – they'd thought it was in the brochure – but had no replies. They'd had nothing from Libby since the first text from the airport saying she'd arrived safely.

'Nikos has emailed her too, with questions about the dinner he's holding in her honour in September, but he hasn't had a reply either. He has started to investigate.'

'Only started!' Zelda was beyond worried. She picked up her car keys. 'I'm coming to Elmsley now, to get the dogs from Janet's. Meet you there?'

Libby had made a deal with Monty. She would go to the lunch party he was so excited about if he would take her to the travel agent's in town. She had checked the night before, in one of the rare moments they had Wi-Fi, that the travel agent's was open on Sunday.

'Rise and shine, darling!' Here he was, by her bed with coffee, looking spruce and clean and smart, wearing one of the blue shirts he favoured and a navy blue and white spotted cravat.

But yesterday was still in Libby's head, all the things that had gone wrong, all the things that didn't work – except when they did work, for Monty. Why was that? She remembered their row, his admission that he was house-sitting and had been lying to her, though he wouldn't call it lying. Monty didn't distinguish between truth and fiction, she now realised, he just said whatever was convenient at the time. He didn't care if one story contradicted another. These thoughts had kept her awake half the night, which was why she'd slept late this morning and had woken up with a headache. The coffee might help. She pulled herself into a sitting position and accepted the cup and a peck of a kiss on her forehead.

'I'm not going to say sorry, darling. You've heard that too many

times before. Deeds not words now. A new man stands before you.'
He straightened up.

Not new, but sober at least. He must have showered already,
from the look of him, but she hadn't heard him. That cravat was
very Noël Coward. She got a whiff of a salty after-shave, quite
refreshing to her pounding head.

'I snuck upstairs to shower so as not to disturb you.'

'Was that wise?'

He shrugged. 'The Kaufmanns left first thing this morning. I
heard them. Must have had an early flight back to the Fatherland.
I'm thinking we could move back upstairs now, perhaps hide our
stuff when that interfering Miss Nose-ring comes. Thursdays, isn't
it? Or even not bother to hide. It was a bloody cheek asking us to
move out, not what usually happens when you house-sit. You live in
the house you're looking after. It's standard practice.'

'You have done it before, then?'

'Yeah, yeah.' He waved dismissively.

'Rokeby Villa, for instance?' Marianna's not knowing where it
was made sense now.

'Yeah, yeah.' He didn't seem to recall that he'd tried to pass it off
as a family property, or didn't care. 'But, darling, shake a leg and get
your glad rags on. We're going out, remember.'

Going out was the last thing she wanted, but she had agreed to
go, thinking she could make it work to her advantage. He had after
all agreed to take her to the travel agent's. She looked at the bedside
clock – half past ten already – and then at the list by her bed,
though she didn't need to as it was in her head.

1. Book a ticket home.
2. Contact her friends, who would be worried stiff when she
   hadn't come home today.

She had a message ready to send to Zelda, who would be home by now.

Sorry not home Sunday. Mix up over dates. Will let you know ETA asap. Please buy food for Cornflake and let Eleanor know.

She'd mentioned Eleanor in case she didn't have time to message her separately. Eleanor might be relying on her to look after Ellie-Jo on Tuesday, when the school term started.

Monty had been very co-operative when she'd said she wanted to go to the travel agent's. That would work well, he'd said. He'd booked a cab to take them to the restaurant, because he'd left the car in town. He said he wasn't going to drink. It was all part of the new reformed Monty, who didn't drive when he was over the limit. The new reformed Monty went outside to water the plants, but popped back to say he'd double-checked the travel agent's. Hellas Travel was definitely open on Sundays.

'Online? You've been online!' He must have been, to check the travel agent's opening times. She grabbed her mobile from where it had been charging by the side of the bed. Yes, her message to Zelda had gone and messages had flooded in. OMG, her friends were going frantic because they hadn't heard from her. They all told her to send them her address. There was one from Nikos wanting her to confirm she'd got Sunday 21 September in her diary. It was for a dinner he was holding in her honour, to celebrate her year of writing Libby's World. He had questions about seating – how did she want the tables arranged? – and about speeches. Sid was going to speak about her. Did she want right of reply? She answered saying she had got the date in her diary – he'd asked her to put it in she remembered but hadn't said why, well not that she could recall – and did want to reply to Sid. But it wouldn't go. Wi-Fi was down again! So-o-o-o frustrating! The sooner she got into town, the better.

She headed for the shower, thinking about what to wear for this lunch. Monty had said 'glad rags'. What did he mean by that? Still in her bathrobe, after her shower, she found him sitting on the terrace outside having a coffee.

'What sort of establishment is it? What's the dress code?'

'Smart,' he said. 'It's a restaurant inside a hotel, so more formal than a beach café, but not The Ritz.'

'And who are we meeting there?'

'A mix of people, the chair of the festival committee and his wife. He's a retired doctor. There's also a vineyard owner and a theatre director – Sophia has a small theatre in Athens – an actor and a musician and another committee member, I think.'

'So what should I wear?'

'Anything goes, darling. Maybe that black and white caftan with red accessories. They look good.'

* * *

They greeted her in a chorus of 'Kalispera' and 'Yassas!'

'Kalispera. Yassas.' Libby returned their friendly greetings, which she knew meant 'Good afternoon' and 'Hello'. Then she sat down at the end of the table on Monty's left, opposite the bald man who she assumed was the chairman. Fortunately, after introductions, everyone then switched to English. Libby listened hard, trying to memorise all the names, but then gave up. Not a chance! She couldn't learn six. Monty seemed to know most of them though, and she, within murmuring distance, hoped he'd keep her in the picture.

On her left was Sophia, the theatre director from Athens, tall, blonde and deeply tanned, a Melina Mercouri lookalike, who could only be described as formidable. Opposite Libby was a dark-haired young man, who might be the actor or the musician, called Dimitris. At the other end of the table was the man she assumed was chair of the festival committee. He was about sixty at a guess and had a similarly aged woman on his right. The other two places on the opposite side of the table were filled by middle-aged women, so in composition it was very like a charity committee back home.

Wine was flowing freely though, not tea or coffee, presided over by the chairman, named Kristos. Someone passed her a bottle of pink fizz, Amalia Brut from the Peloponnese. It had a delicious intense aroma, matched by the taste, very gluggable. She took a photo of the label before making a note for Nikos. She would have to watch herself and go carefully. Monty, she was impressed and very pleased to see, savoured a mouthful when she offered her glass to him, and commented favourably to Kristos, but stuck to his decision not to drink. He would pick up the car later, and drive home, he said, when they'd been to the travel agent's.

'To the festival—' Kristos raised his glass '—and our new director.'

They all raised their glasses and Sophia touched Libby's arm. 'Monty is so proud of you.'

Libby wondered what he'd told them.

'We are so looking forward to your new book. Can't wait to know what it's about.'

'Oh! Thank you.' She was surprised Monty had mentioned her new picture book.

'It will be awesome to launch it at Artemida Fest, when of course all will be revealed. Meanwhile, we'll call you Libby.' Sophia raised her glass with a roguish look in her brown eyes. 'To the mysterious Libby.'

Mysterious? What was she on about? Monty hadn't told her there was going to be a children's section, though most festivals did have one these days. Had he had a change of heart about children's literature? Libby tried to catch his eye and ask for an explanation, but he was talking intently to Dimitris about Stanislavsky and Brecht and his own theory of directing. When that came to an end, he excused himself and went to talk to Kristos and his wife. She watched him doing the rounds of the table then, talking to absolutely everyone, before coming back to sit by her as the food arrived.

'You're good at networking,' she complimented him, 'and obviously have a lot of support.'

She felt better about going home, knowing he'd have so much company.

* * *

The meal was well worth waiting for, an array of the region's best, accompanied by wines chosen by Kristos, or maybe by a vineyard owner, someone had mentioned, who supplied the hotel. But it was nearly two o'clock before they started eating the main, and Libby began to feel anxious about the time. This was looking like one of those meals that could go on all afternoon.

'Darling.' She managed to get Monty's attention when he asked a waiter for water.

'It's all right.' He knew what was on her mind. He tapped his wrist where a watch would once have been. 'I'm keeping an eye on the time.'

And he was! At three o'clock sharp he stood up. 'Sorry, folks, we're going to have to forgo dessert. Libby has to fly, literally!'

She got to her feet. 'Shouldn't we—?' She was going to say *offer to pay our share*, but Monty had her by the hand.

'You've got to fly, darling! You need that ticket. I'll settle up later.'

It took them ten minutes to walk to Hellas Travel at the other end of the town. Even before they reached it Libby saw the blue shutters were down. Closer too they both saw the board outside saying that Sunday opening hours were from 10.00–15.00. Monty was distraught. 'I'm so-o-o-o sorry, darling!' He all but banged his head against the glass of the closed door. It was his fault. He should have checked. He gave every appearance of being desperately sorry. Every *appearance*. He might even have believed in his own misery. 'I'll make this up to you, darling, I really will.'

But it was her fault. *She* should have checked.

48

LIBBY

Monty drove her into Artemida next morning, gripping the steering wheel with steely determination. He'd been up early, he said, hadn't really slept, he was so wracked with guilt, so focussed on waking up to take her to the travel agent's first thing. She, awake beside him, had thought he'd slept very well. Now he had the radio on, a foreign music station, Greek, she presumed, and was concentrating on the traffic, which was slow, busy with people trying to get to their jobs. The business life of the town was waking up, with men and women opening shopfronts and sweeping terraces or hosing them down, sometimes stepping into the street, causing more delays.

'I'll drop you off by the travel agent's and go and park, okay? You'll be the first, I bet.' He pulled up in front of the blue and white façade of Hellas Travel, the shutters up now, she was relieved to see, and the door open.

'Thanks, I'll see you inside as soon as you can,' she said, trying to get out of their little car with dignity, aware of cars behind with horns blowing.

'Kalimera,' the young male assistant greeted her from behind the counter. 'You're bright and early for a Monday morning, madam.'

'Kalimera,' she replied, relieved to hear that his English was excellent, as this transaction would be a bit complicated. 'I'm in a hurry, that's why I'm early. I would like to get home today if I can. I need a flight from Athens to London Luton, leaving as soon as possible, please.' She hoped Monty would arrive before she was asked to pay, so he could show the man they'd already paid and had an open-ended booking. 'With EasyJet,' she added. 'We came by EasyJet, an open-ended booking.'

The young man brought the timetables up on a screen and scrolled down. 'Nothing today, I'm afraid... or tomorrow.' He frowned. 'Sorry, nothing Wednesday... or Thursday. The earliest I can offer you is Friday, midday.'

'Friday!' That was four days away. Much too late to look after Ellie-Jo on Tuesday, or go to the Muscateers lunch on Friday. 'Aren't there any cancellations?'

'That is a cancellation, madam. Airlines are very busy at this time of year. Did you say you had an open-ended return?'

'It's in my partner's name. Charles. Monty Charles.'

He keyed the name in. 'Nothing here.'

'It could be Charles Montgomery.'

He keyed that in. 'Sorry, not in that name either.'

She wondered about asking about flights to Gatwick or Heathrow, but that would mean using a different airline and she really didn't want to pay for a new ticket. At short notice that would be horrendously expensive.

'I don't want to rush you, madam—' the young man's fingers hovered over the keyboard '—but tickets do go very quickly. Do you want the Friday ticket?'

'Okay, yes, thanks, I'll take it.' She was flustered now. Where was Monty? She turned to look at the glass door, hoping to see him approaching, and the young man said something she didn't catch. 'Sorry,' she apologised. 'I'm waiting for someone to join me.'

'You did just want the one ticket, madam?' He looked concerned.

'Yes, yes, please go ahead. I want that one.'

'Are you paying by card, madam?'

'Yes and no. Can you hold on a minute, please? It's paid for actually. The person I'm waiting for, he'll explain when he comes.'

'Would you like a coffee while you're waiting?' He was a very obliging young man. She saw from his lanyard that his name was Marcos.

'No, no, thanks, Marcos. He shouldn't be that long. I'll message him.'

Where are you? I'm waiting.

She hoped that wasn't too terse but there wasn't time for fine-tuning. He replied instantly:

In Yiasemis, café round corner, waiting for you.

Not good. He knew she needed him for the booking.

'Sorry, there's been a mix-up.' She explained a bit. 'All the info's on his phone.'

'No worries,' said Marcos, but he looked worried. He would hold the ticket for as long as he could, and Yiasemis was only round the corner, almost next door.

As she left another customer came in.

* * *

Monty was with Dimitris, the young man at the lunch yesterday. They were sitting at a pavement table drinking coffee, looking at something spread out on the table in front of them.

'Come and look at Dimitris' designs for wine labels, darling.' Monty got up and pulled out a chair for her.

'Later, Monty.' She didn't sit down. 'Sorry, Dimitris, but I've got to go back to the travel agency, pronto. They're holding a ticket for me and I need Monty.'

'What do you need me for, darling?'

What was he playing at?

'To show them the return booking to prove that we've paid.'

'Return booking?' He ran his fingers through his white hair.

'Yes, is it digital or did you print it out? If you've got the paper copy I suppose I could just take it back, but if it's on your phone you'll have to come with me.'

He looked perplexed. 'Sorry, darling, but I'm not following. I didn't book a return. Not sure where you got that idea from. No point in spending money – *your* money, as you kindly offered to pay for travel – till we had to.'

'But...' She didn't know what to say. She couldn't think straight. She couldn't think at all. Her head was full of tangled wool.

'I'm afraid you've got the wrong end of the stick again, old girl.' Monty turned to Dimitris. 'She's doing that a lot these days.'

Am I? Is this all my fault? Am I losing it?

She sat down now because she had to, weak at the knees. She thought of her mother in the care home, another reason she ought to be hurrying back. How old was her mum when she started to become forgetful and confused? In her sixties.

* * *

Monty came back to Hellas Travel with her, for moral support, he said. They hurried but by the time they got there, the ticket for the Friday flight had gone. The earliest Marcos could get her on a flight was Tuesday next, a whole week away. She took it, putting the eye-watering cost on her credit card. On the way home Monty said he was sorry he couldn't help with costs as he'd already nearly maxed out his credit card buying wine. He was waiting for the festival committee to draw up his contract and pay him an advance. Long term his prospects were good, with that and the wine business, but cash flow was still a problem.

She half listened because his words were like a record she'd heard many times before and she was trying to gather her own thoughts. She'd been compos mentis enough in the travel agency to use their Wi-Fi to send all her waiting messages and a new one to Zelda.

Coming home September 9.

She gave flight details and apologised for missing the Musca-teers. She added:

Longing to see you all. Need to talk. Bit worried I'm losing it.

She really was, more than a bit in fact, though pleased she'd managed to send her message.

When they got back to the house, Monty said, 'Cheer up, darling. Another week by the pool isn't the worst thing to happen, is it? Let's think positively about it.'

49

LIBBY

Libby was trying to be positive – and realistic.

Lazing by the pool under a sunny sky, having an occasional swim to cool down, wasn't the worst of fates, but it didn't have the appeal it had when she'd arrived. Now every cell in her body yearned to go home and the yearning made her restless, unable to settle at anything, and she saw Monty differently. When they'd got back from the travel agent's he had sent her down to the pool, saying he'd join her later. Now on a sunbed beside her, drink in one hand, book in the other, he was sure he knew what her problem was. 'You're bored, darling.'

No, I just want to get home.

'It's because you're a writer. Writers get twitchy when they're not writing.'

'But I can't concentrate on writing either.' She'd just given up on the column she'd begun. Sid would have to use another of her reserves.

'Perhaps you need a meaty new project to spark your interest.' He went back to his book without expanding, but she guessed the way his thoughts were tending.

'Is it good?' She nodded at the book, an autobiography of a famous theatre director, to divert him.

'Very.' He turned a page and didn't look up.

On the way back to the villa he'd promised to spend more time with her this week. He could, he said, because he was waiting for other people to do their bit before he could launch his new business. He'd said he was determined to make up for his neglect of her, and he seemed to be trying – he'd made lunch and brought it to the poolside – but the new enlightened Libby suspected his motives. She wasn't bored, she was worried about her mum and the Ellie-Jo and Eleanor situation. She didn't need 'a meaty new project', she needed to go home. At least she had a ticket now, a print version as well as the one on her phone. Belt and braces. And she'd booked a taxi to take her to the airport. Well, Monty had booked it, when she'd turned down his offer to take her, but he'd forwarded the booking to her phone when she insisted. It was for 6 a.m. as her flight was at 9.40 a.m. Monty wasn't reliable. She didn't trust him to get her there. That was why she'd insisted on a taxi. She'd also messaged Zelda, giving her ETA, while she was at the travel agent's. She thought Zelda would offer to meet her from the station, if not the airport, but hadn't had a reply yet. She checked again. Still nothing, so the Wi-Fi must be down.

Monty looked up from his book. 'I've just remembered the very first time I saw you, at auditions for The Central.'

'Really?' She was surprised, though she remembered the first time she saw him. 'I'm sure you hardly noticed me all the time I was there.'

'How could I miss the only girl not wearing a miniskirt?' He laughed.

'Only tarts wore miniskirts, according to my mother. On the knee was as high as she'd let my hems go. My mum made most of my clothes.'

'*Everyone* wore the mini then, well, all the girls. Mary Quant was all the go.'

She did remember feeling old-fashioned and dowdy at the audition, completely out of place. She hadn't fitted in, and had been sure she wouldn't get in. When she'd passed it had been a complete surprise. She'd turned up a few of her hems before she'd started the following October, but when she'd got to her digs, a couple of other girls had taken charge of her wardrobe. They'd made her stand on a table while they'd sliced even more inches off her skirts.

'Libby Allgood.' Monty was still reminiscing or re-imagining. 'I couldn't believe it when I heard your name. What do they call that – nominative determinism?'

'I wasn't such a goody-goody as you seemed to think.' *Wouldn't have got pregnant if I had been.*

'Just me you spurned, then?'

'You didn't ask.' *Except for that invitation to go back to your place.*

'I admired you from afar.' He raised his glass to her.

She laughed.

'I did! Your audition piece was amazing. I can see you now as mad Queen Margaret in Richard III "I am hungry for revenge!"' His deep voice vibrated as he imitated her, with a hint of falsetto. 'Talk about hidden depths. You were terrifying as the old widow queen.'

'Better watch out, then.'

'I do, all the time.' He went back to his book but soon put it down. 'Do you remember the first time you saw me?'

'Yes.'

'Good, because I've just thought of something we could do to pass the time. Let's both write down our earliest memories of each other. Then compare and contrast. That'd be interesting.' He got up. 'I'm going to get another drink. Want one?'

He thinks I don't know what he's doing.

So it was annoying to find herself going along with him when

he came back with their laptops as well as the drinks. She had
one persistent memory of Monty walking away from her down a
long corridor past lots of brown doors, disappearing into the
distance. Head forward, shoulders slightly bowed, he was a man
in a hurry, ambitious, focussed. They'd just had a tutorial
together and she'd wanted to ask him something about Robert
Browning's dramatic monologues. She'd tried to ask in the tutorial but hadn't got a chance, as he and the other male in the
group of five or six students had tended to dominate the discus-
sion. She'd actually plucked up the courage to say, 'There's something I'd like to discuss,' as they'd walked out of the door, but he
hadn't heard, or if he had he'd pretended not to, keen to get
away.

Soon they were both tapping away. Monty's white hair flopped
forward as he typed.

But he was still twenty-five in her mind's eye, breathtakingly
good-looking with his black wavy hair and blue eyes, a six-footer, so
even with that forward thrust of his head he was taller than most.
Ignoring her was a recurring image, she realised. There he was
again, not-seeing her at the union bar, and there were other times,
humiliating to think of now. Not that she'd thrown herself at him.
She certainly hadn't invited him on a date, as girls did now. She'd
just made herself look attractive hoping he'd notice her, but he
hadn't. She was pretty sure of that.

'I knew you fancied me.' He smirked as he read her version.

'How? How did you know?' It was embarrassing even in retro-
spect to think she'd been obvious.

'The pheromones must have drifted over with the adoring looks
you gave me. And I did notice you once in a leotard in a movement
class. I thought you had a good figure, but you didn't stand a
chance, darling. Not then. I wanted lots of sex without strings like
most young men, and you were clearly the sort who wouldn't open

your legs till you had a ring on your finger. It was obvious you were only there to get a husband and babies.'

'Not true! You were *so* wrong. I was very ambitious. I had my career mapped out, a couple of years in rep after drama school, then the RSC, then—'

'Well, that's the impression you gave. Respectability was written all over you. You wore baggy frocks. Matronly, that's the word. It was an odd mix, matronly yet ditzy.'

'Ditzy? I wasn't ditzy.'

'You were, darling.'

She let that go because another memory was surfacing, of walking past an expensive restaurant at night, and seeing him inside with some of the other wealthy students. A meal there would have cost what she'd had to spend on food for a month. She'd been heading back to her digs for beans on toast.

'Let's carry on writing. I think I can get a column from it.' First impressions would be a good subject.

* * *

'Good, darling.' Monty spoke with his mouth full over supper on the barbecue terrace. He'd been reading from her laptop, which was beside him.

'My writing or the kebabs?'

'The writing. The lamb's a bit chewy. I can see the scenes vividly, but you're not a columnist, darling. You're too well balanced, too reasonable. The best columnists are biased, bigoted even.' He waved his fork at her. 'You know what you *are* though...'

She dipped a piece of pitta in olive oil.

'You, my darling, are a novelist.' He reached for her hand.

'And you, Monty, are a fantasist.' She put her hands in her lap. 'I wouldn't know where to begin.'

'But you have begun. Here it is.' He nodded at her laptop. 'Can't you see? That description of me walking away from you, down the long corridor with all the closed doors, closed to your charms, closed to you because of my closed mind. It's the beginning of a novel, a great love story. Ignorant, callous, callow youth, an upper-class snob, meets a beautiful, talented, sensitive, working-class girl but is blind to her charms. *We* were those two people meeting in the wrong place at the wrong time.' He stood up and came round to stand behind her. 'But then we found each other.' He lifted her hair and kissed the nape of her neck. 'You've begun our novel, darling, and you are going to finish it.'

50

ZELDA

Zelda had been in her little office under the stairs on Monday morning when Libby's messages had come in. Phew! At last! She'd had a sleepless night, partly jet lag, partly worry. Yesterday had been horribly worrying. She'd gone round to the neighbour who had been looking after Libby's cat, to see if she had heard from Libby. The neighbour hadn't and she'd used the last packet of cat food. She was worried too because Libby had said she would be home on Sunday morning. It was very un-Libby not to keep her word.

Coming home September 9.

Zelda checked the message again, against the wall calendar in her kitchen. Libby gave flight details and apologised for missing Muscateers on Friday.

Longing to see you all. Need to talk. Bit worried I'm losing it.

Was that a light-hearted remark, like they all made these days, or did she mean it? Libby worried more than most because of her mum's dementia. There was another message obviously written earlier.

> Sorry not home Sunday. Mix up over dates. Will let you know ETA asap. Please buy food for Cornflake and let Eleanor know.

Zelda remembered the tricky Eleanor situation and had rung Viv to see if she had contact details for Libby's daughter – and to update her. Viv had had a message from Libby obviously meant to arrive earlier. She'd read it out. "'Home Sunday. Alone. Will let you know ETA asap but will get train from Luton then taxi home. Looking forward to seeing you all!'" They both thought 'Alone' was a positive but spending another week with Monty Charles a negative. As was the fact that Libby still hadn't given them the address of the Villa Adelos. Zelda's anti-Monty feelings were growing stronger by the minute. She didn't trust the man. Viv had said that Nikos was mobilising his family in Greece to track the house down.

Zelda picked up the landline. It was coming up to midday, but she hoped Nikos wasn't too busy to answer the phone.

* * *

'First Friday, it's in the diary!' Nikos assumed she was ringing to confirm the Muscateers' booking. 'For four, yes?'

'Sorry, Nikos, only three. Libby won't be home. That's what I'm ringing about.'

'Not home?' He sounded alarmed. 'But she was due home yesterday. A red-letter day in my diary.' He had been trying to get in touch with her for over a week now, he said. So had Sid. Neither of them had had a reply. What the hell was going on?

Zelda mentioned the appalling Internet connection and the Wi-Fi always being down.

'What do you mean?' He sounded offended. 'Wi-Fi is very good in Greece, a bit slower than here, but very good. It's not some backward country. Most hotels have it and private houses can get it. Private tends to be better than public, in fact, but you can always find a café or shop if the accommodation you're in doesn't have it.'

'You're saying it's reliable?' Zelda wondered why Libby hadn't availed herself of some of these services.

'Very reliable. It varies of course, some providers' coverage is better than others, like here. In the islands it can be a bit intermittent, but it should be okay in Artemida, which is near Athens.' He got a bit technical then, but she got the gist. 'If the villa Liberty is in has Wi-Fi she should have been able to keep in touch. Has the villa got it?'

'Yes, the brochure says it has. But hardly any of the messages she's written went when she wanted them to go. I got a bunch of them this morning.'

'Perhaps she should check it's plugged in?'

Nikos sounded as if he suspected dark forces, and Zelda remembered her main reason for ringing. 'Nikos, did you have any luck tracking down the address of Villa Adelos?'

'Some, we've narrowed it down to three possibles, and family are working on it. I'll chase them now and get back to you.'

'Thank you, Nikos, see you Friday. Meanwhile, give my regards to...' oh no, a senior moment, or jet lag or stress, made Nikos's wife's name evaporate as names too often did these days '...to, to your wife,' she finished feebly.

Silence. She thought for a moment he'd put down the phone. Then he said, 'Come again? What did you just say?'

'Give my regards to...' Phew! The name was back. 'Evelina!'

Another silence, then, 'Zelda, I need to be clear. Did you just say "give my regards to *your wife*"?'

'Yes, sorry, senior moment, Evelina's name escaped me for the moment.'

There was a sound then, like a laugh, but not a laugh. 'Zelda, Evelina is my sister.'

Your sister?

'Zelda, I am not married. I have not been married for some years, not since my wife left me to go back to Greece. Tell me, is it just you that is under this impression, or do your friends all think, does Liberty think, that I'm married to Evelina?'

'All of us, I think.' She wasn't 100 per cent sure.

'Then please tell them, tell Viv and Janet *and Liberty*, that Evelina is my sister, my older sister, and I am not married to her whatever the Greek gods did.' Now Nikos put the phone down.

Zelda sat for some time looking at the receiver still in her hand. 'Wowee! What do you think of that, Morag?' She would have sat longer processing this new nugget of information if both dogs hadn't reminded her it was their lunchtime. She filled their dishes, then rang Viv.

'Viv, Nikos isn't married. He's single!'

51

LIBBY

This time next week I'll be home.

Libby was counting the days, but also making the best of her extended holiday. Writing helped. As one memory triggered another, she began to wonder if Monty was right. Perhaps she had got the beginning of a novel or an autobiography. Her short life as a drama student was particularly vivid. She felt her confidence draining away as audition after audition led to minor roles. When she'd tried for the lead in *Mother Courage* she'd been given Third Soldier with a single line that she'd never forgotten. 'I am a soldier. My job is to kill and be killed.' Being given a male part seemed to confirm how unattractive she was. Gender-free casting wasn't fashionable like now.

When she got Third Fly in Sartre's *The Flies* she began to think she wasn't cut out to be an actress – or a woman. The only female part she got was as a nun, a non-speaking role. No amount of telling herself there were no small parts, only small actors, raised her spirits. No wonder Charles Montgomery didn't look her way. He *didn't* look her way. He was looking at sexy rich girls with sharp Vidal

Sassoon haircuts and Mary Quant dresses, the genuine article, not the Top Shop replicas.

Luckily, when she wrote about her failures and faux pas they came out as funny, like the time she got sick-drunk at a party. It was a Christmas party, *the* Christmas party at the end of the first term; she wasn't there for the next Christmas party. This one was held at a member of staff's rather grand mews house, where she'd hoped to make a good impression. But the food was a long time coming and, to calm her nerves, she'd knocked back several glasses of mulled red wine before it did, so when the two met... Her description of herself reaching the top of the stairs and seeing the loo door open in front of her, but failing to get there before a fountain of vomit spewed from her mouth and landed on the floor, made her laugh. As it had the crowd on the landing who'd slow-clapped in unison as she'd sunk to her knees in front of the bowl.

Monty was pleased that she was writing, but not so pleased when it kept him awake at night. 'Bloody hell,' he groaned on Monday night, pulling the covers over his head to cut out the light and the sound of her tapping on her laptop. Next morning he said they were moving back upstairs. He'd spoken to Helena on the phone and she'd agreed, impressed by his new status as festival director, and by Libby's as a writer, whose new book was going to be launched at the festival.

Libby, ever-vigilant now for when the Wi-Fi was up – when Monty was making calls – quickly sent off messages to her friends and Eleanor reminding them of her return on Tuesday 9th. She got one straight back from Zelda saying she would meet her at Luton airport, also asking for the full address of the Villa Adelos.

'Haven't got a clue, darling,' Monty said when she asked.

'What do you tell cab drivers?'

He used cabs quite a lot.

'Villa Adelos. They all know it.'

The new sleeping arrangement suited Libby, whose brain was in overdrive. Her bedroom was just as luxurious as the one they'd shared. She could work whenever she wanted, day or night, spreading her notes all over the double bed. It suited Monty too. She heard him on the phone, on Wednesday morning, telling someone she was writing a novel inspired by an idea he gave her. He had given her the outline of the plot he'd scribbled on a sheet of A4, based on *Casablanca*. He was deluded. All she had to do, he said, was substitute Monty and Libby for Rick and Ilsa, changing their names, of course. He rather fancied being Tarquin or maybe Lance. Could she call herself Elsa? She'd have to change the time too, of course, from the 1940s to the 1960s when they first meet, and then again to the 2000s when they meet each other again. He suggested that Libby/Elsa is trapped in a loveless marriage to an insensitive bore, so repressed she is on the brink of a nervous breakdown. Then – ta da! – along comes Lance, the love of her life, and liberates her. It was a travesty of the truth, but it made her laugh – so she hoped it would make readers laugh too. Luckily Monty was so busy with his own projects that he didn't ask to see her writing, which was proving revelatory.

Now she saw why she'd fallen into Jim's arms when she'd gone home that December, and, yes, got pregnant. Jim had been pleased to see her. He'd loved her. He'd thought she was the sexiest woman he'd ever met and the cleverest. It had been as simple as that. He hadn't been a word person, but he'd had no trouble telling her how much he'd loved and admired her. They'd been friends for a year before she went away. He'd been an apprentice with a local engineering firm and her brother's best mate. She had been in the sixth form of the girls' grammar school and had felt very grown-up having a boyfriend who wasn't at school. They hadn't gone to bed together, not because they hadn't fancied each other – they had – but because the opportunity hadn't been there. There had been no question of going upstairs to each other's rooms, never mind staying the night. Parents hadn't allowed it and had rarely left them alone together to try and ensure the not-before-you're-married rule was adhered to.

She might even have believed in it herself. If not, why hadn't she invited Jim to London where there would have been plenty of opportunity? Had she been scared 'it' would have happened? How embarrassing to recall the coy language of the day! Her landlady had had rules about male visitors in digs after dark – how odd the rules had been! – but there had been a friend with a flat who had rented out her double bed for a bottle of wine or a spliff.

But she hadn't invited Jim for any sort of visit. They'd phoned each other from time to time, from the red public phone boxes where it had been hard to synchronise calls. She hadn't gone home during the term, partly due to shortage of cash, mostly because she'd been scared that if she'd gone home she wouldn't have come back. She'd felt completely out of her depth but had still been determined to make a go of it. Had she also been scared Jim wouldn't have fitted in with the drama school set if he'd visited? They wouldn't have fazed him. Even then Jim had been at ease with all sorts of people. At ease in his own skin, that was the phrase people had used about him.

But Jim hadn't been at ease the first time they'd met when she'd got home, after twelve weeks apart. He'd seemed shy, and had said afterwards it had been because he'd fancied her like hell and had been worried she would have gone off him, that she'd have fallen for some posh drama student. She couldn't remember how she'd replied to that, but when he'd invited her to the Christmas dinner-dance at Christies, the firm he and her brother had worked for, she'd accepted. It had been afterwards that 'it' had happened.

'Yours or mine?' he'd asked as they'd kissed under the street lamp's yellow light.

They had just been dropped off by the work's bus, which had picked them up to take them there. It had been shortly after midnight. Jim had been almost the-boy-next-door. He'd lived a few doors away. Neither of them had wanted the night to end. The feeling had been building up all evening, especially during the more old-fashioned dances like waltzes and quicksteps when their hands and bodies had touched. She'd loved being close to him, loved being held by him. She'd sensed his desire, and had felt sexy and safe with him, had known 'heavy-petting' would be as far as it went because they'd agreed on that, though the boundaries had tended to shift depending on where they had been.

'I think my mum and dad will still be up,' she'd said, knowing they would be awake even if they'd gone to bed. Her dad would be banging on the ceiling before Jim had unzipped her mini dress, a daring purchase bought with the money she'd been earning delivering the Christmas mail. It had been black with one white stripe, Mary Quant-ish.

'Mine are away, visiting my gran.' He'd held up the door key and they'd nearly run to his front door.

* * *

'How's it going?'

It took Libby a second or two to realise Monty was standing in the bedroom doorway. Tears were running down her face, tears of joy, as she recalled that first time in Jim's bed, lying exhausted and breathless and happy and amazed, because of course it hadn't stopped when the dress had come off, then her bra and pants, bikini-style, turquoise with white piping from Dorothy Perkins. Silky, they'd slipped off easily...

'Are you okay?' Monty sounded concerned.

She nodded, wiping her eyes.

It had been good, not the debacle you heard so many first times were, though some would say the outcome was. Had she believed that nonsense about not being able to get pregnant the first time? If she had she'd soon learned how wrong she had been. The shocking truth had quickly become clear. All the usual clues. She'd done another term at The Central and left at Easter, to be a wife and mother. Jim, as shocked as she had been at first, had stood by her as she had by him. They'd decided to do their best for the coming baby. They would have got married and had kids eventually – things had just been happening a bit sooner than expected, that was all, in a different order. That was Jim's view anyway. There had been no one else for him. They had been meant for each other. He had been sorry though, for ending her glittering career, and had never stopped trying to make it up to her. They'd got married and it had worked – they'd made it work – with all the ups and downs and plateaus of most marriages...

Monty was still there, looking at his watch.

'What's the time?' Tears were flowing again, sad tears now – for Jim and for how much she missed him.

'Wine o'clock. Eat o'clock. What are we eating?'

She had no idea.

'Eat out, then?' He had lots to tell her, he said. It was such a pity she was going home to all those family demands on Tuesday. Did she really have to? Tuesday was going to be a very exciting day and if she stayed a bit longer she would finish the novel.

52

LIBBY

They ate at Zeus's Taverna on the beach.

They had eaten there once before, and Monty probably more often, it occurred to Libby. The proprietor greeted him like an old friend, throwing his arms round his shoulders. The pink fizz, the *afrothi* – she loved the word – appeared almost instantly and wine talk began. It was yet another wine made from the amazingly versatile Agiorgitiko grape, she learned, and she made a few notes to share with Nikos when she got back as the two men talked. The midday sun was high in the sky burnishing the sea, but thankfully they had seats in the shade, under a blue and white striped umbrella. Monty waited till the man had taken their orders to the kitchen before, at last, sharing his exciting news. 'We're getting our first delivery on Thursday!'

What was he talking about? Libby was still with Jim.

'Keep up, darling.' Monty looked disappointed and she had to excuse herself. 'Sorry, but I've been in the nineteen sixties all day.'

'Delivery of *wine*, of course! A big delivery!'

She tried to concentrate as he explained that he was getting the first delivery of the wine he'd been so busy negotiating for, buying wholesale, to retail under his own label. 'Remember the labels I showed you in the café, for Lord Monty's Cellar?' He got one out of his wallet. It was stylish in black and white, a caricature of a butler, like Jeeves, very P. G. Wodehouse. Things had obviously progressed more quickly than she'd anticipated, because, she remembered with a twinge of guilt, she hadn't had much faith in Monty's business abilities.

'So, how is this wine going to be delivered?' She envisaged a tank, as he had talked about a bottling plant in one of the outhouses.

'No. *No.*' He shook his head, dismissively, when she mentioned it.

He wasn't going to bottle it himself. On advice he'd abandoned that plan. The bottling machinery was obsolete, hadn't been used for years. The wine would come ready-bottled and all he needed to do was put his own label on them. Dimitris, who'd designed the label, said the labelling machine was functioning and he was going to help with that. The young actor-musician was obviously a man of many talents. Libby was glad Monty had help and relieved that he wasn't going in for bottling it himself. She couldn't see him operating machinery to fill bottles, sterilising them beforehand.

'What did you decide, by the way, corks or screw-tops?' She tried to show interest.

'Corks.' He preferred traditional, he said, and was going for the top end of the market.

Libby raised her glass of the delicious pink *afrothi*. 'Here's to Lord Monty's Cellar. Good luck, Monty, I wish you well.' She really did. She wanted him to do well. Without her.

There was more wine talk over their main course, which suited her fine. Remembering Jim and how much she'd loved him had stirred up feelings she'd explore later.

'So what sort of wine will be in the bottles?' She kept the questions coming.

'What do you think of this?' He held up a glass of the red they'd moved onto with their lamb kleftiko.

'Delicious.' She sniffed the bouquet. 'Do I detect raspberries and blackcurrants?'

It was another from the Agiorgitiko grape, he said, a Gran Reserva, from a single vineyard in the Nemea region, very much like the one being delivered on Tuesday. She'd had it, she thought, at The Olive Branch.

'And is there going to be a white?'

'There will be,' he said, but he had still to decide between the Moschofilero and the Malagousia. They were both good, but he was negotiating with two different vineyards and would go with the one who would give him the best deal.

She made approving noises.

The red would be delivered in boxes of twelve, the same as when they ordered from a supermarket. The first delivery on Tuesday would be of four hundred boxes. They'd be delivered straight to the shed with the labelling plant in it, and then stored to await distribution.

'And who's going to unload it from the van?' She couldn't imagine what four hundred boxes would look like, or how long it would take to unload them. 'Will you need to employ people to help?'

He said Dimitris and the van driver could do it between them. She must understand that this wasn't an industrial enterprise. They were going for a home-produced vibe. It was like selling from the farm shop door, though more upmarket than that, not so much farm as castle door. The winery originally at Villa Adelos had been small, serving the local community, with wines made from the vines growing round the house.

'And how are you paying Dimitris?' She wondered if he'd solved his cash-flow problem.

'He's taking a share of the profits.'

She raised her glass. 'Here's to profits. I can't wait to tell Nikos about your venture, by the way. He'll be very interested. He may well buy from you, and if you need any help with the legal side, Customs and Excise, import duties, that sort of thing...' She was going to tell him about Nikos's previous legal career, but tailed off, as Monty was frowning.

'That won't be necessary. In fact I'd rather you didn't mention it to him, just yet. He might tell our competitors. Selling direct to customers is our USP,' Unique Selling Point, he explained, 'bypassing all that customs and excise sort of bureaucracy. Hope that's clear?' He gave her what she could only call a hard stare, as if he was daring her to defy him.

She said, 'Yes, it's clear,' because it was clear he didn't want her to tell Nikos, but not much else was. Her head was full of questions she didn't feel she could ask, and conversation came to a halt.

* * *

Next morning Monty went off after breakfast, not saying where. Andrea arrived soon afterwards. Libby was by the pool with her laptop and saw her drive in. She was surprised as she'd completely forgotten it was cleaning day. But yes, it was last Thursday when the girl had dumped the window-cleaning equipment on the basement terrace, where it still was, though shifted to the side by Libby for safety reasons. Monty hadn't touched it. Andrea disappeared into the house, but soon came out again and Libby saw her striding to the poolside with something in her hand.

There was something in her gait that made Libby anticipate

disapproval, but Andrea's hello was not unfriendly. 'Leebee? Yes? Leebee All Good?'

'Yes.'

It seemed an odd opener for a young person who had been told her name only last week. It was the old who had a problem remembering names. Libby was pleased she'd remembered Andrea's name.

'Meester Mont-gom-er-y not here?' Andrea looked around.

'No.' Libby felt she was being interrogated, though not in a hostile manner.

'He not do jobs?' The something in her hand was the list of house-sitter's duties.

Libby replied that he was doing some. It would have been truer to say *she* was doing some. She had been emptying the toilet bins regularly and changing the litter in the cats' tray.

Andrea looked pointedly at the pool littered with leaves and other debris, which Libby had been planning to rake off later. The turtle was crawling along the bottom hoovering up stuff from the base and the water in the swimming pool looked clean enough, not green anyway. Monty, she thought, was testing it from time to time and adding chemicals. Andrea shook her head, clearly not impressed. 'Come.'

Libby followed her inside, upstairs, where she went straight to the kitchen. 'You use?'

'Yes,' said Libby, 'Helena said...'

But Andrea was now on her way to the stairs and the bedrooms.

'You sleep?' She pointed to the room where Libby was clearly doing more than sleep. Her laptop was on her bed.

'And—' she proceeded to Monty's room '—Mr Mont-gom-er-y he sleep?'

'Yes.' That was obvious too, with male clothes all over the place.

Andrea shook her head slowly from side to side, lips pursed, black eyebrows raised. She didn't think they should be there, it was obvious.

Libby attempted to explain. 'Helena say okay. Monty phoned her.' She acted out Monty talking on the phone to Helena. 'Helena says okay,' she summed up as clearly as she could. 'You don't have to clean for us,' she said, thinking the girl might be cross about the extra cleaning. Andrea shrugged a slow exaggerated shrug that Libby interpreted as 'It doesn't make any difference to me' but she didn't stay to clean.

Libby got on with her writing, pleased to have something absorbing to do to fill the next few days. Thursday, Friday and Saturday passed relatively quickly, but on Sunday the urge to go home was overwhelming. In the afternoon, when Monty said he'd do a barbecue for their evening meal, she went up to her room to start packing her bags and check again she had her ticket and everything she needed to leave first thing Tuesday.

That was when she couldn't find her passport.

53

LIBBY

'I can't find my passport!'

Her cry brought Monty up from the kitchen, where he'd started prepping the barbecue.

'Where did you last have it?'

Was that the most annoying question ever?

'Here. Here in this drawer.' She pointed to the top drawer in her dressing table. 'I put it there with the ticket and other travel documents, insurance, things like that when we came back from the travel agent's. It was here this morning, I'm sure it was.' But she wasn't of course, well, not 100 per cent sure it was this morning when she'd last looked. It might have been yesterday or the day before.

'Wouldn't you have put it in the safe with your valuables?' Monty took a step towards the wardrobe where the safe was hidden.

'No, I haven't used the safe. I haven't got valuables. I wear the only bits of jewellery that are worth anything.' She felt for the gold chain round her neck and the wedding and engagement rings on her finger, switched to the right hand only recently. She hadn't brought her pearls with her.

Monty didn't tut but she sensed a tut, could hear 'ditzy' on his lips.

'I know where you had it last.' He looked thoughtful and calculating, confident that male logic would solve this problem. 'It was at the travel agent's. Could you have left it there?'

'Hellas Travel? No, I'm sure I didn't. I've seen it since. And if I had they'd have got in touch, surely?' She remembered that helpful young man, Marcos.

'How could they, darling?' Monty looked doubtful. 'Did you give them this address at any point?'

Had she? He'd sown doubt in her mind. Had she left it there? Her home address wasn't in her passport, she knew that. Had she given the Villa Adelos's address to the young man at any point? When she paid that astronomical sum for the new ticket home by credit card? No, because she didn't know it. But, anxious now, she checked her wallet to see she'd got her credit card. She tipped everything out of her shoulder bag onto the bed, hoping against hope that her passport would materialise. It didn't, but she found the agent's card and reached for her phone. It was worth a try, but even as she keyed in the number she knew she'd get a recorded message. The time was at the top of the screen: 18.05. They were closed.

'My darling Libby.' Monty didn't say *my darling ditzy Libby* but that was what she heard. 'Try not to worry. We'll go to the travel agent's first thing tomorrow morning and I'm sure it will be there.'

* * *

It wasn't at the travel agent's on Monday morning.

Marcos said he had asked Libby for the expiry date of her passport when she bought the ticket, as that was required by EasyJet, though not by all airlines. He was certain she had got it out of her bag to show him, but he'd only looked at it. He felt sure she had put it back in her bag afterwards.

Monty said, 'What if Ms Allgood dropped it? She was rather flustered because of the misunderstanding.'

'Then someone, most likely me,' said Marcos, 'would have seen it and picked it up. And I didn't.'

'Could a customer have seen it before you had a chance to pick it up?'

'You mean did someone steal it?' Marcos agreed it was an outside chance but thought it very unlikely. But, he said, if they thought it had been stolen, or even lost, they should report it to the police. He gave them directions to the police station, but, when they got outside, Monty said he thought they should search the car again first. So they went back to the car park, and, failing to find the passport in the car, he got in the driving seat saying he thought they should search the villa again.

As Libby searched all the places she'd searched before and some where she hadn't, she started to see the plane flying off without her the next morning. She googled 'What if I've lost my passport in Greece?' Google advised her to contact the police straight away as she would need a police report to get emergency documents to get home. When she'd got the police report she could contact the British Embassy in Athens. How long was this going to take? More googling told her it would take at least two days, probably longer, for emergency travel documents and would cost £100.

It was early afternoon when they got to the police station.

No one had handed her passport in. A policewoman took down all the details Libby gave, but suggested they go back to the villa and search it again along with the grounds, where it might have been dropped. Monty said, 'Are you telling us we haven't looked properly?' and Libby, seeing the policewoman start at his hoity-toity tone, intervened. She said they hadn't searched the grounds yet but she was almost certain she hadn't dropped it outside. The police-woman told them to be sure to be back by six as the desk closed then, unless they'd found it, of course. She wished them luck.

On the drive back to the villa Monty picked up on the 'stolen' theme he'd raised at the travel agent's. He wondered if the passport could have been taken from the villa.

'By whom?' Libby, despairing, managed to sound calm.

'There's only one person, isn't there?' said Monty. 'Only one other person who has been into the house. Into every room. Only one other person who has access to our property. I know you don't like to think badly of others, darling, and nor do I, but...'

'A-Andrea?' Libby was reluctant to think of the girl as a criminal.

When they got back to the villa Libby went to her dressing-table drawer again, as if she believed the passport could have miracu-lously reappeared while she was away. It hadn't, of course. They went for a walk round the grounds, all the areas Libby had ever been to. No luck there either. Back in the kitchen, Libby put the kettle on for a much-needed cup of tea and heard Monty in the sitting room, ringing the police station to say they still hadn't found the passport, and that they would be in next morning to pick up the report so they could get the emergency documents.

'But I want to go now!' Libby ran in to tell him but he waved her away.

'There's another thing, I have a suspect.' She heard him give Andrea's name, only her Christian name because that was all they knew, but with a detailed description of her appearance: shaven hair, nose-ring, tattoo on midriff. Then he pocketed his phone and brushed by her, heading back to the kitchen, where the kettle was boiling. 'Think we need something stronger than tea, darling.' He turned off the kettle and opened the fridge.

'Monty.' She declined the glass of white he offered her. 'I want to go back to the police station *now* and collect the report, then email the embassy and make an appointment to collect the emergency documents. That's what you have to do. I've been on the embassy website. The sooner we get going, the better.'

She still thought there was an outside chance they could sort this today and she could be on the plane tomorrow morning.

Monty gulped down a mouthful of wine. 'No hurry, darling. A few hours isn't going to make any difference. We'll go first thing tomorrow morning. Meanwhile, I'll get in touch with Helena to say we don't want that cleaning girl on the premises.'

'Monty—' she grabbed hold of his wrist '—if you won't go, I will go, by myself. Give me the car keys.'

He shook his head. 'Sorry, darling. You know you're not on the insurance.'

'Then drive me, please.' She hated pleading.

'Sorry, darling.' He did a sad face. 'I don't drink and drive.'

'Since when?' It slipped out.

His eyebrows went up. 'Are you turning into a shrew?'

'Are you trying to tame me?'

He walked out, taking the bottle with him.

54

LIBBY

Libby tried to keep calm. She finished making a cup of tea and took it upstairs to her bedroom. She obviously wasn't getting any help from Monty, not tonight, so she would have to do what she could by herself. First, sitting on her bed, laptop propped against her knees, she emailed the embassy. She asked for an appointment as soon as possible, explaining that she had reported the loss of her passport to the police and would bring in the official report the next day, Tuesday 9 September, she wrote for clarity. It was six o'clock now but the embassy operated 24/7, it said on the website, so she might get an answer this evening, if – big if – she could send the email. She was now reconciled – no, that wasn't the word! – she now reluctantly recognised that she wasn't flying home tomorrow. But if she could get an appointment in the next couple of days – the website said there was a two-day wait at least – she might be able to rebook her flight for Wednesday or Thursday.

But when she tried to send the email the Wi-Fi was down.

Determined to keep trying all night if necessary, she messaged Zelda to say she wouldn't be home. Then she wrote one to Marcos at Hellas Travel, saying she wouldn't be able to use the ticket she'd bought, but would need him to rearrange a flight later in the week.

But when she pressed send, nothing went.

Keep calm. What did she do at home when the Wi-Fi was down? Switching it off, unplugging and trying again sometimes worked. She reached beside the bed where her laptop and her phone were plugged in and unplugged, waited a few minutes, then plugged in again.

No connection.

Keep calm. Think. But it was hard to think when her brain felt as if it were made of sticky toffee. She had no new ideas, that was the trouble, only the old ones going round and round in her head. Should she drive herself into the town – if she could get hold of the car key – or have another go at cajoling Monty into driving her? She would have to be quick, before he'd finished the bottle. Where was he? It was hard to know these days, as he operated in so many different places. She tried resending a few more times before heading downstairs. He wasn't anywhere she could see so she opened the front door and stepped outside, where she got a whiff of burning charcoal. Monty was barbecuing on the terrace above the pool.

'Darling.' He held his arms open wide as he saw her approaching. 'I was about to come and look for you. Hug?'

It was the last thing she wanted, but if he could play *everything's fine* so could she. If it was the only way to get him on her side.

'Darling—' his arms round her felt like iron bands '—I just want to say how sorry I am for being a heartless brute. Mea culpa. Mea culpa. Mea culpa. Of *course* you're longing to get back home to see your family as soon as you can. I was insensitive not to see things from your point of view.'

She stayed in his arms. 'Apology accepted, Monty, but deeds not words, as you keep on saying. Please can we drive into Artemida now?'

'Sweetheart.' She felt him kissing the top of her head and made herself not shrink away. 'Sorry, but I've had far too much of the vino.' He released her now to point to the nearly empty bottle beside the barbecue.

'Monty.' She tried not to show her fury. 'Give me the car keys, then, so I can go to the police station to pick up that report, while they're still open. I also need to send messages and emails *tonight*, from the police station, or find an Internet café. It's not just the embassy. I must let Zelda know I won't be home tomorrow. She's expecting to meet me from the airport. She knows the arrival time. And yes, there's another thing, I need to tell Marcos at Hellas Travel that I'm not going tomorrow and will need to transfer my ticket to another day soon.'

'*That*,' said Monty, beaming, 'is one thing you don't need to do.'

'What don't I need to do?' She wasn't following.

'Cancel your ticket. I did it this morning for you, so you wouldn't lose your money. You'll get a refund on your credit card.'

'But I don't want a refund. I don't want a cancellation.' Something was feeling very wrong. 'I want a transfer to a new ticket later in the week.'

He looked hurt. It was *so* hard to please her. He was trying his best, he really was. Wasn't it better to have the money in her account, ready to pay for the new ticket when it was ready?

She didn't know but thought not. Refunds took time and there was something else not right. Her toffee-brain started to function, as he said he'd also helpfully cancelled the taxi to take her to the airport. *He must have cancelled my ticket before we went to the police station to see if anyone had handed my passport in.* It was as if he knew she wouldn't find it.

Monty was back at the barbecue now, placing kebabs on the hot charcoal. He said they'd try the Internet again after supper, before they went to bed. He thought it odd that he didn't have as much trouble as she seemed to have. Maybe it was her phone. Her server probably wasn't as good as his. Or perhaps she was doing something wrong? He'd check her settings. Ditzy, she heard ditzy again, but she wasn't ditzy. She wasn't as computer savvy as she'd like to be, but she wasn't completely clueless.

'Sit down, darling.' He pointed to olives and hummus and pitta bread on the bistro table and urged her to help herself. 'If your messages don't go tonight, I'll drive you straight to an Internet café in the morning. Yiasemis will be perfect, as I'm meeting Dimitris there for coffee. Or we might be able to send them from the police station. We'll go there first thing.'

He refused to give her the car keys, which must be in one of his pockets. Looking round, she couldn't see them anywhere, and she was, she realised, desperate enough to pick them up and drive if she got a chance. Her messsage to Zelda must go tonight or very early tomorrow to warn her not to go to the airport. Later tomorrow would be too late to save Zelda a wasted journey.

She made one drink, a spritzer with very little wine, last all evening, determined to keep a clear head. And after supper when they moved to comfortable chairs on the balcony for coffee, she declined the Metaxa. Monty urged her to try and send her messages, and offered to try for her when they didn't go. Clutching her phone – *he mustn't get his hands on it* – she declined his offer with as much grace as she could muster. The sun was setting and there was a new moon, a sliver of silver, in the purple sky.

'Doesn't that make you feel hopeful, darling?' Monty leaned across the table to touch her hand, making her shudder. 'A little bit willing to see the silver lining in this small dark cloud that has

briefly descended? What is a mislaid passport in the grand scheme
of things, after all? Why go home? I must admit I love it here, and
I've started to picture a future for us two together, you and me, you
writing your wonderful novels, me discovering delicious wines for
the delight of our friends back home. Couldn't you try, just try,
darling, to see it like that too?'

55

LIBBY

'Libby hasn't arrived! She's not on the flight!'

Zelda was on the phone to Viv. 'I'm here at the airport. She didn't board the flight, Viv! She wasn't even listed on it.' Zelda was at the information desk at Luton airport extracting as much info from the staff as she could. 'She didn't come on an earlier flight either. And she isn't booked on a flight later today. Or tomorrow.'

She'd checked the details Libby had sent her umpteen times. Her message said clearly she was going to be on flight EZY8182 departing Athens 9.40 ETA London Luton 11.38. It was a four-hour flight but the two-hour time difference made it look like two hours. She had messaged Libby to say she would meet her at the airport, but hadn't heard from her since.

'What's gone wrong, Viv?' Zelda was more than worried.

'With the travel arrangements or the relationship?'

'Both. I'm sure they're connected. I never did trust that man. Viv, have you got plans for lunch? It's twelve thirty now. I could meet you at The Olive Branch in an hour and a bit.'

'Good idea. I'll see if Janet's free too. I'll ring Nikos to tell him we're coming.'

Before she went to get her car, Zelda messaged again.

Don't worry, Libby! The Muscateers are coming!

If the others wouldn't join her, she'd go alone. Greece wasn't that far, not compared with the USA. She would find Libby somehow. Rescue her from that possessive bastard. Praying that Libby would get her message in the very near future, she pressed 'send' then headed for the exit.

56

LIBBY

Libby was at the police station when she got Zelda's message.

Don't worry, Libby! The Muscateers are coming!

It brought tears to her eyes, but this was no time to emote. She had to take advantage of the Wi-Fi connection while she could. She had only just got here, though it was half past two. Monty had found reasons not to come all morning. He couldn't see why she was in such a hurry. Couldn't she use the time to get on with the novel?

She had used the time going round the villa plugging in her phone, trying to find a place where there was a Wi-Fi connection. There must be one, or several, because Monty managed to send his messages. Desperate to contact the embassy and her friends, especially Zelda to apologise for her wasted journey to the airport, she had also written messages. Now afraid of losing contact, she sent them off, and skimmed the incoming messages. There were lots from her friends, including Nikos, and Sid demanding another column. But 'Keep in touch by any means possible' was the gist of all of them. Nikos said check the router was plugged in. Greece had good Internet. The villa should have good connections. The router, where was it? She should have thought of that before. She knew what it was, as she'd had a new one installed back home recently, when she'd upgraded her broadband, on Eleanor's advice. It was on her desk at home in her mini-study, a black square thing. She remembered asking Eleanor why it was described as 'wireless' when there were so many wires, well, cables, plugged into the back of it? Eleanor had sighed but hadn't explained. Mum was too dim to understand, obviously. Did everyone think she was ditzy?

Monty, tapping her arm, clearly did. 'The officer has just asked you your home address, darling.' He was being the charming Englishman today, the caring protective male, the proud partner, and the patronising bastard. He turned to the policeman behind the counter, an oldish man with a walrus moustache. 'Libby's a very bright lady, but she tends to have her head in the clouds. She's a writer, you know.'

Libby butted in before he could start telling the man that he was a theatre director in charge of next year's festival and she was the guest star. 'Monty, I want to go back to the villa.' She wanted to find the router.

'But, darling—' he looked at her fondly '—we're here to get the police report, remember? Then we'll take it to the embassy in Athens and deliver it personally.'

It seemed like a good plan, so why was she wary?

57

ZELDA

When Zelda arrived at The Olive Branch, later than she'd hoped, Viv and Janet were already there. It was two o'clock. As she walked in she saw them sitting at the back of the restaurant with Nikos. The restaurant wasn't crowded because most of the lunchtime eaters had gone back to work. When she got nearer she saw there was something spread out on the table in front of them.

'Here, have my seat.' Nikos stood up and Zelda saw the something was a map of the Artemida area, the part of Greece where Libby had gone. Clearly, they were on the case. Good. Nikos was pointing to the spot where he thought the Villa Adelos was. He'd got the address from a great-niece who actually worked as a cleaner there. He said that Andrea hadn't at first been 100 per cent sure that the blonde lady staying with the house-sitter was called Libby, but she'd gone back and checked when Uncle Nikos requested.

'House-sitter?' Zelda looked from one to the other.

'Yes,' said Nikos. 'It seems that Monty Charles is employed by the owner as a house-sitter, while she is in the USA. But he's not very good at it, according to my great-niece.'

'You mean he isn't paying out huge sums of money to rent a

luxurious holiday home? Why aren't I surprised?' Zelda shook her head.

'No, the man's a liar.' Nikos was curt.

'But—' Zelda looked for silver linings '—you say we have a mole on the premises? Your niece? That's good.'

'*Was* good,' said Nikos. 'She was only on the premises for a short time once a week. And even that isn't happening now. Andrea has been accused of stealing Liberty's passport. She has been told to keep away from the Villa Adelos.'

'Stealing her passport!' Zelda's brain was whirring. 'Hang on.' She reached for her mobile, which she'd glanced at from time to time during the many traffic jams on the way here. 'I think I saw the word passport. Yes.' She scrolled down. 'Here's a message from Libby saying her passport has disappeared so she can't get home. Unfortunately I didn't get it before I set off for the airport, till I was on my way from it, in fact. This is looking very...'

'...fishy.' Viv and Janet finished her sentence.

'Stinks to high heaven – the situation, not this wine.' Nikos paused as Evelina arrived with a tray of meze and a bottle of white, an Assyrtiko.

It was the first time Zelda had seen Evelina since Nikos had told her she was his sister. Now she wondered why she had ever thought they were married to each other. They looked like brother and sister, had the same strong features and possibly the same colouring. They both had brown eyes, but Nikos's bronze pate was shaved and it was impossible to say what colour Evelina's iron-grey hair had once been.

Evelina put the tray on the table. 'Wine-loving ladies, we all worry about friend, Libby, and must keep the clear head, but also keep up the spirit. Yes?' She filled their glasses and they all drank to Libby's health. 'And to wish Nikos good luck,' said Evelina, raising her glass again. 'To my leetle brother, not husband.' She giggled. 'He go soon like Greek hero to sort out mess.'

Nikos was flying to Greece on Monday, Zelda learnt, to help the family in their dealings with the police and, of course, find Libby.

'But that's nearly a week away! Why not today?' Zelda feared for Libby's safety and there was something else. The anniversary of Jim's death was coming up: 13 September. That was Saturday. Couldn't they get Libby home for that?

That sadly was impossible, Nikos said. He'd got the first available flight. Recent industrial disputes hadn't helped.

Viv said she would get there on Monday too, as she was driving there with Patrick. 'We're leaving Sunday morning, cross Channel, then overland.' She was going to work on the garden of the property Patrick was restoring in the Peloponnese. 'It's not that far from Artemida.'

'Couldn't you go earlier?' Zelda felt things were moving at a snail's pace.

'Sorry no. Ferry crossings are hard to come by at this time of year. But I'll bust a gut to make contact as soon as we get there if Nikos tells me where to look.'

Viv and Nikos exchanged contact details and Nikos gave Viv Libby's address. One of them at least could be at the Villa Adelos on Monday evening, or Tuesday at the latest they thought. They arranged to keep in touch.

Zelda messaged Libby.

Help on way!

But she wasn't entirely happy. A week seemed an age away.

58

LIBBY

Help on way!

Libby's heart leaped as she saw the words on her phone, which she shoved back in her pocket. She'd stopped on the stairwell on the way to bed to check the time.

'Did I hear your phone go?' Monty was on the step below. She hadn't heard him coming up behind her, or her phone pinging. The batteries in her hearing aids must have run out.

Ignoring his question, she carried on climbing, keen to get to her room and reply to the message while there was still Wi-Fi, but she paused on the landing. It would be better to find out where the router was before she went to bed, so if the Wi-Fi went down again – because it had been unplugged, most likely – she could go and plug it in again. It was even more important now because without Wi-Fi she couldn't receive communications from the embassy.

They hadn't been in long. Monty had kept her out all day, finding one person after another that he 'had' to see. That was after the useless, time-wasting trip to the embassy, where they'd been told that applications for emergency documents had to be submitted online. Only then could a meeting in person be arranged for collection of documents. An official told them they had to supply a valid up-to-date digital passport photo, contact telephone numbers, an email address and debit or credit card details for the £100 fee. They'd had to go and find a photo booth and take a photo. Then an Internet café so they could submit the application.

'Where's the router, Monty?' About to go into his room, he sighed heavily, but she didn't care. 'I need to know.'

'In the morning, darling. Too late now for technicalities. And I need some shut-eye, unless you're up for a bit of rumpy-pumpy?'

Why did she ever think she fancied the man?

'I'll sleep in my own room tonight, Monty. I've got things on my mind and don't think I'll sleep very well.'

Back in her own room, she thought she heard him going downstairs again and opened her door to see. He called out, 'Just checking I've locked up!' and she tried to send a message to Zelda, but couldn't because the Wi-Fi was already down. He'd moved fast. She wished she had followed him downstairs to wherever the router was. It was obvious what he'd been doing.

* * *

She didn't sleep well and hadn't for several nights. Her body seemed to be reliving that last awful week of Jim's life, when she'd sat by his bedside not daring to close her eyes. And she was aching to see Ellie-Jo. What had Eleanor told her about her granny to explain her absence? It was a week into term already. Who was taking her to nursery school? Who had looked after her on Tuesday, the day she didn't go to nursery? Was Ellie-Jo missing her granny as much as Libby was missing Ellie-Jo? Was she missing her grandad? Libby hoped not, because she didn't want her to be hurting as much as she was.

When she did eventually get off she slept fitfully, reaching for Jim's hand when she woke up, panicking when she couldn't find it, till she realised where she was. At six o'clock she got out of bed to go for a pee and on the way back pulled out the dressing-table drawer, hoping stupidly that she'd see her passport lying there.

'Believe in poltergeists, darling?' Monty was peering round the door, looking tired and seedy in his paisley dressing gown. 'Sorry.' He'd noticed she hadn't laughed. 'Too early for joshing. I'll go down and make coffee. Shall we have it here in your bed or on the balcony?'

'On the balcony.' She didn't want him near her.

She picked up her phone as soon as he'd gone. Some messages had come in overnight, so the Wi-Fi had been up at some point. Interesting. There was a message from Zelda repeating that she should check the router. There was one from Simon asking where she would be on Jim's anniversary. He must be thinking of sending her flowers. There was also an email from the embassy, acknowledging receipt of her request for an appointment. At least the process had begun. She messaged Zelda saying she would check the router asap, and one to Simon saying she was stuck in Greece. Then she messaged Eleanor sending love to Ellie-Jo. But when she pressed send nothing happened. The Wi-Fi was down again, surprise, surprise. She showered and got dressed as quickly as she could, then went downstairs.

'Monty, where's the router?'

He was still in his dressing gown, sitting at the table on the balcony where he'd laid breakfast. 'I'll show you when I'm dressed, darling. Come and eat.' There was yogurt and fruit and bread with cherry jam, but she wasn't hungry.

'Show me now. Please,' she added, hating herself for pleading.

'What's the hurry, darling? Look at that view.' He raised his arm to take in the vista of sea and sky and distant mountains. 'I still don't understand why you want to go home.'

'To see my granddaughter.'

'Who wouldn't be allowed to see you.'

'Who said?'

'You said. You told me that Eleanor said that if you came on holiday with me she wouldn't allow you to see Ellie-Jo ever again. Don't you remember, darling?' He shook his head, the picture of concern. *Poor Libby, you're losing it, just like your mother.* But she did remember, clearly. Eleanor hadn't said that. She'd said that she'd have to think about letting her look after Ellie-Jo, which, with the benefit of hindsight, was just Eleanor shooting her mouth off.

'Honestly, darling.' Monty beckoned. 'Come and sit down. There's no point in rushing back. Term's started, hasn't it? Eleanor will have made other arrangements by now.'

'Monty, I *want* to get back. I *want* to see Ellie-Jo and help my daughter!'

But she was wasting her breath.

'Eleanor doesn't need your help, darling. She's made that clear. But I do.'

'Monty,' she shouted. 'You are a grown man!'

'Libby dear, Eleanor is a grown woman!'

'But Ellie-Jo isn't! She needs me!'

* * *

Confrontation wasn't a good tactic with Monty.

She sat down and apologised for losing her temper, but only because she had to, to get his co-operation. She buttered a piece of bread and waited before asking him again.

'Why are you obsessed with the router?' He shook his head.

She ignored *obsessed*, with its implication of mental instability, and kept her voice light, playing the not-too-clever little woman. 'Because I gather it's the device that connects our mobiles and laptops to the Internet. I think cables can come loose, causing the Wi-Fi to go down. If I knew where it was I wouldn't have to keep bothering you to reconnect it.'

He went into the kitchen to make more coffee. She followed him, putting a little laugh in her voice. 'It sometimes feels that you don't want me to know.'

'That's silly, darling. It's in my office, and always has been.'

'But I didn't know you had an office.' She hadn't seen one when they first looked round.

Now he had a laugh in his voice. 'It's been there all the time, darling, in the lobby at the back of the lounge. Not hard to find.'

'May I go and look?'

'I said I'd show you when I'm dressed.'

And he did, presumably because he couldn't think of any more delaying tactics.

* * *

It was a room she had noticed when they'd first looked round. Well, she'd noticed the door, but it was one of several that were locked. She had assumed it was because they were rooms the owner didn't want guests to use.

'Ta da!' Monty, his cheery self again, unlocked the door and stood back for her to enter. 'Welcome to the hub of my new business empire!'

It was a very smart office, compact but well equipped. Photographs and charts on the walls suggested that some sort of travel business, property letting perhaps, was run from here. Monty gestured that she should sit down in a dark green leather chair and he sat down opposite her in its twin, with his back to a PC screen.

The CEO of the business empire swivelled in his chair, lifting his feet above the marble floor. Her chair didn't swivel, but she didn't need to turn round to get a good view of the galley-style office, furnished with pale beechwood desks and filing cabinets along both long walls. The window at the far end looked over the outbuildings at the back of the property. Ah. There it was. She spotted the router, behind a tier of in-trays, close to the PC, but she couldn't see any cables. They presumably were at the back and Monty could come here whenever he wanted and plug them in or pull them out.

'This is Helena's office.' Libby stated the obvious.

'When she's here, but she's okay with me using it to run my businesses. Which is what I want to talk to you about, darling. First, though...' he leaned forward and reached for her hands '...I want to apologise for losing my temper this morning, and for being needlessly harsh.'

She let him talk, waiting for a chance to free her hands.

Of *course* she would see Ellie-Jo again, he said. He hadn't meant to imply that she wouldn't. Of *course* her disagreement with Eleanor would blow over – given time. That was his point. Eleanor needed *time*, time *away* from her mother to appreciate her. Absence would make her heart grow fonder. Eleanor needed Libby but not in the way she, Libby, thought she needed her. She didn't need Libby there, all the time, for childcare. Nor did Ellie-Jo need her there. There was no substitute for the *relationship* Libby had with Ellie-Jo, of course, but Libby could sustain that with letters and parcels and phone calls and Skype. He, on the other hand – he gripped her hands harder – couldn't be doing with substitutes.

'I need you here, darling, and so do your fans.'

Need. The word tugged at something deep inside her despite the feeling she was being worked on. He let go of her hands to run his fingers through his white hair. 'I'm not as young as I was, darling, not as *able*.' Now he was going for sympathy. 'I've been out of things for so long and need your support. I need you to help me like you helped your husband set up his business. Everyone loves you, you know.' The change of tack took her by surprise. 'You enchanted everyone at the lunch. The festival committee were thrilled to meet the great Libby Allgood.'

'You don't need to big me up, Monty.' Bemused, she got up. It was time to inspect the router, which wasn't plugged in, she'd spotted straight away. Well, one cable wasn't, so she plugged it in and heard the phone in her pocket ping.

'Darling, they're thrilled you're going to launch your novel at the festival. They feel you're writing it for them.'

Still on her feet, she scrolled to find the new message. Monty tapped her hand. 'I said they're thrilled you're going to launch your novel at the festival.'

The message was from Zelda. It took maybe ten seconds to take in what Monty had said.

'Novel? But, Monty, when that woman at the lunch mentioned launching my latest book at the festival, I thought she was talking about *Lovely Old Lion*.' It was a picture book about a lion with dementia.

'You can't launch a festival with a kiddies' book!'

'Monty, I am *not* writing a novel.'

'But you are, darling, you're writing a wonderful novel. I've told them the title. Did I mention I'd thought of that too? It's called *A Second Summer*, because that's what we're having, aren't we? A second summer in which we're both flowering even more brightly than we did in the first.' He swivelled round in his seat, switched on his PC and pressed some keys. 'Look, publishers of romantic fiction!' The screen was full and he scrolled down to reveal more. 'Dozens of them. Hundreds. Which one do you fancy?'

She couldn't believe that he knew so little about publishing, how little he knew about writing, or *anything*. Now he was saying that she needed to finish the novel by the end of the year, so that he could send it out. He would act as her agent and invite publishers to an auction. He wouldn't just sell to the highest bidder though; he'd go for the one who could publish quickest. The launch was scheduled for the first day of the festival next October.

'It isn't like that, Monty. You...' But there was no point in explaining.

He was swivelling back to her, not listening. 'And the book is only the beginning. I've already started talking to people about the film. Sophia—' that was the blonde statuesque Melina Mercouri lookalike, Libby thought '—knows several film producers who are looking for a project exactly like this to back and I've started to think about casting.'

'But, Monty—'

'That's why you can't go home, darling. If you went home you'd get distracted. You've got to stay here till it's finished.'

The message from Zelda said help would arrive on Tuesday 16, but that was a whole week away!

59

Libby took advantage of the Wi-Fi working. First she replied to Zelda:

> Great but hope to get myself back before that. Will get a flight asap.

It went and she got one back.

> Hurray! Give flight details and I'll be there to meet you! Z

With luck and help from the embassy she'd be back at the weekend. Next morning she got to work. Having Wi-Fi made all the difference. Her attempts to Skype with Eleanor – and Ellie-Jo, she hoped – kept failing, but only, she surmised, because Eleanor was declining her calls. It strengthened her resolve to get home asap. She had to sort things out with her daughter. Now sure that Monty had been unplugging the router when he didn't need Wi-Fi, to prevent her using it, she wondered how to prevent him from doing it again. She must persuade him to leave the study unlocked for a start. Would being sweet and submissive, pretending she was going along with his plan, get him to loosen up a bit?

She gave it her best shot, acting her socks off, but maintained her celibate 'I must put all my energy into my writing' stance, spending even more time in her own room, writing. She wrote a lot more, reliving her past, imagining what she couldn't remember. In fact her imagination was fired, and characters were taking shape on the page. She even began to think she might be writing something publishable, not Monty's novel but her own.

And it helped to stop missing Jim, but time still passed slowly.

There was an awkward moment on Thursday morning, just after breakfast – they were on the balcony – when at last she got a reply from the embassy offering her an appointment on Monday afternoon, not as early as she hoped. She asked Monty if he could take her there. He said he didn't see why she wanted to go. If she'd decided to stay, she didn't need emergency travel documents. She said that she did, in case of an emergency like her mother dying, and – phew! – he conceded the point. He said he would take her there as he had to go into Athens that day to see Sophia. He left quickly then as he'd seen a white van at the gates. It was the wine he was expecting, four hundred cases, for relabelling.

For the rest of the day he didn't take a lot of interest in what she was doing and when she went outside for a dip in the pool, she could hear the clunk and whir of machinery. The labelling was under way. This was good because she was busy too. She had a lot of things to do like packing and searching for her passport. She was now convinced it hadn't been stolen. Well, not by Andrea. She thought it could be somewhere in the house, hidden by Monty, if he hadn't destroyed it. She wanted to find it because she didn't trust Monty to keep his word and take her to the embassy on Monday. Knowing him better now, she anticipated another hitch and wanted to forestall it, by getting herself home before that. But when she

started looking for the slim, maroon, book-like object in a house
full of furniture and books and filing cabinets and ornaments and
pictures on the walls, needles and haystacks came to mind.

Fortunately, Monty and Dimitris kept out of her way on
Thursday and Friday. They worked all through the weekend too,
coming into the villa only for lunch, at Libby's invitation. It was part
of her sweet and co-operative act. She said she wanted to do everything she could to help. She even volunteered to help in the sheds,
but they declined. The sheds were no place for a woman, Monty
said – too many spiders! Libby really did want this wine-exporting
enterprise to be viable. She wanted Monty to prosper at something
– without her.

But she didn't find her passport.

60

LIBBY

She had to wait till Monday.

But it started to feel as if she really might be going home. In the morning Marcos messaged to say they'd had a cancellation and therefore a ticket was available for a flight late that night. She had accepted eagerly. With luck she'd get her emergency travel documents that afternoon, and proceed to the airport. At lunch Monty reminded her to be ready to leave at two for the drive to the British Embassy. Her appointment was at four, so that would give them plenty of time. It actually did look as if he was going to keep his word, when he and Dimitris went back to the shed to do another hour's labelling. He said he'd meet her by the car at 2 p.m. sharp, and she was ready a good ten minutes early. But when she went to the side of the house where the car was usually parked it wasn't there. Nor was Dimitris's car, though he'd come in it that morning.

Why am I surprised?

Libby's mouth went dry as she noticed the silence. No clunking or whirring. Just the ever-present chirruping of cicadas. Knowing it was a waste of time, she hurried to the shed, but even before she reached it she saw the padlock on the door. Had they nipped out for a few minutes? Would they be back any minute now? Despite knowing the answer, she messaged Monty:

I'm ready and waiting. Where are you?

But her message didn't go. Of course it didn't. She went back into the house. The office door was locked. Of course it was. She went outside again. The gates were locked. Suddenly she felt very alone, and sick with self-loathing. Why hadn't she been prepared for this?

* * *

It was dark when Monty came home.

Libby was on the terrace, glass in hand but with a clear head. She had made herself eat something but had had hardly anything to drink. She didn't get up from the swing-seat to greet him and she didn't ask where he'd been, just sat back to listen to his story, his *story*. A tiny bit of her was ready to be entertained.

He looked abject, his face creased with misery.

'So-o-o-o sorry, darling, but it was an emergency. Had to rush off. No time to waste. Must admit I completely forgot about your appointment till too late.' He reached for the bottle of red on the table. 'Dimitris's mother had a stroke and was rushed to hospital. Had to go with him. He was in bits, darling. Loves his mum. Just like you.' He poured himself a glass.

'But you let him drive? In bits?'

'Yes, why not? Er...' He took a gulp. 'I needed mine to get back *for you*.'

'But you didn't come back for me.'

'Because...' He was standing in front of her now holding out the bottle, but she covered her glass with her hand. What had he said once? *You're not like other women. You don't try to trip a chap up.* But you didn't have to trip Monty up. He tripped himself up.

'And how is Dimitris's mother now? Did you get there in time?' She watched him wondering whether to kill Dimitris's mother off now for maximum pathos, or keep her alive for later use.

'Yes, yes, we did. We got there. She was unconscious, still is, and sadly they're not holding out much hope. Dimitris is there now by her bedside.'

'Poor Dimitris. How did he find out that she was in hospital?'

A flicker of annoyance crossed his face. 'Sorry, darling. I'm knackered. Questions in the morning, okay?' He lowered himself onto the swing seat beside her.

But she got up and faced him, her head full of words. She wanted to say, *Monty, listen to me. I missed an appointment today, an appointment you promised to take me to. I couldn't order a taxi to take me to it because the Wi-Fi was down. I also missed a flight I'd booked but couldn't cancel because the Wi-Fi was down. The Wi-Fi was down because you disconnected it and locked the office door so I couldn't recon-nect it. I can't help thinking that you locked the door deliberately, to stop me going home. I won't get another appointment for days now, which means I won't get a flight home this week. I want to go home, Monty, I want to go home to be with my family as soon as possible, because I wasn't with them on the anniversary of their father's death!*

But she would be wasting her breath and in this situation honesty wasn't the best policy. She had to go on pretending, so she just said that she'd wanted to order a taxi but the office was locked so she couldn't connect the Wi-Fi.

'It wasn't, darling. I'm quite sure I left it open. Let's go and look.' He stood up and held out his hand as if she were a child. *You're ditzy if not yet demented,* was the recurring message.

She didn't take his hand, but did follow him to the office, where the door opened as soon as Monty turned the handle. He must have unlocked it as soon as he came in. She went straight to the router where the Wi-Fi cable was out. She plugged it in as he watched, muttering about loose connections, and her phone starting to vibrate in her pocket. Straight away, while he was standing there, she emailed the embassy, choosing her words carefully because he was watching:

Dear Sir/Madam

Please accept my apologies for not coming to my appointment today. It was for reasons out of my control. I desperately need a new appointment as I need to get home as soon as possible.

Libby Allgood.

'Desperately, darling?' He was close to her. 'I thought you were happy here?'

She deleted desperately and pressed send without adding 'I am being kept against my will', though she wanted to. Then she messaged Zelda:

Setbacks. Still no passport and haven't managed to get to embassy yet. Libby x

Monty said, 'Come to bed, darling. We can sort everything out in the morning.'

It wasn't a bad idea, as long as she slept in her own bed. She planned to write more to Zelda if by any chance the Internet was still connected when she got to her bedroom. She needed more details about the 'help on the way'. Tomorrow she suddenly realised! What sort of help? When exactly was it coming? Now she needed her friends like never before. Her own efforts were being thwarted at every turn by Monty and always would be. As she headed for the stairs she heard Monty turning the key in the office door. With sickening certainty she knew he'd disconnected the router first.

61

LIBBY

Keys, I need Monty's keys.

Libby woke up with this thought in her head. She needed to be
able to get in and out of the office to make sure the Internet was
working, so she could get in touch with her friends, and they with
her. She needed to be able to get out of the property if possible,
because they wouldn't be able to get in.

Without keys she was trapped. Without keys she was under
house arrest. Monty would keep putting obstacles in her path to
prevent her leaving, because he needed her, he said. He couldn't
manage without her. It was emotional blackmail. She would have to
steal the keys. Stealing went against everything she believed, but
there was no point in asking politely. If he said he would lend them
to her or get a set copied for her, he wouldn't.

'Darling.' He got up from the table to greet her with a kiss when
she came onto the balcony in the morning. 'How are you? How did
you sleep? Sit down and have breakfast. Coffee? I'll make some
more.'

She thought she could see the shape of keys in the righthand
pocket of his slacks.

'Thank you.' She sat at the table where he had clearly already eaten. There was half a loaf of bread and butter and cherry jam, cubed melon and yogurt. When he brought fresh coffee he said he'd been up early because he had such a lot to do. Labelling the bottles was a big job.

She said, 'How are you going to manage without Dimitris?'

He frowned and for a moment she thought he'd forgotten the yarn he'd spun last night. But then he recovered his aplomb. 'No worries. Dimitris is coming. The doctors said there was no point in him sitting by his mother's bedside. It's going to be a long time before she recovers consciousness.'

Libby thought small talk was the best option. 'What a shame to be cooped inside on such a lovely morning!'

It was a lovely morning, the sky cloudless, the view of sea and mountains stunning, and the air was already warm on her bare arms. She'd dressed practically in cut-off denims and T-shirt for what she hoped was going to be an active day. Three kittens play-hunting under the table helped to keep the mood light. Who didn't laugh at kittens? She was lifting her toes out of the way of a speckled black one, when she saw the gates open and Dimitris's car driving in. Monty got up. 'Sorry, darling, can't sit around enjoying myself any longer, but we'll both be in for lunch at one o'clock.'

'Would you open the study door before...' *you go?* she started to say, but he had already gone. Perhaps best, she decided. She must give the impression she was content and happy to stay.

* * *

She spent the time writing – on the balcony so she could keep a look-out – then made a very nice lunch. It was a Greek version of salade niçoise, with tuna steaks and lots of black olives. Monty and Dimitris didn't appear at one o'clock, so she messaged Monty to say lunch was ready, but it didn't send. Of course it didn't! For a few minutes she considered eating on her own. Then she remembered that she was trying to keep the atmosphere amicable, if only to further her chances of 'borrowing' those keys, so she went outside to tell them.

There were no padlocks on the door today. The machinery was clunking and whirring away so they didn't hear her entering the building. Nor did they see her because they both had their backs to the door. Monty was sitting at one end of a conveyor belt feeding bottles into a machine, a labelling machine presumably, which then dropped them onto the conveyor belt. Dimitris stood at the other end of the belt, picking up the bottles and putting them into a box. It looked like an efficient operation. When the box was full Dimitris moved it to one side and got another. They'd already filled quite a lot of boxes, some of which, she noticed, were piled up near her on her right. Something struck her as slightly odd, so she moved closer to get a better look. Yes, the writing on the side of the box said, 'Produit de France, Chateau Jarmaine, Bordeaux.'

Is Monty into fraud?

Libby was shocked that the thought crossed her mind. There must be a reasonable explanation why they were using French wine boxes. People often put things in cardboard boxes with a different product's name on the side. When you brought groceries home from the supermarket, it might say Whiskas on the side of the box, but it wasn't cat food inside, and no one was trying to deceive anyone.

These aren't groceries that Monty has brought home from the supermarket.

Checking that Monty and Dimitris still had their backs to her, Libby edged sideways to be nearer the boxes. She needed to look inside. The box nearest to her didn't seem to be sealed firmly. She edged closer and got her fingers under a flap, managed to break through the dry glue with her nails, lift the flap and grasp the neck of a bottle. But the clunking stopped as she lifted it out, and the conveyor belt whined to a halt. She froze.

'Stop for lunch, shall we?' Monty was standing up, rubbing his back.

'I'm ready for it.' Dimitris stretched and groaned.

Can I sidle out before they turn round? Too late. Monty had seen her.

'Hi.' She held the bottle aloft. 'I was just coming to tell you lunch was ready. Shall we try this with it?'

'Er...' Monty shook his head. 'Don't think red's right with fish, darling. Aren't we having tuna?'

'Oh, that old rule.' She headed for the door. 'Made to be broken, I think.'

How was Monty going to play this? Libby wondered as they walked back to the house, she on one side of Monty, Dimitris on the other. How was *she* going to play it? The bottle hung from her hand. She hadn't had time to more than glance at the label yet, but that glance had told her that the writing on it was French. From the look on his face, Monty was thinking hard.

Dimitris complained about his aching back, and she sympathised. She recommended getting up and walking at regular intervals and asked him about his mother. He said his mother was comfortable but still unconscious. They made small talk then about the meal they were about to eat. She said she had picked basil and lemons for the dressing in the garden – what a joy that had been! – and wittered on about the recipe she'd followed, one she'd found on the Internet years back. She hoped she'd remembered all the ingredients. She'd even picked some black olives from the tree by the pool, and thought of using them, till she'd tasted one. Monty nodded and said he was sure it would all be delicious but wasn't, she thought, really listening. Dimitris said olives had to be cured to make them palatable. When they got inside Monty said he was going to the bathroom to wash his hands and Dimitris followed – no doubt to confer. What were they going to tell her? She said she'd be outside on the terrace when they got back. The meal was already on the table under a white cloth.

She opened the bottle and decanted it into a carafe, as befitted a wine of this quality. According to the labels, front and back, it was an *édition limitée* from the Chateau Pierre Jarmaine, Bordeaux, Appellation d'Origine Controlée. Made from the Merlot grape, vintage 1982, it was of course Produit de France. Quickly she photographed the bottle then sat down at the table to wait. She wished she could talk to Jim. He liked Bordeaux wines and knew a lot about them. They were a bit oaky for her taste and she preferred something lighter and fruitier. She knew Bordeaux was supposed to improve with age and this one was over thirty years old, so should be very good. People bought it young as an investment, to 'lay down', beneath their floorboards if they didn't have a cellar to keep it in. Jim had done a bit of that. The grey and white label, slightly brown at the edges with a gold medallion in the corner, looked old. How different from the cartoony label Monty had shown her that day in the café. Why had they abandoned the Lord Monty's Cellar brand? Perhaps they hadn't, perhaps they were using old bottles with old labels, and were going to put the new labels over them? Still unwilling to think of them as fraudsters, she clutched for honesty straws as Monty and Dimitris reappeared.

'Could eat the proverbial horse,' said Monty, rubbing his hands, as he sat down at one end of the table.

'Me too,' said Dimitris, sitting at the other.

'Sorry, it's tuna,' she replied, keeping her tone light, as she sat on the long side of the table nearest the kitchen. 'Fresh, not tinned.'

Monty poured the wine. 'Let's give it a try.' He raised his glass. 'Yamas!'

'Yamas!' Libby raised her glass, sniffed and took a mouthful. Not bad. Not gluggable but fruitier and lighter than she'd expected. She urged them to help themselves to the salade niçoise and soon they were all tucking in.

Then Monty paused, frowning. 'Sorry, I may be old-fashioned but this meal needs white wine. We can keep the red for cheese, yes?'

Dimitris agreed and, after another mouthful, so did Libby. After fish, the red tasted metallic. Monty went inside to get a white from the fridge, and Libby saw an opportunity.

'What happened to your fun label, Dimitris? I thought it a great design.' A compliment was never wasted.

'Change of plan,' the young man said, looking at his plate. 'I'm sure Monty will explain.'

Monty, back with the white, had heard. 'Not upmarket enough.' He sat down. 'Too jokey. And upmarket drinkers don't drink Greek wine.'

'So—' she nodded at the glass of red '—you've decided to buy and sell French wine?'

'If you say so,' said Monty.

'Sorry, what do you mean?'

'Do you think it's French?' he said. 'Does it taste French to you?'

'I don't know, Monty. My palate isn't sophisticated enough. It says French on the label so I am assuming it's French.'

'Exactly. Like everyone else. Wait till you've tried it with cheese, darling, you'll be sure you're drinking a lovely Merlot.'

'And it is?' She really didn't want him to say what she thought he was going to say.

'Our old friend, the very versatile Agiorgitiko.'

Now she knew why Monty didn't want her to tell Nikos about his project. Nikos knew about Greek wine. He was trying to promote Greek wines because they were delicious and as good as some of the best wines in the world. He'd be appalled by this fraud.

'But that's fraud.' She couldn't stop herself. There was no other word for it.

'Not really, darling. We'll be duping a few wine snobs with more money than sense, that's all. They won't know the difference.' He wasn't ashamed, that was the worst of it. Far from it. He seemed proud that he was going to try and pass off a newish Greek wine as vintage Bordeaux.

'You'll end up behind bars, Monty. You'll both end up behind bars.' She remembered Dimitris was there.

'Not if we have your support, darling. Not if Miss Goody Good doesn't blab, which wouldn't be wise, by the way, as she's implicated too.'

'What do you mean? I've got nothing to do with this.'

'Oh, yes, you have! You're our business partner, darling, so you'd better stick by our story.' He filled her glass with white. 'This is an Assyrtiko, by the way, perfect with seafood, elegant and crisp, like you. You won't let us down, will you?'

62

LIBBY

Libby sat at the table, after the men had gone back to the shed, too stunned to drink the glass of white Monty had poured. How was she *implicated*? In what way was she their *business partner*? She checked her mobile. No reply from the embassy or from Zelda. She messaged Zelda.

Failing to get myself home. Really do need your help. Please contact embassy.

She pressed send, but of course it didn't send. She went to the office and the door was locked.

I must get Monty's keys.

Back on the balcony she leaned over the balustrade and studied her surroundings like never before. Where once, many times, she'd focussed on the beautiful view, the gleaming glittering sea, the changing colours of the low mountain range and the wondrous blue sky, she now homed in on Villa Adelos's solid boundaries. There was a stone wall right round the property for as far as she could see, which extended round the back of the building. The wall was probably no more than a metre high but it was topped by metal railings another metre high. In total the boundary was taller than she was, taller than a tall man. The spaces between the railings were filled-in with what looked like metal mesh. In a couple of places there was a flight of steps leading to the top of the wall, easy enough to climb, she thought. But what was the drop down to the other side where the road was? More than on this side, she was pretty sure. The Villa Adelos was built on a raised site, which was why she could see for miles. So, if she climbed up to the top of the wall could she get over the metal fence by doing a five-bar roll? She'd done one recently on a country walk, horrifying Eleanor, who'd yelled, 'No, Mum!' as she'd leaned over the top bar of a five-bar gate, then thrown her legs over and landed on the other side, safely. Ellie-Jo had laughed so much she'd wet her knickers. Ellie-Jo! Her heart skipped a beat as she thought of her. If she needed another incentive to renew her efforts to get home, that girl was it! Grandgirl, here I come! What a celebration they would have when she broke free!

Broke free!

What was she thinking? This wasn't *Cell Block H*. The surrounding wall wasn't topped with rolls of barbed wire. There weren't searchlights flooding the area at night. Stone-faced warders weren't watching her. But Monty, the keeper of the keys, iron hand in a velvet glove, was doing everything he could to stop her leaving.

Libby plotted her escape.

When she got out, *when* she got over that wall, what would she do? The nearest other building was a long way off. A blue and white Greek flag flew from it, but she couldn't tell if it was a public building or a house. Was there someone inside who would help her – give her a lift into Athens perhaps? The quietness struck her. She could hear cicadas clicking and pigeons cooing but couldn't see any birds. From time to time a dog barked in the distance but there weren't many other sounds, maybe a far-off rumbling from that plane drawing a white line across the sky. If, no, *when* she managed to get outside what would she do? Thumb down a passing car and get it to take her to the embassy? How many passing cars were there likely to be? She'd been standing here – for what, ten minutes? – but hadn't seen a single vehicle going by.

She took a gulp from the glass but stopped herself refilling it. She must keep a clear head to think things out. She had to get to the embassy. Their website said people needing emergency travel documents had to appear in person once they had an appointment. She needed another appointment. Where were Monty's keys? In his pocket. She was wondering how she could steal them, to give her access, not just to the study and the Wi-Fi, but also to the front door and the gate and the car, when she noticed a bright yellow taxi going by. No, not going by. Stopping. Stopping at the gate of Villa Adelos. Was this the promised help?

She hurried downstairs and made her way to the side gate.

'Mrs Liberty Allgood?' The voice on the other side of the gate was male and Greek.

Libby peered through a gap and thought she recognised the taxi driver who had brought them here, what seemed an age ago. 'Yes, yes, that's me.'

'I come for you.'

'Come for me?'

'Yes, Nikos sent me. He was coming today but is stuck at Heathrow. Like lion in cage. The plane he had boarded is grounded. Technical error. He will come as soon as problem solved.'

Nikos! Libby felt herself welling up at the sound of his name, but saw through her tears that the driver had a bunch of sunflowers in his hand.

'Can you open the gate, Mrs Liberty?'

Libby said she couldn't because she didn't know the combination to open the side-gate, or the main gate where Monty drove the car in and out. She hadn't got the digital key that Monty used to open and close the gates. She tried pushing and pulling, but nothing happened.

'Can you get someone to open the gate for you?' said the cab driver.

Libby hesitated. Did she want Monty to know about this meeting? If he came and opened the gate what would she do? Rush out? Would he let her? No, he wouldn't. What would he do? He wouldn't open the gate. She'd be wasting her time asking – and give too much away.

'Have flowers from Nikos,' said the taxi driver. 'He ask how are you? What I say? My name Georgios, by the way.'

Tears were now streaming down her face.

'What I say?' insisted the taxi driver.

'That I want to get out of here. I want to come ho-ome!' Now she was blubbing.

'Okay. Don't cry, lady. He working on it. They working on it. They send message "All for One!" Here are my contact details. You ring when you can leave.' He slid a business card through a narrow gap.

Libby forced her brain to work.

'Georgios, please go to the British Embassy and say I – Liberty Allgood – I've been trying to contact them. Tell them I need emergency travel papers very quickly. Say I've lost my passport and I'm being prevented from getting to the embassy myself. I've submitted my application. I can't come in person. Could you bring the papers here?'

'I try.' His voice sounded as if it were further away.

'You're going?' Her mouth went dry.

'Yes, but no worry, I return.'

'Georgios, one thing more. I sent one hundred pounds to the British Embassy for the emergency papers.'

'Okay.' His voice sounded even further away.

'And another thing, I want those flowers.'

'Okay, stand back.'

She took a step back as a bouquet of golden sunflowers came flying over the gate and landed at her feet.

63

LIBBY

Libby headed for the villa, clutching the sunflowers by their sturdy stems.

Nikos was coming today. Georgios's words were in her head. He will come when problem solved.

Hoping Monty was busy in the shed, she planned to take the flowers to her bedroom. Thank God she had that to herself. She would close the door, calm down and plan. As she climbed the steps to the front door, dodging bendy branches of pale blue plumbago and spiky tangles of purple bougainvillea – how everything had grown in a month! – she tried to put herself in Monty's shoes. If he wanted to keep her here – which he definitely did – how would he react if he knew people on the outside knew she was being held against her will? Would he realise the game was up and see there was no point in preventing her leaving? Or would he panic and tighten security? Her friends were 'working on it', Georgios had said. What did that mean? That the Muscateers were planning one of their rescue missions? If only! But where were they? Nikos was stuck at Heathrow. This was Greece, not a pub or a house up the road from where Viv and Janet and Zelda lived.

Puffed now, she paused before tacking the next flight of steps.

The front door was closed. But she had left it open. This wasn't good. She had propped it open so it couldn't close in a sudden breeze. She had put the catch on to be double sure so that if it closed it wouldn't lock. She didn't want to be locked out till she could get Monty to let her in. So what had happened? That became clear even as she asked the question. Monty was now opening the door, looking down at her, looking down at the bouquet in her hands, which she went to hide behind her back, till that instinct was overtaken by a better one. She thrust the flowers in front of her. 'Darling! Thank you!' She hurried up the second flight of steps. 'They're so lovely, but why? It isn't my birthday!'

He was flummoxed, as she'd hoped he would be. It gave her time to think.

* * *

'They're gorgeous.' She kept the tone light as, in the kitchen now, she looked for a jug to hold the flowers. She'd decided to carry on with her 'grateful partner' act and appeal to his better side. 'It is lovely to feel appreciated.'

He'd followed her into the kitchen, saying he'd come in for a cup of tea.

She found an earthenware jug in a lower cupboard. 'Still not sure why you need me here right now though.'

'To write the novel, darling. Look, we've been over this before.' He was at the sink, filling the kettle, waiting for the water to run cold, looking preoccupied. He must be wondering who had sent the flowers.

As she straightened up she noticed the bulge of keys in his left-hand pocket, saw that it was a side pocket not buttoned or zipped. Moving the jug to her left hand so her right hand was free, she went and stood beside him at the sink, hoping he'd think she was there only to fill the jug with water. Now the keys were inches from her hand. 'Darling—' she leaned towards him '—I can't believe I haven't given you a thank-you kiss. There.' She landed a smacker on his lips as her hand reached out...

'Feeling me up, darling?' He laughed, but it wasn't a nice laugh.

'No, I was auditioning for the Artful Dodger.' She realised she'd made a bad move as he removed her hand.

He'd sussed her. From now on he'd be on the alert. Not good. 'The novel's going well,' she said, to steer the subject to one she hoped he'd enjoy. It was in fact going surprisingly well. Her enforced stay had given her time to write several more chapters.

'Who delivered them?' He jerked his head at the flowers.

'A taxi driver. I think the same one that brought us here at the beginning of the holiday.'

'How did he give them to you with the gate closed?' He was suspicious.

'He threw them over.'

'Was there a card?'

'No. Should there have been?' The card was in her pocket. She hadn't had time to read it yet. 'Must have fallen out. I just assumed they were from you...' She tailed off, leaving him an opening, but he didn't fill it, so she burbled on. 'Back to the novel, Monty. As I said, it's going well. I'm starting to think of plot twists of my own to add to your brilliant ideas. There's only one thing holding me up – as the first part is set in the sixties I really need to google for information, brand names, things like that...'

But he was standing up, preoccupied, not listening. He went onto the balcony and looked over the balustrade, and she stood up too, hope triumphing over experience. 'If you could open the study before you go back to work, I could go and check the Wi-Fi connection, to save you the bother, and get googling.'

'Sorry, darling, let's talk later.' He turned back towards the kitchen. 'I've got to get back to work.'

And he was gone, forgetting that he'd come in for a cup of tea.

Where was he going? Libby went back to the balcony and leaned over the balustrade. There he was coming out of the front door, then going down the outside steps. She could see his head, some of the time. It was now you see it, now you don't as he bobbed past all the potted plants on the stairway. He was at the bottom now in clear view, walking in a zigzag, slowly, head down looking for the card that she'd said must have fallen out of the bouquet.

Monty wanted to know who had sent her flowers. She watched him search for a while, then give up. She saw him turn round, and for a scary moment she thought he was coming back in to demand to know where the flowers came from. But – phew! – he disappeared round the side of the villa, to discuss with Dimitris, she guessed. Monty was worried. Someone on the outside knew where Libby was. Someone was in touch with her. Someone who might thwart his plans. He also knew that she was desperate to leave, desperate enough to try and steal his keys. Libby read the card again.

Get well soon, Liberty!
Just stay put and stay safe.
All for one!

It didn't completely make sense. *Get well soon?* She guessed that whoever wrote it was using words carefully in case Monty got hold of it. They didn't want to give too much away. *All for one!* The Muscateers were obviously working with Nikos. But he was stuck at Heathrow! Where were they? She read the card again. *Just stay put and stay safe.* Well, stay put was all she could do, though doing nothing went against the grain. She felt like a helpless princess in an old-fashioned fairy tale, passively waiting for a knight on a white charger, but she wanted to be the modern sort fighting her way to freedom. She wanted to *do* something.

64

LIBBY

It was good that she had writing to distract her – to some extent. Sitting on her bed, knees bent, she opened her laptop, and read what she'd written most recently. Tarquin, the character based on Monty at his request, had just fallen from his pedestal. Libby – she hadn't thought of another name for herself yet – had realised he was a bumbling idiot, a Bertie Wooster figure, or an upper-class Del Boy. He wasn't the dashing figure she'd thought he was when she had a crush on him. For yes, she'd had a crush, not just when she was young, but as an older woman too. How could she have been so deluded? She blushed to remember how passionately she'd wanted him. Tarquin was comical, incompetent and deluded, living in a dream world, but harmless.

Is Monty harmless? Was her depiction of him too benign?

She remembered with a jolt her recent discovery – hard to believe it was only earlier today – that he was a fraudster. Selling Greek wine in French bottles! Did he really think he would get away with a scam like that? She hoped he hadn't got the organisational skills to sell any, because if he had he would surely end up behind bars. Despite everything, she'd hate that to happen to him.

But what a great scene it would make! She saw Tarquin in the dock, protesting his innocence to judge and jury. She saw the judge banging down his gavel. Guilty as charged! Send him down! She made a note then picked up her phone. Time to check the Wi-Fi again. From time to time, when he needed it, Monty went into his office and plugged in the router. He didn't tell her when, of course, so she had to keep checking. The Wi-Fi was down.

It was nearly five o'clock. Monty and Dimitris would be finishing work for the day soon. Monty would be coming in for his dinner, unless she could persuade him to take her out for a meal. If they went to a taverna she could use the Wi-Fi there. She went downstairs, checked the study door, locked, of course, then headed for the shed. The production line was in full swing, clunking and whirring away. She heard it even before she opened the door. As soon as she did she noticed they had changed positions. Dimitris was now feeding the labelling machine and Monty was putting the bottles into boxes, facing the door. He was on the other side of the conveyor belt so he saw her coming in, and shouted to Dimitris to stop the belt, then to her.

'What is it, darling?'

'I've come to see if we could go out for dinner tonight.' Her voice was loud in the quietness when the belt stopped. 'The cupboards are a bit bare.'

'Oh, I'm sure you can rustle something up, darling, just for you and me. Dimitris is going home.'

He wanted to keep her inside.

'Okay, I'll do my best.' She turned to go, then turned back, hoping to make it sound like an afterthought. 'Did you know the Wi-Fi's down again? I need to look something up to move on with the novel. Lack of info is holding me up.'

Monty got his mobile from his pocket, glanced at the screen and pressed something. 'So it is.' He really was keen for her to write the novel. 'I'll come and open the office for you, darling. Back soon, Dimitris!' He left his post and joined her. 'What is it you want to know?'

'Names of shops on the old King's Road, for authenticity, you know.' She was thinking on her feet. 'That's where the other girls bought their clothes, if I'm remembering rightly.'

'Hoped you'd be a bit further on than our student days, darling.'

'Oh, I am, it's a flashback.'

They reached the office and he unlocked the door. Then he went straight to the router and plugged in a cable. 'There. Be as quick as you can, sweetie. These things cost money, you know.'

Interesting. Unplugging it to save money was a new tack. He wasn't even pretending that the cable kept going in and out of its own accord, that there was a loose connection. He was concocting a reason for disconnecting it most of the time, for keeping control. Now he was watching, but not looking closely as she googled, so she went straight into her bank account, where one glance made her blood run cold. She sank into the chair behind her.

'What's the matter, darling?' Monty's voice seemed to come from a long way off.

You know what's the matter. You know more about this than I do.

Her bank account was empty. Her account frozen.

Opening her eyes, she looked at the figures again, still not believing. Worse than empty, she was in the red, by a wide margin. She had been in the red before, by small amounts when she'd gone overdrawn by mistake, or sometimes knowingly when she'd had to pay for something over a few months, but never as much as this. She was well over her overdraft limit. There wasn't enough to buy a ticket home. There wasn't enough to pay for a taxi to the airport. There wasn't enough to pay the embassy's £100 fee. She felt sick, her stomach heaving. Someone had been drawing money out of her account, lots of money, huge sums. Someone had been using her card.

No prizes for guessing who.

She had been financing his crazy scheme. The payees' names showed her that – all of them were vine growers. And she saw how she'd made it possible. She'd given him her bank details so he could use her card from time to time, to save his manly pride. In restaurants she'd let him take it to the desk to pay, because he was embarrassed, he'd said, when a woman paid the bill. He felt his manhood shrinking. His bloody manhood!

'Darling, you look ill.' He was close now.

'You've been stealing from me.' She couldn't pretend any longer.

'How can you say that?' He looked hurt.

'You've cleaned me out.'

'No, darling.' He shook his head. 'You've cleaned yourself out, if that's the expression you want to use, by investing in our company. Our company, yours, Dimitris's and mine.'

Now she understood *implicated*. She was in this up to her neck.

I didn't! I didn't! I didn't! She wanted to scream.

'But, sweetie—' he stooped, taking hold of her hands '—please don't worry. It's an investment. You'll get your money back. We'll get our just rewards when the money starts rolling in.'

Just rewards – that was what she feared.

'In fact—' he kept hold of her hands '—it's all going rather better than expected. We're ahead of schedule. We'll have finished the labelling by the end of today, and—' he straightened up, releasing her hands at last '—I was going to tell you this over dinner, but I'll tell you now...' He paused for dramatic effect. 'We are going on a little vacation.'

Alarm bells clanged.

'We've got a couple of days before the wine will be collected, so we're heading out to the islands, where Dimitris has a little house.'

Just stay put.

'Nice.' Libby got to her feet. 'You and Dimitris deserve a break. You've worked hard. Enjoy!' She took a step towards the office door.

'But you're coming too, darling. Can't leave our partner behind.'

'Sorry, but I need to carry on writing, Monty. No holidays for me, I'm afraid, not till I've finished the novel.'

'But you can carry on writing while you're there. You can take your laptop with you. I'm not leaving you behind, darling.' He grasped her wrist, a new steely note in that gravelly voice.

He suspects. He knows that my friends know where I am.

'Okay.' She had to seem to comply. 'That's really kind. How exciting! Which island is the house on and when exactly are we leaving?'

'Tomorrow at 9 a.m., to catch an early ferry.' He didn't say which island. 'So pack a bag tonight.'

'Okay, but first I'd better go and rustle up something for dinner.' She had to think fast. She had to act.

65

LIBBY

Stay put.

She had to stay. She must not leave the Villa Adelos. She had to wait here for her friends. Georgios said they were 'working on it'. That must mean they were coming here. But if she left... Could Monty make her go with him? Would he, could he, use force? He was bigger than her and possibly stronger, but not strong enough to carry her into the car. Passive resistance, that was the answer. *Just say no. Make yourself into a dead weight. Sit down and refuse to move. Lock yourself in the bedroom. Tie yourself to the railings.* Ideas buzzed in her head as she made her way to the kitchen. But what if Monty got nasty? So far he hadn't – though there was still a red mark where his fingers had circled her wrist none too gently – and she wasn't completely naïve. Even the nicest of men...

Monty isn't the nicest of men. And Dimitris might be there too. Monty hadn't said how they were getting to the ferry. If Dimitris was picking them up there would be two of them...

She was standing in front of the fridge now, her brain flipping to food and supper. She had lied when she'd said the cupboard was bare. There were still a few things in the fridge, mince of some kind and a couple of aubergines, so moussaka came to mind. She took them out and closed the door. The mince was beef, not lamb, but it would do. What else had she got? Onions? Yes, in the hopper under the sink. Herbs and spices? She opened cupboard doors to see what else there was, and her eyes wandered to the top shelf where there was a plastic box full of everyday medicines. She had raided it before, looking for a sticking plaster or an indigestion tablet, from time to time, but as she perused it now her thoughts returned to her current predicament.

Brain against brawn was one of her dad's favourite sayings, which Libby thought of as she reached for the box of medicines and selected a packet and a bottle or two. Then she made moussaka, which she cooked in four separate dishes, two for the freezer, two for tonight, his and hers. She left out the brown sugar from Monty's portion, but added a secret sweetener, never to be divulged. California syrup of figs. Quite a lot of California syrup of figs. Helena's family must suffer from constipation. There were three bottles. She added cinnamon and oregano to take the edge off the sweetness, though Monty luckily had a sweet tooth. He loved chocolate brownies, so she made a batch of those too. She would tell him they were a snack for the journey, but knew that if he didn't nab one as soon as he came in, he wouldn't be able to resist a couple for pudding tonight. Little chocolatey squares of Ex-lax added texture to the brownies. Broken into little pieces, they looked and would taste just like dark chocolate chips. Laxatives! Re-laxatives! What fun! Monty was always telling her to 'relax' and 'loosen up'. It would be fun watching him take a taste of his own medicine.

Monty came in at seven o'clock, complaining about his aching back, but affable enough. 'Dinner smells great, darling. Oh! May I?' He spotted the brownies and put one in his mouth before Libby could say, 'Later, darling!'

Obviously, everything was fine in Monty's world, positively

hunky-dory. People defrauding other people was normal. Stealing was normal. Lying was what you did. He washed his hands at the kitchen sink then went and sat down at the table on the balcony and tipped the dish of moussaka onto his plate. Then, helping himself to salad, he said he wanted to talk about the novel. When would it be finished? How many words did she do a day?

Libby sat down opposite him. 'Five hundred,' she said, 'a thousand on a good day. Sorry.' She saw his shocked face, knew some writers did a lot more.

'How many words are there in a novel?'

Libby said she wasn't sure. She thought shorter ones, novellas, were around 60,000 words, big fat sagas well over 100,000. She was aiming for something in between.

Monty got a pen and did some calculations on a paper serviette. 'At one thousand a day, ninety thousand would take you three months, double that if you're only doing five hundred! You've got to speed up, darling!'

'I'll try but I'm only on the first draft. I've never written a novel before, but I do several drafts of my column before it's right.'

'Several drafts? How many? How long will that take?'

'Another couple of months?'

He was horrified. It took more wine and moussaka and another chocolate brownie to soothe him.

By nine o'clock he was quite mellow. She was tired after playing compliant little woman all night. Now she was sitting beside him on the swing seat, watching a glorious sunset set sea and sky ablaze.

'Early night, darling?' He touched her hand and raised a white eyebrow in the way that had once made her heart skip, but now made her stomach heave.

'Sorry, darling, not for me, I'm afraid. Work to do.' Sleeping with him might make it easier to take the keys from his trouser pocket, but the price was too high. 'You go up, darling. I'll stay here and do a few more words.' She reminded him of Freud's theory of sublimation, that creativity was suppressed sexual desire. 'I really do find I'm more creative if I don't have sex while I'm writing. So it's hands-off till the novel is finished, I'm afraid. Can't tell you how much I want to get to The End.'

She was lying for her life.

He muttered something she didn't hear properly but got to his feet rather unsteadily. She said she'd also got her packing to do for their little holiday in the islands and asked him what time they were leaving. He said they had to be at the gate at nine o'clock sharp, where a cab would be waiting – not Dimitris, phew! – so he was setting his alarm for seven.

* * *

But at seven Monty had been up for an hour. Libby, awake and alert for longer than that, heard him getting up and saw him going downstairs fully dressed. Disappointed at first, she thought the laxatives hadn't worked, but then heard a bellowing groan from downstairs and soon afterwards the pipes started to gurgle. The pipes continued to gurgle and more groans emanated from the downstairs loo. Hurray! The plumbing was working overtime and so were Monty's bowels. The timing was perfect. Monty would have to stay near the loo for the next few hours at least.

First, she searched his bedroom just in case he'd left the keys – and maybe her passport – in there. But he hadn't, well, not unless he'd hidden them very cleverly. More likely they were still in his pocket. Back to Plan A. She got dressed – no time to shower – and made sure she'd packed everything essential in her large suitcase. Her plan was to direct the cab at the gate to take her to the embassy in Athens. She would work out what to do from there. Only when she'd hauled her case downstairs and stowed it by the front door did she knock on the downstairs loo door, praying that he had his keys with him.

'Are you okay, darling?' She was the voice of concern.

It was some time before he replied, saying he'd got the most godawful gut ache he'd ever had in his life. Food poisoning, he thought. She encouraged him to drink water to avoid dehydration and said she would fetch him some. He said not to bother. She recommended Imodium to relieve the symptoms and he said he'd give them a go, so she went to look for some, but unfortunately – ha ha! – couldn't find any. Returning to the fray, she advised him not to eat for a couple of days and he said he never wanted to eat again. Then another spasm of gut ache had him calling out for more toilet paper. Off she went dutifully to fetch him some from an upstairs loo. How she managed to keep a straight face when she opened the door she would never know. There he was sitting on the loo with his trousers round his ankles, his hands covering his nether regions, his face a picture of misery.

'Poor darling,' she was sympathy personified, 'I do hope you're remembering to put the loo paper in the bin. Don't flush it away, will you? Or you'll clog up the plumbing!'

'Sod the plumbing,' was the politest of his replies and the bin looked empty. Never mind, she was leaving very soon and wouldn't have to deal with the consequences.

But first there were things she must do.

'I need your keys, Monty.' She held out her hand to save what little was left of his dignity.

'So you can depart and ditch me?' He suspected.

So she moved decisively. Stepping forward, bending down, and grabbing hold of his trousers, she jerked them off over his shoes, lifting his feet and legs into the air, exposing his bare bum. As he grabbed the loo with both hands to stop himself falling off, she backed out of the door, curses exploding in her ears.

'Come back with my f****** trousers!'

On the kitchen balcony she shook the trousers briskly and the keys fell out with a satisfying clunk. Then she searched the other pockets. Yes! There was her passport in the buttoned back pocket. That was where it had probably been all the time, since he'd taken it from her drawer. Within minutes she'd thrown the trousers over the balcony, used the key to open the office, reconnected the Wi-Fi and begun a message to Zelda. But before she could finish a message came in:

We are on our way! Z

When was that sent? Yesterday? Today? And where had Zelda sent it from? England? Greece? She had no idea. And who were 'we'? It was eight thirty in the morning and the cab to take her to the ferry was coming at nine. With luck Monty would still be stuck on the loo she was thinking, when something made her turn and there he was standing in the doorway. What a sight, clutching a small towel round his middle! But before she had the nouse to push him out of the way he'd managed to step inside, kicking the door shut behind him.

'You're not going anywhere, Miss Too Good! You're not leaving this effing room!'

* * *

Meanwhile, in a lay-by three kilometres away, a small fleet of assorted vehicles was assembling, about to converge on the Villa

Adelos. Nikos had flown in overnight and Georgios had met him at Athens airport in his yellow taxi. Viv and Patrick had come straight to Artemida once they'd convinced Customs and Excise who were holding them up, that they had nothing illegal in their Range Rover. And Nikos's second cousin, Stefanos, was testing the blue flashing light of his shiny blue and white police car.

66

LIBBY

'Where are my bloody trousers?' Monty had his back to the office door.

'On the bloody balcony!' Libby saw him scanning the room. 'They're not here, Monty.' That much was true.

'Give me those keys!' He tried masterful male. Then, seeing her stony face, wheedling male. 'Have a heart, Libby.'

'I've got a heart, Monty, but it's hardening by the second.' Libby reprised her audition piece. She became Queen Margaret in her mad rage as she caught sight of the paper knife on the desk beside the PC. It was for opening letters no doubt, but the blade was long and metal and sharp enough.

'Turn round and face the door, Monty.' She held the knife in front of her. 'Then open it and put both hands back on your towel.'

He shuffled round to face the door then hesitated.

'Open it!'

She was the mad queen as she heard the handle turn and saw the door opening inwards, as he shuffled backwards clutching the towel with one hand.

'Now face the wall.' She *was* the vengeful widow, enjoying the fear on his face, as she watched him turn and saw his trembling white shins. Then an avenging furie as she swept past, slamming and locking the door behind her. Keys in hand, she headed for the front door.

Exit Libby, herself again, dragging her case down the first flight of steps, bumpety bump, not dignified but totally focussed.

Only when halfway down and puffed out did she pause to check her phone for messages. Nothing from her friends or anyone else. Then, as she was about to tackle the second flight downwards, she heard screeching brakes. What was that on the other side of the gates? Standing on tiptoe, she saw a flashing band of blue on the roof of a white car. And a yellow taxi? And a— She couldn't see clearly what it was, but now there were three vehicles parked on the road, then four as another police car with flashing blue lights screeched to a halt. She heard doors opening and banging shut, then a crackling sound, then an amplified voice as if someone was speaking through a megaphone.

Someone was speaking through a megaphone.

'Open these gates immediately! We are police officers with a warrant to enter this building! If you do not open these gates we will force entry!'

A stunned Libby came to her senses. 'I've got keys! I'm coming! Hold on!' Leaving the suitcase, she hurried down the steps, as quickly as she could, trying not to fall headlong in her eagerness.

Minutes later, after opening the side-gate, she was running into the open arms of Nikos, who wrapped them round her, cheered on by Viv and Zelda and a taxi driver called Georgio.

'Liberty Allgood,' said Nikos, 'we have come to take you home.'

I am home, she thought but didn't say, breathing the man in. *I am home.*

Libby travelled back with Zelda on a flight the next day. Tickets had appeared as if by magic, but it had all been carefully planned – at great speed she came to understand. Money, not hers, must have been spent, which was problematic. The Muscateers and Nikos had worked together to make things happen and get her home for the celebratory dinner at The Olive Branch on Sunday night.

'But first you must rest,' said Zelda as they buckled their seat belts.

'I rested last night, thank you,' said Libby from the window seat. She'd had the best night's sleep she'd had for weeks, in a hotel near the airport, also paid for by A.N. Other or Others. 'Now I need to write a column for Sid.' Her laptop was in the bag under her seat. She needed to start earning again.

'Sid's still got one of your reserves, one he's been wanting to use for ages, he said, about knickers?' Zelda lowered her voice, with a glance at the man in the aisle seat beside her, fortunately plugging something into his ears.

'Inspired by you.' Libby laughed. 'Well, by the Muscateers.'

The Muscateers set great store by knickers, smart knickers.

Saggy, faded knickers were a big NO. She'd gathered it was Viv's theory originally that the knickers you put on in the morning coloured your mood for the rest of your day. They affected your morale so you had to be careful. Put on slogged-out Sloggis and you crept around like a worn-out has-been, no confidence at all. Put on snug new Sloggis or something snazzy with a bit of elasticity, you had a spring in your step and felt you could conquer your to-do list, if not the world.

Zelda said she knew the theory and subscribed to it but didn't see how Libby could write a whole column on the subject. 'More to the point, what are you going to wear that's visible for the dinner chez Nikos, where, may I remind you, you're the star?'

Libby didn't mind the reminder, not at all, well, not about what to wear. Clothes were important, outer garments even more than knickers. She closed her eyes to visualise the contents of her wardrobe. What had she got that would do?

'You could treat yourself to something new.' Zelda loved a shopping spree.

'No, I couldn't!' Libby's eyes opened with alarm.

They were flying over the Alps by the time she'd finished telling Zelda about her current disastrous financial situation and events leading up to it. Zelda's jaw dropped lower and lower as Libby revealed one Monty rip-off after another, but amazingly didn't once say, 'I told you so.' Nor did she say that she'd warned Libby to *never ever* hand over her credit card. She didn't need to. She was in Libby's head, telling her very clearly back in March on that Sunday afternoon walk, when she'd just revealed that she'd let Monty use her credit card to buy her a drink at the theatre bar. Zelda must have bitten her tongue off not-saying – Libby appreciated – but she did say, 'You've got to let Nikos help sort this out, Libby. With his legal hat on, I mean. That man—' she obviously couldn't bear to say

Monty's name '—must be reported to the police, Greek or British or both.'

'But I'm not sure he's done anything illegal, or anything that could be proved to be illegal.' Libby thought this was true. 'He'll say I spent the money willingly, that I was their business partner.' She'd explained about Dimitris.

'But he's lying, Libby. And he used your card to buy wine for his fraudulent enterprise, which, the wine scam, I mean, is undoubtedly criminal.'

That was horribly true.

'I've been an idiot, such an idiot.'

Zelda reached for Libby's hand. 'Yes, but don't beat yourself up. No one's blaming you, least of all Viv, Janet and me. We know what that first year is like. None of us was sane. We all made mistakes.'

The drinks trolley arrived. 'Ladies?' The steward stood by.

'Two Prosecco,' said Zelda.

'It's two o'clock in the afternoon!'

'Not in the UK and we need the lift.' Zelda paid with her credit card, ignoring Libby's protests.

'To you, Zelda,' said Libby when the fizz was in their glasses. 'A role model. You've got the right idea, going it alone, I mean.'

'To you, Libby, onwards and upwards.' Zelda raised her glass. 'That man should be behind bars, for hurting you if nothing else.'

The thought of Monty in prison didn't give Libby any pleasure at all, though she felt sick thinking about what he had done – and what *she* had done unwittingly. What a fool she'd been! She'd let herself be duped because she'd *fancied* him, worse, because she'd fancied him years ago, and had thought she could pick up where she'd left off and take the road not travelled. She'd thought she could go back in time and make him love her now, as he hadn't loved her then, because she'd longed to be loved. Because there was an aching gap in her life. An expression of her father's came into her head. When she was getting speculative, he'd say, 'You know what thought thought, Libby? He thought he'd bought a car but he'd only bought the hooter.' Yes, she'd bought the hooter *and* convinced herself that the hooter loved her. How could she ever trust her feelings again?

'Oh, by the way, don't think I've said.' Zelda touched her arm to get her attention. 'We've discovered that Nikos isn't married.'

'So?' Libby shrugged.

'I *mean*,' said Zelda, 'that he *isn't* married to Evelina.' She sounded as if it mattered.

'I assumed that's what you meant, but what's the big deal? Viv's not married to Patrick. My youngest son isn't married to his partner.'

'I *mean*...' Zelda put her glass into the holder. 'Sorry, I'm not making myself clear. The interesting thing is that Evelina isn't Nikos's wife, she's his sister. Big sister. She's older than him and they don't even live together. In a word, he's single.'

'S-single?' Libby felt her eyes opening wide.

'Divorced actually.' Zelda picked up her glass. 'Several years ago. Ex-wife went back to Greece, but they're still—'

'Zelda, stop it!' Libby converted a shout into a hiss, aware of other passengers all around. The woman on the other side of the aisle was agog. Heaven knew what the ones in the seats in front of theirs were thinking.

'Stop what?' Zelda whispered.

'Matchmaking.'

'I'm not!' Zelda spluttered, spraying fizz. 'I most certainly am not! I'm the last person. I was just saying—'

'That I'm not capable of going it alone like you? That I should shack up with Nikos and save on the legal fees? That I should jump from one failed relationship—'

'That's not fair, Libby! I implied nothing of the sort!'

'Well, I wish you hadn't told me. It changes things. I was looking forward to this dinner, but now I'm not.'

'Why ever not?' Zelda's face creased with incredulity.

'Because...' Wasn't it obvious?

'No.' Zelda asked for an explanation.

'Because, because,' – it was hard to explain – 'now I can't show him I love him.'

'Why not?' Zelda shook her head.

'B-because... I do?'

She answered her own question. She loved Nikos. It hit her. She'd always loved Nikos, well, since she'd got to know him when she and Jim had started going to The Olive Branch. Nikos was loveable, trustworthy, decent, and kind, all the important things. Jim had thought so too. They had been like brothers. That was it – she thought of him *as a brother* and the best of men.

'But you don't fancy him?'

'Fancy?' The word seemed so trite. 'I don't *know*, Zelda. I've never allowed myself to think that way.'

And she didn't want to start thinking that way. She was having memories of all the hugs she'd given him over the years, the pleased-to-see-you hugs, the that-was-a-great-meal hugs, the thanks-for-a-great-evening hugs, given freely because she'd thought he was married to Evelina as she had been married to Jim. Shrinking in her seat, she remembered the hug she'd given him yesterday. She had *thrown* herself into his arms, and wanted to stay there forever because it felt spontaneous and natural and safe.

But now it didn't.

68

ZELDA

'Libby accused me of thinking what I'm sure had suddenly occurred to her, that she and Nikos could be together, should be together. What's that called, Janet? I'm sure there's a word for it. You're into psychology.'

Zelda was sitting on the sofa in Janet's conservatory, Mack and Morag either side of her, snuggled up close. She'd driven to Janet's as soon as she'd got home, to collect the dogs and offload, Libby having made it clear she'd had enough of her company for the time being, probably for ever. Libby had almost run up her garden path to get away from her.

Mack and Morag had been with Janet for nearly a week, a month if you counted Zelda's time in North Carolina. She'd left them again when she'd hitched a lift to Greece with Viv and Patrick, to go and search for Libby. The little dogs loved Janet, but of course loved their mistress more. Still smarting at Libby's unfair accusations, Zelda needed the dogs' commiserations, and Janet's and Viv's. Viv, still in Greece, had just joined them by Skype. She was on the screen of Janet's iPad, which was propped against a potted plant on the table in the conservatory.

'Projection,' said Janet, putting a chair by the sofa, so she could see the screen too. 'It's called projection. You project onto another person what you're feeling because you don't feel comfortable with that feeling yourself.'

'Why would loving Nikos make Libby feel uncomfortable? They're made for each other,' said on-screen Viv, who had a glass in her hand. It was eight o'clock in Greece, she reminded them. Six o'clock in UK.

'Yes, well, probably.' Zelda wasn't sure about 'made for each other' as a concept. 'I think Libby suddenly thought that too, but she doesn't trust her feelings any more, which may be wise after recent events. There's a lot going on in her head. She's afraid Nikos will think she's using him, and she may even be punishing herself. She's definitely blaming herself for being an idiot, much more than she's blaming the idiot who's been using her for the last six months.'

'You did tell her...' Viv interrupted.

'Yes, of course I did. I told her we'd all done mad things in that first year, and that she'll start to see things more clearly now. It was Jim's anniversary last week.'

'And what about Nikos? Where is he at the moment?' Janet got up to get a bottle from the fridge.

'Still in Greece.' Zelda declined the offered glass and Janet poured herself one. 'He's coming back tomorrow to be here for the dinner on Sunday. Evelina's been doing most of the prep. He stayed on to make sure the police dropped charges against his niece or great-niece or whatever she is, the one Monty accused of stealing Libby's passport. I've texted him with a few more things I learned from Libby on the way back, not least Monty's fraudulent wine so-called business. I'm sure he'll share that with the police.'

'Does Nikos need to be told to proceed slowly with Libby?' Janet sipped thoughtfully. 'I assume we're all of the opinion that the man adores her?'

They both nodded but Viv said, 'I don't think Nikos needs to be told to go softly-softly. He's adored her quietly for a long time now. I mean, he must have loved her when Jim was alive, but, honourable bloke that he is, he didn't say. And when Jim died he was kind and supportive but nothing more. He's sensitive. He was giving her time, which was why he was so taken aback, I mean bloody furious, when Monty jumped in.'

'And what about Libby?' said Janet. 'Does she love Nikos?'

'She said "like a brother" but I'm not so sure.'

Zelda recalled the moment she told Libby that Nikos was single. 'I saw something flicker in her eyes, which opened wide as if she was seeing something amazing. Then they snapped shut and she started accusing me of matchmaking.'

'An insight.' Viv was certain. 'It was a moment of truth. She was seeing them as a couple, shacked up together, to use her own words.'

'Which she instantly put into your mouth, Zelda.' Janet sounded certain too. 'So how do we proceed?'

Zelda got to her feet. 'Carefully. She doesn't think she deserves Nikos, that's part of the problem, but I'm going home now to pick up a bottle to take round to Libby's. If she'll let me in, I'll volunteer my services as wardrobe mistress for Sunday night. When I last saw her she was veering towards sackcloth and ashes.'

* * *

Zelda arrived with Libby in the cab that Nikos had sent to pick them both up. Libby looked amazing in the black velvet dress that Zelda had chosen for her, with the pearl necklace with matching earrings that Jim had given her for their thirtieth anniversary. It was her understated Grace Kelly look, her blonde hair held back to the nape of her neck with a diamond clip, 'foisted on her' by Janet. She hadn't shown a lot of interest in getting dressed up – Zelda had had an almost-free hand – but the trooper in Libby perked up when she saw the packed restaurant. Zelda, observing closely from behind as the two of them followed Nikos to the top table, saw Libby's back straighten as she acknowledged, with a little wave of her hand, the applause of those already seated.

Zelda had already noted that Nikos, at the door standing between the two olive trees, waiting to greet them, had received only a handshake from Libby and the lightest of pecks on the cheek. But Nikos, Zelda also noted, hadn't greeted Libby with his customary open arms. What would she have done if he had? Were they both going to play I'm-not-going-to-show-you-how-keen-I-am all night?

Nikos was keen. That wasn't the word. He was devoted. He loved and admired Libby. That became even more obvious when he made his welcoming speech saying the night was in honour of Libby, whose first column, Libby's World, had appeared just one year ago, soon after the passing-away of her husband and his old friend, Jim. Always one to choose his words carefully, he seemed to be choosing them even more carefully tonight, speaking from the heart, Zelda had no doubt, but also fully engaging his brain, so as to say what he wanted to say to Libby while addressing a crowded room. He looked at her from time to time, surely hoping for a response, but she looked down at her plate.

Look at him, Libby. Look at his face.

Zelda, sitting next to her, wanted to give her the nudge of all nudges as Nikos said how much he admired Libby's bravery in sharing her sadness with her readers. How much he admired her bravery in sharing her search for happiness with readers, her openness, her humour, her generosity, matched only by the generosity of her husband. He spoke of Jim, his friend, and Jim's love for Libby and his wish that she would be happy after he'd gone.

Did Jim say this? To Nicos? Zelda longed to ask.

'It's too easy to live in the past after a great loss. It takes great courage to move on. Mistakes are made, inevitably...'

Was Libby listening? Did she hear what he was saying? Viv, on her other side, nudged her.

Nikos was drawing to a close, or changing the subject, rather abruptly, she thought. Did he think he'd said too much? Today was, he was saying, by amazing coincidence, International Day of Peace, so there was a double reason why Evelina had decorated their tables with mini olive branches, trimmings from their own olive trees. He urged everyone to take one home at the end of the evening and make their peace with whoever they were at odds with. Then he asked them to raise their glasses to Peace and Love and Liberty, before disappearing, rather suddenly, into the kitchen. Soon afterwards, waiters came out with the meal, an array of Libby's favourites.

He totally got her, Zelda thought. Why wasn't she melting?

After the meal Sid made a speech, praising Libby to high heaven in his laconic manner, saying she was the best columnist he'd ever had, and announcing that Libby's World was going to be syndicated, so she would soon be known countrywide. 'A local treasure will become national.' Thanks to her the paper was now viable and would continue into the foreseeable future in both its digital and paper editions. She'd saved their jobs.

Sid sat down and Libby got up.

She was as self-deprecating as ever, telling jokes against herself. Sid was exaggerating. It was a team effort et cetera. He'd helped her hone her skills. 'If you've only got five hundred words to say your piece you can't use ten words where two will do.' She thanked him for being the first person to commission her to write, for having faith in her. 'For boosting my confidence, for making me believe that others would enjoy what are, after all, only the ramblings of an old woman.' She urged everyone to enjoy their lives, but especially the last chapters, to try new things, to take risks. 'With one proviso. Don't *assume* that, because you get older, you get wiser. You've learned a lot, yes, but can still be as daft as a teenager, without the excuse of being a teenager. So keep your friends close, to ensure damage limitation. To friendship.' She raised her glass then sat down.

It wasn't Libby's best-ever speech, in Zelda's opinion. 'Ramblings of an old woman' was not a good choice of words, even said ironically. She consulted her notes a bit too often, was too *careful*. Zelda had hoped that, mellowed by food and drink, she would have dropped her guard a little by this time in the evening. But she drank very little and her guard was high when she said goodbye to Nikos, as formally as she'd said hello. She thanked him graciously, pecked his cheek, and walked out to the waiting cab, her expression hard to read. Zelda, looking out of the cab window, saw Nikos watching them drive away.

69

ZELDA

The Muscateers didn't see as much of Libby as they would have liked for the next few months. She came to their monthly lunches at The Wagon and Horses and at The Olive Branch, reporting on her ups and down as they all did, but she didn't linger long to chat. Zelda saw more of her, living nearby, but not a great deal more. The morning coffee they used to have at least once a week stopped. Libby was too busy, she said.

She wrote every morning, even on Tuesdays when she looked after Ellie-Jo. She simply got up earlier and wrote before she set off, or before Ellie-Jo arrived at her house. One of the ups was that she'd sorted things out with Eleanor. A down was the sad experience of visiting her increasingly demented mother every Wednesday afternoon and sometimes more often as the poor woman became more distressed. Then her mother died in February, which hit her hard, though it brought release and relief to them both. Zelda, and the others to a lesser extent, gave her as much support as she would allow, but their meetings didn't become more frequent. She was writing a novel, she revealed at their March meeting, but didn't say what it was about.

Then Libby got an invitation, which she did discuss with Zelda. She asked her round for a glass-of-something one Tuesday evening in April. Greek fizz, Zelda noted, reading the label on the bottle in front of her. They were in Libby's sitting room. 'Afrodi?' she sounded it out.

'*Afrothi*,' Libby corrected.

'*Afrothi*,' Zelda repeated, the word fizzing in her mouth like the tiny bubbles in the glass.

Then Libby handed her a printed-out email. 'It's from Monty, though written by the festival secretary. He's inviting me to launch my picture book, *Lovely Old Lion*, at this year's festival in October.' Libby sounded doubtful. Good.

'I think I should do it.' Not so good. *Monty wants her back,* was Zelda's first thought, as Libby went on to say it was an opportunity to educate people about dementia and proof that Monty was at last recognising the importance of children's literature.

Zelda thought Monty was recognising that he could end up behind bars if Libby told the police everything she knew. Nikos was urging the Greek police to investigate Monty, for theft and fraud, but they'd said they could only bring charges if Libby testified against him, for using her credit and debit cards if nothing else. Libby was refusing to do this. She was outraged by his scam to sell Greek wine as vintage French, and was determined to stop that, but not outraged enough by what he'd done to her, in Zelda's opinion. Libby said she'd told Monty she would testify against him if he didn't close down his so-called business. He'd told her he had seen the error of his ways and would show her that the labelling machinery was no longer at the Villa Adelos, if she came to see. He was still living at the Villa Adelos, by all accounts, in his role as house-sitter.

* * *

Zelda told all this to Viv and Janet next morning. 'I'm sure Monty's trying to keep her on his side.'

'He wants to get back in her knickers.' Viv was as graphic as ever.

'Or her wallet.' Janet was terse.

They were sitting round Viv's kitchen table drinking coffee from her stylish black and white cups.

'I'm sure she won't be daft enough to allow him access to either, but I have told her that if she goes, and she seems determined to, that I would be happy to go with her. I've checked my diary and could be free. Libby's happy with that, by the way, but I also wondered if we were due another Muscateers overseas jaunt?' Zelda looked from one to the other.

'Sounds as if you've got a plan?' Viv got her diary out.

Janet got her phone; her diary had gone digital. They could both be free, they said, after a minute's perusing, given it was six months away.

'And,' said Zelda, 'I wondered if we should take a Greek interpreter?'

'One with legal expertise?' Janet put her phone away.

How to manage it, that was the question. Nikos was a straight-speaking guy, Viv opined, so wouldn't it be best to be straight speaking? And didn't he usually head for Greece at that time of year? Zelda was assigned to sound him out.

* * *

And so it happened that the five of them met in the departures lounge of Luton airport on the morning of Monday 5 October. Nikos had booked a one-way ticket as he was staying on for a few months. Zelda had booked two-way tickets for the Muscateers, but they all found themselves looking at flight EZY688, on the same departures screen, at just before twelve noon. It was pre-planned; there was no subterfuge. Well, only a little.

* * *

Libby

Libby was aware Nikos would be there because, on the previous Friday, he had told the Muscateers that their meal at The Olive Branch was the last he would cook for them that year, because he was heading for Greece to hibernate. Janet had asked him when he was leaving and there had been expressions of amazement when they'd discovered they were on the same flight. *What a coincidence, I don't think!* Libby suspected machinations and wasn't surprised to see him at the airport, but she was more than a little disconcerted when she found herself sitting next to him on the plane. She had just sat down by the window in row five, after Viv, Janet and Zelda had taken the three seats on the opposite side of the aisle, when he appeared in the aisle. Then, after an exchange of words with the woman in front of him, he sat down beside Libby. The woman, who was taller than him, needed the legroom, he said. 'Sorry.'

She said it was okay, but the words *coercive control* came into her head. Was she going to be trapped with this man for the next three hours forty-five minutes? The words came into her head because Nikos had used the phrase several times in the past six months when the Muscateers met at The Olive Branch. He'd told them about a much-needed law coming into force at the end of next year. It would be used to prosecute men who abused women by keeping them under control by non-violent means, and would, he hoped, be a deterrent. Libby, listening, had guessed what he was thinking.

She'd immediately thought about her longer-than-wanted sojourn in the Villa Adelos, and didn't need to be told how a woman could be deprived of her liberty by non-violent means. Nikos, she noted, hadn't yet buckled his safety belt.

'I'm sure Viv or Janet or Zelda would swap places with me if that's what you'd prefer.'

She shook her head.

He said, 'We have, I think, been manoeuvred so we can discuss things. Is that what you want?'

She nodded, and they talked, haltingly at first, but gathering momentum even before they took off. He said that he would like to bring a charge against Monty for theft under Greek and British law. She said she would prefer to persuade Monty to return the money he'd taken from her. He said he'd like to help to try and persuade him. She said that was okay as long as he used legal means. He said, 'Of course.' By the time they reached Athens she had agreed that it would be lovely to be shown the sights by him, but along with the Muscateers. She'd also said she would like him to be nearby when she gave her talk on Thursday.

She'd gathered Monty was coming to hear her.

70

LIBBY

'You'll be a triumph.' Nikos was by her side as she waited to go on stage. They were in the wings at the small community theatre in Artemida.

'It's a niche-market children's book. They've only sold half the tickets.'

'To a discriminating minority.' He checked the microphone clipped to the edge of her linen dress, upping her pulse-rate, already quite fast with pre-performance nerves. 'It's a very good children's book that is being translated into eleven languages.'

Libby wasn't the star of the Artemida Festival of Art. She wasn't even the star of the children's section, which she had insisted they have. It was part of her price for keeping Monty out of jail. There were other bigger names here, people she'd recommended, because she wanted the festival to honour children's literature and art and theatre and music alongside that for adults. Art for children was important. It was formative, so they must have the best. *Lovely Old Lion*, her picture book about a lion with dementia, was one of several books being showcased. A plea for kindness and under-standing, it was a tribute to her mum and a very good story –

though she said so herself – that taught children what dementia was and showed them how they could help if their granny or granddad was afflicted. It was, several reviewers said, an empowering book.

'You're on.'

She felt his hand on the small of her back pressing her gently forward.

'Ladies and gentlemen, boys and girls...' she addressed the half-full hall, with Zelda, Viv and Janet, ever supportive, on the front row. 'I wrote this story because I was asked to by a librarian called Karen. Karen was concerned because children were coming into the library worried about their grandparents who couldn't remember their names, or who kept forgetting the rules of games like snakes and ladders...'

She hadn't said much more, choosing to let the story with Susan Varley's brilliant illustrations, projected onto a screen, speak for her. It went down well, if the applause and the queue to buy books, now forming, was significant. It looked as if everyone in the room wanted to buy a copy or several and have them signed. But not her friends who had disappeared. Well, of course they had copies already, but they usually hung around...

'Better get signing, Liberty.' Nikos pointed to the queue forming in front of her. And was that really Monty hovering near the end of it? He didn't do queuing. But yes, she saw when she looked up again, it was Monty. With a woman, she noted, of hard-to-say age, plump and short, motherly, or grandmotherly, holding onto his arm. Monty was carrying what looked like several *Lovely Old Lions*, presumably for his companion, unless he'd remembered he had a granddaughter. Libby signed a few more copies then Monty was in front of her, fanning five copies onto the table.

'Well *done*, Libby dear. Nice talk. Nice little story.'

'It's a beautiful story, Libby, and much needed.' The woman

with him stepped forward. 'My husband, sadly, is a lovely old lion but the grandchildren don't always see it that way. I'm hoping this will help. We met at lunch last year, by the way. I'm on the festival committee.'

Monty remembered his manners. 'Libby, meet Hermione – again.'

Hermione, a nice jolly lady, Libby recalled, didn't so much ooze as glimmer with wealth. She was fashionably dressed in a mini-skirted dress in a gold-brocade fabric, and rings crusty with diamonds adorned the fingers clutching the chain handle of her Louis Vuitton micro-trunk handbag. If half those sparklers were real she was worth a fortune. It looked as if Monty had found someone else to keep him in the style he was sure he deserved, so her friends needn't worry about him raiding her bank account again.

'My grandchildren love your children's books,' said Hermione, 'but I am looking forward to your novel for adults that Monty talked about last year.'

Libby read Monty's thoughts from the smirk on his face. *Poor old Libby. She hasn't finished it. She can't have, not without my help. Not while she's pandering to friends and family...*

'It's coming out next year.' Nikos was still by her side.

As she carried on signing books for Hermione's grandchildren, she heard Nikos telling them the name of the publisher and the publication date and the title, and she couldn't help feeling proud. Because, in a year of hard work, she had finished her novel *and* sold it. *Widows on the Wine Path!* was a romantic comedy with a princi-pled Greek lawyer as hero, a failed actress as heroine and a former very posh theatre director as a not-very-clever villain. Nikos didn't tell them all that, but when she glanced up, she saw Monty's jaw dropping so low it almost reached his polka-dotted cravat.

'Congratulations,' he said, picking up the books.

'And?' Nikos was the head teacher prompting a naughty schoolboy.

'Yes, yes, of course, thanks for the reminder, old chap. Been meaning to say, Libs, I've set up a standing order to repay the loan you made me. Very grateful, thanks.'

'We'll be looking out for it,' said Nikos. 'And sending you a receipt each month.'

'Isn't it great,' he said as they left the auditorium, now starting to fill up for the next speaker, 'how effective a visit from a lowly lawyer can be, when accompanied by the Lieutenant General of the Hellenic Police Force?'

'I'm glad you didn't take the heavy mob.' Libby's phone pinged as she linked her arm in his. The incoming text said:

> Sorry had to rush off but leaving you in good hands. We know where he lives. Z V and J.

Did they, now? Well, that was more than she did. She put her phone away. 'I'm glad you're so well connected, Nikos, but didn't you say you lived a life of monastic simplicity in the smallest flat in Athens?' He'd called it his eyrie. 'Well, I'd rather like to see that.'

* * *

'You sit there and I'll cook you something.'

Were those the most appealing words ever in the language of seduction? Definitely, Libby answered her own question, when spoken by a good-looking, bronze-pated chap with a spatula in his hand, to a hungry woman with a bubbling glass of *afrothi* in hers. Nikos was becoming more attractive with every sip, and more like a golden eagle in her rather overactive imagination, which now had the eagle reaching out for the food processor...

Slow down, Libby. You're not sure yet. She put the glass on the floor beside the surprisingly comfortable wooden chair she was sitting on. Modern, like the flat that was at the top of a five-storey high-rise, the chair, carved from a single piece of wood, had looked at first like a piece of sculpture. Now she had her feet up on it, in the middle of the open-plan flat and through the plate-glass windows on three sides of her, turning only a little, she could see the dark plains of Attica in the twilight. Earlier, before the light faded, she'd seen the outline of misty blue mountains in the distance. Now, shifting her focus to the interior, she could see nearly all the flat, including the kitchen where Nikos was working in front of her. A door on the fourth windowless wall led, she supposed, to his bedroom. Am I going to see that? *Do I want to?* The apartment was Shaker-like in its simplicity, with minimal furnishings, but the kitchen was well equipped, she gathered from watching Nikos complete an array of tasks. As he'd chopped the veg for her favourite fasolakia, the knife had moved so fast over the green beans, onions, tomatoes and potatoes that she'd feared for his fingers, but they had stayed intact and now the veg were simmering softly, filling the air with the fragrant scent of olive oil seasoned with garlic, cumin and oregano.

'Are you sure you wouldn't feel better with the bastard behind bars?' Nikos paused after deftly pouring tahini into the processor to make his signature hummus. Competence, she thought, was seriously underrated as a seductive technique. What couldn't this man do? He'd already got back her hundred quid from that near-criminal car-park company.

'Very sure.' She nodded, disappointing him, she knew. Nikos had put in a lot of time on her behalf exploring UK and European law and thought Monty should be convicted for theft in either the UK or Greece. But that was before, at her request, he'd gone to see Monty and persuaded him to start paying back the money he'd taken from her. It was also before the police had visited Villa Adelos and closed down the fraudulent wine operation before Monty and Dimitris had sold a single bottle of wine. What a couple of bumbling idiots! There was, of course, the not unimportant matter of his keeping her in the Villa Adelos against her will, cutting her off from family and friends. He was guilty of that but the law against coercive control wasn't coming in till the end of next year, and then only in England and Wales till other countries caught up, and it couldn't be applied retrospectively. Good, because she didn't want to see Monty behind bars.

'Still can't see why not. Here, try this.' Nikos held out a piece of pitta with a generous dollop of hummus on top.

'Because it wasn't all Monty's fault, that's why. I was partly to blame. No, don't shake your head, Nikos, he told me from the start how he worked.'

She tried to explain later when they were eating on the balcony, the night still warm with stars starting to appear between the scudding clouds.

'Monty was honest in his way,' she insisted. 'I just love them, he said or words to that effect, when I asked him to explain how he got actors to give him their best. *If you love people, they love you and give you what you want*, because they want you to go on loving them. What I didn't realise was that he used the same method outside the theatre, on everyone he wanted something from including me.'

'But did he love you – and indeed the actors – or just say that he did?' Nikos, the lawyer, made a fine distinction.

'Say, in my case, definitely.' Monty she'd realised loved only himself. 'And only when he needed a particular performance from me.' She remembered the exact moment with useless hindsight. It was the day he'd got the letter telling him he must leave Rokeby Villa, when he'd realised he needed a roof over his head and she could provide it. 'We'd been to the theatre to see *Blithe Spirit*, a comedy, but it had upset me and made me miss Jim badly, and, well, we'd gone back to his place, as I then thought it was. Anyway, I came downstairs from the bathroom, and he was deep in thought reading a letter looking very cross. Then he saw me, stuffed the letter in his pocket, and his expression suddenly changed. His body language changed. He was a pretty good actor too, I now know. He held out his arms, looking so loving and concerned that I walked into them. Then he said, "I do love you, you know," and I believed him and kept on believing, despite everything, because I wanted to be loved. I so missed being loved...'

'But you were loved.' Nikos reached across the table and took her hand. 'You *are* loved. I've loved you for years and years, and more so since Jim passed away, but, stupidly, I thought I shouldn't show my hand...'

'You weren't stupid, you were wise. It was too soon, but oh...' – she caught sight of something out of the corner of her eye – 'it isn't now!' Suddenly filled with certainty she kissed the tips of his fingers one by one, because while they'd been eating and drinking a breeze had blown the clouds away, unveiling the moon, so low in the sky, so big and round and full it looked like a lamp you could reach out and switch on and off, or a giant peach about to take off on a magical journey, and it had sparked a happy memory of long, long ago.

'Nikos, look at that moon, look at that wonderful moon and I'll tell you a story. Are you sitting comfortably? Well, once upon a time —' she kept hold of his hand '—long ago, when I was a girl, eleven or twelve perhaps, I asked my granny, my mum's mum, how I would know when I'd found true love. I think I was just beginning to be interested in boys, or perhaps I'd read too many fairy tales or teen romances or even bowdlerized retellings of stories from Shakespeare. Anyway, I was vain enough to think that one day I might have suitors queuing up, competing for my hand, and I would need to know how to choose the right one. My granny laughed and called me an old-fashioned one, as she often did, and carried on washing up. But, annoying, persistent child that I was, I kept on asking her, "Granny, how will I know?" and in the end she wiped her hands on her apron and said, "Well, Libby, my girl, you will know when you meet Mr Right because you'll look up at the sky one night and see that the moon has turned pink." She said that, she really did. And what colour is the moon right now, would you say?'

They turned to look at it together.

'Orange?' said Nikos, his eyes smiling as he looked into hers.

'Pink,' said Libby firmly. 'That moon is pink.'

ACKNOWLEDGEMENTS

The list of acknowledgments isn't quite as long as for my first novel. That's because I've written it much more quickly, consulting fewer people. It may also be because I've had a senior moment and forgotten some names in my haste. Please forgive me if that includes – or excludes – you. Any faults are very much my own. Top of the list for thanks though, are writer-friends Linda Newbery, Celia Rees and Cindy Jefferies whose cries of 'Course you can!' blew away most of my self-doubt, when Boldwood Books said they would like to publish *The Widows' Wine Club* but only if I would write more books about my widows. We were staying in Lyme Regis at the time, so the shades of Jane Austen and John Fowles, to name only two gone-before writers, also urged me on in my fevered imagination. Even better, Cindy remembered me once saying something which she'd said at the time would make a great premise for a story. On the strength of that jogged memory I made a tentative beginning to *Widows on the Wine Path* and the story gained momentum when I got home with more encouragement from my writer-friend-and-neighbour, Georgia Bowers. Family and non-writing friends joined in with the 'You can do its' and my supportive agent, Caroline Walsh, assured me I could up my pace and deliver in months rather than the years I usually took.

Thank you to youngest daughter Mary for finding the Greek location, and to Lois, Josie, Jon, Ursula and Faith for their help researching Greek food and wine and pool-sides. Newly-weds

Sandra and John Withey also merit thanks for dedicated research into Greek wine. Sam Jarman was house-sitting consultant and Maya cheered on from afar.

In this novel I draw on my background as a drama student in the nineteen-sixties, and the theatre scene in the twenty-tens. The characters however are all the product of my imagination – with the exception of certain famous actors and directors whom I have named. I have used poetic licence here and, as I'm sincerely complimentary about all these performances, I hope those mentioned approve. All the performances attended by my fictional characters actually took place, just not on the dates specified. I have also drawn on my experience as a writer for children and the picture book *Lovely Old Lion* does exist.

My first draft was read by four trusted friends, Sue Davies, Trevor Arrowsmith, Linda Newbery and Val Cumine before being revised in the light of their comments, and then sent off to editor Sarah Ritherdon at Boldwood. My friends all loved it, but well, they are my friends and therefore biased. Fingers crossed, I waited to hear from Sarah, who – phew! – loved it too. Never has an editor been more full of praise! Thank you, Sarah, for your enthusiasm and reassurance. Thank you too, Sue Smith for meticulous copy-editing, Rachel Sargeant for enlightened proof-reading and the whole Boldwood Team for not just producing another beautiful-to-hold-and-look-at book, but getting it out there. I've been thrilled by the success of *The Widows' Wine Club* and thank every single one of you who has read, bought, borrowed, and/or listened to it and then spread the word by telling your friends or even writing a review. Special thanks are due to Rachel Gilbey and her team of enthusiastic reviewers. May *Widows on the Wine Path* give you all just as much pleasure and then – dare I mention? – you may want to read even more about Viv, Janet and Zelda when they take to the sea in *Widows Waive the Rules*. Better get writing!

Julia Jarman
December 2023

ABOUT THE AUTHOR

Julia Jarman has written over a hundred books for children, and is now turning her hand to uplifting, golden years women's fiction. Julia draws on her own experience of bereavement, female friendship and late-life dating.

Sign up to Julia Jarman's mailing list here for news, competitions and updates on future books.

Visit Julia's website: https://juliajarman.com/

Follow Julia on social media:

facebook.com/juliajarman
x.com/JuliaJarman

ALSO BY JULIA JARMAN

The Widows' Wine Club

Widows on the Wine Path

Boldwood

Boldwood Books is an award-winning fiction publishing company seeking out the best stories from around the world.

Find out more at www.boldwoodbooks.com

Join our reader community for brilliant books, competitions and offers!

Follow us
@BoldwoodBooks
@TheBoldBookClub

Sign up to our weekly deals newsletter

https://bit.ly/BoldwoodBNewsletter